The Tinder Box

'If there wasn't a recognised school of crime writing called Home Counties noir before, there is now. Minette Walters invented it and remains the undisputed Head Girl'
Mike Ripley, *Birmingham Post*

The Devil's Feather

'One of the most powerful yet nuanced practitioners of the psychological thriller . . . always keeps the narrative momentum cracked up to a fierce degree'
Daily Express

Chickenfeed

'A marvellous little story, thoroughly intimate with human nastiness'
Evening Standard

The Chameleon's Shadow

'No wonder Minette Walters is the country's bestselling female crime writer. But even this label does not exactly do justice to the scope and breadth of her gripping, terrifying novels . . . *The Chameleon's Shadow* is another classic'
Daily Mirror

Also by Minette Walters

The Ice House

The Sculptress

The Scold's Bridle

The Dark Room

The Echo

The Breaker

The Shape of Snakes

Acid Row

Disordered Minds

The Tinder Box

The Devil's Feather

Chickenfeed
(Quick Reads)

The Chameleon's Shadow

MINETTE WALTERS

Fox Evil

PAN BOOKS

First published 2002 by Macmillan

This edition published 2012 by Pan Books
an imprint of Pan Macmillan, a division of Macmillan Publishers Limited
Pan Macmillan, 20 New Wharf Road, London N1 9RR
Basingstoke and Oxford
Associated companies throughout the world
www.panmacmillan.com

ISBN 978-1-4472-0799-3

A CIP catalogue record for this book is available from
the British Library.

Typeset by SetSystems Ltd, Saffron Walden, Essex
Printed and bound by CPI Group (UK) Ltd, Croydon, CR0 4YY

For all my Jebb and Paul cousins, near or far.

Blood is always thicker than water.

The Lion, the Fox and the Ass

The Lion, the Fox and the Ass entered into an agreement to assist each other in the chase. Having secured a large booty, the Lion on their return from the forest asked the Ass to allot his due portion to each of the three partners in the treaty. The Ass carefully divided the spoils into three equal shares and modestly requested the two others to make the first choice. The Lion, bursting into a great rage, devoured the Ass. Then he requested the Fox to do him the favour of making the division. The Fox accumulated all that they had killed into one large heap and left to himself the smallest possible morsel. The Lion said, 'Who has taught you, my excellent fellow, the art of division? You are perfect to a fraction.' He replied, 'I learned it from the Ass, by witnessing his fate.' Happy is the man who learns from the misfortunes of others.

– AESOP

fox evil, 'a disease in which the hair falls off' (1842 Johnson *Farmer's Encycl.*), alopecia

– *Oxford English Dictionary*, 2002

alopecia areata – baldness occurring in patches on the scalp, possibly caused by a nervous disturbance. [**Gr.** *alōpekiā*, fox-mange, a bald spot, *alōpekoeidēs*, fox-like—*alōpēx*, fox.]

– *Chambers English Dictionary*

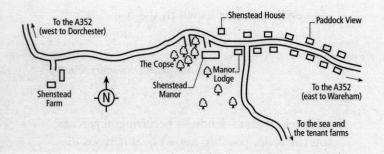

Shenstead Valley, Dorset

Fox Evil

One

THE FOX SLIPPED quietly through the night in search of food, with only the occasional flash of his white-tipped brush flagging his presence. The scent of a badger set his nose quivering, and he skirted the piece of track where the territorial marker had been laid. A shy, nervous creature, he had more sense than to cross the path of a voracious fighter with powerful jaws and poisonous teeth.

He had no such fear of the smell of burning tobacco. It spoke to him of bread and milk for himself, and pieces of chicken for his vixen and her cubs – easier plunder than a night-time's wearisome hunting for voles and field mice. Ever suspicious, he stood for several minutes, watching and listening for alien movement. There was none. Whoever was smoking was as quiet and still as he. Finally, in trustful response to the Pavlovian stimulus, he crept towards the familiar smell, unaware that a rolled cigarette was different from the pipe he was used to.

The illegal trap, a maiming device of metal teeth, sprang shut on his delicate foreleg with the biting power of a huge badger, tearing the flesh and snapping the bone. He screamed in pain and anger, lashing at the empty night in search of his imagined adversary. For all his supposed cunning, he hadn't been clever enough to recognize that the motionless figure beside a tree bore no resemblance to the patient old man who regularly fed him.

The woodland burst with sound in response to his terror. Birds fluttered on their perches, nocturnal rodents scurried into hiding. Another fox – perhaps his vixen – barked an alarm from across the field. As the figure turned towards him, drawing a hammer from his coat pocket, the shaved tracks in the mane of hair must have suggested a bigger, stronger foe than the fox could cope with, because he ceased his screaming and dropped in whimpering humility to his belly. But there was no mercy in the deliberate crushing of his little pointed muzzle before the trap was forced open and, still alive, his brush was sliced from his body with a cut-throat razor.

His tormentor spat his cigarette to the ground and mashed it under his heel before tucking the brush in his pocket and seizing the animal by its scruff. He slipped as quietly through the trees as the fox had done earlier, coming to a halt at the edge of the wood and melting into the shadow of an oak. Fifty feet away, across the ha-ha ditch, the old man was on his feet on the terrace, staring towards the treeline, a shotgun levelled at shoulder height towards his unseen watcher. The backwash from the lights inside his open French windows showed his face grim with anger. He knew the cry of an animal in pain, knew that its abrupt cessation meant the creature's jaw had been smashed. He should have done. This wasn't the first time a broken body had been tossed at his feet.

He never saw the whirl of the black-sleeved, black-gloved arm as it lobbed the dying fox towards him, but he caught the streaks of white as the tumbling paws flashed in the lamplight. With murder in his heart he aimed below them and fired both barrels.

TRAVELLER INVASION

THE ROLLING DOWNLAND of Dorset's Ridgeway has become home to the largest illegal caravan park in the county's history. Police estimate that some 200 mobile homes and over 500 gypsies and travellers have gathered at scenic Barton Edge for an August Bank Holiday rave.

From the windows of Bella Preston's psychedelic bus, the soon-to-be-designated World Heritage site of Dorset's Jurassic coastline unfolds in all its glory. To the left, the majestic cliffs of Ringstead Bay, to the right the stunning crag of Portland Bill, ahead the dazzling blue of the English Channel.

'This is the best view anywhere in England,' says Bella, 35, cuddling her three daughters. 'The kids love it. We always try to spend our summers here.' Bella, a single mother from Essex, who describes herself as a 'social worker', was one of the first to arrive. 'The rave was proposed when we were at Stonehenge for the solstice in June. Word spread quickly, but we hadn't expected so many.'

Dorset police were alerted when an abnormal number of traveller-style vehicles entered the county yesterday morning. Road blocks were set up along the routes leading to Barton Edge in an attempt to stop the invasion. The result was a series of jams, some five miles long, that angered locals and bona fide tourists who were caught in the net. With the travellers' vehicles unable to turn round in the confined space of the narrow Dorset lanes, the decision was taken to allow the gathering to happen.

Farmer Will Harris, 58, whose fields have been taken over by the illegal encampment, is angered by police and local authority impotence to act. 'I've been told I'll be arrested if I provoke these people,' he fumed. 'They're destroying my fences and crops, but if I complain and someone gets hurt then it's my fault. Is that justice?'

Sally Macey, 48, Traveller Liaison Officer for the local authority, said last night that the travellers had been served with a formal notice to quit. She agreed that the serving of notices was a game. 'Travellers operate on the basis that seven days is the usual length of stay,' she said. 'They tend to move on just before the order comes into effect. In the meantime we ask them to refrain from intimidatory behaviour and to ensure that their rubbish is disposed of in nominated sites.'

This cut no ice with Mr Harris who pointed to the sacks of litter dumped at the entrance to his farm. 'This will be all over the place tomorrow when the foxes get at these bags. Who's going to pay for the clean-up? It cost a farmer £10,000 to clear his land in Devon after an encampment half this size.'

Bella Preston expressed sympathy. 'If I lived here I wouldn't like it either. Last time we held a rave of this size, 2000 teens came from the local towns to join in. I'm sure it will happen again. The music goes on all night and it's pretty loud.'

A police spokesman agreed. 'We are warning local people that the noise nuisance will last throughout the weekend. Unfortunately there is little we can do in these situations. Our priority is to avoid unnecessary confrontation.' He confirmed that an influx of youngsters from Bournemouth and Weymouth was likely. 'A free open-air rave is a big draw. Police will be on hand, but we expect the event to pass off peacefully.'

Mr Harris is less optimistic. 'If it doesn't, my farm will be in the middle of a war zone,' he said. 'There aren't enough policemen in Dorset to shift this lot. They'll have to bring in the army.'

Two

Barton Edge – August Bank Holiday, 2001

TEN-YEAR-OLD Wolfie pumped up his courage to confront his father. His mother had seen that others were leaving and she was frightened of attracting unwelcome attention. 'If we stay too long,' she told the child, wrapping her thin arms around his shoulder and keening against his cheek, 'the do-gooders will come in to check for bruises, and when they find them they'll take you away.' She had had her first child removed years before and had imbued her two remaining children with an undying terror of the police and social workers. Bruises were minor inconveniences in comparison.

Wolfie climbed onto the front bumper of the coach and peered through the windscreen. If Fox was asleep, there was no way he was going inside. The geezer was a devil if you woke him. One time he'd slashed Wolfie's hand with the cut-throat razor he kept under his pillow when Wolfie had touched his shoulder by mistake. Most of the time he and Cub, his little brother, sat under the coach while their dad slept and their mum cried. Even when it was cold and raining, neither of them dared go inside unless Fox was out.

Wolfie thought Fox was a good name for his father. He hunted at night under cover of darkness, slipping invisibly from shadow to shadow. Sometimes Wolfie's mother sent him after Fox to see what he was doing, but Wolfie was too afraid of the razor to follow far. He'd seen Fox use it on animals, heard the death rattle of a deer as he slowly slit its throat and the gurgling squeal of a rabbit. He never killed quickly. Wolfie didn't know why – but instinct told him that Fox enjoyed fear.

Instinct told him a lot about his father, but he kept it bottled inside his head along with strange, flimsy memories of other men and times when Fox hadn't been there. None of them was substantial enough to persuade him they were true. Truth for Wolfie was the terrifying reality of Fox and the gnawing pangs of permanent hunger that were assuaged only in sleep. Whatever thoughts might be in his head, he had learnt to keep a still tongue. Break any of Fox's rules and you tasted the razor, and the strongest rule of all was 'never talk to anyone about the family'.

His father wasn't in the bed, so with wildly beating heart Wolfie mustered his nerve and climbed in through the open front door. He had learnt over time that the best way to approach this man was to play an equal – '*never show how afraid you are*,' *his mother always said* – so he dropped into a John Wayne swagger and sauntered up what had once been the aisle between the seats. He could hear splashing water and guessed his father was behind the curtain that gave privacy to the washing area.

'Hey, Fox, what ya doing, mate?' he said, pausing outside.

The splashing stopped immediately. 'Why do you want to know?'

'It don't matter.'

The curtain rattled aside, revealing his father stripped to the waist with beads of water dripping down his hairy arms from immersion in the old tin bowl that served as bath and basin. '*Doesn't!*' he snapped. 'It *doesn't* matter. How many times do I have to tell you?'

The child flinched but stood his ground. Most of his confusion about life came from the illogical disparity between his father's behaviour and the way he spoke. To Wolfie's ear, Fox sounded like an actor who knew stuff that no one else knew, but the anger that drove him was nothing like Wolfie had ever seen on the movies. Except, maybe, Commodus in *Gladiator* or the bog-eyed priest in *Indiana Jones and the Temple of Doom* who ripped people's hearts out. In Wolfie's dreams, Fox was always one or other of them, which was why his surname was Evil. 'It doesn't matter,' he repeated solemnly.

His father reached for his razor. 'Then why ask what I'm doing if you're not interested in the answer?'

'It's just a way of saying hi. They do it in the movies. Hey, mate, what's happening, what ya doing?' He raised his hand to reflect in the mirror by Fox's shoulder, palm showing, fingers spread. 'Then you do a high five.'

'You watch too many damn films. You're beginning to sound like a Yank. Where do you see them?'

Wolfie picked the least alarming explanation. 'There was this boy me and Cub made friends with at the last place. He lived in a house . . . let us watch his mum's videos when she was at work.' It was true . . . up to a point. The boy had taken them into his house until his mother found out and sent them packing. Most of the time Wolfie filched money from the tin box under his parents' bed when Fox was out, and used it to buy cinema tickets when they were near towns. He didn't know where the money came from, or why there was so much of it, but Fox never seemed to notice when it went.

Fox gave a grunt of disapproval as he used the tip of the razor to scrape at the shaven tracks on his close-cropped crown. 'What was the bitch doing? Was she there, too?'

Wolfie was used to his mother being called 'bitch'.

He even called her 'bitch' himself sometimes. 'It was when she was sick.' He never understood why his father didn't cut himself with the razor. It wasn't natural to drag a sharp point down your scalp and never once draw blood. Fox didn't even use soap to make it easier. Sometimes he wondered why Fox didn't just shave off all his hair instead of turning the bald patches into irregular tracks and letting the bits at the back and sides hang down below his shoulders in dreadlocks that got more and more straggly as the hair dropped out. He guessed that going bald really worried Fox, though Wolfie couldn't account for it. Hard guys in the movies often shaved their heads. Bruce Willis did.

He met Fox's eyes in the mirror. 'What are you staring at?' the man growled. 'What do you want?'

'You gonna be bald as a coot if this keeps up,' the child said, pointing to the strands of black hair that were floating on the surface of the water. 'You should go to a doctor. It ain't normal to have your hair fall out every time you shake your head.'

'How would you know? Maybe it's in my genes. Maybe it'll happen to you.'

Wolfie stared at his own blond reflection. 'No chance,' he said, emboldened by the man's willingness to talk. 'I don't look nuffink like you. I reckon I'm like Ma, and she ain't going bald.' He shouldn't have said it. He knew it was a mistake even as the words came out and he saw the narrowing of his father's eyes.

He tried to duck but Fox clamped a massive hand around his neck and snicked the soft flesh under his chin with the razor. 'Who's your dad?'

'You is,' the boy wailed, tears smarting in his eyes. 'You is, Fox.'

'Jesus Christ!' he flung the child aside. 'You can't remember a fucking thing, can you? It's *are* . . . you *are* . . . he *is* . . . I *am*. What's the word for that, Wolfie?' He went back to scraping at his hair.

'G-g-grammar?'

'Conjugation, you ignorant little shit. It's a verb.'

The boy stepped back, making damping motions with his hands. 'There ain't no call to get cross, Fox,' he said, desperate to prove he wasn't as stupid as his father thought him. 'Mum and me looked the hair thing up on the Net the last time we went to the library. I reckon it's called—' he'd memorized the word phonetically – 'all-oh-peck-ya. There's loads on it . . . and there's things you can do.'

The man's eyes narrowed again. 'Alopecia, you idiot. It's Greek for fox-mange. You're so *fucking* uneducated. Doesn't that bitch teach you anything? Why do you think I'm called Fox Evil?'

Wolfie had his own ideas. In his child's mind, Fox denoted cleverness and Evil denoted cruelty. It was a name that suited this man. His eyes filled with tears again. 'I was only trying to help. There's loads of guys go bald. It's no big deal. Most times—' he took his best stab at the sound he'd heard – 'aypeesha goes away and the hair grows back. Maybe that'll happen with you. You don't wanna be nervous – they reckon it's worrying that can make hair fall out.'

'What about the other times?'

The boy gripped the back of a chair because his knees were trembling with fright. This was further than he wanted to go – with words he couldn't pronounce and ideas that would make Fox angry. 'There was some stuff about cancer—' he took a deep breath – ''n' dybeets 'n' arthrytes that can make it happen.' He rushed on before his father turned nasty again. 'Mum and me reckon you should see a doctor, because if you is ill it won't get no better by pretending it ain't there. It's no big deal to sign on at a surgery. The law says travellers got the same rights to care as everyone else.'

'Did the bitch say I was ill?'

Wolfie's alarm showed in his face. 'N-n-no. She don't n-n-never talk about you.'

Fox stabbed the razor into the wooden wash-board. 'You're lying,' he snarled, turning round. 'Tell me what she said or I'll have your fucking guts.'

'*Your father's sick in the head . . . your father's evil . . .*' 'Nothing,' Wolfie managed. 'She don't never say nothing.'

Fox searched his son's terrified eyes. 'You'd better

be telling the truth, Wolfie, or it's your mother's innards that'll be on the floor. Try again. What did she say about me?'

The child's nerve broke and he made a dash for the rear exit, diving beneath the bus and burying his face in his hands. He couldn't do anything right. His father would kill his mother, and the do-gooders would find his bruises. He would have prayed to God if he knew how, but God was a nebulous entity that he didn't understand. One time his mother had said, if God was a woman she'd help us. Another time: God's a policeman. If you obey the rules he's nice, if you don't he sends you to hell.

The only absolute truth that Wolfie understood was that there was no escape from the misery of his life.

*

Fox fascinated Bella Preston in a way that few other men had. He was older than he looked, she guessed, putting him somewhere in his forties, with a peculiarly inexpressive face that suggested a tight rein on his emotions. He spoke little, preferring to cloak himself in silence, but when he did his speech betrayed his class and education.

It wasn't unheard of for a 'toff' to take to the road – it had happened down the centuries when a black sheep was kicked out of the family fold – but she would have expected Fox to have an expensive habit. Crackheads were the black sheep of the twenty-first century, never mind what class they were born into. This guy wouldn't even take a spliff, and that was weird.

A woman with less confidence might have asked herself why he kept singling her out for attention. Big and fat with cropped peroxided hair, Bella wasn't an obvious choice for this lean, charismatic man with pale eyes and shaven tracks across his skull. He never answered questions. Who he was, where he came from and why he hadn't been seen on the circuit before were no one's business but his own. Bella, who had witnessed it all before, took his right to a hidden past for granted – *didn't they all have secrets?* – and allowed him to haunt her bus with the same freedom that everyone else did.

Bella hadn't travelled the country with three young daughters and an H-addict husband, now dead, without learning to keep her eyes open. She knew there were a woman and two children in Fox's bus, but he never acknowledged them. They looked like spares, chucked out along the way by someone else and taken on board in a moment of charity, but Bella saw how the two kids cowered behind their mother's skirts whenever Fox drew near. It told her something about the man. However attractive he might be to strangers – *and he was attractive* – Bella would bet her last cent that he showed a different character behind closed doors.

It didn't surprise her. What man wouldn't be bored by a spaced-out zombie and her by-blows? But it made her wary. The children were timid little clones of their mother, blond and blue-eyed, who sat in the dirt under Fox's bus and watched while she wandered aimlessly from vehicle to vehicle, hand held out for anything that would put her to sleep. Bella wondered how often she gave happy pills to the kids to keep them quiet. Too often, she suspected. Their lethargy wasn't normal.

Of course she felt sorry for them. She dubbed herself a 'social worker' because she and her daughters attracted waifs wherever they camped. Their battery-operated television had something to do with it, also Bella's generous nature that made her a comfortable person to be around. But when she sent her girls to make friends with the two boys, they slithered under Fox's bus and ran away.

She made an attempt to engage the woman in conversation by offering to share a smoke with her, but it was a fruitless exercise. All questions were greeted with silence or incomprehension, except for wistful agreement when Bella said the hardest part about being on the road was educating the kids. 'Wolfie likes libraries,' the skinny creature said, as if Bella should know what she was talking about.

'Which one's Wolfie?' asked Bella.

'The one that takes after his father . . . the clever

one,' she said, before wandering away to look for more handouts.

The subject of education came up again on the Monday night when prone bodies littered the ground in front of Bella's purple and pink bus. 'I'd chuck it all in tomorrow,' she said dreamily, staring at the star-studded sky and the moon across the water. 'All I need is for someone to give me a house with a garden that ain't on a fucking estate in the middle of a fucking city full of fucking delinquents. Somewhere round here would do . . . a decent place where my kids can go to school 'n' not get their heads fucked by wannabe jail meat . . . that's all I'm asking.'

'They're pretty girlies, Bella,' said a dreamy voice. 'They'll get more 'n' their heads fucked the minute you turn your back.'

'Yeah, and don't I know it. I'll chop the dick off the first man who tries.'

There was a low laugh from the corner of the bus where Fox was standing in shadow. 'It'll be too late by then,' he murmured. 'You need to take action now. Prevention is always better than cure.'

'Like what?'

He detached himself from the shadows and loomed over Bella, straddling her with his feet, his tall figure blotting out the moon. 'Claim some free land through adverse possession and build your own house.'

She squinted up at him. 'What the hell are you talking about?'

His teeth flashed in a brief grin. 'Winning the jackpot,' he said.

Three

Lower Croft, Coomb Farm,
Herefordshire – 28 August 2001

UNUSUALLY FOR twenty-eight years ago, Nancy Smith had been delivered in her mother's bedroom, but not because her mother had avant-garde views on a woman's right to home birthing. A wild and disturbed teenager, Elizabeth Lockyer-Fox had starved herself for the first six months of her pregnancy and, when that failed to kill the incubus inside her, ran away from boarding school and demanded her mother rescue her from it. Who would marry her if she was saddled with a child?

The question seemed relevant at the time – Elizabeth was just seventeen – and her family closed ranks to protect her reputation. The Lockyer-Foxes were an old military family with distinguished war service from the Crimea to the stand-off in Korea on the 38th parallel. With abortion out of the question because Elizabeth had left it too late, adoption was the only option if the stigmas of single motherhood and illegitimacy were to be avoided. Naively perhaps, and even in 1973 with the women's movement well under way, a 'good' marriage was the Lockyer-Foxes' only solution to their daughter's uncontrollable behaviour. Once settled down, they hoped, she would learn responsibility.

The agreed story was that Elizabeth was suffering from glandular fever, and there was muted sympathy amongst her parents' friends and acquaintances – none of whom had much affection for the Lockyer-Fox children – when it became clear that the fever was debilitating and contagious enough to keep her quarantined for three months. For the rest, the tenant farmers and workers on the Lockyer-Fox estate, Elizabeth remained her usual wild self, slipping her mother's leash at night to drink and shag herself stupid, unrepentant about the damage it might do to her fetus. If it wasn't going to be hers, why should she care? All she wanted was rid of it, and the rougher the sex the more likely that was.

The doctor and midwife kept their mouths shut, and a surprisingly healthy child emerged on the due date. At the end of the experience, interestingly pale and frail, Elizabeth was sent to a finishing school in London from where she met and married a baronet's son who found her fragility and ready tears endearing.

As for Nancy, her stay in Shenstead Manor had

been of short duration. Within hours of her birth she had been processed through an adoption agency to a childless couple on a Herefordshire farm where her origins were neither known nor relevant. The Smiths were kindly people who adored the child that had been given to them and made no secret of her adoption, always attributing her finer qualities – principally the cleverness that took her to Oxford – to her natural parents.

Nancy, by contrast, attributed everything to her only-child status, her parents' generous nurturing, their insistence on a good education and their untiring support of all her ambitions. She rarely thought about her biological inheritance. Confident in the love of two good people, Nancy could see no point in fantasizing about the woman who had abandoned her. Whoever she was, her story had been told a thousand times before and would be told a thousand times again. Single woman. Accidental pregnancy. Unwanted baby. The mother had no place in her daughter's story . . .

. . . or wouldn't have done but for a persistent solicitor who traced Nancy through the agency's records to the Smith home in Hereford. After several unanswered letters, he came knocking on the farmhouse door, and by a rare stroke of fate found Nancy home on leave.

*

It was her mother who persuaded her to speak to him. She found her daughter in the stables where Nancy was brushing the mud of a hard ride from Red Dragon's flanks. The horse's reaction to a solicitor on the premises – a scornful snort – so closely mimicked Nancy's that she gave his muzzle an approving kiss. There's sense for you, she told Mary. Red could smell the devil from a thousand paces. So? Had Mr Ankerton said what he wanted or was he still hiding behind innuendo?

His letters had been masterpieces of legal sleight of hand. A surface read seemed to suggest a legacy – '*Nancy Smith, born 23.05.73 . . . something to your advantage . . .*' A between-the-lines read – '*instructed by the Lockyer-Fox family . . . relative issues . . . please confirm date of birth . . .*' – suggested a cautious approach by her natural mother which was outside the rules governing adoption. Nancy had wanted none of it – '*I'm a Smith*' – but her adoptive mother had urged her to be kind.

Mary Smith couldn't bear to think of anyone being rebuffed, particularly not a woman who had never known her child. She gave you life, she said, as if that were reason enough to embark on a relationship with a total stranger. Nancy, who had a strong streak of realism in her nature, wanted to warn Mary against opening a can of worms, but as usual she couldn't bring herself to go against her soft-hearted mother's wishes. Mary's greatest talent was to bring out the best in people, because her refusal to see flaws meant they didn't exist – in her eyes at least – but it laid her open to a legion of disappointments.

Nancy feared this would be another. Cynically, she could imagine only two ways this 'reconciliation' could go, which was why she had spurned the solicitor's letters. Either she would get on with her biological mother or she wouldn't, and the only thing on offer in both scenarios was a guilt trip. It was her view that there was room for only one mother in a person's life, and it was an unnecessary complication to add the emotional baggage of a second. Mary, who insisted on putting herself in the other woman's shoes, couldn't see the dilemma. No one's asking you to make a choice, she argued, any more than they ask you to choose between me and your father. We all love many people in our lives. Why should this be different?

It was a question that could only be answered afterwards, thought Nancy, and by then it would be too late. Once contact was made, it couldn't be unmade. Part of her wondered if Mary was motivated by pride. Did she want to show off to this unknown woman? And if she did, was that so wrong? Nancy wasn't immune to the sense of satisfaction it would give. *Look at me. I'm the child you didn't want. This is what I've made of myself with no help from you.* She might have resisted more firmly had her father been there to support her. He understood the dynamics of jealousy better than his wife, having grown up between a warring mother and stepmother, but it was August, he was harvesting, and in his absence she gave in. She told herself it was no big deal. Nothing in life was ever as bad as imagination painted it.

*

Mark Ankerton, who had been shut into a sitting room off the hall, was beginning to feel extremely uncomfortable. The Smith surname, coupled with the address – Lower Croft, Coomb Farm – had led him to assume that the family were farm labourers who lived in a tied cottage. Now, in this room of books and worn leather furniture, he was far from confident that the weight he'd given in his letters to the Lockyer-Fox connection would cut much ice with the adopted daughter.

A nineteenth-century map on the wall above the fireplace showed Lower Croft and Coomb Croft as two distinct entities, while a more recent map next to it showed the two within a single boundary, renamed Coomb Farm. As Coomb Croft farmhouse fronted a main road, it was obvious that the family would have chosen the more secluded Lower Croft as their residence, and Mark cursed himself for jumping to easy conclusions. The world had moved on. He should have known better than to dismiss a couple called John and Mary Smith as labourers.

His eye was constantly drawn to the mantelpiece, where a photograph of a laughing young woman in gown and mortar board with 'St Hilda's, Oxford, 1995' inscribed at the bottom held pride of place. It had to be the daughter, he thought. The age was right, even if she bore no resemblance to her foolish, doll-like mother. The whole thing was a nightmare. He had pictured the girl as easy meat – a coarser, ill-educated version of Elizabeth – instead he was faced with an Oxford graduate from a family probably as well-to-do as the one he was representing.

He rose from the armchair when the door opened and strode forward to grip Nancy's hand in a forceful clasp. 'Thank you for seeing me, Miss Smith. My name's Mark Ankerton and I represent the Lockyer-Fox family. I realize this is a terrible intrusion, but my client has put considerable pressure on me to find you.'

He was in his early thirties, tall and dark, and much as Nancy had imagined from the tone of his letters: arrogant, pushy, and with a veneer of professional charm. It was a type she recognized and dealt with daily in her job. If he couldn't persuade her by pleasantry, then he'd resort to bullying. He was certainly a successful lawyer. If his suit had cost less than a thousand pounds then he'd found himself a bargain, but she was amused to see mud on his shoes and trouser cuffs where he'd picked his way round the slurry in the farmyard.

She, too was tall and more athletic-looking than her photograph suggested, with cropped black hair and brown eyes. In the flesh, dressed in loose-fitting sweatshirt and jeans, she was so different from her blonde, blue-eyed mother that Mark wondered if there'd been an error in the agency's records, until she gave a slight smile and gestured to him to sit down again. The smile, a brief courtesy that didn't reach her eyes, was so precise an imitation of James Lockyer-Fox's that it was startling.

'Good lord!' he said.

She stared at him with a small frown before lowering herself into the other chair. 'It's *Captain* Smith,' she corrected mildly. 'I'm an officer in the Royal Engineers.'

Mark couldn't help himself. 'Good lord!' he said again.

She ignored him. 'You were lucky to find me at home. I'm only here because I'm on two weeks' leave from Kosovo, otherwise I'd be at my base.' She watched his mouth start to open. 'Please don't say "good lord" again,' she said. 'You're making me feel like a performing monkey.'

God! She was like James. 'I'm sorry.'

She nodded. 'What do you want from me, Mr Ankerton?'

The question was too blunt and he faltered. 'Have you received my letters?'

'Yes.'

25

'Then you know I'm representing the Lock—'

'So you keep saying,' she broke in impatiently. 'Are they famous? Am I supposed to know who they are?'

'They come from Dorset.'

'*Really!*' She gave an amused laugh. 'Then you're looking at the wrong Nancy Smith, Mr Ankerton. I don't know Dorset. Off the top of my head, I can't think of anyone I've ever met who *lives* in Dorset. I *certainly* have no acquaintance with a Lockyer-Fox family . . . from Dorset or anywhere else.'

He leaned back in his chair and steepled his fingers in front of his mouth. 'Elizabeth Lockyer-Fox is your natural mother.'

If he'd hoped to surprise her, he was disappointed. He might as well have named royalty as her mother for all the emotion she showed.

'Then what you're doing is illegal,' she said calmly. 'The rules on adopted children are very precise. A natural parent can publicize his or her willingness for contact, but the child isn't obliged to respond. The fact that I didn't answer your letters was the clearest indication I could give that I have no interest in meeting your client.'

She spoke with the soft lilt of her Herefordshire parents, but her manner was as forceful as Mark's and it put him at a disadvantage. He had hoped to switch tack and play on her sympathies but her lack of expression suggested she didn't have any. He could hardly tell her the truth. It would only make her angrier to hear that he had done his damnedest to prevent this wild goose chase. No one knew where the child was or how she'd been brought up and Mark had advised strongly against laying the family open to worse problems by courting a common little gold-digger.

(*'Could it* **be** *any worse?' had been James's dry response.*)

Nancy ratcheted up his discomfort by glancing pointedly at her watch. 'I don't have all day, Mr Ankerton. I return to my unit on Friday, and I'd like to make the most of the time I have left. As I have never registered an interest in meeting either of my biological parents, could you explain what you're doing here?'

'I wasn't sure if you'd received my letters.'

'Then you should have checked with the post office. They were all sent by registered delivery. Two of them even followed me out to Kosovo, courtesy of my mother who signed for them.'

'I hoped you'd acknowledge receipt on the pre-paid cards I enclosed. As you never did, I assumed they hadn't found you.'

She shook her head. *Lying bastard!* 'If that's as honest as you can be, then we might as well call a halt now. There's no obligation on anyone to answer unsolicited mail. The fact that you registered delivery—' she stared him down – 'and I didn't answer, was proof enough that I didn't want a correspondence with you.'

'I'm sorry,' he said again, 'but the only details I had were the name and address that were recorded at the time of your adoption. For all I knew, you and your family had moved . . . perhaps the adoption hadn't worked out . . . perhaps you'd changed your name. In any of those circumstances, my letters wouldn't have reached you. Of course I could have sent a private detective to ask questions of your neighbours, but I felt that would be more intrusive than coming myself.'

He was too glib with his excuses and reminded her of a boyfriend who stood her up twice and then got the elbow. *It wasn't his fault . . . he had a responsible job . . . things came up . . .* But Nancy hadn't cared enough to believe him. 'What could be more intrusive than an unknown woman claiming title to me?'

'It's not a question of claiming title.'

'Then why did you give me her surname? The implied presumption was that a common-or-garden Smith would fall over herself to acknowledge a connection with a Lockyer-Fox.'

God! 'If that's the impression you received then you read more into my words than was there.' He leaned forward earnestly. 'Far from claiming title, my client is in the position of supplicant. You would be doing a great kindness if you agreed to a meeting.'

Loathsome little toerag! 'The issue is a legal one, Mr Ankerton. My position as an adopted child is protected by law. You had no business to give me information that I've never requested. Did it occur to you that I might not know I was adopted?'

Mark took refuge in lawyer-speak. 'There was no mention of adoption in any of my letters.'

Any amusement Nancy had found in pricking his rehearsed defences was rapidly giving way to anger. If he in any way represented the views of her natural mother then she had no intention of 'doing a kindness'. 'Oh, *please*! What inference was I supposed to draw?' It was a rhetorical question, and she looked towards the window to calm her irritation. 'You had no right to give me the name of my biological family or tell me where they live. It's information I've never requested or wanted. Must I avoid Dorset now in case I bump into a Lockyer-Fox? Must I worry every time I'm introduced to someone new, particularly women called Elizabeth?'

'I was working to instruction,' he said uneasily.

'Of course you were.' She turned back to him. 'It's your get-out-of-jail card. Truth is as alien to lawyers as it is to journalists and estate agents. You should try doing my job. You think about truth all the time when you hold the power of life and death in your hands.'

'Aren't you following instructions, just as I am?'

'Hardly.' She flicked her hand in a dismissive

wave. '*My* orders safeguard freedom . . . *yours* merely reflect one individual's attempts to get the better of another.'

Mark was stung to mild protest. 'Do individuals not count in your philosophy? If numbers bestowed legitimacy, then a handful of suffragettes could never have won the right for women to vote . . . and you would not be in the army now, Captain Smith.'

She looked amused. 'I doubt that citing the rights of women is the best analogy you could have drawn in the present circumstances. Who has precedence in this case? The woman you represent or the daughter she gave up?'

'You, of course.'

'Thank you.' Nancy pushed herself forward in her chair. 'You can tell your client I'm fit and happy, that I have no regrets about my adoption and that the Smiths are the only parents I recognize or wish to have. If that sounds uncharitable, then I'm sorry, but at least it's *honest*.'

Mark moved to the edge of his seat to keep her sitting down. 'It's not Elizabeth who's instructing me, Captain Smith. It's your grandfather, Colonel James Lockyer-Fox. He assumed you'd be more inclined to respond if you thought your mother was looking for you—' he paused – 'though I gather from what you've just said that his assumption was wrong.'

It was a second or two before she answered. Like

James, her expression was difficult to read and it was only when she spoke that her contempt was obvious. '*My God!* You really are a piece of work, Mr Ankerton. Supposing I *had* replied . . . supposing I'd been desperate to find my biological mother . . . when were you planning to tell me that the best I could hope for was a meeting with a geriatric Colonel?'

'The idea was always to introduce you to your mother.'

Her voice was heavy with sarcasm. 'Did you bother to inform Elizabeth of this?'

Mark knew he was handling this badly, but he couldn't see how to retrieve the situation without digging bigger holes for himself. He deflected attention back to her grandfather. 'James may be eighty but he's very fit,' he said, 'and I believe you and he would get on well together. He looks people in the eye when he speaks to them and he doesn't suffer fools gladly . . . rather like yourself. I apologize unreservedly if my approaches have been—' he sought a word – '*clumsy* – but James wasn't confident that a grandfather would appeal over a mother.'

'He was right.'

It might have been the Colonel speaking. A quick, scornful bark that left the other person floundering. Mark began to wish that the gold-digger of his imagination was the reality. Demands for money he could have dealt with. A complete disdain for the

31

Lockyer-Fox connection fazed him. Any minute now she would ask him why her grandfather was looking for her, and that was a question he wasn't at liberty to answer. 'Yours is a very old family, Captain. There have been Lockyer-Foxes in Dorset for five generations.'

'Smiths have been in Herefordshire for two centuries,' she snapped back. 'We've farmed this land without interruption since 1799. When my father retires, it'll be my turn. So, yes, you're right, I do come from a very old family.'

'Most of the Lockyer-Fox land is rented out to tenant farmers. There's a lot of it.'

She fixed him with a furious gaze. 'My *great-grandfather* owned Lower Croft and his brother owned Coomb. My *grandfather* inherited both farms and incorporated them into one. My *father* has been farming the entire valley for the last thirty years. If I marry and have kids, then my father's *grandchildren* will own the two thousand acres after me. As I fully intend to do both, *and* add Smith to my children's surname, then there's a good chance these fields will be farmed by Smiths for another two centuries. Is there anything more I can say that will make my position clear to you?'

He gave a resigned sigh. 'Have you no curiosity?'

'Absolutely none.'

'Can I ask why not?'

'Why fix something that isn't broken?' She waited

for him to respond, and when he didn't: 'I may be wrong, Mr Ankerton, but by the sound of it it's your client whose life needs fixing . . . and off the top of my head I can't think of a single reason why that burden should fall on me.'

He wondered what he'd said that had led her to so accurate a conclusion. Perhaps his persistence had suggested desperation. 'He just wants to meet you. Before she died his wife asked him several times to try to find out what had happened to you. I think he feels it's his duty to honour her wishes. Can you respect that?'

'Were they party to my adoption?'

He nodded.

'Then please reassure your client that it was completely successful and he has nothing to feel guilty about.'

He gave a baffled shake of his head. Phrases like 'unresolved anger' and 'fear of rejection' hovered on the tip of his tongue, but he had the sense not to say them. Even if it were true that her adoption had left her with a lingering resentment – which he doubted – psychobabble would only irritate her more. 'What if I were to repeat that you'd be doing a great kindness if you agreed to meet the Colonel? Would that persuade you?'

'No.' She watched him for a moment, then raised a hand in apology. 'Look, I'm sorry, I've obviously disappointed you. You might understand my refusal better if I take you outside and introduce you to Tom Figgis. He's a nice old boy, and he's worked for Dad for years.'

'How will that help?'

She shrugged. 'Tom knows more about the history of Coomb Valley than anyone. It's an amazing heritage. You and your client might like to learn a little of it.'

He noticed that every time she said 'client' she lent a slight emphasis to it, as if to distance herself from the Lockyer-Foxes. 'It's not necessary, Captain Smith. You've already convinced me that you feel a strong connection to this place.'

She went on as if she hadn't heard him. 'There was a Roman settlement here two thousand years ago. Tom's the expert on it. He rambles a bit but he's always willing to pass on his knowledge.'

He declined politely. 'Thank you, but it's a long drive back to London and I've a stack of paperwork in the office.'

She flashed him a sympathetic glance. 'You're a busy man . . . no time to stand and stare. Tom will be disappointed. He loves chewing the cud, particularly with Londoners who have no idea of Herefordshire's ancient traditions. Round here we take them seriously. It's our link to our past.'

He sighed to himself. *Did she think he hadn't got the message already?* 'Yes, well, with the best will in the world, Captain Smith, talking to a total stranger about a place I'm not acquainted with isn't a top priority for me at the moment.'

'No,' she agreed coolly, standing up, 'nor for me. We both have better things to do with our time than listen to elderly strangers reminisce about people and places that have no relevance to us. If you explain my refusal to your client in those terms, then I'm sure he'll understand that what he's suggesting is a wearisome imposition that I could do without.'

He'd walked into that with his eyes wide open, thought Mark ruefully as he, too, rose to his feet. 'Just for the record,' he asked, 'would it have made any difference if I'd said from the start that it was your grandfather who was looking for you?'

Nancy shook her head. 'No.'

'That's a relief. I haven't made a complete dog's breakfast of it, then.'

She relaxed enough to give him a smile of genuine warmth. 'I'm not unusual, you know. There are as many adopted children who are perfectly content with their lot as there are who need to go looking for the lost pieces in their jigsaws. Perhaps it has something to do with expectation. If you're satisfied with what you have, then why court trouble?'

It wouldn't do for Mark, but then he didn't share her confidence in herself. 'I probably shouldn't say this,' he told her, reaching for his briefcase, 'but you owe the Smiths a lot. You'd be a very different person if you'd grown up a Lockyer-Fox.'

35

She looked amused. 'Should I take that as a compliment?'

'Yes.'

'It'll make my mother's day.' She led him to the front door and held out her hand. 'Goodbye, Mr Ankerton. If you have any sense you'll tell the Colonel he's got off lightly. That should kill his interest.'

'I can try,' he said, taking her hand, 'but he won't believe me . . . not if I describe you accurately.'

She pulled out of his grip and stepped back inside the doorway. 'I was talking about legal action, Mr Ankerton. I'll certainly sue if you or he ever approach me again. Will you make that clear to him, please?'

'Yes,' he said.

She gave a brief nod and closed the door, and Mark was left to pick his way through the mud, less concerned with failure than with regret for an opportunity missed.

Fox hunters and saboteurs resume hostilities

Boxing Day will see a return to fox hunting after foot-and-mouth restrictions were lifted yesterday. The sport was voluntarily suspended in February after hunts nationwide agreed to support the ban on animal movements during the epidemic. It has been the most peaceful 10 months since the crusade against fox hunting began 30 years ago, but the Boxing Day meets will rekindle the antagonism between the pro- and anti-hunting groups which has been on a back burner for most of 2001.

'We expect a huge turnout,' said a spokesman for the Countryside Alliance Campaign for Hunting. 'Many thousands of ordinary people recognize that hunting is a necessary part of rural life. Fox numbers have doubled in the 10-month layoff, and sheep farmers are worried about the number of lambs they are losing.'

Hunt saboteurs have pledged to be out in force. 'People feel strongly about this,' said one activist

37

from west London. 'All saboteurs are united in their desire to protect foxes from people who want to kill them for fun. There is no place for this kind of savage blood sport in the 21st century. It's a lie to say fox numbers have doubled. The summer has always been a closed season to hunting, so how could extending the layoff by three months result in a "plague"? Such claims are pure propaganda.'

According to a recent Mori survey, 83% of people polled found hunting with dogs either cruel, unnecessary, unacceptable or outdated. But even if the Prime Minister makes good his recent pledge to ban fox hunting before the next election, the debate will continue.

The pro-lobby argues that the fox is vermin and will need to be controlled whether hunting is banned or not. 'No government can legislate against the fox's predatory instincts. Once inside the wire, he will kill every chicken in the run, not because he's hungry but because he enjoys killing. Currently 250,000 foxes are culled annually to keep the numbers at an acceptable level. Without hunting, the fox population will grow out of control and people's attitudes will change.'

The anti-lobby disagrees. 'Like any other animal, the fox adapts to its environment. If a farmer fails to protect his stock then he can expect it to be preyed upon. That's Nature. Cats kill for enjoyment but no one's suggesting we set a pack of hounds on the family moggy. Where's the sense in blaming the fox when the debate should be about animal husbandry?'

The pro-lobby: 'Hounds dispatch cleanly and quickly while snares, traps and shooting are unreliable methods of control, often leading to severe injury with no guarantee that the fox is the animal captured. Injured animals die slowly and painfully, and the public mood will shift when this becomes apparent.'

The anti-lobby: 'If the fox is as dangerous as hunts claim, why do they use artificial earths to encourage their numbers? A gamekeeper recently admitted that for 30 years he's been producing foxes and pheasants for the hunt. If you're a keeper in hunting country, it's obligatory to provide an animal for the kill, otherwise you're out of a job.'

The accusations and recriminations are bitter. The Countryside Alliance's pretence that it's a rural v urban issue is as absurd as the League Against Cruel Sports' claim that no jobs will be lost if fox hunters make a 'wholesome switch to drag hunting'. Dislike of killing a native animal for sport is as strongly felt in rural areas as it is in the town, and the Woodland Trust, for one, refuses to allow hunts across its land. By contrast, drag hunting will only secure jobs if huntsmen, many of whom are farmers, can be persuaded that signing up to a group activity which offers no useful benefit to the community is worth their time and money.

Each side would like to paint the other as destroyers – of a way of life or of a vulnerable animal – but the verdict on whether or not hunting should be banned will rest on the public perception of the fox. It's not good news for the hunting lobby. Another recent opinion poll posed this choice: Place the following in order of the damage they do to the countryside: 1) Foxes; 2) Tourists; 3) New Age travellers. 98% of the respondents put Travellers at the top. 2% (presumably huntsmen suspecting a trap) put Foxes; 100% found Tourists the least damaging because of the money they bring into rural economies.

Brer Fox in his red coat and white slippers appeals to us. A man on the dole in an unlicensed vehicle does not. The government should take note. *Vulpes vulgaris* is not an endangered species, yet he is busy acquiring protection status through the many campaigns to preserve him. It is the Traveller who now enjoys the status of vermin. Such is the might of public opinion.

But since when was might right?

Anne Cattrell

Four

BOB DAWSON LEANED on his spade and watched his wife pick her way across the frost-covered vegetable garden to the back door of Shenstead Manor, her mouth turned down in bitter resentment against a world that had defeated her. Small and bent, her old face creased with wrinkles, she muttered to herself continuously. Bob could predict exactly what she was saying because she repeated it over and over again, day after day, in an unending stream that made him want to kill her.

It wasn't right for a woman of her age to be working still . . . She'd been a skivvy and a slave all her life . . . A seventy-year-old should be allowed her rest . . . What did Bob ever do except sit on a lawnmower in the summer . . .? How dare he keep ordering her up to the Manor . . . It wasn't safe to be in the house with the Colonel . . . Everyone knew that . . . Did Bob care . . .? Of course not . . . 'You keep your mouth shut,' he'd say, 'or you'll feel the back of my hand . . . Do you want us to lose the roof over our heads . . .?'

Insight had faded a long time ago, leaving Vera's head full of martyred resentment. She had no understanding that she and Bob paid nothing for their house because Mrs Lockyer-Fox had promised it to them for life. All she understood was that the Colonel paid her wages in return for cleaning, and her aim in life was to keep those wages from her husband. Bob was a bully and tyrant, and she squirrelled away her earnings in forgotten hiding places. She liked secrets, always had done, and Shenstead Manor had more than most. She had cleaned for the Lockyer-Foxes for forty years, and for forty years they had taken advantage of her, with the help of her husband.

A clinical psychologist would have said that dementia had released the frustrated personality she had repressed since she married at twenty to improve herself and chose the wrong man. Bob's ambition had been satisfied by a rent-free tied cottage in return for lowly paid gardening and cleaning duties at Shenstead Manor. Vera's ambitions had been to own a house, raise a family and select her customers herself.

The few close neighbours they'd had had long since moved away, and the new ones avoided her, unable to cope with her obsessional loops. Bob might be a taciturn man who eschewed company, but at least he still had his marbles and patiently tolerated her attacks on him in public. What he did in private was his own concern, but the way Vera smacked him whenever he contradicted her suggested they were no strangers to physical conflict. Nevertheless, sympathy tended to be with Bob. No one blamed him for pushing her out of the house to work up at the Manor. A man would go mad with Vera for company all day.

Bob watched her feet drag as she looked towards the south-west corner of the Manor. Sometimes she talked about seeing Mrs Lockyer-Fox's body on the terrace . . . shut out in the cold night and left to freeze to death with next-to-nothing on. Vera knew about cold. She was cold all the time, and she was ten years younger than Mrs Lockyer-Fox.

Bob threatened her with the back of his hand if she repeated in public the stuff about the door being locked, but it didn't stop the muttering. Her affection for the dead woman had grown exponentially since Ailsa's death, all recriminations forgotten in sentimental remembrance of the many kindnesses Ailsa had shown her. *She* wouldn't have insisted on a poor old woman working beyond her time. *She* would have said the time had come for Vera to rest.

The police had paid her no attention, of course – not after Bob had screwed his finger into his forehead and told them she was gaga. They smiled politely and said the Colonel had been cleared of any involvement in his wife's death. Never mind that he'd been alone in the house . . . and the French windows onto the terrace could only be locked and bolted from the inside. Vera's sense of injustice remained strong but Bob cursed her roundly if she expressed it.

It was a can of worms that shouldn't be opened. Did she think the Colonel would take her accusations lying down? Did she think he wouldn't mention her thieving or how angry he'd been to find his mother's rings gone? You don't bite the hand that feeds you, he warned her, even if the same hand had been raised in anger when the Colonel found her rifling through his desk drawers.

Occasionally, when she looked at him out of the corner of her eye, Bob wondered if she was more lucid than she pretended. It worried him. It meant there were thoughts inside her head that he couldn't control . . .

*

Vera opened the gate into Mrs Lockyer-Fox's Italian courtyard and scurried past the withered plants in the huge terracotta pots. She fished in her pocket for the key to the scullery door, and smiled to herself when she saw the fox's brush pinned to the jamb beside the lock. It was an old one – probably from the summer – and she plucked it down and stroked the fur against her cheek before concealing it in her coat pocket. In this matter, at least, there had never been any confusion. The brush was a calling card that she never failed to remember or recognize.

Out of sight of her husband the muttering had taken a different direction. Bloody old bugger . . . she'd show him . . . he wasn't a real man and never had been . . . a real man would have given her babies . . .

Five

Shenstead – 25 December 2001

VEHICLES MOVED ONTO the tract of unregistered woodland to the west of Shenstead Village at eight o'clock on Christmas evening. None of the inhabitants heard their stealthy approach, or if they did there was no linkage of ideas between engine sound and New Age invasion. It was four months since the events at Barton Edge, and memories had dimmed. For all the hot air expended over the pages of the local rag, the 'rave' had inspired a Nimby *Schadenfreude* in Shenstead, rather than fear that the same thing might happen there. Dorset was too small a county for lightning to strike twice.

A bright moon allowed the slow-moving convoy to negotiate the narrow lane across the valley without headlights. As the six buses neared the entrance to the Copse, they drew into the side of the road and killed their engines, waiting for one of their party to explore the access track for pitfalls. The ground was frozen to a depth of two feet from the bitter east wind that had been blowing for days, with another hard frost promised for the morning. There was absolute silence as a torch beam flickered from side to side, showing the width of the track and the crescent-shaped clearing at the entrance to the wood that was large enough to accommodate vehicles.

On another, warmer, night the ramshackle convoy would have become bogged down in the soft, damp clay of the track before it reached the relative safety of the root-toughened woodland floor. But not on this night. With careful marshalling, as precisely dictated as aircraft movements on a carrier, the six vehicles followed the gesturing torch beam and parked in a rough semicircle under the skeletal branches of the outer trees. The torch bearer had a few minutes' conversation with each driver before windows were obscured with cardboard and the occupants retired for the night.

Although unaware of it, Shenstead Village had had its resident population more than doubled in under an hour. Its disadvantage was its situation in a remote valley which cut through the Dorset Ridge-way to the sea. Of its fifteen houses, eleven were holiday homes, owned by either rental businesses or distant city dwellers, while the four that remained in full-time occupation contained just ten people, three of whom were children. Estate agents continued to describe it as an 'unspoilt gem' whenever the holiday homes came up for sale at exorbitant prices, but the truth was very different. Once a thriving community of fisher folk and workers of the land, it was now the casual resting place of strangers who had no interest in fighting a turf war.

And what could the full-time residents have done if they had realized their way of life was about to be threatened? Called the police and admit the land had no owner?

Dick Weldon, half a mile to the west of the village, had made a half-hearted attempt to enclose the acre strip of woodland three years earlier when he bought Shenstead Farm, but his fence had never remained intact for more than a week. At the time he had blamed the Lockyer-Foxes and their tenants for the broken rails as theirs was the only other property with a competing claim, but it soon became apparent that no one in Shenstead was ready to let a Johnny-come-lately increase the value of his property for the cost of some cheap wooden posts.

It was well known that it took twelve years of uninterrupted usage to claim a piece of wasteland in law, and even the weekenders had no intention of surrendering their dog-walking territory so tamely. With planning permission for a house the site would be worth a small fortune, and there was little doubt in anyone's mind, despite Dick's protests to the contrary, that that was his goal. What other use was woodland to an arable farmer unless he felled the trees and ploughed the land? Either way, the Copse would fall to the axe.

Weldon had argued that it must have belonged to Shenstead Farm at some point because it cut a U-shaped loop into his curtilage with only a meagre hundred yards bordering the Lockyer-Foxes at the Manor. Privately most people agreed with him, but without the documents to prove it – almost certainly a careless oversight by a solicitor in the past – and with no guarantee of success, there seemed little point in arguing the case in court. The legal costs could amount to more than the land was worth, even with planning permission, and Weldon was too much of a realist to risk it. As ever in Shenstead, the issue died through apathy, and the 'common land' status of the wood was restored. At least in the minds of the villagers.

The pity was that no one had troubled to record it as such under the 1965 Commons Registration Act which would have given it status in law. Instead, unclaimed and unowned, it remained tantalizingly available to the first squatter who took up residence on it and was prepared to defend his right to stay.

*

Contrary to the instructions he had given his convoy to stay put, Fox stole down the lane and prowled from house to house. Apart from the Manor, the only property of any size was Shenstead House, home to Julian and Eleanor Bartlett. It was set back from the road down a short gravel driveway, and Fox picked his way along the grass verge to deaden his footsteps. He stood for several minutes beside the drawing-room window, watching through a gap in the curtains as Eleanor made serious inroads into her husband's cellar.

She was a good sixty, but HRT, Botox injections and regular home aerobics were doing their bit to keep her skin firm. From a distance, she looked younger, but not tonight. She lay on the sofa, eyes glued to the television screen in the corner where *EastEnders* was playing, her ferrety face puffed and blotchy from the bottle of Cabernet Sauvignon on the floor. Unaware of a peeping Tom, she kept delving her hand into her bra to scratch her breasts, making her blouse gape and showing the tell-tale sags and wrinkles around her neck and cleavage.

It was the human side of a nouveau riche snob and it would have amused Fox if he had any liking for her. Instead, it increased his contempt. He moved around the side of the house to see if he could locate her husband. As usual, Julian was in his study, *his* face, too, flushed with alcohol from the bottle of Glenfiddich on the desk in front of him. He was talking on the telephone and his hearty laugh rattled against the pane. Snippets of the conversation drifted through the glass. '. . . don't be so paranoid . . . she's watching telly in the sitting room . . . of course not

. . . she's far too self-centred . . . yes, yes, I should be there by nine thirty at the latest . . . Geoff tells me the hounds are out of practice and saboteurs are expected in droves . . .'

Like his wife he didn't look his age, but he kept a secret stash of Grecian 2000 in his dressing room which Eleanor didn't know about. Fox had found it on a stealthy tour of the house one afternoon in September when Julian had gone out and left the back door unlocked. The hair dye wasn't the only thing that Eleanor didn't know about, and Fox toyed with the razor in his pocket as he thought of his satisfaction when she found out. The husband couldn't control his appetites, but the wife had a vicious streak that made her fair game to a hunter like Fox.

He abandoned Shenstead House to stalk the weekender cottages, looking for life. Most were boarded up for the winter, but in one he found a foursome. The overweight twin sons of the London banker who owned it were with a couple of giggly girls who clung to the men's necks and shrieked hysterically every time they spoke. The fastidious side of Fox's nature found the spectacle distasteful: Tweedledum and Tweedledee, with the sweat of overindulgence staining their shirts and glistening on their brows, looking to score over Christmas with a couple of willing scrubbers.

The twins' only attraction for women was their

father's wealth – which they vaunted – and the fervour with which the drunken girls were throwing themselves into the party spirit suggested a determination to be part of it. If they had any intention of emerging before their libidos wore out, Fox thought, they wouldn't be interested in the encampment at the Copse.

Two of the commercial rents had staid-looking families in them, but otherwise there were only the Woodgates at Paddock View – the husband-and-wife-team who looked after the commercial properties, and their three young children – and Bob and Vera Dawson at Manor Lodge. Fox couldn't predict how Stephen Woodgate would react to travellers on his doorstep. The man was deeply lazy, so Fox's best guess was that he would leave it to James Lockyer-Fox and Dick Weldon to sort out. If nothing happened by the beginning of January, Woodgate might make a phone call to his employers, but there'd be no urgency until the letting season got under way in spring.

By contrast, Fox could predict exactly how the Dawsons would react. They would bury their heads in the sand as they always did. It wasn't their place to ask questions. They lived in their cottage courtesy of James Lockyer-Fox and, as long as the Colonel honoured his wife's promise to keep them there, they would pay lip service to supporting him. In a bizarre echo of the Bartletts, Vera was glued to

EastEnders and Bob was closeted in the kitchen, listening to the radio. If they spoke at all that night, it would be to have a row, because whatever love they had once shared was long since dead.

He lingered for a moment to watch the old woman mutter to herself. In her way she was as vicious as Eleanor Bartlett but hers was the viciousness of a wasted life and a diseased brain, and her target was invariably her husband. Fox had as much contempt for her as he had for Eleanor. In the end, they had both chosen the lives they led.

He returned to the Copse and picked his way through the wood to his vantage point beside the Manor. It was all good, he thought, catching sight of Mark Ankerton sitting hunched over the old man's desk in the library. Even the solicitor was on hand. It wouldn't suit everyone, but it suited Fox.

He held them all to blame for the man he had become.

*

The first person to see the encampment was Julian Bartlett, who drove past at eight o'clock on Boxing Day morning on his way to the West Dorset meet at Compton Newton. He slowed as he spotted a rope across the frontage with a painted notice saying 'keep out' hanging from its centre, and his gaze was drawn to the vehicles amongst the trees.

Dressed for the hunt, in yellow shirt, white tie and

buff breeches, and towing a horsebox behind his Range Rover, he had no intention of becoming involved and speeded up again. Once out of the valley, he drew into the side of the road and phoned Dick Weldon, whose farm the land abutted.

'We have visitors in the Copse,' he said.

'What sort of visitors?'

'I didn't stop to find out. They're almost certainly fox lovers, and I didn't fancy taking them on with Bouncer in the back.'

'Saboteurs?'

'Maybe. More likely travellers. Most of the vehicles look like they've come from a scrap-metal yard.'

'Did you see any people?'

'No. I doubt they're awake yet. They've slung a notice across the entrance saying "keep out", so it might be dangerous to tackle them on your own.'

'Damn! I knew we'd have a problem with that piece of land eventually. We'll probably have to pay a solicitor to get rid of them . . . and that's not going to be cheap.'

'I'd call the police if I were you. They deal with this kind of thing every day.'

'Mm.'

'I'll leave it with you then.'

'*Bastard!*' said Dick with feeling.

There was a faint laugh. 'It'll be chicken feed compared with the melee I'm heading for. Word is the sabs have been seeding false trails all night, so

God only knows what sort of a shambles it's going to be. I'll call when I get home.' Bartlett switched off his mobile.

Irritably, Weldon pulled on his Barbour and summoned his dogs, calling up the stairs to his wife that he was going to the Copse. Bartlett was probably right that it was a job for the police, but he wanted to satisfy himself before he phoned them. His gut feeling said they were saboteurs. The Boxing Day meet had been well publicized and, after the ten months' layoff because of foot-and-mouth, both sides were spoiling for a fight. If so, they'd be gone again by the evening.

He bundled the dogs into the back of his mud-spattered Jeep and drove the half-mile from the farmhouse to the Copse. The road had a hoar of frost on it and he picked up Bartlett's tyre tracks coming from Shenstead House. There was no sign of life anywhere else and he guessed that, like his wife, people were making the most of their bank-holiday lie-in.

It was a different story at the Copse. As he drew into the entrance, a line of people spread out behind the rope barrier to block his way. They made an intimidating array with balaclavas and scarves hiding their faces and thick coats bulking out their bodies. A couple of barking Alsatians on leads lunged forward as the vehicle stopped, teeth bared aggressively, and Dick's two Labradors set up an answering clamour. He cursed Bartlett for driving on by. If the man had had the sense to demolish the barrier and call for reinforcements before these buggers could organize, instructions to keep out would have had no validity. As it was, Dick had a nasty suspicion they might be within their rights.

He opened his door and climbed out. 'OK, what's this all about?' he demanded. 'Who are you? What are you doing here?'

'We might ask you the same thing,' said a voice from the middle of the line.

Because of the scarves across their mouths, Dick couldn't make out who had spoken, so he homed in on the one at the centre. 'If you're hunt saboteurs, I don't have much of an argument with you. My views on the subject are well known. The fox is not a pest to arable farmers so I don't allow the hunt across my land because of the damage it does to my crops and hedgerows. If that's why you're here, then you're wasting your time. The West Dorset Hunt will not come into this valley.'

This time it was a woman's voice that answered. 'Good on yer, mate. They're all fucking sadists. Riding around in red coats so the blood won't show when the poor little fing gets ripped to pieces.'

Dick relaxed slightly. 'Then you're in the wrong place. The meet's in Compton Newton. It's about ten miles to the west of here, on the other side of Dorchester. If you take the bypass and head towards

Yeovil, you'll see Compton Newton signed to the left. The hunt is assembling outside the pub, and the hounds will be called for an eleven o'clock start.'

The same woman answered again, presumably because she was the androgynous figure he was looking at: big and burly in an army-surplus overcoat and with an accent straight from the Essex marshes. 'Sorry, mate, but I'm the only one that agrees with you. The rest couldn't give a shit one way or the other. You can't eat foxes, see, so they ain't much good to us. It's different with deer 'coz they're edible, and none of us can see the point of letting dogs 'ave their meat . . . not when there's humans like us needs it.'

Still hoping for saboteurs, Dick allowed himself to be drawn into discussion. 'There's no deer hunting with dogs in Dorset. Devon possibly . . . but not here.'

'Sure there is. You think any hunt will pass up the chance of a buck if the hounds get wind of it? It ain't no one's fault if a little Bambi gets killed 'coz the dogs go after the wrong scent. That's life. There ain't nothing you can do about it. Numbers of times we've set traps for somefink to eat, and we end up with a poor little moggy's foot in the workings. You can bet your bottom dollar there's an old lady some-where, weeping her heart out 'coz Tom never came home . . . but dead is dead, never mind it ain't what you planned.'

58

Dick shook his head, recognizing that argument was futile. 'If you're not prepared to tell me why you're here, then I'll have to call the police. You've no right to trespass on private property.'

The remark was greeted with silence.

'All right,' said Dick, taking a mobile from his pocket, 'though be warned, I *will* prosecute if you've caused any damage. I work hard for the environment and I'm sick to death of types like you ruining it for the rest of us.'

'Are you saying it's your property, Mr Weldon?' said the same well-spoken voice that had answered him at the beginning.

For the briefest of moments he had a sense of recognition – it was a voice he knew, but without a face he couldn't put it in context. He searched the line for the speaker. 'How do you know my name?'

'We checked the electoral register.' This time there was a rougher edge to the vowels as if the speaker had noticed his sharpened interest and wanted to deflect it.

'That wouldn't help you recognize me.'

'R. Weldon, Shenstead Farm. You said you were an arable farmer. How many others are there in the valley?'

'Two tenant farmers.'

'P. Squires and G. Drew. Their farms are to the south. If you were one of them you'd have come the other way.'

'You're too well informed to have got all that from the electoral register,' said Dick, scrolling through his mobile menu for the local police station. His calls usually concerned poachers or burnt-out cars in his fields – an increasing nuisance since the government had declared zero tolerance on unlicensed vehicles – which was why he had the number on file. 'I recognize your voice, my friend. I can't place it at the moment—' he selected the number and punched the call button, raising the phone to his ear – 'but I'm betting this lot will know who you are.'

The watching people waited in silence while he spoke to the sergeant at the other end. If any of them smiled as he became increasingly irritated at the advice he was being given, the smiles remained hidden behind their scarves. He turned his back towards them and walked away, making an effort to keep his voice down, but the angry hunching of his shoulders was the best indication they could have that he didn't like what he was hearing.

Six vehicles or less were considered an acceptable size for an encampment, particularly if it was at a distance from neighbours and posed no threat to road safety. The landowner could apply for eviction, but it would take time. The best course was to negotiate the length of stay through the Traveller Liaison Officer at the local authority and avoid unnecessary confrontation with the visitors. The sergeant reminded Dick that farmers had recently been arrested in Lincolnshire and Essex for using threatening behaviour against groups who had invaded their land. The police were sympathetic to landowners but their first priority was to avoid anyone getting hurt.

'Godammit!' Dick rasped, cupping his hand across his mouth to muffle the words. 'Who wrote these rules? You telling me they can park wherever they fancy, do whatever they like, and if the poor sap who owns the bloody land objects, you bastards'll arrest him? Yeah . . . yeah . . . I'm sorry . . . no offence intended. So what rights do the poor sods who live here have?'

In return for occupying the site, travellers were asked to agree to certain conditions. These concerned appropriate disposal of household and human waste, the proper control of animals, health and safety issues, and agreements not to reoccupy the same site within a period of three months or use threatening or intimidatory behaviour.

Dick's ruddy face turned apoplectic. 'You call those *rights*?' he hissed. 'We're expected to offer house-room to a bunch of crooks and all we get in exchange is a promise that they'll behave in a halfway civilized manner.' He shot an angry glance towards the line. 'And how do you define threatening and intimidating behaviour anyway? There's a dozen of them blocking my way and they're all wearing masks over their faces . . . not to mention some damn dogs and the "keep out" notice they've slung across the track. What's that if it's not intimidating?' He hunched his shoulders lower. 'Yes, well, that's the problem,' he muttered, 'no one knows who owns it. It's an acre of woodland on the edge of the village.' He listened for a moment. '*Jesus wept!* Whose side are you on, for Christ's sake? . . . Yeah, well, it might not be an issue for you but it sodding well is for me. You wouldn't have a job if I didn't pay my taxes.'

He snapped the mobile closed and shoved it into his pocket before returning to the Jeep and yanking the door open. A ripple of laughter ran along the line.

'Got a problem, have you, Mr Weldon?' said the voice in a mocking tone. 'Let me guess. The busies have told you to phone the council negotiator.'

Dick ignored him and climbed behind the wheel.

'Don't forget to tell her that no one owns this land. She lives in Bridport, and she'll be mighty stroppy if she has to drive all this way on her holiday to learn it from us.'

Dick started the engine and turned the Jeep broadside to the line. 'Who are you?' he demanded through the open window. 'How do you know so much about Shenstead?'

But the question was greeted with silence. Furiously grinding his gears, Dick made a three-point turn and returned home to discover that the negotiator was indeed a woman, did live in Bridport and refused to give up her holiday to negotiate over a piece of unclaimed land that squatters had as much right to occupy as anyone in the village.

Mr Weldon should never have mentioned that the land was in dispute. Without that knowledge she could have negotiated a length of stay that would have suited neither party. It would have been too short for the travellers and too long for the villagers. All land in England and Wales was owned by someone, but a failure to register left it open to opportunists.

For whatever reason, Mr Weldon had volunteered information that suggested solicitors would become involved – '*No, I'm sorry, sir, you were a fool to take advice from the squatters. This is a grey area of law . . .*' – and there was little she could do until agreement was reached on who owned the land. *Of course* it was unjust. *Of course* it went against every norm of legal fairness. *Of course* she was on the side of the taxpayers.

But . . .

Shenstead Manor, Shenstead, Dorset

1st October, 2001

Dear Captain Smith,

My solicitor informs me that if I attempt to contact you, you will sue. For that reason I should make it clear that I am writing without Mark Ankerton's knowledge and that the entire responsibility for this letter is mine. Please be assured, too, that any suit you bring will not be contested and I will pay any compensation that a court sees fit to award.

In these circumstances, I am sure you are wondering why I am writing so potentially costly a letter. Call it a gamble, Captain Smith. I am wagering the cost of damages against a one in ten – perhaps even a one in a hundred – chance that you will respond.

Mark has described you as an intelligent, well-balanced, successful and brave young woman, who feels an absolute loyalty to her parents and has no desire to learn anything about people who are strangers to her. He tells me your family has a long history, and that your ambition is to take over your father's farm when you leave the army. In addition, he says you are a credit to Mr and Mrs Smith, and suggests that your adoption was the best thing that could have happened to you.

Please believe there is nothing he could have said that

would have given me greater pleasure. My wife and I always hoped that your future was in the hands of good people. Mark has repeated several times that you have no curiosity about your relations, to the extent that you do not wish even to know their names. Should your determination remain as strong, then throw this letter away now and do not read on.

I have always been fond of fables. When my children were small I used to read Aesop to them. They were particularly fond of stories about the Fox and the Lion, for reasons that will become obvious. I am reluctant to put too much information into this letter, for fear of giving you the impression that I care little for your strongly held feelings. To that end, I enclose a variation on an Aesop fable and two newspaper clippings. From what Mark tells me, you will certainly be able to read between the lines of all three and draw some accurate conclusions.

Suffice it to say that my wife and I failed dismally to achieve the same high standard of parenting with our two children as the Smiths achieved with you. It would be easy to lay the blame for this at the door of the army – the absence of a father figure whenever I was away on duty, foreign postings when neither parent was at home, the influences they fell under at boarding school, the lack of supervision during holidays at home – but that would be wrong, I think.

The fault lay with us. We overindulged them to compensate for our absences and interpreted their wild behaviour as attention-seeking. We also took the view – shamefully, I fear – that the family name was worth something and rarely, if ever, did we ask them to face up to their mistakes. The greatest loss was you, Nancy. For the worst of reasons –

snobbery – we helped our daughter find a 'good husband' by keeping her pregnancy secret, and in the process gave away our only grandchild. If I were a religious man, I would say it was a punishment for setting so much store by family honour. We abandoned you rashly to protect our reputation without any understanding of your fine qualities or what the future might hold.

The irony of all this hit me very strongly when Mark told me how unimpressed you were by your Lockyer-Fox connection. In the end, a name is only a name and a family's worth resides in the sum of its parts not in the label they have chosen to attach to themselves. Had I come to this view earlier, I doubt I would be writing this letter. My children would have grown up to be stable members of society, and you would have been welcomed for who you were, not banished for what you were.

I will finish by saying that this is the only letter I shall write. If you don't reply or if you instruct a solicitor to sue, I shall accept that the gamble is lost. I have purposefully not explained my real reason for wanting to meet you, although you may suspect that your status as my only grandchild has something to do with it.

I believe Mark told you that you would be doing a great kindness by agreeing to see me. May I add that you would also be offering the hope of redress to someone who is dead.

Yours sincerely,

James Lockyer-Fox

The Lion, the elderly Fox and the generous Ass

The Lion, the Fox and the Ass lived together in intimate friendship for several years until the Lion grew scornful of the Fox's age
and derided the Ass for her generosity to strangers. He demanded
the respect due his superior might, and insisted her generosity be
shown only to him. The Ass, in great trepidation, assembled all
her wealth into one large heap and offered it to the Fox for safe
keeping until the Lion mended his ways. The Lion burst into a
great rage and devoured the Ass. Then he requested the Fox do
him the favour of making the division of the Ass's wealth. The
elderly Fox, aware that he was no match for the Lion, pointed to
the pile and invited the Lion to take it. The Lion, assuming the
Fox had learnt sense from the death of the Ass, said, 'Who has
taught you, my very excellent fellow, the art of division? You are
perfect to a fraction.' The Fox replied, 'I learnt the value of
generosity from my friend, the Ass.' Then he raised his voice and
called upon the animals of the jungle to put the Lion to flight
and share the Ass's fortune amongst themselves. 'In this way,'
he told the Lion, 'you will have nothing and the Ass will be
avenged.'

But the Lion devoured the Fox and took the Fox's fortune instead.

Lockyer-Fox – Ailsa Flora, unexpectedly at home on 6 March 2001, aged 78. Dearly loved wife of James, mother of Leo and Elizabeth, and generous friend to many. Funeral service at St Peter's, Dorchester on Thursday 15 March at 12.30. No flowers please, but donations if desired to Dr Barnardo's or the Royal Society for the Prevention of Cruelty to Animals.

Coroner's Verdict

A coroner's inquest ruled yester-day that Ailsa Lockyer-Fox, 78, of Shenstead Manor died of natural causes despite an inconclusive post mortem and pathologist's report which failed to identify a reason for death. A police investigation was launched after bloodstains were found near the body and neighbours alleged an angry argu-ment on the night of her death.

Mrs Lockyer-Fox was dis-covered on the terrace of Shen-stead Manor on the morning of 6 March by her husband. She was wearing nightclothes and had been dead for some time. Colonel Lock-yer-Fox, who gave evidence at the inquest, said he believed she must have risen during the night to feed the foxes that were regular visitors to Shenstead Manor. 'I can only assume she lost consciousness and died of cold.' He denied that the French windows were locked on the inside when he came down-stairs, or that Mrs Lockyer-Fox was unable to regain entry to the house had she wished.

The coroner referred to one neighbour's claim that she heard a man and woman arguing shortly after midnight on 6 March. Colonel Lockyer-Fox denied that he and his wife were the people in question, and the coroner accepted his state-ment. He also accepted that blood-stains found on flagstones two metres from the body were animal and not human. In dismissing the speculation that has surrounded Ailsa Lockyer-Fox's death, he said: 'Rumour in this case was entirely unfounded. I hope today's verdict will bring an end to it. For what-ever reason, Mrs Lockyer-Fox decided to go outside on a cold night, inadequately dressed, and tragically collapsed.'

The daughter of a wealthy Scot-tish landowner, Ailsa Lockyer-Fox was well known for her campaigns against cruelty to animals. 'She will be greatly missed,' said a spokesman for the Dorset branch of the League Against Cruel Sports. 'She believed that all life had value and should be treated with respect.' She was also a generous benefactor of local and national children's homes and charities. Her personal estate, valued at £1.2m, passes to her husband.

Debbie Fowler

Kosovo

Tuesday, 6th November

Dear Colonel Lockyer-Fox,

Your letter was forwarded to me by my mother. I, too, have an interest in fabular culture. The bones of your fable are 'The Lion, the Fox and the Ass', one of whose morals could be described as: 'Might makes Right'. You could have applied a similar moral to your own tale: 'The Might of Many makes Right', since the implication is that you are dismantling your wife's fortune in order to give it away to more deserving causes than your son – presumably children and animal charities. This seems to me a very sensible course, particularly if he was responsible for her death. I am not a great believer in leopards (or Lions) changing their spots, so I remain cynical that he will 'mend his ways'.

I am not entirely clear from the clipping re: the coroner's verdict who was the subject of the speculation following your wife's death, although I suspect it may have been you. However, if I have read your fable correctly then your son is Leo the Lion, your wife was Ailsa the Ass and you are the Fox who witnessed her murder. So why didn't you inform the police of this instead of allowing speculation to grow? Or is this another case of hiding family 'mistakes' under the carpet? Your strategy would seem to be that redress for your wife is best achieved by denying your son his inheritance, but isn't justice through the courts the only true redress? Whatever instability problems your son has will not be improved by allowing him to get away with murder.

You seem to refer to this in your last sentence. 'The Lion devoured the Fox and took the Fox's fortune instead.' This is obviously a prediction and not a fact, otherwise you could not have written to me, but I strongly question how acknowledging me as your only grandchild can shift this prediction in your favour. I fear it will do the exact opposite and force your son into precipitate action. In view of the fact that I have no interest at all in your or your wife's money – and have no wish to confront your son over it – I suggest it would be infinitely wiser to seek the advice of your solicitor, Mark Ankerton, in respect of putting the money beyond your son's reach.

Without wishing to be offensive, I see no reason at all why you should allow yourself to be 'devoured' so tamely, nor why I should be proposed as a stalking horse.

Yours sincerely,

Nancy Smith

Nancy Smith (Captain, Royal Engineers)

Shenstead Manor, Shenstead, Dorset

30th November 2001

Dear Nancy,

Please think no more about it. Everything you say is completely justified. I wrote in a moment of depression and used emotive language that was unforgivable. I did not wish in any way to give you the impression that you would be in confrontation with Leo. Mark has constructed a will that honours my obligations to my family while giving the bulk of the estate to worthy causes. It was an old man's foolish whim and arrogance that wanted the 'family silver' to pass intact to family.

I fear my last letter may have given you a false impression of both myself and Leo. Inadvertently I may have suggested that I am perceived in warmer terms than he. This is far from the truth. Leo is extraordinarily charming. I, by contrast – indeed Ailsa, too, when she was alive – are (were) rather shy people who appear stiff-necked and pompous in company. Until recently I would have said that our friends perceived us differently, but the isolation in which I now find myself has shattered my confidence. With the honourable exception of Mark Ankerton, suspicion, it seems, is more easily attracted than dispelled.

You pose the question: how will acknowledging you as my only grandchild benefit me? It won't. I see that now. It was an idea conceived some time ago when Ailsa came to share my view that we would do our children more harm than good by giving them access to large amounts of money on our deaths. However, Mark's view was that Leo would challenge any will that gave large bequests to charities on the basis that the money was family money and should pass to the next generation. Leo may or may not have won, but he would certainly have found it harder to challenge a legitimate heir in the shape of a grandchild.

My wife was always a believer in giving people second chances – the 'mending of ways' that you referred to – and I believe she also hoped that recognition of our grandchild would persuade our son to rethink the future. Since hearing from you, I have decided to abandon this plan. It was a selfish attempt to keep the estate intact, and took no account at all of your love and loyalty to your rightful family.

You are an admirable and wise young woman with a marvellous future ahead of you, and I wish you long life and happiness. As the money is of no interest to you, nothing can be gained by involving you in my family's difficulties.

Be confident that your identity and whereabouts will remain a secret between Mark and myself, and that you will under no circumstances feature in any legal documents relating to this family.

With gratitude for your response and the warmest good wishes for whatever comes your way in life,

James Lockyer-Fox

Six

Shenstead Manor – Christmas Eve
to Boxing Day, 2001

MARK ANKERTON'S faith that James Lockyer-Fox
would never have harmed his wife was under assault
on all sides, not least from James himself. True, Mark
had forced his presence in the house, refusing to
accept the Colonel's cool assurances that he was
quite able to face his first Christmas alone in nearly
fifty years, but James's secretive behaviour and
inability to carry a conversation for more than a few
minutes were deeply worrying to his lawyer.

He wouldn't look Mark in the eye, and there were
tremors in his hands and voice. His weight had
decreased alarmingly. Always meticulous about his
appearance in the past, he had become dirty and
unkempt, with straggly hair, stained clothes, and
patches of silver stubble on his chin. To Mark, for
whom the Colonel had always been an authoritative
figure, such a dramatic change in physical and mental

strength was shocking. Even the house smelt of dirt and decay, and Mark wondered if Vera Dawson had compounded her legendary laziness by ceasing to work at all.

He blamed himself for not having come down since August, when he'd delivered Nancy Smith's verdict to the old man. At the time James had taken it well and had instructed Mark to draw up a will which would result in the break-up of the Lockyer-Fox estate with only minimum bequests going to his two children. It had remained unsigned, however, with James sitting on the draft document for months, apparently reluctant to take what he perceived as an irrevocable step. When urged over the telephone to voice his concerns, his only answer had been an angry one: 'Stop harassing me. I still have my faculties. I'll make the decision in my own good time.'

Mark's worries had increased a few weeks back when an answerphone had suddenly appeared on the Manor line, as if James's naturally reclusive nature now extended to a ban on all access. Letters, which had previously been dealt with by return, went unanswered for days. On the few occasions when James bothered to return Mark's calls, his voice had sounded remote and indifferent, as if the affairs of the Lockyer-Fox estate no longer interested him. He excused his lack of enthusiasm on grounds of tiredness. He wasn't sleeping well, he said. Once or twice, Mark had asked him if he was depressed, but each time the question was greeted with tetchiness. 'There's nothing wrong with my mind,' James had said, as if it were something he feared nevertheless.

Certainly Mark had feared it, hence his insistence on this visit. He had described James's symptoms to a doctor friend in London, who told him they sounded like full-blown depression or post-traumatic stress disorder. These were normal reactions to unbearable situations: avoidance of social contact – withdrawal from responsibility – listlessness – insomnia – anxiety about incompetence – *anxiety*, full stop. Use your imagination, his friend had advised. Anyone of the Colonel's age would suffer loneliness and distress when his wife died, but to be suspected of killing her and questioned about it . . .? It was delayed shock. When had the poor old fellow been given a chance to grieve?

Mark had arrived on Christmas Eve, armed with advice about bereavement counselling and the ability of mild doses of antidepressants to lift the mood and restore optimism. But he had prepared himself for sadness, and sadness was absent. Talk of Ailsa only made James angry.

'The woman's dead,' he snapped on one occasion. 'Why this need to resurrect her?' On another: 'She should have dealt with her estate herself instead of passing the buck to me. It was pure cowardice. Nothing was ever gained by giving Leo a second chance.' An enquiry about Henry, Ailsa's elderly

Great Dane, brought an equally curt response. 'Died of old age. Best thing for him. He was always mooching around trying to find her.'

Mark's contribution to the holiday was a hamper from Harrods after his doctor friend told him that depression didn't eat. The truth of that was starkly obvious when he opened the fridge to store his brace of pheasant, pâté de foie gras and champagne. No wonder the old man had lost so much weight, he thought, eyeing the empty shelves. The chest freezer in the scullery was fairly well stocked with meat and frozen vegetables, but thick layers of frost suggested most of it had been put there by Ailsa. Announcing that he needed bread, potatoes and dairy products, even if James didn't, he drove to the Dorchester Tesco's before it closed for the holiday and stocked up on essentials – throwing in detergents, bleach, shampoo, soap and shaving equipment for good measure.

He set to with a will, scrubbing and disinfecting the surfaces in the kitchen before mopping the stone-flagged hall. James pursued him like an angry wasp, locking the doors of rooms that he didn't want him entering. All questions were greeted with half-answers. Was Vera Dawson still cleaning for him? '*She was senile and lazy.*' When did he last have a decent meal? '*He wasn't expending much energy these days.*' Were his neighbours watching out for him? '*He preferred his own company.*' Why hadn't he been answering letters? '*It was a bore to walk to the post box.*' Had he thought about replacing Henry, and giving himself an excuse for a walk? '*Animals were too much trouble.*' Wasn't it lonely living in that rambling great house with no one to talk to? Silence.

At regular intervals the phone rang in the library. James ignored it even though the drone of voices leaving messages was audible through the locked door. Mark noticed that the jack to the phone in the drawing room had come out of its socket, but when he attempted to plug it back in, the old man ordered him to stop. 'I'm neither blind nor stupid, Mark,' he said angrily, 'and I would prefer it if you ceased treating me as if I had Alzheimer's. Do I come into your house and question your arrangements? Of course not. I wouldn't dream of being so crass. Please do not do it in mine.'

It was a flicker of the man he had known, and Mark responded to it. 'I wouldn't need to if I knew what was going on,' he said, jerking his thumb towards the library. 'Why aren't you answering that?'

'I don't choose to.'

'It might be important.'

James shook his head.

'It sounds like the same person each time . . . and people don't keep calling unless it's urgent,' Mark objected, raking ashes out of the fireplace. 'At least let me check if it's for me. I gave my parents this number in case of emergencies.'

Anger flared again in the Colonel's face. 'You take too many liberties, Mark. Do I need to remind you that you invited yourself?'

The younger man relaid the fire. 'I was worried about you,' he said calmly. 'I'm even more worried now that I'm here. You may think I'm imposing, James, but you really don't have to be rude about it. I'll happily stay in a hotel for the night, but I'm not leaving till I'm satisfied you're looking after yourself properly. What does Vera *do*, for Christ's sake? When did you last have a fire? Do you want to die of hypothermia like Ailsa?'

His remarks were greeted with silence and he turned his head to assess the reaction.

'Oh lord,' he said in distress as he saw tears in the old man's eyes. He stood up and laid a sympathetic hand on James's arm. 'Look, everyone suffers from depression at some time or another. It's nothing to be ashamed of. Can't I persuade you to talk to your doctor, at least? There are various ways of dealing with it . . . I've brought some leaflets for you to read . . . all the advice says the worst thing to do is suffer in silence.'

James pulled his arm away abruptly. 'You're very keen to persuade me I'm mentally ill,' he muttered. 'Why is that? Have you been talking to Leo?'

'No,' said Mark in surprise, 'I haven't spoken to him since before the funeral.' He shook his head in perplexity. 'What difference would it have made if I had? You won't be ruled incompetent just because you're depressed . . . and, even if you were, enduring power of attorney is invested in me. There's no way Leo can register with the Court of Protection unless you revoke the document I hold and issue one in his name. Is that what's been worrying you?'

A strangled laugh caught in James's throat. 'Hardly *worrying* me,' he said bitterly before dropping into a chair and lapsing into a morose silence.

With a resigned sigh, Mark squatted down again to light the fire. When Ailsa was alive the house had run like clockwork. Mark had spent a couple of working holidays in Dorset, 'learning' the estate, and he'd thought his ship had come in. Old money – *well invested*; rich clients – *without pretensions*; people he liked – *with chemistry that worked*. Even after Ailsa's death the bond with James had remained strong. He'd held the old man's hand throughout his questioning, and he'd come to know him better than his own father.

Now he felt estranged. He had no idea if a bed was made up. It seemed unlikely, and he didn't fancy poking around looking for sheets. In the past he had stayed in the 'blue' room where the walls were covered in photographs from the nineteenth century, and the shelves were filled with family diaries and leather-bound legal documents relating to the lobster industry that had flourished in Shenstead Valley during James's great-grandfather's tenure. 'This room was made for you,' Ailsa told him the first time he came. 'Your two favourite subjects – history and law. The diaries are old and dusty, my dear, but they deserve a read.'

He had felt more saddened by Ailsa's death than he'd ever been able to say because he, too, had not been given time to grieve. So much turbulent anguish had surrounded the event – some of it affecting him personally – that he had retreated into coolness in order to cope. He had loved her for a number of reasons: her kindness, her humour, her generosity, her interest in him as a person. What he had never understood was the gulf that existed between her and her children.

Occasionally she talked of siding with James, as if the breach were not of her making, but more usually she cited Leo's sins of omission and commission. 'He kept stealing from us,' she said once, 'things that we didn't notice . . . most of them quite valuable. It made James so angry when he finally found out. He accused Vera . . . it made for a lot of unpleasantness.' She fell into a troubled silence.

'What happened?'

'Oh, the usual,' she sighed. 'Leo owned up. He thought it was very funny. "How would an idiot like Vera know what was valuable?" he said. Poor woman – I think Bob gave her a black eye over it because he was afraid they'd lose the Lodge. It was awful . . . she treated us as tyrants from then on.'

'I thought Leo was fond of Vera. Didn't she look after him and Elizabeth when you were away?'

'I don't think he had any feelings for her – he doesn't have feelings for anyone except possibly Elizabeth – but Vera adored *him*, of course . . . called him her "blue-eyed darling" and let him wrap her round his little finger.'

'Did she never have children of her own?'

Ailsa shook her head. 'Leo was her surrogate son. She bent over backwards to protect him, which wasn't a good thing in retrospect.'

'Why?'

'Because he used her against us.'

'What did he do with the money?'

'The usual,' she repeated dryly. 'Blew it on gambling.'

On another occasion: 'Leo was a very clever child. His IQ was 145 when he was eleven. I've no idea where it came from – James and I are very average – but it caused terrible problems. He thought he could get away with anything, particularly when he discovered how easy it was to manipulate people. Of course, we asked ourselves where we went wrong. James blames himself for not taking a stronger line earlier. I blame the fact that we were abroad so often and had to rely on the school to control him.' She shook her head. 'The truth is simpler, I think. An idle brain is the devil's workshop, and Leo was never interested in hard work.'

Of Elizabeth: 'She lived in Leo's shadow. It made her desperate for attention, poor child. She adored her father, and used to throw tantrums whenever he was in uniform, presumably because she knew it meant he was going away again. I remember once, when she was eight or nine, she cut the legs off his regimental trousers. He was furious with her, and she screamed and yelled and said he deserved it. When I asked her why, she said she hated him dressed up.' Another shake of her head. 'She had a very disturbed adolescence. James blamed Leo for introducing her to his friends . . . I blamed our absences. We lost her effectively by the time she turned eighteen. We set her up in a flat with some girlfriends but most of what we were told about her lifestyle was lies.'

She was ambivalent about her own feelings. 'It's impossible to stop loving your children,' she told him. 'You always hope things will change for the better. The trouble is, somewhere along the line they abandoned the values we taught them and decided the world owed them a living. It's led to so much resentment. They think it's their father's bloody-mindedness that's caused the money to dry up instead of recognizing that they took the pail to the well once too often.'

Mark sat back on his heels as the fire roared to life. His own feelings for Leo and Elizabeth were anything but ambivalent. He disliked them intensely.

Far from taking the pail to the well once too often, they had installed permanent taps that worked through emotional blackmail, family honour and parental guilt. His own view was that Leo was a psychopath with a gambling addiction, and Elizabeth was a nymphomaniac with an alcohol problem. Nor could he see any 'mitigating circumstances' for their behaviour. They had been given every advantage in life, and had failed spectacularly to build on them.

Ailsa had been putty in their hands for years, torn between maternal love and maternal guilt for her failures. To her, Leo was the same blue-eyed boy that Vera adored, and all James's attempts to contain his son's excesses had been met with pleas to give him a 'second chance'. It was no surprise that Elizabeth had been desperate for attention, no surprise either that she was incapable of sustaining relationships. Leo's personality dominated the family. His mood swings created strife or calm. At no point was anyone allowed to forget his existence. When he wanted, he could charm the birds from trees; when he didn't, he made life miserable for everyone. Including Mark . . .

The sound of the phone intruded into his thoughts, and he glanced up to find James looking at him.

'You'd better go and listen,' the Colonel said, offering him a key. 'They might stop if they see you in the library.'

'Who?'

A tired shake of the head. 'They obviously know you're here,' was his only answer.

*

When he first entered the room, Mark assumed the caller had hung up till he leaned towards the answerphone on the desk and heard the sound of stealthy breathing through the amplifier. He lifted the receiver. 'Hello?' No response. 'Hello? . . . hello? . . .' The line went dead. *What on earth . . .?*

Out of habit, he dialled 1471 and scouted round for a pen to jot down the caller's number. It was an unnecessary exercise, he realized, as he listened to the computerized voice and noticed a piece of card, propped against an old-fashioned inkstand, with the same number alongside the name 'Prue Weldon' already written on it. Puzzled, he replaced the receiver.

The answerphone was an old-fashioned one with tapes rather than voicemail. A light flashed at the side, indicating messages, with the number 5 showing in the 'calls' box. Miniature tape boxes were piled in stacks behind the machine, and a quick search showed that each one was dated, suggesting a permanent record rather than regular erasure. Mark pressed the 'new messages' button and listened to the tape rewinding.

After a couple of clicks, a woman's voice filled the speaker.

'*You won't be able to pretend innocence much longer . . . not if your solicitor listens to these messages. You think by ignoring us we'll go away . . . but we won't. Does Mr Ankerton know about the child? Does he know there's living proof of what you did? Who does she take after, do you think . . .? You? Or her mother? It's all so easy with DNA . . . just one hair will prove you a liar and a murderer. Why didn't you tell the police that Ailsa went to London to talk to Elizabeth the day before she died? Why won't you admit that she called you insane because Elizabeth told her the truth . . .? It's why you hit her . . . it's why you killed her . . . How do you think your poor wife felt to find out that her only grandchild was your daughter . . .?*'

*

After that, Mark had little choice but to stay. In a bizarre reversal of roles, it was James who now set out to reassure. He hoped Mark understood that none of it was true. James wouldn't have kept the tapes if there was any question of guilt. It had started in the middle of November, two or three calls a day accusing him of all manner of beastliness. Recently the frequency of the disturbance had risen, with the phone ringing through the night to stop him sleeping.

This fact was certainly true. Even though the bell was muffled by the shut library door, and the phones in other rooms had been disconnected Mark, infinitely more sensitive to the sound than his host, lay awake, his ears waiting for the distant jangle. It was a relief each time it came. He told himself he had an hour to try for sleep before the next one, and each time his brain went into overdrive. If none of it were true, why was James so frightened? Why hadn't he told Mark when it first began? And how – *why?* – did he endure it?

Some time during the night the smell of burning pipe tobacco told him James was awake. He toyed with the idea of getting up and talking to him, but his thoughts were too confused to attempt a discussion in the dark hours. It was a while before he questioned how he could smell tobacco when James's room was on the other side of the house, and curiosity drew him to his window where a pane was open. He saw with astonishment that the old man was sitting on the terrace where Ailsa had died, swathed in a heavy coat.

On Christmas morning, James made no mention of his vigil. Instead he took the trouble to spruce himself up with a bath, a shave and clean clothes, as if to persuade Mark that he had slept soundly in recognition that personal care – or lack of it – was an indication of a disordered mind. He made no objection when Mark insisted on playing the tapes in order to understand what was going on – he said it was one of the reasons why he had made them – but reminded Mark that it was all lies.

The difficulty for Mark was that he knew much of it wasn't. Various details were constantly repeated, and he knew for a fact they were true. Ailsa's trip to London the day before she died . . . the constant references to Elizabeth's hatred of her father in uniform . . . James's fury that the child had been put up for adoption instead of aborted . . . Prue Weldon's certainty that she had heard Ailsa accuse James of destroying her daughter's life . . . the undeniable fact that Elizabeth was a damaged woman . . . the suggestion that if the grandchild were found she might resemble James . . .

One of the voices on tape was disguised with an electronic distorter. It sounded like Darth Vader's. It was the most chilling and the best informed. There was no escaping the conclusion that it was Leo. There were too many historical descriptions, in particular of Elizabeth's bedroom when she was a child, for a stranger to know: her teddy bear, called Ringo after the Beatles' drummer, which she still had in her London house; the posters of Marc Bolan and T-Rex on her walls, which Ailsa had carefully stored because someone had told her they were valuable; the predominant colour of her patchwork bedspread – blue – that had since been moved to the spare room . . .

Mark knew that just by questioning James he was giving the impression that his mind was open to the allegations of incest. Even his assertion at the outset that the calls were clearly malicious was qualified by his admission that he didn't understand what the intention was. If it was Leo, what was he hoping to achieve? If it was blackmail, why didn't he make demands? Why involve other people? Who was the woman who seemed to know so much? Why did Prue Weldon never say anything? How could anyone unconnected with the family know so many details about it?

Everything he said sounded half-hearted, more so when James flatly refused to involve the police because he didn't want Ailsa's death 'resurrected' in the press. Indeed, resurrection seemed to be an obsession with him. He didn't want Mark resurrecting Elizabeth's 'blasted teddy bear' or the row over the adoption. He didn't want Leo's thieving resurrected. It was history, over and done with, and had no relevance to this campaign of terror. And, yes, of course he knew why it was happening. Those damned women – Prue Weldon and Eleanor Bartlett – wanted him to admit he'd murdered Ailsa.

Admit . . .? Mark tried to keep the anxiety out of his voice. 'Well, they're right about one thing,' he said. 'These allegations are easily disproved with a DNA test. Maybe the best strategy would be to make a tactful approach to Captain Smith. If she's prepared to cooperate then you could take these tapes to the police. Whatever the reason for the calls, there's no question they constitute menace.'

James held his gaze for a moment before his eyes slid away. 'There's no tactful way of doing it,' he said. 'I'm not stupid, you know, I have thought about it.'

Why this tiresome defence of his faculties? 'We needn't involve her at all. I could ask her mother for a sample of hair from her bedroom. She must have left something behind that will give a reading. It's not illegal, James . . . not at the moment, anyway. There are companies on the Internet who specialize in giving DNA analysis in questions over paternity.'

'No.'

'It's my best advice. Either that, or inform the police. A temporary solution might be to change your phone number and go ex-directory . . . but if Leo's behind it, he'll soon find out the new one. You can't let it go unchecked. Apart from the fact that you'll be dead of exhaustion in another month, the gossips will talk and mud will stick if you don't challenge these allegations.'

James opened a drawer in his desk and took out a file. 'Read this,' he said, 'then give me one good reason why I should turn this child's life into a nightmare. If one thing is certain, Mark, she neither chose – *nor is responsible for* – the man who fathered her.'

*

'*Dear Captain Smith, My solicitor informs me that if I attempt to contact you, you will sue . . .*'

*

An hour later, telling James he needed a walk to clear his mind, Mark crossed the vegetable garden and made his way to Manor Lodge. But if he expected enlightenment from Vera Dawson, he didn't get it. Indeed he was shocked by how much her brain had deteriorated since August. She kept him at the door, her old mouth sucking and working through her resentments, and he was less surprised than he had been that the Manor was filthy. He asked her where Bob was.

'Out.'

'Do you know where? Is he in the garden?'

A pleased smile flickered in her rheumy eyes. 'Said he'd be gone eight hours. That's usually fishing.'

'Even on Christmas Day?'

The smile vanished. 'He wouldn't spend it with me, would he? Only good for work, that's all I am. You get up there and clean for the Colonel, he says, never mind there's mornings I can hardly rise from my bed.'

Mark smiled uncomfortably. 'Well, could you ask Bob to come up to the house for a chat? Later this evening, perhaps, or tomorrow? If you have a pen and paper, I'll write him a note in case you forget.'

Her eyes narrowed suspiciously. 'There's nothing wrong with my memory. I've still got my marbles.'

It might have been James talking. 'Sorry. I thought it might help.'

'What do you want to talk to him about?'

'Nothing in particular. Just general things.'

'Don't you go talking about me,' she hissed angrily. 'I've got rights, same as everyone else. It wasn't me stole the Missus's rings. It was the boy. You tell the Colonel that, you hear. Bloody old bugger – it was him murdered her.' She slammed the door.

Shenstead Village

Boxing Day, 2001

Seven

AFTER A FRUITLESS attempt to contact his solicitor
– the office answerphone advised callers that the
partnership was on holiday until January 2nd – Dick
Weldon gritted his teeth and dialled Shenstead
Manor. If anyone had a lawyer on tap, it would be
James Lockyer-Fox. The man was in permanent
danger of arrest if Dick's wife, Prue, was to be
believed. 'You'll see,' she kept saying, 'it's only a
matter of time before the police are forced to act.'
More to the point, as the only other property-owner
with a boundary on the Copse, James would be
involved in the discussion sooner or later, and it
might as well be now. Nevertheless, it wasn't a call
that Dick wanted to make.

There had been no communication between Shenstead Farm and the Manor since Prue had told police
of the row she'd heard the night Ailsa died. She
always said it was Fate that intervened to turn her
into an eavesdropper. In three years she had never
felt the need to walk the dogs through the Copse in
the dark, so why that night? She had been on her

way home from a visit to their daughter in Bourne-mouth and one of the Labradors started to whine halfway across the valley. By the time she reached the Copse, the agitation in the back of the estate was intense and, with a groan, she pulled onto the mud track and let the two dogs free.

It should have been a brief lavatory stop, but the bitch, untroubled by her bowels, got wind of a scent and vanished into the woodland. Damned if she was going after it without a torch, Prue reached inside the car for the dog whistle on the dashboard. As she straightened again an angry argument broke out somewhere to her left. Her first assumption was that the Labrador had caused it, but one of the voices was clearly Ailsa Lockyer-Fox's and curiosity kept Prue from blowing her whistle.

She had an ambivalent attitude towards the Lock-yer-Foxes. The social climber in her wanted to become a frequent visitor to the Manor, to count them among her friends and drop their name into casual conversation. But the fact that she and Dick had been invited only once since their arrival in Shenstead three years ago – and then only for a drink – annoyed her, particularly as her reciprocal invita-tions to dinner at the farm had all been politely declined. Dick couldn't see what the fuss was about. They're not comfortable with formal socializing, he said. Go and talk to them in their kitchen. That's what everyone else does.

So Prue had turned up a few times, only for Ailsa to give the impression that she had more important things to do than hang around the kitchen gossiping. After that, their encounters were confined to brief exchanges in the road if they chanced to meet, and irregular appearances by Ailsa in Prue's kitchen when she was looking for donations to her many charities. Prue's private view was that Ailsa and James looked down on her, and she wasn't above a little muck-raking to find something that would give her an edge.

It was rumoured – principally by Eleanor Bartlett who claimed to have heard them in full flow one time – that the Lockyer-Foxes had vicious tempers, despite the reserve they showed in public. Prue had never seen any evidence of this, but she'd always thought it likely. James, in particular, appeared incapable of showing emotion, and in Prue's experience such rigid repression had to break out somewhere. Every so often one of their children announced a visit, but neither parent showed much enthusiasm at the prospect. There were stories of skeletons in cupboards, mostly to do with Elizabeth's reputation for being sex-mad, but the Lockyer-Foxes were as close-lipped about that as they were about everything.

To Prue, such restraint was unnatural and she was always pestering Dick to dig out the dirt. The tenant farmers must know something, she would say. Why don't you ask them what these skeletons are? People say the son's a thief and a gambler, and the daughter was awarded a pittance from her divorce because she'd had so many affairs. But Dick, being a man, wasn't interested, and his advice to Prue was to keep her mouth shut if she didn't want a reputation as a gossip. The community was too small to make an enemy of the oldest family there, he warned.

Now, with Ailsa's rapidly rising voice carrying on the night air, Prue greedily turned her head to listen. Some of the words were swallowed by the wind but the gist was unmistakable. 'No, James . . . won't put up with it any more! . . . it was *you* destroyed Elizabeth . . . such cruelty! It's a sickness . . . had my way . . . seen a doctor a long time ago . . .'

Prue cupped a hand to her ear to make out the man's voice. Even if Ailsa hadn't addressed him as James, she would have recognized the clipped baritone as the Colonel's, but none of the words were audible and she guessed he was facing the other way.

'. . . money's *mine* . . . no question of giving in . . . rather *die* than let you have it . . . Oh, for God's sake . . . *No, don't! Please . . . DON'T!'*

The last word was a shout, followed by the sound of a punch and James's grunted: 'Bitch!'

Somewhat alarmed, Prue took a step forward, wondering if she should go to the other woman's aid, but Ailsa spoke again almost immediately.

'You're insane . . . I'll never forgive you . . . should have got rid of you years ago.' A second or two later, a door slammed.

It was five minutes before Prue thought it safe to put the dog whistle to her lips and blow for the Labrador. The whistles were advertised as silent to the human ear, but they rarely were, and her curiosity had given way to embarrassment as her menopausal system flushed overtime in sympathy with Ailsa's imagined shame if she ever learnt there had been a witness to her abuse. What a dreadful man James was, she thought over and over again in amazement. How could anyone be so holier-than-thou in public and so monstrous in private?

As she gathered the dogs back into the car, her mind was busy filling in the gaps in the conversation, and by the time she reached home to find her husband already asleep it had become a lucid whole. She was shocked but not surprised, therefore, when Dick returned from the village the following morning full of news that Ailsa was dead and James was being questioned by the police about bloodstains found near the body.

'It's my fault,' she said in distress, telling him what had happened. 'They were arguing about money. She said he was insane and should see a doctor, so he called her a bitch and hit her. I should have done something, Dick. Why didn't I *do* something?'

Dick was appalled. 'Are you sure it was them?' he asked. 'Perhaps it was one of the couples from the rented cottages.'

'Of course I'm sure. I could make out most of what she said, and she called him James at one point. The only thing I heard him say was "bitch" but it was definitely his voice. What do you think I should do?'

'Call the police,' said Dick unhappily. 'What else can you do?'

Since then, the coroner's verdict and James's continued freedom from arrest had led to a prolonged whispering campaign. Some of it – speculation about the existence of untraceable poisons, freemasonry membership, even black-magic sacrifices of animals with James as chief warlock – Dick dismissed as patently absurd. The rest – the man's refusal to leave his house and grounds, his ducking out of sight on the one occasion when Dick happened to see him near his gate, his children's cold-shouldering of him at the funeral, his rumoured abandonment of Ailsa's charities and friends with the door being slammed in the faces of well-wishers – all suggested the mental disorder of which Ailsa, and by dint of overhearing their final altercation, Prue – had accused him.

*

The phone was answered after the second ring. 'Shenstead Manor.'

'James? It's Dick Weldon.' He waited for an acknowledgement that never came. 'Look . . . er . . . this isn't easy . . . and I wouldn't be ringing if it wasn't urgent. I realize it's not what you want to hear on Boxing Day morning, but we have a problem at the Copse. I've spoken to the police but they've passed the buck to the local authority – some woman called Sally Macey. I've had a word with her but she's not prepared to do anything till we give her the name of the owner. I told her there wasn't one . . . pretty damn stupid of me, I know . . . so now we need a solicitor . . . and mine's on holiday. It's likely to impact on you as much as anyone – these bastards are right on your doorstep . . .' He wallowed to a halt, intimidated by the silence at the other end. 'I wondered if we could use your man.'

'This isn't James, Mr Weldon. I can ask him to come to the phone if you like, but it sounds as if I'm the person you want. My name's Mark Ankerton. I'm James's solicitor.'

Dick was taken aback. 'I'm sorry. I didn't realize.'

'I know. Voices can be confusing—' a slight pause – 'words, too, particularly when taken out of context.'

It was an ironic reference to Prue, but it passed Dick by. Instead he stared at the wall, remembering the familiar tone of the traveller. He still hadn't worked out who he was. 'You should have said,' he answered lamely.

'I was curious to know what you wanted before I bothered James. Few calls to this house are as civil as yours, Mr Weldon. The usual mode of address is "you murdering bastard" – or words to that effect.'

Dick was shocked. Such a possibility had never occurred to him. 'Who would do a thing like that?'

'I can supply you with a list if you're interested. Your number features on it regularly.'

'It can't do,' Dick protested. 'I haven't phoned James for months.'

'Then I suggest you take it up with BT,' said the other dispassionately. 'Dialling 1471 has produced your number on ten separate occasions. All the calls are being taped, and the contents noted. Nobody speaks from your number—' his voice grew very dry – 'but there's a great deal of unpleasant panting. The police would say they're more in the nature of heavy-breathing calls, although I don't understand the sexual element as the only recipient is a man in his eighties. The most recent was on Christmas Eve. You realize, of course, that it's a criminal offence to make abusive or threatening telephone calls.'

God! Who the hell could have been so stupid? Prue?

'You mentioned you had a problem at the Copse,' Mark went on when there was no response. 'I'm afraid I didn't follow the rest so would you like to go through it again? When I have it straight in my mind, I'll discuss it with James . . . though I can't guarantee he'll come back to you.'

Dick accepted the change of tack with relief. He was a straightforward man who found the idea of his wife panting down a telephone line both alarming and distasteful. 'James is going to be the worst affected,' he said. 'There are six busloads of travellers parked about two hundred yards from the Manor terrace. As a matter of fact, I'm surprised you haven't heard them. There was a bit of argy-bargy when I went down there earlier.'

There was a short pause as if the man at the other end had taken his ear away from the receiver. 'Obviously sound doesn't carry as well as your wife claims it does, Mr Weldon.'

Dick wasn't trained to think on his feet. The nature of his business was to assess problems slowly and carefully, and make long-term plans to carry the farm through glut and famine as profitably as possible. Instead of ignoring the remark – the wiser option – he tried to override it. 'This isn't about Prue,' he said. 'It's about an invasion of this village. We need to pull together . . . not snipe at each other. I don't think you appreciate how serious the situation is.'

There was a small laugh at the other end. 'You might like to reflect on that statement, Mr Weldon. In my opinion, James has a case against your wife for slander . . . so it's naive to suggest I don't understand the seriousness of the situation.'

Riled by the man's patronizing tone, Dick piled in again. 'Prue knows what she heard,' he said aggressively. 'She'd have spoken to Ailsa in private if the poor soul had been alive the next morning – neither of us agrees with hitting women – but Ailsa was dead. So what would you have done in Prue's place? Pretended it hadn't happened? Swept it under the carpet? Tell me that.'

The cool voice came back immediately. 'I'd have asked myself what I knew of James Lockyer-Fox . . . I'd have asked myself why the post mortem showed no evidence of bruising . . . I'd have asked myself why an intelligent and wealthy woman would remain married to a wife-beater for forty years when she was intellectually and financially able to leave . . . I'd *certainly* have questioned whether my own passion for gossip had led me to embroider what I heard in order to make myself interesting to my neighbours.'

'That's offensive,' said Dick angrily.

'Not as offensive as accusing a loving husband of murder and inciting other people to do the same.'

'I'll have *you* for slander if you say things like that. All Prue ever did was tell the police what she heard. You can't blame her if idiots draw their own conclusions.'

'I suggest you talk to your wife before you sue me, Mr Weldon. You might end up with a very expensive legal bill.' There was the sound of a voice in the background. 'Hang on a moment.' The line was muted for several seconds. 'James has come into the room. If you want to go over this business of the travellers again, I'll put you on loudspeaker so we can both hear it. I'll call you back with a decision after we've discussed it . . . though I wouldn't hold your breath for a favourable one.'

Dick had had a lousy morning, and his volatile temper exploded. 'I couldn't give a damn what you decide. It isn't my problem. The only reason I phoned is because Julian Bartlett didn't have the guts to deal with it himself and the police aren't interested. You and James can sort it yourselves. Why should I care? My house is half a mile away. I'm out of it.' He thumped the phone down and went in search of Prue.

*

Mark replaced the handset as the line went dead. 'I was merely giving him some facts of life,' he explained, in belated response to James's agitated reaction when he entered the room and heard Mark talking about incitement to slander. 'Mrs Weldon's a menace. I don't understand why you're so reluctant to do something about her.'

James moved to the window and peered out over the terrace, his head bent forward as if he couldn't see very well. They'd been through this the day before. 'I have to live here,' he said, repeating the same arguments he'd used then. 'Why stir up a hornets' nest unnecessarily? It'll blow over as soon as the women get bored.'

Mark's eyes strayed to the answerphone on the desk. 'I can't agree,' he said bluntly. 'There were five calls last night, and none of them was from a woman. Do you want to listen to them?'

'No.'

Mark wasn't surprised. There was nothing new. They were simply repeat liturgies of the information that was on the stack of tapes he'd worked through the previous day, but the anonymous voice, distorted electronically, rasped on the listener's nerves like a dentist's drill. He turned his chair to address the elderly man directly. 'You know as well as I that this won't go away of its own accord,' he said gently. 'Whoever it is knows he's being recorded and he'll just keep on with it until you agree to involve the police. That's what he's angling for. He wants them to hear what he's saying.'

The Colonel continued to stare through the window as if reluctant to meet the younger man's gaze. 'It's all lies, Mark.'

'Of course it is.'

'Do you think the police will agree with you?' There was a tiny inflection in his voice that sounded like irony.

Mark ignored it and gave a straightforward

answer. 'Not if you keep putting off the decision to involve them. You should have told me about these calls when they began. If we'd acted immediately we could have nipped it in the bud. Now I'm worried the police will ask what you've been trying to hide.' He massaged the back of his neck where a sleepless night, beset by doubt and punctuated by the ringing of the telephone, had given him a headache. 'Put it this way, this bastard has obviously been passing information to Mrs Bartlett or she wouldn't be so well informed . . . and, if he's spoken to her, what makes you think he hasn't been to the police already? Or that *she* hasn't?'

'The police would have questioned me.'

'Not necessarily. They may be conducting an investigation behind your back.'

'If he had any evidence he'd have gone to them before the inquest – that was the time to destroy me – but he knew they wouldn't listen.' He turned round and stared angrily at the telephone. 'It's a form of terror, Mark. When he sees he can't break me, he'll stop. It's a waiting game. All we have to do is hold our nerve.'

Mark shook his head. 'I've been here two days and I haven't slept at all. How long do you think you can last before you keel over?'

'Does it matter?' said the old man wearily. 'I don't have much left except my reputation and I'm damned if I'll give him the satisfaction of placing

107

these lies in the public domain. The police won't keep their mouths shut. Look how the details of their investigation into Ailsa's death leaked out.'

'You have to trust someone. If you die tomorrow these allegations will become fact simply because you failed to challenge them. What price your reputation then? There are always two sides to a story, James.'

The remark brought a faint smile to the Colonel's face. 'Which is precisely what my friend on the telephone is saying. He's really quite persuasive, isn't he?' There was a painful beat of silence, before he went on. 'The only thing I've ever been good at is soldiering, and a soldier's reputation is won on the battlefield, not by kowtowing to grubby little black-mailers.' He rested a light hand on his solicitor's shoulder before walking towards the door. 'I'd rather deal with this in my own way, Mark. Would you care for a coffee? It's about time for one, I think. Come into the drawing room when you've finished.'

He didn't wait for an answer and Mark remained where he was until he heard the latch click. Through the window he could see the discoloured paving stone where animal blood had sunk into the worn surface. A yard or two to the left beside the sundial was where Ailsa had lain. Was the caller right? he wondered. Did people die of shock when truth was unpalatable? With a sigh he turned back to the desk and rewound the last message. It had to be Leo, he thought, pressing 'play' to listen to the 'Darth Vader' voice again. Apart from Elizabeth, no one knew so much about the family, and it was ten years since Elizabeth had been able to string two coherent words together.

'*Do you ever ask yourself why Elizabeth's such an easy lay . . . and why she's drunk all the time . . .? Who taught her to debase herself . . .? Did you think she'd keep the secret for ever . . .? Perhaps you thought your uniform would protect you? People look up to a man with bits of metal pinned to his chest . . . You probably felt like a hero every time you brought out your swagger stick . . .*'

Sickened, Mark closed his eyes, but he couldn't prevent his mind playing relentless images of Captain Nancy Smith, whose likeness to her grandfather had been remarkable.

*

Dick Weldon found his wife in the spare room, making up beds for their son and daughter-in-law who were arriving that evening. 'Have you been phoning James Lockyer-Fox?' he demanded.

She frowned at him, stuffing a pillow into its case. 'What are you talking about?'

'I've just been on to the Manor, and his solicitor said someone from here has been making abusive calls to James.' His ruddy face was dark with irritation. 'It flaming well wasn't me, so who was it?'

Prue turned her back on him to pat the pillow

into shape. 'You'll have a heart attack if you don't do something about your blood pressure,' she told him critically. 'You look as if you've been on the bottle for years.'

Dick was well used to her habit of deflecting unwelcome questions by sticking the knife in first. 'So it *was* you,' he snapped. 'Are you *mad*? The lawyer said you were panting.'

'That's ridiculous.' She turned round to pick up another pillowcase before flicking him a disapproving glance. 'There's no need to look so huffy. As far as I'm concerned, that brute deserves everything he gets. Have you any idea how guilty I feel about leaving Ailsa in his clutches? I should have helped her instead of walking away. She'd still be alive if I'd shown some spirit.'

Dick sank onto a blanket chest by the door. 'Supposing you're wrong? Supposing it was someone else you heard?'

'It wasn't.'

'How can you be so sure? I thought the solicitor was James till he told me he wasn't. It certainly sounded like him when he said "Shenstead Manor".'

'Only because you expected James to answer.'

'The same applies to you. You expected Ailsa to be rowing with the Colonel. You were always asking me to find out the dirt on them.'

'Oh, for goodness sake!' she countered crossly.

'How many times do I have to tell you? She *called* him James. She said, "No, James, I won't put up with this any more." Why would she do that if she was talking to somebody else?'

Dick rubbed his eyes. He'd heard her say this a number of times, but the solicitor's remark about words out of context had unsettled him. 'You told me the next day that you couldn't hear anything James said . . . well, maybe you didn't hear Ailsa too well either. I mean, it makes a hell of a difference if she was talking *about* him instead of *to* him. Maybe the "I" wasn't there . . . maybe she said, "James won't put up with this any more".'

'I know what I heard,' Prue said stubbornly.

'So you keep saying.'

'It's true.'

'All right . . . what about this punch you said he gave her? Why didn't the post-mortem find any bruises?'

'How would I know? Maybe she died before they could develop.' Irritably, she pulled the coverlets over the beds and smoothed them flat. 'What were you phoning James for, anyway? I thought we agreed to take Ailsa's side.'

Dick stared at the floor. 'Since when?'

'It was you who told me to go to the police.'

'I said you didn't have much choice. That's not an agreement to take a side.' Another vigorous rub of his eyes. 'The solicitor said there's a case against you for slander. According to him, you've been inciting people to call James a murderer.'

Prue was unimpressed. 'Then why doesn't he sue? Eleanor Bartlett's says that's the best evidence there is that he's guilty. You should hear what *she* says about him.' Her eyes gleamed at some memory that amused her. 'Plus if anyone's making abusive phone calls, it's her. I've been there when she's made one. She calls it "smoking him out".'

Dick took stock of his wife for the first time in years. She was dumpier than the girl he'd married but a great deal more assertive. At twenty, she'd been mild-mannered and mousy. At fifty-four, she was a dragon. He hardly knew her now except as the woman who shared his bed. They hadn't had sex or talked about anything personal for years. He was out all day on the farm, and she was playing either golf or bridge with Eleanor and her snobbish friends. Evenings were passed in silence in front of the television, and he was always asleep before she came upstairs.

She sighed impatiently at his shocked expression. 'It's fair enough. Ailsa was Ellie's friend . . . mine, too. What did you expect us to do? Let James get away with it? If you'd shown a blind bit of interest in anything other than the farm, you'd know there's far more to the story than the nonsense verdict the coroner produced. James is a complete brute, and the only reason you're making a fuss now is because you've been listening to his solicitor . . . and he's *paid* to take his client's side. You're so *slow* sometimes.'

There was no arguing with that. Dick had always taken his time to think things through. What he blamed himself for was his indifference. 'Ailsa can't have died that quickly,' he protested. 'You said the reason you didn't interfere was because she spoke to him after the punch. OK, I'm no pathologist, but I'm pretty sure a person's circulation would have to stop immediately to prevent the damaged blood vessels leaking into the skin. Even then I wouldn't bet on it.'

'There's no point browbeating me, it's not going to change my mind,' announced Prue with a return to irritability. 'I expect the cold had something to do with it. I heard a door slam afterwards, so James obviously locked her out and left her to die. If you're so interested, why don't you call the pathologist and talk to him? Though you probably won't get much joy. Eleanor says they're all in the funny-handshake brigade, which is why James hasn't been arrested.'

'That's ridiculous. Why do you take any notice of what that stupid woman says? And since when were either of you friends of Ailsa? The only time she ever spoke to you was when she was after money for her charities. Eleanor was always complaining about what a scrounger she was. I remember how mad you both were when the paper said she'd left £1.2m. Why did she ask us for money, you both said, when she was rolling in it?'

Prue ignored the remark. 'You still haven't explained why you were phoning James.'

'Travellers have taken over the Copse,' he grunted, 'and we need a solicitor to get rid of them. I hoped James would put me in touch with his.'

'What's wrong with ours?'

'On holiday till the second.'

Prue shook her head in disbelief. 'Then why on earth didn't you phone the Bartletts? They have a solicitor. What possessed you to phone James? You're such an idiot, Dick.'

'Because Julian had already passed the buck to me,' hissed Dick through clenched teeth. 'He's gone to the Compton Newton meet, dressed up like a dog's dinner, and he thought they were saboteurs. Didn't want to get his blasted clothes dirty, as per bloody usual. You know what he's like . . . lazy as hell and didn't fancy a run-in with some thugs . . . so ducked the whole damn issue. It makes me mad, frankly. I work harder than anyone in this valley but I'm always expected to pick up the pieces.'

Prue gave a scornful snort. 'You should have told me. I'd have sorted it with Ellie. She's perfectly capable of putting us in touch with their solicitor . . . even if Julian can't.'

'You were in bed,' Dick snapped. 'But be my

guest. Go ahead. It's all yours. You and Eleanor are probably the best people to deal with invaders, anyway. It'll scare the living daylights out of them to have a couple of middle-aged women shouting abuse at them through a megaphone.' He stomped angrily from the room.

*

It was Mark Ankerton who answered the peal of the old-fashioned brass bell that hung from a spring in the Manor hall and was operated by a wire pull in the porch. He and James were sitting in front of a log fire in the panelled drawing room, and the sudden noise caused them both to jump. Mark's reaction was relief. The silence between them had become oppressive, and he welcomed any diversion, even an unpleasant one.

'Dick Weldon?' he suggested.

The older man shook his head. 'He knows we never use that entrance. He'd have come to the back.'

'Should I answer it?'

James shrugged. 'What's the point? It's almost certainly a nuisance ring – usually the Woodgate children. I used to shout at them . . . now I don't bother. They'll grow tired of it eventually.'

'How often?'

'Four or five times a week. It's very boring.'

Mark pushed himself to his feet. 'At least let me

take out injunctions for that,' he said, reverting to the subject that had brought on the long silence. 'It's easily done. We can stop them coming within fifty yards of your gate. We'll insist that the parents take responsibility . . . threaten them with jail if the children continue with the nuisance.'

James smile faintly. 'Do you think I want accusations of fascism added to all my other problems?'

'It's nothing to do with fascism. The law puts the onus on parents to take responsibility for underage children.'

James shook his head. 'Then I haven't a leg to stand on. Leo and Elizabeth have done worse than the Woodgate children will ever do. I won't take cover behind a piece of paper, Mark.'

'It's hardly taking cover. Think of it more as a weapon.'

'I can't. White paper. White flag. It smacks of surrender.' He waved the lawyer towards the hall. 'Go and give them a tongue-lashing. They're all under twelve,' he said with a small smile, 'but it'll make you feel better to see them run away with their tails between their legs. Satisfaction, I find, has nothing to do with the calibre of the opponent, merely the routing of him.'

He steepled his fingers under his chin and listened to Mark's footsteps cross the flagged stone floor of the hall. He heard the bolts being drawn and caught the sound of voices before the black depression, his constant companion these days, briefly in abeyance because of Mark's presence in the house, struck without warning and flooded his eyes with shameful tears. He leant his head against the back of the chair and stared at the ceiling, trying to force them into retreat. Not now, he told himself in desperation. Not in front of Mark. Not when the young man had come so far to help him through his first Christmas alone.

Eight

WOLFIE WAS CURLED under a blanket in a corner of the bus, cradling a fox's brush against his mouth. It was soft, like a teddy bear's fur, and he sucked his thumb surreptitiously behind it. He was so hungry. His dreams were always about food. Fox had been ignoring him since his mother and brother had vanished. That was a long time ago – weeks maybe – and Wolfie still didn't know where they were or why they'd gone. Once in a while a lingering terror at the back of his mind told him he did know, but he avoided visiting it. It had something to do with Fox razoring off his dreadlocks, he thought.

He had cried for days, beseeching Fox to let him go, too, till Fox threatened him with the razor. After that, he'd hidden under the blanket and kept his mouth shut while he made fantasy plans about running away. As yet, he hadn't found the courage – his fear of Fox, the police and social workers – his fear of *everything* – was too ingrained, but he'd leave one day, he promised himself.

Half the time his father forgot he was there. Like

now. Fox had brought some of the others from the camp into the bus, and they were drawing up a 24-hour rota to guard the entrance to the site. Wolfie, lying as still as a terrified mouse, thought his father sounded like a general instructing his troops. Do this. Do that. I'm the boss. But Wolfie was worried because the people kept contradicting him. Did they know about the razor, he wondered?

'Whichever way you look at it, we've got seven days before anyone takes action,' said Fox, 'and by then we'll have turned this place into a fortress.'

'Yeah, well, you'd better be right about there being no owner,' came a woman's voice, ''coz I sure as hell don't fancy breaking my back to build a stockade just to have bulldozers break it down the day after it's finished. Plus, it's fucking freezing out there, in case you hadn't noticed.'

'I am right, Bella. I know this place. Dick Weldon had a try at enclosing it three years ago but gave up because he wasn't prepared to pay a fortune in legal fees with no guarantee that he'd win. The same'll happen now. Even if the rest of the village agrees to let him stake a claim to this land, he'll still have to pay a solicitor to force us out and he's not that altruistic.'

'What if they all gang up together?'

'They won't. Not in the short term, anyway. There are too many conflicting interests.'

'How do you know?'

'I just do.'

There was a short silence.

'Come on, Fox, give,' said a man. 'What's your connection with Shenstead? Did you live here? What do you know that the rest of us don't?'

'None of your business.'

'Sure it's our business,' said the other man, his voice rising angrily. 'We're taking a hell of a lot on trust here. Who's to say the filth won't come in and arrest us for trespass? First you want us to rope the place off . . . then turn it into a fortress . . . And all for what? A million-to-one gamble that in twelve years anything we've built on it will be ours? The odds suck. When you put it to us back in August, you said it was open countryside . . . land for the taking. There was no mention of a fucking village rammed up against it.'

'Shut up, Ivo,' said another woman. 'It's a short-arse Welsh thing,' she added for the benefit of the rest. 'He's always picking fights.'

'I'll pick one with you if you're not careful, Zadie,' said Ivo furiously.

'Enough. The odds *are* good.' There was a steely edge to Fox's voice that sent shivers up Wolfie's spine. If the other bloke didn't shut up, his dad would bring out his razor. 'There are only four houses permanently occupied in this village – the Manor, Shenstead House, Manor Lodge and Paddock View. Otherwise it's weekenders or rentals . . .

and *they* won't get exercised till women come down for extended breaks in the summer and start complaining to their husbands about their kids consorting with the trash at the Copse.'

'What about the farms?' asked Bella.

'The only one that matters is Dick Weldon's. His land makes up most of the boundary, but I know for a fact there aren't any documents to prove Shenstead Farm ever owned it.'

'How?'

'Not your business. Just accept that I do.'

'What about that house we can see through the trees?'

'The Manor. There's an old man living there on his own. He won't be giving us any trouble.'

'How do you know?' It was Ivo's voice again.

'I just do.'

'Jesus Christ!' There was the sound of a fist thumping on the table. 'Can't you say anything else?' Ivo fell into mimicry of Fox's more educated tones. '"I just do . . . not your business . . . accept it." What's the deal, man? Because I'm telling you now, I'm not hanging around listening to you spout crap without some fucking explanations. For starters, why won't this old guy give us any trouble? I sure as hell would if I lived in a manor and some New Agers moved onto my turf.'

Fox didn't answer immediately and Wolfie closed his eyes in fright, picturing him slicing at the other man's face. But the expected screams didn't come. 'He knows this land doesn't belong to him,' said Fox calmly. 'He had his solicitors look into it when Weldon tried to take it, but there are no documents supporting his claim either. The reason we're here now is because he's the only person with enough money to foot the bill for the rest of them . . . and he won't do it. Might have done a year ago. Not now.'

'Why not?'

Another short silence. 'I suppose you'll hear soon enough. The rest think he murdered his wife and they're trying to have him arrested. He's a recluse, doesn't go out any more, doesn't see anyone . . . his food's delivered to the door. He's not going to bother us . . . not with the problems he's got.'

'Shit!' said Bella in astonishment. 'Did he do it?'

'Who cares?' said Fox indifferently.

'Maybe I do. Maybe he's dangerous. What about the kids?'

'If you're worried, tell them to steer clear of that side of the wood. He only ever comes out at night.'

'Shit!' she said again. 'He sounds like some sort of weirdo. Why isn't he in a loony bin?'

'There aren't any left,' said Fox dismissively.

'How old is he?'

'Eighty-odd.'

'What's his name?'

'What the hell does it matter what his name is?' snapped Fox. 'You won't be talking to him.'

'So? Maybe I want to know who he is when he's talked *about*. It's not a secret, is it?' She paused. 'Well, well . . . perhaps it is at that. Know him from before, do you, Fox? He the one give you all this information?'

'I've never met him in my life . . . I just know a hell of a lot about him. *How* is none of your business.'

'Sure. What's his name then?'

'Lockyer *fucking* Fox. Satisfied?'

There was a ripple of laughter.

'Worried about the competition, are you?' said the woman. 'Reckon there ain't room for two foxes in this place, maybe?'

'Shut up, Bella,' said Fox with the edge back in his voice.

'Yeah . . . yeah. It was a joke, sweetheart. You've gotta learn to relax . . . get stoned . . . take happy pills. We're with you, darlin' . . . all the way. You've just gotta trust us.'

'Obey the rules and I will. Break them and I won't. First rule, everyone works to the rota and no one shirks their turn. Second rule, no one fucks with the locals. Third rule, no one leaves this campsite after dark . . .'

*

123

Wolfie crawled out from his hiding place when he heard the bus door close and tiptoed to one of the windows overlooking the entrance to the Copse. It was hung with fox brushes, and he pushed them aside to watch his father take up position behind the rope barrier. There was so much he didn't understand. Who were these people in the other buses? Where had Fox found them? What were they doing there? Why weren't his mother and brother with them? Why were they building a fortress?

He pressed his forehead to the glass and tried to find meaning in what he'd heard. He knew that Fox's full name was Fox Evil. He had asked his mother once if that meant Evil was his surname, too, but she'd laughed and told him, no, you're just Wolfie. Only Fox is Evil. From then on, Wolfie transposed the words and thought of his father as Evil Fox. To his child's mind, always seeking balance and answers, it made more sense than Fox Evil, and Fox immediately assumed the virtue of a surname.

But who was this old man called Lucky Fox? And how could his father not know him if they had the same name? Excitement and fear collided in the child's heart. Excitement that Lucky Fox might be related to him . . . might even know where his mother was; fear of a murderer . . .

*

124

Mark retreated, closing the drawing-room door quietly behind him. He turned to the visitor with an apologetic smile. 'Would you mind if we left the introductions for a few minutes? James is . . . er . . .' He broke off. 'Look, I know he's going to be thrilled to see you, but just at the moment he's asleep.'

Nancy had seen more than Mark realized and nodded immediately. 'Why don't I come back after lunch? It's no trouble. I need to book into Bovington Army Camp by five o'clock this evening . . . but there's nothing to stop me doing it now. I can come back later.' This was far more embarrassing than she'd imagined it would be. She certainly hadn't expected Mark Ankerton to be there. 'I should have rung first,' she finished lamely.

He wondered why she hadn't. The number was in the book. 'Not at all.' He placed himself between her and the front door as if afraid she might make a run for it. 'Please don't go. James would be devastated.' He gestured to a corridor on the right, rushing his words to make her feel welcome. 'Let's go down to the kitchen. It's warm in there. I can make you a cup of coffee while we wait for him to wake up. It shouldn't be more than ten minutes or so.'

She allowed herself to be shepherded forward. 'I lost my nerve at the last minute,' she admitted, answering his unspoken question. 'It was all rather spur of the moment and I didn't think he'd appreciate a phone call late last night or first thing this morning. I had visions of it getting very complicated if he didn't catch on to who I was. I thought it would be easier to come in person.'

'It's not a problem,' Mark assured her, opening the kitchen door. 'It's the best Christmas present he could have had.'

But was it? Mark hoped his anxiety wasn't showing for he had no idea how James was going to react. Would he be pleased? Would he be afraid? What would a DNA test show? The timing was crazy. He could pluck a hair from Nancy's shoulder and she wouldn't even know he'd done it. The smile froze on his face as he looked into her eyes. *God, they were so like James's!*

Discomfited by his stare, Nancy pulled off her woollen hat and fluffed her dark hair with her fingertips. It was a feminine gesture that belied the otherwise masculine way she was dressed. Thick fleece over a polo-neck jumper, cargo trousers tucked into heavy boots, all black. It was an interesting choice, particularly as she was visiting an elderly man whose tastes and opinions on dress and behaviour were bound to be conservative.

Mark guessed it was a deliberate challenge to James's willingness to accept her because it said effectively, no compromise. Take me as I am or not at all. If a butch-looking woman doesn't fit the Lockyer-Fox mould, then tough shit. If you expected me to woo you with feminine charm, think again. If you wanted a manipulable granddaughter, forget it. The irony was that, quite unconsciously, she had presented herself as the antithesis of her mother.

'I'm on temporary secondment to Bovington as an instructor in field operations in Kosovo,' she told him, 'and when I looked at the map . . . well . . . I thought if I left at the crack of dawn I could use today . . .' She broke off to give an embarrassed shrug. 'I didn't realize he had guests. If there'd been cars in the drive I wouldn't have rung the bell, but as there weren't . . .'

Mark made what he could of this. 'Mine's in a garage at the back, and he and I are the only ones here. Truly, Captain Smith, this is—' he sought for a word that would put her at ease – '*brilliant*. You've no idea *how* brilliant, as a matter of fact. This is his first Christmas since Ailsa died. He's putting on a damn good show, but having your solicitor to stay isn't much of a replacement for a wife.' He pulled out a chair for her. 'Please. How do you like your coffee?'

The kitchen was warmed by an Aga, and Nancy could feel herself blushing in the heat. Her awkwardness deepened. She couldn't have picked a worse time to walk in unannounced. She imagined the Colonel's shame if he came looking for Mark with the tears still in his eyes and found her sitting at the table. 'Actually, I don't think this is a good idea,' she said abruptly. 'I saw him over your shoulder, and he's not asleep. Supposing he wonders where you are? It'll devastate him to find me here.' She glanced towards a door in the corner. 'If that leads outside I can sneak away without him ever knowing I was here.'

Perhaps Mark, too, was having second thoughts because he looked irresolutely towards the corridor. 'He's having a pretty bad time of it,' he said. 'I don't think he's sleeping much.'

She pulled on her hat again. 'I'll come back in two hours, but I'll phone first to give him time to compose himself. It's what I should have done this time.'

He searched her face for a moment. 'No,' he said, taking her lightly by the arm and turning her towards the corridor. 'I don't trust you not to change your mind. My coat and wellies are in the scullery and the door from there takes us out on the other side from James. We'll go for a walk instead, blow the cobwebs away after your drive. We can take a discreet look through the drawing-room window in half an hour to see how he's getting on. How does that sound?'

She relaxed immediately. 'Good,' she said. 'I'm much better at walking than coping with uncomfort-able social situations.'

He laughed. 'Me, too. This way.' He turned to the right and took her into a room with an old stone sink on one side and a litter of boots, horse blankets, waterproofs and ulsters on the other. The floor was covered with lumps of mud that had dropped from the treads of rubber soles, and dust and grime had accumulated in the sink and on the draining board and window sills.

'It's a bit of a mess,' he apologized, swapping his Gucci loafers for some old wellingtons, and shrugging into a Dryzabone oilskin. 'I sometimes think everyone who's ever lived here has abandoned bits of themselves as proof of passage.' He flicked an ancient brown ulster hanging from a peg. 'This belonged to James's great-grandfather. It's been hanging here for as long as James can remember, but he says he likes to see it every day . . . it gives him a sense of continuity.'

He opened the outer door on to a walled court-yard and ushered Nancy through. 'Ailsa called this her Italian garden,' he said, nodding to the large terracotta urns that were scattered around it. 'It's a bit of a suntrap on a summer evening and she used to grow night-scented flowers in these pots. She always said it was a pity it was at the scrag-end of the Manor because it was the nicest place to sit. That's the back of the garage.' He nodded to a single-storey building to their right. 'And this—' he lifted the latch of an arched wooden door in a wall ahead of them – 'leads into the kitchen garden.'

The courtyard looked curiously neglected, as if it hadn't been entered since the death of its mistress.

Weeds grew in profusion between the cobbles, and the terracotta tubs contained only the brittle skeletons of long-dead plants. Mark seemed to take it for granted that Nancy knew who Ailsa was, even though he hadn't told her, and Nancy wondered if he knew about the Colonel's letters.

'Does James have any help?' she asked, following him into the vegetable garden.

'Only an elderly couple from the village . . . Bob and Vera Dawson. He does the gardening and she does the cleaning. The trouble is, they're almost as old as James, so not much gets done. As you can see.' He gestured round the overgrown vegetable garden. 'I think mowing the lawn is about all Bob can manage these days, and Vera's virtually senile so dirt just gets moved around. It's better than nothing, I suppose, but he could do with some energy about the place.'

They picked their way along a vestigial gravel path between the beds with Nancy admiring the eight-foot-high wall that surrounded the garden. 'It must have been splendid when they had staff to manage this properly,' she said. 'It looks as though they grew espalier fruit trees all along that south wall. You can still see the wires.' She pointed to a raised plateau of earth in the middle. 'Is that an asparagus bed?'

He followed her gaze. 'God knows. I'm a complete ignoramus when it comes to gardening. How does asparagus grow? What does it look like when it's not in a packet in a supermarket?'

She smiled. 'Just the same. The tips push up out of the ground from a massive root system. If you keep banking up the earth, the way the French do, then the tips stay white and tender. That's how my mother does it. She has a bed at the farm that produces pounds of the stuff.'

'Is she the gardener in the family?' he asked, steering her towards a wrought-iron gate in the western wall.

Nancy nodded. 'It's her profession. She has a huge nursery complex down at Coomb Croft. It's amazingly profitable.'

Mark remembered seeing the signs when he passed on his way to Lower Croft. 'Did she train for it?'

'Oh, yes. She went to Sowerbury House as an under-gardener when she was seventeen. She stayed for ten years, rose up the ranks to head gardener, then married my father and moved to Coomb Croft. They lived there till my grandfather died, which gave her time to develop the nursery. She started as a one-man band, but now she has a staff of thirty . . . it virtually runs itself.'

'A talented lady,' he said with genuine warmth, opening the gate and standing back to let Nancy through. He found himself hoping she would never meet her real mother. The comparison would be too cruel.

They entered another enclosed garden, with L-shaped flanks of the house forming two sides of the square and a hedge of thickly growing evergreen shrubs running from the kitchen wall to the quoin on the left. Nancy noticed that all the windows overlooking this space were shuttered on the inside, giving them a blind white stare from the painted wood behind the glass. 'Isn't this wing used any more?' she asked.

Mark followed her gaze. If he had his bearings right, then one of the second-floor rooms was Elizabeth's – where Nancy had been born – and beneath it was the estate office where her adoption papers had been signed. 'Not for years,' he told her. 'Ailsa closed the shutters to protect the furnishings.'

'It's sad when houses outgrow their occupants,' was all she said, before returning her attention to the garden. In the centre was a fish pond, heavily iced over, with reeds and the dead stalks of water plants poking above the surface. A bench seat, green with mould, nestled amongst clumps of azaleas and dwarf rhododendrons beside it, and a crazy-paving path, much degraded by weeds, wound through dwarf acers, delicate bamboos and ornamental grasses towards another gate on the far side. 'The Japanese garden?' Nancy guessed, pausing beside the pond.

Mark smiled as he nodded. 'Ailsa loved creating rooms,' he said, 'and they all had names.'

'It must be stunning in the spring when the azaleas are in bloom. Imagine sitting here with their scent filling the air. Are there any fish?'

Mark shook his head. 'There certainly were when Ailsa was alive, but James forgot to feed them after she died and he says he couldn't see any the last time he came here.'

'They wouldn't die from lack of feeding,' she said. 'It's big enough to provide insect life for dozens of fish.' She squatted down to peer through the sheet of ice. 'They were probably hiding in the water plants. He ought to ask his gardener to thin them out when the weather improves. It's like a jungle down there.'

'James has given up on the garden,' said Mark. 'It was Ailsa's preserve, and he seems to have lost interest in it completely since she died. The only part he ever visits now is the terrace, and then only at night-time.' He gave an unhappy shrug. 'It worries me, to be honest. He parks his chair just to the right of where he found her and sits there for hours.'

Nancy didn't bother to pretend ignorance of what he was talking about. 'Even in this weather?' she asked, glancing up at him.

'He's certainly been doing it for the last two nights.'

133

She pushed herself upright again and walked beside him along the path. 'Have you talked to him about it?'

Another shake of the head. 'I'm not supposed to know he's doing it. He vanishes off to bed at ten o'clock every night, then creeps out again after I've switched off my bedroom light. He didn't come in till nearly four o'clock this morning.'

'What does he do?'

'Nothing. Just huddles into his chair and stares into the darkness. I can see him from my window. I nearly went out on Christmas Eve to give him a rocket for being stupid. The sky was so clear that I thought he'd die of hypothermia – even wondered if that was the intention – it's probably what killed Ailsa – but he kept relighting his pipe so I knew he wasn't unconscious. He didn't mention it yesterday morning . . . or this . . . and when I asked him how he'd slept, he said, fine.' He turned the handle on the next gate and shouldered it open. 'I suppose it *may* have been a Christmas vigil for Ailsa,' he finished without conviction.

They emerged onto an expanse of parkland with the bulk of the house lying to their right. Frost still lay in pockets under the shrubs and trees that formed an avenue facing south, but the bright winter sun had warmed it to a glistening dew on the sweep of grass that sloped away and gave an unrestricted view of Shenstead Valley and the sea beyond.

'Wow!' said Nancy simply.

'It's stunning, isn't it? That bay you can see is Barrowlees. It's only accessible via the dirt track that leads to the farms . . . which is why this village is so expensive. All the houses have a right of way attached to them which allows them to drive their cars down to the beach. It's a complete disaster.'

'Why?'

'They're priced outside local people's reach. It's turned Shenstead into a ghost village. The only reason Bob and Vera are still here is because their cottage is tied to the Manor and Ailsa promised it to them for life. I wish she hadn't, as a matter of fact. It's the only cottage that still belongs to James, but he insists on honouring Ailsa's word even though he desperately needs help. He had another cottage up until four years ago, but sold it off because he had trouble with squatters. I'd have advised short-term lets rather than sale – precisely for this eventuality – but I wasn't his lawyer at the time.'

'Why doesn't he have someone living in the house with him? It's big enough.'

'Good question,' said Mark dryly. 'Maybe you can persuade him. All I get is—' he adopted a quavery baritone – ' "I'm not having some damn busybody poking her nose in where it isn't wanted." '

Nancy laughed. 'You can't blame him. Would you want it?'

135

'No, but then I'm not neglecting myself the way he is.'

She nodded matter-of-factly. 'We had the same problem with one of my grandmothers. In the end my father had to register his power of attorney. Have you set up a document for James?'

'Yes.'

'In whose name?'

'Mine,' he said reluctantly.

'My father didn't want to exercise it either,' she said sympathetically. 'In the end it was forced on him when Granny was threatened with having her electricity cut off. She thought the red bills were prettier than the others, and lined them up along her mantelpiece to brighten her room. It never occurred to her to pay them.' She smiled in response to his smile. 'It didn't make her any less lovable,' she said. 'So, who else lives in Shenstead?'

'Hardly anyone permanently. That's the trouble. The Bartletts in Shenstead House – retired early and made a fortune selling up in London; the Woodgates at Paddock View – they pay a peppercorn rent to the company that owns most of the holiday cottages in return for managing them; and the Weldons at Shenstead Farm.' He pointed at a woodland that bordered the parkland to the west. 'They own the land that way so, strictly, they're outside the village boundary. As are the Squires and the Drews to the south.'

'Are they the tenant farmers you told me about?'

He nodded. 'James owns everything from here to the shoreline.'

'Wow!' she said again. 'That's some acreage. So how come the village has a right of way across his land?'

'James's great-grandfather – the fellow whose ulster you saw – granted rights to fishermen to transport boats and catches to and from the coast in order to build a lobster industry in Shenstead. Ironically, he was faced with the same problem that exists today – a dying village and a dwindling workforce. It was the time of the industrial revolution and youngsters were leaving to find better-paid work in the towns. He hoped to tap into the successful Weymouth and Lyme Regis operations.'

'Did it work?'

Mark nodded. 'For about fifty years. The entire village was geared to lobster production. There were carriers, boilers, preparers, packers. They used to freight ice by the ton and store it in ice-houses round the village.'

'Do the ice-houses still exist?'

'Not as far as I know. They became redundant as soon as the fridge was invented and electricity was brought in.' He nodded towards the Japanese garden. 'The one that was here became that pond we've just been looking at. James has a collection of copper boiling pans in one of the outhouses, but that's about all that's survived.'

'What killed it off?'

'The First World War. Fathers and sons went off to fight and didn't come back. It was the same story everywhere, of course, but the effects were devastating in a small place like this which relied on its menfolk to heave the boats in and out of the water.' He led her out to the middle of the lawn. 'You can just about see the shoreline. It's not a good anchorage so they had to haul the boats onto dry land. There are photographs of it in one of the bedrooms.'

She shielded her eyes against the sun. 'If it was that labour-intensive then it was always doomed,' she said. 'Prices would never have kept up with the cost of production and the industry would have died anyway. Dad always says the greatest destroyer of countryside communities was mechanization in farming. One man on a combine harvester can do the work of fifty, and he does it quicker, better and with far less waste.' She nodded towards the fields in front of them. 'Presumably these two farms contract out their ploughing and harvesting?'

He was impressed. 'How can you tell just by looking at them?'

'I can't,' she said with a laugh, 'but you didn't mention any labourers living in the village. Does the farmer to the west contract out as well?'

'Dick Weldon. No, he's the contractor. He built up a business on the other side of Dorchester, then bought Shenstead Farm for peanuts three years ago when the previous owner went bankrupt. He's no fool. He's left his son in charge of the core business to the west and now he's expanding here.'

Nancy eyed him curiously. 'You don't like him,' she said.

'What makes you think that?'

'Tone of voice.'

She was more perceptive than he was, he thought. Despite her smiles and her laughs, he still hadn't learnt to read her face or inflection. Her manner wasn't as dry as James's but she was certainly as self-contained. Anywhere else, and with a different woman, he would have flattered to seduce – either to be fascinated or disappointed – but he was reluctant to do anything to queer James's pitch. 'Why the change of heart?' he asked abruptly.

She turned to look at the house. 'You mean, why am I here?'

'Yes.'

She shrugged. 'Did he tell you he wrote to me?'

'Not till yesterday.'

'Have you read the letters?'

'Yes.'

'Then you ought to be able to answer your question yourself . . . but I'll give you a clue.' She flicked him an amused glance. 'I'm not here for his money.'

Nine

THE HUNT WAS the shambles Julian Bartlett had predicted. The saboteurs had kept a surprisingly low profile at the start but, as soon as a fox was put up in Blantyre Wood, cars raced ahead to create avenues of safety by using hunting horns to divert the hounds onto false trails. Out of practice after the long layoff, the dogs quickly became confused and the huntsman and his whippers-in lost control. The riders circled impatiently until order was restored, but a return to Blantyre Wood to raise a second fox was no more successful.

Hunt followers in their cars attempted to block the saboteurs and shout to the huntsman the direction the fox had taken, but an amplified tape of a pack in full cry, played through loudspeakers on a van, drew the hounds away. The aggravation levels amongst the riders – already high – mounted alarmingly as saboteurs invaded the field and waved their arms at the horses in a criminal and dangerous attempt to unseat the riders. Julian lashed out at a foolhardy lad who tried to catch Bouncer's reins, then swore profusely when he saw he'd been photo-graphed by a woman with a camera.

He circled and came up beside her, wrestling to keep Bouncer in check. 'I'll sue if you publish that,' he said through gritted teeth. 'That man was fright-ening my horse and I was within my rights to protect myself and my mount.'

'Can I quote you?' she asked, pointing the lens at his face and clicking off a fusillade of shots. 'What's your name?'

'None of your damn business.'

She lowered the camera on its neck strap and patted it with a grin, before pulling a notebook from her jacket pocket. 'It won't take me long to find out . . . not with these pictures. Debbie Fowler, *Wessex Times*,' she said, retreating to a safe distance. 'I'm a neutral . . . just a poor little hack trying to make a living. So—' another grin – 'do you want to tell me what you have against foxes . . . or shall I make it up?'

Julian scowled ferociously. 'That's about your level, isn't it?'

'Talk to me, then,' she invited. 'I'm here . . . I'm listening. Put the hunt's side.'

'What's the point? You'll paint me as the aggressor and that idiot there—' he jerked his chin at the skinny saboteur who was backing away, rubbing his arm where the crop had caught him – 'as the hero, never mind he made a deliberate attempt to break my neck by unseating me.'

'That's a bit of an exaggeration, isn't it? You're hardly an inexperienced rider, so you must have been in this situation before.' She glanced around the field. 'You know you're going to face the sabs at some point, so presumably taking them on is part of the fun.'

'That's rubbish,' he snapped, reaching down to ease his left stirrup, which had jammed against his heel in the fracas with the saboteur. 'You could say the same thing about these blasted hooligans with their horns.'

'I do and I will,' she said cheerfully. 'It's gang fighting. Sharks against Jets. Toffs against proles. From where I'm standing the fox seems fairly irrelevant. He's just an excuse for a rumble.'

It wasn't Julian's habit to back away from an argument. 'If you print that you'll be laughed out of court,' he told her, straightening again and gathering in his reins. 'Whatever your views on the fox, at least credit all of us – saboteurs and huntsmen alike – with doing what we do for love of the countryside. It's the wreckers you should be writing about.'

'Sure,' she agreed disingenuously. 'Tell me who they are, and I'll do it.'

'Gyppos . . . travellers . . . whatever you want to call them,' he growled. 'Busloads of them arrived in Shenstead Village last night. They muck up the environment and steal off the locals, so why aren't you writing about them, *Ms* Fowler? They're the real vermin. Focus on them and you'll be doing everyone a favour.'

'Would you set your dogs on them?'

'Damn right I would,' he said, wheeling Bouncer away to rejoin the hunt.

*

Wolfie was crouched in the woodland, watching the people on the lawn. He thought it was two men until one of them laughed and the voice sounded like a woman's. He couldn't hear what they were saying because they were too far away, but they didn't look like murderers. Certainly not the old murderer that Fox had talked about. He could see more of the man in the long brown coat than he could of the person with the hat pulled low, and he thought the man's face was kind. He smiled often and, once or twice, put his hand behind the other's back to steer him in a different direction.

A terrible longing grew in Wolfie's heart to run from hiding and ask this man for help, but he knew it was a bad idea. Strangers turned away whenever he begged for money . . . and money was a little thing. What would a stranger do if he begged for rescue? Hand him over to the police, he guessed, or take him back to Fox. He turned his frozen face towards the house and marvelled again at its size. All the travellers in the world could fit inside it, he thought, so why was a murderer allowed to live there alone?

His sharp eyes caught a movement in the downstairs room at the corner of the house, and, after several seconds of concentrated staring, he made out a figure standing behind the glass. He felt a thrill of terror as a white face turned towards him and sunlight glinted on silver hair. The old man! And he was looking straight at Wolfie! With heart knocking, the child scrambled backwards until he was out of sight, then ran like the wind for the safety of the bus.

*

Mark thrust his hands into his pockets to keep his circulation going. 'I can only think it was James's change of mind about involving you that persuaded you to come,' he told Nancy, 'though I don't understand why.'

'It has more to do with the suddenness of his decision,' she said, marshalling her thoughts. 'His first letter implied he was so desperate to make contact that he was prepared to pay a fortune in compensation just to get a reply. His second letter suggested the exact opposite. Keep away . . . no one will ever know who you are. My immediate idea was that I'd done the wrong thing by replying. Maybe the plan was to provoke me into suing as a way of draining the family finances away from his son—' she broke off on an upward inflection, making the statement a question.

Mark shook his head. 'That wouldn't have been

his reason. He's not that devious.' Or never used to be, he thought.

'No,' she agreed. 'If he were, he'd have described himself and his son in very different terms.' She paused again, recalling her impressions of the correspondence. 'That little fable he sent me was very strange. It effectively said that Leo killed his mother in anger because she refused to go on subsidizing him. Is that true?'

'You mean did Leo kill Ailsa?'

'Yes.'

Mark shook his head. 'He couldn't have done. He was in London that night. It was a very solid alibi. The police investigated it thoroughly.'

'But James doesn't accept it?'

'He did at the time,' said Mark uncomfortably, 'or at least I thought he did.' He paused. 'Don't you think you might be reading too much into the fable, Captain Smith? If I remember correctly, James apologized in his second letter for using emotive language. Surely it was symbolic rather than literal. Supposing he'd written "ranted at" instead of "devoured"? It would have been a lot less colourful . . . but far closer to the truth. Leo was prone to shout at his mother, but he didn't kill her. Nobody did. Her heart stopped.'

Nancy nodded abstractedly as if she were only half listening. 'Did Ailsa refuse to give him money?'

'In so far as she rewrote her will at the beginning

145

of the year to exclude both her children.' He shook his head. 'As a matter of fact, I've always regarded that as a reason for Leo *not* to kill her. Both he and his sister were informed of the changes, so they knew they had nothing to gain by her death . . . or not the half-million they were hoping for, anyway. They had a better a chance of that if they kept her alive.'

She looked towards the sea with a thoughtful frown between her eyes. 'This being the "mending of ways" that James referred to in the fable?'

'Effectively, yes.' He took his hands from his pockets to blow on them. 'He's already told you they're a disappointment, so I'm not giving anything away by stressing that. Ailsa was always looking for leverage over their behaviour, and changing her will was one way to exert pressure for improvement.'

'Which is where the search for me came in,' Nancy said without hostility. 'I was another lever.'

'It really wasn't as callous as that,' said Mark apologetically. 'It was more about finding the next generation. Both Leo and Elizabeth are childless . . . and that makes you the only genetic link to the future.'

She turned to look at him. 'I never thought about my genes until you turned up,' she said with a small smile. 'Now they terrify me. Do the Lockyer-Foxes ever consider anyone but themselves? Are selfishness and greed my only inheritance?'

Mark thought about what was on the tapes in the

library. How much worse would she feel if she ever heard them? 'You need to speak to James,' he said. 'I'm just the poor bloody solicitor who takes instruction, though for what it's worth I wouldn't describe either of your grandparents as selfish. I think James was very wrong to write to you – and I told him so – but he was clearly depressed when he did it. It's no excuse, but it might explain some of the apparent confusion.'

She held his gaze for a moment. 'His fable also suggested that Leo will kill him if he gives any of the money away. Is *that* true?'

'I don't know,' he said honestly. 'I read the damn thing for the first time yesterday and I haven't a clue what it's about. James isn't very easy to talk to at the moment, as you probably realize, so I'm not sure myself what's going on inside his head.'

She didn't answer immediately, but seemed to be mulling over ideas to see if they were worth voicing. 'Just for the sake of argument,' she murmured then, 'let's say James wrote exactly what he believes: that Leo killed his mother in anger because money was denied him and is threatening his father with a similar fate if he dares give the money away. Why did he back off involving me between his first and second letters? What changed between October and November?'

'You wrote extremely forcefully to say you didn't want his money and didn't want to confront Leo over it. Presumably he took that to heart.'

147

'That's not the issue, though, is it?'

He looked puzzled. 'Then what is?'

Nancy shrugged. 'If his son is as dangerous as the fable implies, why wasn't he always worried about involving me? Ailsa had been dead several months before he sent you to look for me. He believed when he wrote his first letter that Leo had something to do with her death, but it didn't stop him writing to me.'

Mark followed her logic step-by-step. 'But doesn't that prove you're assuming too much from what he wrote? If James had thought he was putting you in danger, he wouldn't have asked me to go looking for you . . . and, if I'd had any doubts, I wouldn't have done it.'

Another shrug. 'So why do an about-turn in his second letter and fill it with guarantees of non-involvement and anonymity? I was expecting a bull-ish reply, saying I'd got the wrong end of the stick entirely; instead I had a rather confused apology for having written in the first place.' She assumed from his suddenly worried expression that she wasn't explaining herself very well. 'It suggests to me that someone put the fear of God into him between the two letters,' she said, 'and I'm guessing it's Leo, because he's the one James seems to be afraid of.'

She was studying his face and saw the guarded look that had come into his eyes. 'Let's trade infor-mation on that bench over there,' she said abruptly, setting off towards a seat overlooking the valley. 'Was James's description of Leo accurate?'

'Very accurate,' said Mark, following her. 'He's a charmer until you cross him . . . then he's a bastard.'

'Have you crossed him?'

'I took James and Ailsa as clients two years ago.'

'What's wrong with that?' she asked, rounding the bench and looking at the saturated wooden slats.

'The family affairs were managed by Leo's closest friend until I arrived on the scene.'

'Interesting.' She nodded towards the seat. 'Do you want to lend me a flap of your Dryzabone to keep my bum dry?'

'Of course.' He started to undo the metal poppers. 'My pleasure.'

Her eyes twinkled mischievously. 'Are you always this polite, Mr Ankerton, or do clients' granddaughters get special treatment?'

He shrugged out of his Dryzabone and threw it across the seat like Sir Walter Raleigh subduing a puddle before Queen Elizabeth. 'Clients' granddaughters get special treatment, Captain Smith. I never know when . . . or if . . . I'm going to inherit them.'

'Then you'll freeze to death in a lost cause,' she warned, 'because this is one granddaughter who won't be inherited by anyone. Doesn't that make this gesture a little OTT? All I need is a triangle . . . if you open out the flap, you can go on wearing it.'

He lowered himself onto the middle of the seat. 'I'm far too frightened of you,' he murmured, stretching his legs in front of him. 'Where would I put my arm?'

'I wasn't planning on getting that close,' she said, perching awkwardly beside him in the small gap that remained.

'It's unavoidable when you sit on a man's coat . . . and he's still in it.'

He had deep brown eyes that were almost black, and there was too much recognition in them. 'You should go on a survival course,' she said cynically. 'You'd soon discover that keeping warm is more important than worrying about what you're touching.'

'We're not on a survival course, Captain,' he said lazily. 'We're sitting in full view of my client who won't be at all amused to see his solicitor put his arm round his granddaughter.'

Nancy glanced behind her. 'Oh, my God, you're right!' she exclaimed, surging to her feet. 'He's coming towards us.'

Mark leapt up and whipped round. 'Where? Oh, ha-bloody-ha!' he said sarcastically. 'I suppose you think that's funny.'

'Hilarious,' she said, sitting down again. 'Were the family affairs in order?'

Mark resumed his seat, this time pointedly putting distance between himself and her. 'Yes, in so far as my predecessor followed James's instructions at the time,' he said. 'I replaced him when James wanted to change the instructions without Leo being given advance warning.'

'How did Leo react?'

He stared thoughtfully towards the horizon. 'That's the million-dollar question,' he answered slowly.

She eyed him curiously. 'I meant, how did he react towards you?'

'Oh . . . wined me and dined me until he realized I wasn't going to betray his parents' confidence, then took his revenge.'

'How?'

He shook his head. 'Nothing important. Just personal stuff. He can be very charismatic when he wants to be. People fall for it.'

His voice sounded bitter and Nancy suspected the 'personal stuff' had been very important. She leaned forward to prop her elbows on her knees. For 'people' read 'women', and for 'it' read 'Leo', she thought. *Women fall for Leo . . .* One woman? Mark's woman?

'What does Leo do? Where does he live?'

For someone who hadn't wanted to know anything about her biological family, she was suddenly extremely curious about them. 'He's a playboy gambler and lives in a flat in Knightsbridge that belongs to his father.' He was amused by her expression of disapproval. 'More accurately, he's unemployed and unemployable because he stole from the bank he used to work for, and only avoided prison and bankruptcy because his father made good the debt. It wasn't the first time, either. Ailsa had bailed him out a couple of times before because he couldn't control his gambling.'

'*God!*' Nancy was genuinely shocked. 'How old is he?'

'Forty-eight. He spends every night in the casinos, has done for years . . . even when he was working. He's a con artist, pure and simple. People get taken for a ride all the time because he's good at selling himself. I don't know what his situation is at the moment – I haven't spoken to him in months – but it won't be healthy since Ailsa's will was published. He was using his projected inheritance to guarantee private loans.'

It explained a lot, thought Nancy. 'No wonder his parents changed their wills,' she said dryly. 'Presumably he'd sell this place and blow it on roulette if it was left to him?'

'Mm.'

'What a *fuckhead*!' she said contemptuously.

'You'd probably like him if you met him,' Mark warned. 'Everyone else does.'

'No chance,' she said firmly. 'I knew a man like that once, and I'll never get taken in again. He was a casual labourer on the farm when I was thirteen.

Everyone thought the sun shone out of his arse – including me – till he threw me onto the straw in one of the stables and pulled out his prick. He didn't get very far. I suppose he thought he was so much stronger than I was that I wouldn't fight back, so the moment he relaxed his grip I wriggled out from under him and went for him with a pitchfork. I probably ought to have run away but I kept thinking what a fake he was . . . pretending one thing and doing another. I've always hated people like that.'

'What happened to him?'

'Four years for sexual assault of a minor,' she said, staring at the grass. 'He was a right little shit . . . tried to pretend I'd attacked him for relieving himself against the stable wall – but I was screaming so much that two of the other labourers came piling in and found him curled up on the floor with his trousers round his ankles. If it hadn't been for that, I think he might have won. It was his word against mine and Mum said he was very convincing on the witness stand. In the end, the jury took the view that a man didn't need to expose his buttocks to urinate against a wall, particularly as the outside loo was only twenty yards away.'

'Did you attend the court?'

'No. They said I was too young to be cross-examined. My version was presented in the form of a written statement.'

'What was his defence?'

She glanced at him. 'That I'd launched in without provocation and he refused to defend himself for
fear of injuring me. His barrister argued that because
the defendant was more damaged than I was, and
because a thirteen-year-old couldn't have inflicted
such harm on a grown man unless he allowed her to
do it, I must have been the aggressor. It made me
mad when I read the report of the trial. He painted
me as a spoilt, rich brat with a bad temper, who
didn't think twice about lamming into the hired
help. You end up feeling you're the one in the dock
when that kind of thing happens.'

'How much damage did you do?'

'Not enough. Ten stitches in a slash across the
bum and fuzzy vision after one of the prongs caught
the corner of his eye. It was a lucky shot . . . meant
he couldn't focus properly . . . which is why he didn't
fight back. If he'd been able to see the fork, he'd
have grabbed it off me, and I'd have been the one in
hospital.' Her expression hardened. 'Or dead, like
Ailsa.'

Ten

BELLA CLIMBED THE steps of her bus and pulled off her balaclava, running her thick fingers over her stubbly hair where her skin was beginning to itch. The army-surplus overcoats, balaclavas and scarves had been handed out by Fox the day before at the rendezvous, with instructions to wear them every time they went outside. It hadn't been worth arguing about at the time, the cold alone made everyone grateful for them, but Bella was very curious now about why disguise was necessary. Fox knew this place too well, she thought.

A sound from her curtained kitchen area caught her attention. She assumed it was one of her daughters and reached out to pull the drape aside. 'What's up, darlin'? I thought you were with Zadie's kids—' But it wasn't one of hers. It was a skinny little boy with shoulder-length blond hair, and she recognized him immediately as one of the 'spares' who had been in Fox's bus at Barton Edge. 'What the fuck are you doing?' she asked in surprise.

'It weren't me,' muttered Wolfie, cringing away and waiting for the slap.

Bella stared at him for a moment before dropping onto the banquette seat beside her table and pulling a tin of snout from her coat pocket. 'What weren't you?' she asked, prizing open the tin and removing a packet of Rizlas.

'I didn't take nothing.'

Out of the corner of her eye, she watched him squash a piece of bread inside his fist. 'Who did then?'

'I don't know,' he said, mimicking Fox's classy speech, 'but it wasn't me.'

She eyed him curiously, wondering where his mother was and why he wasn't with her. 'So what are you doing here?'

'Nothing.'

Bella spread the Rizla on the table and ran a thin line of tobacco down its centre. 'Are you hungry, kid?'

'No.'

'You look it. Ain't your mum feeding you properly?'

He didn't answer.

'The bread's free,' she said. 'You can take as much as you like. All you have to do is say please.' She rolled the Rizla and ran her tongue along its edge. 'You wanna eat with me and my girls? You want me to ask Fox if that's OK?'

The child stared at her as if she were a gorgon, then took to his heels and belted it out of the bus.

*

Mark lowered his head into his hands and massaged his tired eyes. He'd hardly slept at all in two nights and his energy reserves were at zero. 'James is certainly the suspect in this case,' he told Nancy, 'though God knows why. As far as the police and coroner are concerned, there's no case to answer. It's a crazy situation. I keep asking him to challenge the rumours that are flying around but he says there's no point . . . they'll die down of their own accord.'

'Perhaps he's right.'

'I believed that at the beginning, but not any more.' He ran a worried hand through his hair. 'He's been having nuisance calls and some of them are vicious. He's been recording them on an answerphone and they're all accusing him of killing Ailsa. It's destroying him . . . physically and mentally.'

Nancy plucked at a blade of grass between her feet. 'Why wasn't natural causes accepted? Why does suspicion remain?'

Mark didn't answer immediately and she turned her head to find him grinding his knuckles into his eyes in a way that suggested lack of sleep. She wondered how often the phone had rung the previous night. 'Because at the time all the evidence seemed to suggest an *unnatural* death,' he said wearily. 'Even James assumed she'd been murdered. The fact that Ailsa went out in the middle of the night . . . the blood on the ground . . . her normally robust health. He was the one who whipped up the police to look for evidence of a burglar and, when they couldn't find any, they shifted their attention to him. It's standard procedure – husbands are always first in the firing line – but he got very angry about it. By the time I arrived he was accusing Leo of killing her . . . which didn't help.' He fell silent.

'Why not?'

'Too many wild accusations. First a burglar, then his son. It smacked of desperation when he was the only one there. It only needed evidence of an alter-cation to make him look doubly guilty. He was put through the wringer about the nature of his and Ailsa's relationship. Did they get on? Was he in the habit of hitting her? The police accused him of locking her out in anger after a row, until he asked them why she wouldn't have broken a window pane or gone to Vera and Bob for help. He was pretty shocked by the end of it.'

'But that all happened in the police station pre-sumably . . . so how does it explain the continuing suspicion?'

'Everyone knew he was being questioned. He was taken away in a police car for two days on the trot and you can't keep a thing like that secret. The police backed off when the post-mortem findings came up negative and the blood on the ground was shown to be animal, but it didn't stop the rumour-mongers.' He sighed. 'If the pathologist had been more specific about cause . . . if his children hadn't cold-shouldered him at the funeral . . . if he and Ailsa had been more open about their family problems instead of pretending they didn't exist . . . if the blasted Weldon woman wasn't so puffed up with her own importance . . .' He broke off. 'I keep likening it to chaos theory. A small uncertainty triggers a chain of events that results in chaos.'

'Who's the Weldon woman?'

He flicked a thumb to the right. 'Wife of this farmer over here. The one who claims she heard James and Ailsa arguing. It's the most damaging accusation against him. She said Ailsa accused him of destroying her life, so he called her a bitch and punched her. Now he's tarred as a wife-beater as well as everything else.'

'Did Mrs Weldon see them arguing?'

'No, which is why the police and the coroner rejected her evidence . . . but she's adamant about what she heard.'

Nancy frowned. 'She's been watching too many movies. You can't tell a punch by sound . . . or not against a person, anyway. Leather on leather . . . a hand clap . . . it could have been anything.'

'James denies the argument ever took place.'

'Why would Mrs Weldon lie?'

Mark shrugged. 'I've never met her but she certainly sounds like the type to invent or exaggerate a story to give herself some kudos. James says Ailsa was driven mad by her gossiping. Apparently she was always warning James to watch what he said around the woman because she'd use it against him at the first opportunity.' He gave his jaw a troubled stroke. 'And that's exactly what she's done. The more distance there is between herself and the event the more certain she becomes of who and what she heard.'

'What do *you* think happened?'

He skated round the question and produced what sounded like a rehearsed answer. 'James suffers from arthritis and he hadn't slept all that week. The doctor was able to confirm that he picked up a prescription for barbiturates the day of Ailsa's death and two were missing from the bottle. The traces were still in his system when he insisted the police take a blood sample to prove he was comatose at the time the argument is supposed to have happened. It didn't satisfy his doubters, of course – they say he took the pills after Ailsa was dead – but it satisfied the coroner.' He fell into a brief silence that Nancy didn't break. 'It wouldn't have done if there'd been proof she'd been murdered, but as there wasn't . . .' He didn't bother to finish.

'Your chaos theory sounds about right,' she said sympathetically.

He gave a hollow laugh. 'It's a hell of a mess,

frankly. Even the fact that he armed himself with barbiturates is considered suspicious. Why that day? Why take two? Why insist the police take a blood sample? They keep saying he needed an alibi.'

'Are these the phone calls you were talking about?'

'Mm. I've been going through the recordings . . . and it's getting worse rather than better. You asked if something happened between October and November . . . well, these calls certainly did. He'd had the odd one during the summer – nothing unpleasant, just long silences – but there was a step change in November when the frequency went up to two or three a week.' He paused, clearly wondering how much to tell her. 'It's unbearable,' he said abruptly. 'It's five a *night* now and I don't think he's slept in weeks . . . which is maybe why he goes out to sit on the terrace. I suggested he change his number but he says he's damned if he'll be seen as a coward. He says malicious calls are a form of terrorism and he refuses to kowtow to it.'

Nancy had some sympathy with that view. 'Who's doing it?'

Another shrug. 'We don't know. Most of them are from a number or numbers that have been withheld . . . probably because the caller dials 141 to block number recognition. James has managed to trace a few by dialling call-return on 1471, but not many. He's keeping a list, but the worst offender—' he paused – 'or *offenders* – it's hard to know if it's always the same person – isn't stupid enough to advertise who he is.'

'Does he speak? Don't you recognize the voice?'

'Oh, yes, he speaks all right,' said Mark bitterly. 'The longest call goes on for half an hour. I think it's one man – almost certainly Leo, because he knows so much about the family – but he uses a voice distorter which makes him sound like Darth Vader.'

'I've seen those things. They work just as well for women.'

'I know . . . which is most of the trouble. It would be fairly straightforward if we could say it was Leo . . . but it could be anyone.'

'Isn't it illegal? Can't you ask BT to do something?'

'They can't act without police authority, and James won't have the police involved.'

'Why not?'

Mark took to grinding his eye sockets again, and Nancy wondered what was so difficult about the question. 'I think he's scared it'll make matters worse if the police hear what the Darth Vader voice is saying,' he said finally. 'There are details of events—' a long pause – 'James denies them, of course, but when you hear them over and over again . . .' He lapsed into silence.

'They sound convincing,' she finished for him.

'Mm. Some of it's certainly true. It starts to make you wonder about the rest.'

Nancy recalled the Colonel's reference to Mark Ankerton being an 'honourable exception' amongst the ranks of those rushing to condemn him, and she wondered if he knew that his lawyer had begun to waver. 'Can I listen to these tapes?' she asked.

He looked appalled. 'No way. James would have a fit if he thought you'd heard them. They're pretty damn awful. If I was on the receiving end of them, I'd have changed my number and gone ex-directory immediately. The bloody Weldon woman doesn't even have the guts to speak . . . just phones in the middle of the night to wake him . . . then sits and pants for five minutes.'

'Why does he answer?'

'He doesn't . . . but the phone still rings, he still wakes up, and the tape records her silence.'

'Why doesn't he disconnect at night?'

'He's collecting evidence . . . but won't use it.'

'How far away is the Weldons' farmhouse?'

'Half a mile up the road towards Dorchester.'

'Then why don't you go and read the riot act to her? She sounds like a lump of jelly to me. If she doesn't even have the courage to speak, then she'll probably faint if his solicitor turns up.'

'It's not that easy.' He blew on his hands to bring back some warmth. 'I had a go at her husband this morning over the phone, told him there was a case against his wife for slander. James came in in the middle and gave me hell for even suggesting it. He refuses to consider injunctions . . . calls them white flags . . . says they smack of surrender. To be honest, I don't understand his reasoning at all. He uses siege metaphors all the time as if he's content to wage a war of attrition instead of doing what I want him to do, which is take the fight to the enemy. I know he's worried that legal action might put the story back on the pages of the newspapers – something he doesn't want – but I also think he's genuinely afraid of renewed police interest in Ailsa's death.'

Nancy pulled off her hat and tucked it over his hands. 'That doesn't make him guilty,' she said. 'I imagine it's far more frightening to be innocent of a crime, and unable to prove it, than guilty and covering your tracks all the time. The one's a passive state, the other's proactive, and he's a man who's used to action.'

'Then why won't he take my advice and start attacking these bastards?'

She stood up. 'For the reasons you've already given. Look, I can hear your teeth chattering. Put your coat back on and let's start walking again.' She waited while he redonned the Dryzabone then purposefully retraced their steps towards the Japanese garden. 'There's no point him putting his head above the parapet if it's likely to be blown off,' she pointed out. 'Maybe you should suggest guerrilla warfare instead of formal troop deployment in the shape of injunctions and police involvement. It's a perfectly honourable course of action to send out a sniper to pick off an enemy in a dugout.'

'My God!' he said with a groan, surreptitiously tucking her hat into his pocket, very conscious that it was a DNA gold mine. If she forgot it, the problem could be solved. 'You're as bad as he is. Do you want to put that into English?'

'Take out the people you can identify, like the Weldon woman, then concentrate on Darth Vader. He'll be easier to neutralize once you've isolated him.' She smiled at his expression. 'It's bog-standard tactics.'

'I'm sure it is,' he said sourly. 'Now tell me how to do it without injunctions.'

'Divide and rule. You've made a start on Mrs Weldon's husband. How did he react?'

'Angrily. He didn't know she'd been making calls.'

'That's good. Who else has 1471 identified?'

'Eleanor Bartlett . . . lives in Shenstead House, about fifty yards down the road. She and Prue Weldon are close friends.'

'Then that'll be the strongest axis against James. You need to split them.'

He bared his teeth in a sarcastic grimace. 'And how do I do that?'

'Start believing in the cause you're fighting for,'

she said dispassionately. 'It's no use being half-hearted about it. If Mrs Weldon's version of events is true, then James is lying. If James is telling the truth then it's Mrs Weldon who's lying. There are no grey areas. Even if Mrs Weldon believes she's telling the truth – but it *isn't* the truth – then it's a lie.' She bared her teeth back at him. 'Pick a side.'

To Mark, for whom the entire issue was a confusing collage of greys, this was an extraordinarily simplistic argument and he wondered what she'd read at Oxford. Something with defined parameters; engineering, he guessed, where torque and thrust had defined limits and mathematical equations produced conclusive results. In fairness, she hadn't heard the tapes, but even so . . . 'Reality is never so black and white,' he protested. 'What if both sides are lying? What if they're being honest about one thing and lying about another? What if the event they're disputing has no bearing on the alleged crime?' He jabbed a finger at her. 'What do you do then . . . assuming you have a conscience and you don't want to shoot the wrong person?'

'Resign your commission,' Nancy said bluntly. 'Become a pacifist. Desert. All you do by listening to enemy propaganda is compromise your morale and the morale of your troops. It's *bog-standard* tactics.' She jabbed a finger back at him to stress the words. 'Propaganda is a powerful weapon. Every tyrant in history has demonstrated that.'

Eleven

ELEANOR BARTLETT was satisfyingly bullish when Prue phoned to relay the news about travellers in the Copse. She was an envious woman who enjoyed a grievance. Had she been wealthy enough to indulge her whims, she would have taken her grievances to court and been dubbed a 'malicious litigant'. As she wasn't, she contented herself with destabilizing relationships under the guise of 'straight-speaking'. It made her generally disliked, but also gave her influence. Few wanted her as an enemy, particularly the weekenders whose absences meant they couldn't guard their reputations.

It was Eleanor who had urged her husband to accept early-retirement in order to move to the country. Julian had agreed reluctantly, but only because he knew that his days with the company were numbered. Nevertheless, he had serious doubts about the wisdom of leaving the city. He was content with where he was in life – senior-management level, a decent portfolio on the stock market which would pay for a cruise or two during retirement, like-minded friends who enjoyed a drink after work and a game of golf at weekends, easy-going neighbours, cable television, his children by his previous marriage within a five-mile radius.

As usual, he was overruled by a mixture of silence and tantrums, and the sale four years ago of their modest (by London standards) home on the outer fringes of Chelsea had allowed them to trade up to a more impressive address in a Dorset village where inflationary city prices overwhelmed provincial ones. Shenstead House, a fine Victorian building, lent tradition and history to its owners where 12 Croydon Road, a 1970s construction, had not, and Eleanor invariably lied about where she and Julian had lived before – '*down the road from Margaret Thatcher*' – what his position had been within the company – '*director*' – and how much he had been earning – '*a six-figure salary.*'

Ironically, the move had proved more successful for him than it had for her. While the isolation of Shenstead, and its tiny resident population, had given Eleanor the status of a large fish in a small pond – something she had always craved – those same factors had made the victory a hollow one. Her attempts to ingratiate herself with the Lockyer-Foxes had come to nothing – James had avoided her, Ailsa had been polite but distant – and she refused to lower herself by befriending the Woodgates or, worse, the Lockyer-Foxes' gardener and his wife.

The Weldons' predecessors at Shenstead Farm had been depressing company because of their money problems, and the weekenders – all wealthy enough to own a house in London *and* a cottage by the sea – were no more impressed by the new mistress of Shenstead House than the Lockyer-Foxes had been.

Had Julian shared her ambitions to break into Dorset society, or made more of an effort to support them, it might have been different, but, freed from the shackles of earning a living and bored with Eleanor's criticism of his laziness, he had cast around for something to do. A naturally gregarious man, he homed in on a friendly pub in a neighbouring village and drank his way slowly into the agricultural community, unconcerned whether his boon companions were landowners, farmers or farm labourers. Born and bred in Wiltshire, he had a better idea than his London-born wife of the pace at which things happened in the countryside. Nor, to his wife's disgust, did he have a problem sharing a pint with Stephen Woodgate or the Lockyer-Foxes' gardener, Bob Dawson.

He did not invite Eleanor to join him. Spending time with her and her sharp tongue had made him realize why he had viewed retirement with such reluctance. They had been able to tolerate each other for twenty years because he had been out of the house all day, and it was a pattern he stuck to now. Over a period of months he resurrected his boyhood love of riding, took lessons, reappointed the stable at the back of his house, fenced off half the garden as a paddock, purchased a horse and joined the local hunt. Through these connections he found satisfactory golfing and snooker partners, enjoyed a sail now and then, and after eighteen months pronounced himself entirely satisfied with life in the country.

Predictably, Eleanor was furious, accusing him of wasting their money on selfish pursuits that benefited only him. She harboured a continuing resentment that they had missed the housing boom by a year, particularly when she learnt that their ex-neighbours in Chelsea had sold an identical house two years later for a hundred thousand more. With typical doublethink, she conveniently forgot her part in the move, and blamed her husband for selling out too soon.

Her tongue grew teeth. His redundancy hadn't been that generous, in all conscience, and they couldn't afford to splash out whenever they felt like it. How could he waste money on doing up the stable when the house needed redecorating and recarpeting? What sort of impression would faded paint and shabby carpets make on visitors? He'd joined the hunt deliberately to scupper her chances with the Lockyer-Foxes. Didn't he know that Ailsa supported the League Against Cruel Sports?

Julian, intensely bored with both her and her social climbing, advised her to try less hard. There was no point getting uppity if people didn't socialize the way she wanted, he said. Ailsa's idea of a good time was to sit on charitable committees. James's was to shut himself in his library in order to compile his family's history. They were private people, and they weren't remotely interested in wasting time on trivial chatter or dressing up for drinks and dinner parties. How did he know all this? Eleanor had asked. A chap in the pub had told him.

The Weldons' purchase of Shenstead Farm had been a lifesaver for Eleanor. In Prue, she found a bosom pal who could restore her confidence. Prue was the admiring acolyte with a circle of contacts from her ten years on the other side of Dorchester that Eleanor needed. Eleanor was the sophisticated London steel in Prue's backbone that gave her permission to voice her criticism of men and marriage. Together they joined a golf club, learnt to play bridge and went on shopping expeditions to Bournemouth and Bath. It was a friendship made in heaven – or hell, depending on your viewpoint – two women in perfect tune with each other.

Julian had remarked sourly to Dick some months before, during a particularly dire supper party when Eleanor and Prue had ganged up drunkenly to abuse them, that their wives were *Thelma and Louise* going through the menopause – but without the sex appeal. The only mercy was they hadn't met earlier, he said, otherwise every man on the planet would be dead – irrespective of whether he'd found the nerve to rape them or not. Dick had never seen the movie, but he laughed nonetheless.

It wasn't surprising, therefore, that Prue distorted the facts when she spoke to Eleanor that Boxing Day morning. Julian's 'passing the buck' became 'a typical male reluctance to be involved'; Dick's 'idiocy in phoning Shenstead Manor' became 'a panic reaction to something he couldn't handle'; and the solicitor's 'abusive calls' and 'slander' became 'cowardly threats because James was too frightened to sue'.

'How many travellers are there?' asked Eleanor. 'It's not a repeat of Barton Edge, I hope. The *Echo* gave a figure of four hundred for that.'

'I don't know – Dick went off in a huff without giving any details – but there can't be many or their vehicles would be clogging the street. The traffic jams to Barton Edge were five miles long.'

'Did he call the police?'

Prue gave an irritated sigh. 'Probably not. You know how he shies away from confrontation.'

'All right, leave it with me,' said Eleanor, who was used to taking control. 'I'll have a look, then ring the police. There's no point wasting money on solicitors before we have to.'

'Call me back when you know what's happening. I'm in all day. Jack and Belinda are due this evening . . . but not till after six.'

'Will do,' said Eleanor, adding a cheerful 'goodbye' before going through to the back porch to find her padded candy-stripe jacket and designer walking boots. She was a few years older than her friend, rapidly approaching sixty, but she always lied about her age. Prue's hips were spreading disastrously, but Eleanor worked hard to keep hers in trim. HRT had kept her skin in good condition for eight years but she was obsessive about keeping her weight down. She didn't want to be sixty; she certainly didn't want to *look* sixty.

She sidled past her BMW in the drive, and thought how much better everything had been since Ailsa died. There was no question who was the leading lady of the village now. The money situation had improved by leaps and bounds. She boasted to Prue about bull markets and the wisdom of investing offshore, while being grateful that her friend was too stupid to understand what she was talking about. She didn't want to answer difficult questions.

Her route to the Copse took her past Shenstead Manor and she paused to fire her usual inquisitive glance up the driveway. She was surprised to see a dark green Discovery parked in front of the dining-room window and wondered who it belonged to. Certainly not the solicitor, who had arrived in a silver Lexus on Christmas Eve, nor Leo, who had driven her round London a couple of months ago in a black Mercedes. Elizabeth? Surely not. The Colonel's daughter could barely string a sentence together, let alone drive a car.

*

Mark put out a hand to hold Nancy back as they rounded the corner of the house from the garage block. 'There's that bloody Bartlett woman,' he said crossly, nodding towards the gate. 'She's trying to work out who your car belongs to.'

Nancy took stock of the distant figure in its pink jacket and pastel ski pants. 'How old is she?'

'No idea. Her husband admits to sixty, but she's his second wife – used to be his secretary – so she's probably a lot younger.'

'How long have they lived here?'

'Not sure. Three years . . . four years.'

'What did Ailsa think of her?'

'Called her "Pokeweed" . . . common as muck, pokes her nose in where it isn't wanted, stinks to high heaven and lives in a bog.' Mark watched Eleanor move out of sight, then turned to Nancy with a grin. 'It's a poisonous plant in America. Gives you headaches and nausea if you're unwise enough to swallow it. Your mother probably knows about it if she's interested in global flora. Ailsa certainly did. It has pretty berries and edible shoots but the root and stem are poisonous.'

Nancy smiled. 'What did she call Prue Weldon?'

'Staggerbush. A poisonous shrub that affects sheep.'

'You?'

He moved out onto the drive. 'What makes you think she called me anything?'

'Instinct,' she murmured, following him.

'Mandrake,' he said dryly.

It was Nancy's turn to laugh. 'Was that meant as a compliment or an insult?'

'I was never too sure. I looked it up once. The root is said to look like a man and gives a terrible shriek when it's pulled from the ground. The Greeks used it as both an emetic and an anaesthetic. It's poisonous in large doses and soporific in small ones. I prefer to think she looked at my name, M. Ankerton . . . saw Man . . . and added drake.'

'I doubt it. Pokeweed and Staggerbush are brilliantly evocative, so presumably Mandrake was intended to be, too. Man. Drake.' Her eyes twinkled again as she made a deliberate separation between the words. 'Doubly macho, therefore. I'm sure it was meant as a compliment.'

'What about the poisonous aspect?'

'You're not giving credit to its other properties. It's fabled to have magical powers, particularly against demonic possession. In the Middle Ages people put the roots on their mantelpieces to bring happiness and prosperity to their houses and ward

175

off evil. It was also used as a love potion and a cure for infertility.'

He looked amused. 'You've got Ailsa's genes as well,' he said. 'That's almost word for word what she said when I accused her of lumping me in with Pokeweed and Staggerbush.'

'Mm,' she said coolly, leaning against her car, still indifferent to her genetic heritage. 'What did she call James?'

'Darling.'

'I don't mean to his face. What was her nickname for him?'

'She didn't have one. She always referred to him as "James" or "my husband".'

She crossed her arms and stared at him with a thoughtful expression. 'When she called him "darling", did she sound as if she meant it?'

'Why do you ask?'

'Most people don't. It's a term of endearment that means very little . . . like: "I love you with all my heart". If someone said that to me, I'd stick my fingers down my throat.'

He recalled how often he'd called women 'darling' without thinking about it. 'What do you like to be called?'

'Nancy. But I'm happy to accept Smith or Captain.'

'Even by lovers?'

'Particularly by lovers. I expect a man to know

who I am when he shoves his prick up my fanny. "Darling" could be anyone.'

'Christ!' he said with feeling. 'Do all women think like you?'

'Obviously not, otherwise they wouldn't use endearments on their men.'

He felt an irrational need to defend Ailsa. 'Ailsa seemed to mean it,' he said. 'She never used it for anyone else . . . not even for her children.'

'Then I doubt James ever lifted a finger against her,' Nancy said matter-of-factly. 'It sounds to me as if she used names to define people, not reinforce their violence with pretty words. What did she call Leo?'

Mark looked interested, as if her more objective eye had seen something he hadn't. 'Wolfsbane,' he said. 'It's a form of aconite, highly poisonous.'

'And Elizabeth?'

'Foxbane,' he said with a wry smile. 'Smaller . . . but no less deadly.'

*

Eleanor felt only irritation as she walked towards the barrier and saw a fire smouldering in the middle of the deserted encampment. It was the height of irresponsibility to leave burning wood untended, even if the ground was frozen with ice. Ignoring the 'keep out' notice, she put a hand on the rope to lift it, and suffered a pang of alarm when two hooded figures stepped out from behind trees on either side of the path.

'Can we do something for you, Mrs Bartlett?' asked the one to her left. He spoke with a soft Dorset accent, but there was nothing else to judge him by except a pair of pale eyes that watched her closely over the scarf that covered his mouth.

Eleanor was more taken aback than she cared to admit. 'How do you know my name?' she asked indignantly.

'Electoral register.' He tapped a pair of binoculars on his chest. 'I watched you come out of Shenstead House. How can we help you?'

She was at a loss for words. A courteous traveller was not a stereotype she recognized, and she immediately questioned what sort of encampment this was. For no logical reason – except that the muffled faces, army-surplus overcoats and binoculars suggested manoeuvres – she decided she was dealing with a soldier.

'There's obviously been a mistake,' she said, preparing to lift the rope again. 'I was told travellers had taken over the Copse.'

Fox advanced and held the rope where it was. 'The sign says "keep out",' he said. 'I suggest you obey it.' He nodded towards a couple of Alsatians that lay on the ground near one of the buses. 'They're on long tethers. It would be sensible not to disturb them.'

'But what's going on?' she demanded. 'I think the village has a right to know.'

'I disagree.'

The bald response left her scrabbling. 'You can't just . . .' She waved an ineffectual hand. 'Do you have permission to be here?'

'Give me the name of the landowner and I'll discuss terms with him.'

'It belongs to the village,' she said.

He tapped the 'keep out' notice. 'I'm afraid not, Mrs Bartlett. There's no record of it belonging to anyone. It's not even registered as common land under the 1965 Act, and the Lockean theory of property says that when a piece of land is vacant then it may be claimed through adverse possession by anyone who encloses it, erects structures and defends his title. We claim this land as ours unless and until someone comes forward with a deed of ownership.'

'That's outrageous.'

'It's the law.'

'We'll see about that,' she snapped. 'I'm going home to call the police.'

'Go ahead,' said the man, 'but you'll be wasting your time. Mr Weldon's already spoken to them. You'd do better to find yourselves a good solicitor.' He jerked his head towards Shenstead Manor. 'Maybe you should ask Mr Lockyer-Fox if you can use Mr Ankerton . . . at least he's in situ and probably knows something about the rules and regulations re. *terra nullius.* Or have you burnt your boats in that direction, Mrs Bartlett?'

Eleanor's alarm returned. Who was he? How did he know the name of James's solicitor? That certainly wasn't in the electoral register for Shenstead. 'I don't know what you're talking about.'

'*Terra nullius.* Land with no owner.'

She found his pale stare unnerving – familiar even – and glanced towards the smaller, bulkier figure next to him. 'Who are you?'

'Your new neighbours, darlin',' said a woman's voice. 'We're gonna be here a while, so you'd better get used to us.'

This was a voice and gender that Eleanor felt she could deal with – the chewed diphthongs of an Essex Girl. Also the woman was fat. 'Oh, I don't think so,' she said condescendingly. 'I think you'll find Shenstead is well out of your reach.'

'It don't look that way at the moment,' said the other. 'Just two of you's turned up since your old man drove by at eight thirty. Hardly a fuckin' stampede to get rid of us, is it, bearin' in mind it's Boxing Day and everyone's on holiday? What's wrong with the rest of them? Ain't no one told them we're here . . . or don't they care?'

'The word will spread quickly, don't you worry.'

The woman gave an amused laugh. 'I reckon it's you needs to start worrying, darlin'. You've got lousy communications here. So far, it looks like your man alerted Mr Weldon and he's alerted you . . . or maybe it was your man alerted you and it's taken you four hours to get dolled up. Either way, they've dropped you in it without telling you what's going on. Mr Weldon was so fired up we thought he was gonna set a whole posse of solicitors on us . . . and all we get is a piece of candyfloss. How does that work, then? Are you the most terrifying thing this village has got?'

Eleanor's lips thinned angrily. 'You're absurd,' she said. 'You obviously know very little about Shenstead.'

'I wouldn't bet on it,' the woman murmured.

Neither would Eleanor. She was disturbed by the accuracy of their information. How did they know it was Julian who drove past at eight thirty? Had someone told them what car he owned? 'Well, you're right about one thing,' she said, jamming the fingers of both hands together to tighten her gloves, 'a posse of solicitors is exactly what you're going to face. Mr Weldon's and Colonel Lockyer-Fox's have both been informed and, now that I've seen for myself what sort of people we're dealing with, I shall be instructing ours.'

The man attracted her attention by tapping the notice again. 'Don't forget to mention that it's an issue of ownership and adverse possession, Mrs

Bartlett,' he said. 'You'll save yourself a lot of money if you explain that when Mr Weldon tried to enclose it, no deeds to this piece of land could be found.'

'I'm not taking advice from you on how to talk to my solicitor,' she snapped.

'Then perhaps you should wait for your husband to come home,' he suggested. 'He won't want to run up bills on a piece of land he has no claim to. He'll tell you the responsibility lies with Mr Weldon and Mr Lockyer-Fox.'

Eleanor knew he was right, but the suggestion that she needed her husband's permission to do anything sent her blood pressure soaring. 'How very misinformed you are,' she said scathingly. 'My husband's commitment to this village is one hundred per cent . . . as you will discover in due course. He's not in the habit of backing away from a battle just because his interests aren't threatened.'

'You're very sure of him.'

'With reason. He upholds people's rights . . . unlike you who are intent on destroying them.'

There was a short silence, which Eleanor interpreted as victory. With a tight little smile of triumph, she turned on her heel and stalked away.

'Maybe you should ask him about his lady friend,' the woman called after her, 'the one that comes visiting every time your back's turned . . . blonde . . . blue-eyed . . . and not a day over thirty . . . that sure as hell don't look like a hundred per cent commitment to us . . . more like a replacement model for a beat-up old banger in need of a facelift.'

*

Wolfie watched the woman walk away. He could see her face going pale as Fox whispered into Bella's ear and Bella shouted after her. He wondered if she was a social worker. At the very least she was a 'do-gooder', he guessed, otherwise she wouldn't have frowned so much when Fox put his hand on the rope to stop her coming in. Wolfie was glad of that, because he hadn't liked the look of her. She was skinny and her nose was pointy, and there were no smiley lines around her eyes.

His mother had told him never to trust people without smiley lines. It means they can't laugh, she said, and people who can't laugh don't have souls. What's a soul? he'd asked. It's all the kind things that a person's ever done, she said. It shows in their face when they smile, because laughter is the music of the soul. If the soul never hears music then it dies, which is why unkind people don't have smiley lines.

He was sure it was true even if his understanding of the soul was confined to counting wrinkles. His mother had loads. Fox had none. The man on the lawn had creased his eyes every time he smiled. Confusion began when he thought about the old man at the window. In his simplistic philosophy age bestowed soul, but how could a murderer have a soul? Wasn't killing people the unkindest thing of all?

*

Bella, too, watched the woman walk away. She was angry with herself for repeating Fox's words verbatim. It wasn't her business to wreck other people's lives. Nor could she see the point. 'How's that gonna help us get on with the neighbours?' she said aloud.

'If they're at each other's throats, they won't be at ours.'

'You're a bit of a ruthless bastard, ain't you?'

'Maybe . . . when I want something.'

Bella glanced at him. 'And what's that, Fox? Because you sure haven't brought us here to be sociable. I reckon you've tried that already, and it didn't work.'

A flash of humour gleamed in his eyes. 'What's that supposed to mean?'

'It means you've been here before and got sussed, darlin'. I reckon the posh accent didn't go down as well with this lot—' she jabbed a thumb towards the village – 'as it does with a bunch of ignorant travellers . . . and you got slung out on your arse. It's not just your face you're hiding, it's your fucking voice . . . so are you gonna tell me why?'

His eyes went cold. 'Mind the barrier,' was all he said.

Twelve

NANCY BACKED UP towards the gate, narrowing her eyes against the sun to stare at the Manor facade, while Mark dragged his heels several yards behind. Aware that Eleanor Bartlett could return at any moment, he wanted to keep Nancy away from the road, but she was more interested in a vigorous wisteria that was dislodging slates from the roof. 'Is the building listed?' she asked him.

Mark nodded. 'Grade Two. It's eighteenth century.'

'What's the local council like? Does it monitor for structural damage?'

'I've no idea. Why do you ask?'

She pointed to the bargeboards beneath the eaves, which were showing signs of wet rot in the shredding wood. There had been similar damage at the back of the house, where the beautiful stone walls were streaked with lichen from water leaking out of the gutters on that side. 'There's a lot of repair work needs doing,' she said. 'The gutters are coming away because the wood underneath is rotten.

It's the same at the back. All the bargeboards need replacing.'

He moved up beside her and glanced along the road. 'How do you know so much about houses?'

'I'm a Royal Engineer.'

'I thought you built bridges and mended tanks.'

She smiled. 'Obviously our PR isn't as good as it ought to be. We're jacks of all trades. Who do you think builds accommodation for displaced people in war zones? Certainly not the cavalry.'

'That's James.'

'I know. I looked him up in the army list. You really ought to persuade him to have the repairs done,' she said seriously. 'Damp wood's a breeding ground for the dry-rot fungus when the temperature heats up . . . and that's a nightmare to get rid of. Do you know if the timber's been treated inside?'

He shook his head, drawing on his knowledge of property conveyancing. 'I wouldn't think so. It's a mortgage requirement, so it's usually done when a house changes hands . . . but this one's been in the family since before wood preservative was invented.'

She cupped both hands over her forehead. 'He could end up with a huge bill if he lets it go. The roof looks as if it's sinking in places . . . there's a hell of a dip under the middle chimney.'

'What does that mean?'

'I don't know without looking at the rafters. It depends how long it's been like that. You need to check with some old photographs of the house. It may just be that they used green wood in that part of the construction and it bowed under the weight of the slates. If not—' she lowered her hands – 'the timber in the attic may be as rotten as the bargeboards. You can usually smell it. It's pretty unpleasant.'

Mark remembered the odour of decay when he arrived on Christmas Eve. 'That's all he needs,' he remarked grimly, 'the bloody roof to cave in as well. Have you ever read Poe's "The Fall of the House of Usher"? Do you know what the symbolism is?'

'No . . . and no.'

'Corruption. A corrupt family infects the fabric of their house and brings the masonry down on their heads. Remind you of anything?'

'Colourful but entirely improbable,' she said with a smile.

A flustered voice spoke behind them. 'Is that you, Mr Ankerton?'

Mark swore under his breath as Nancy gave a start of surprise and swung round to find Eleanor Bartlett, looking every bit her age, on the other side of the gate. Nancy's immediate reaction was sympathy – the woman looked frightened – but Mark was cool to the point of rudeness. 'This is a private conversation, Mrs Bartlett.' He put his hand on Nancy's arm to draw her away.

'But it's important,' Eleanor said urgently. 'Has Dick told you about these people at the Copse?'

'I suggest you ask him,' he told her curtly. 'I don't make a habit of passing on what people may or may not have said to me.' He put his mouth to Nancy's ear. 'Walk away,' he begged. 'Now!'

She gave a brief nod and wandered down the drive, and he thanked God for a woman who didn't ask questions. He turned back to Eleanor. 'I've nothing to say to you, Mrs Bartlett. Good day.'

But she wasn't about to be rebuffed so easily. 'They know your name,' she said rather hysterically. 'They know *everybody's* names . . . what sort of cars they drive . . . *everything*. I think they've been spying on us.'

Mark frowned. 'Who's "they"?'

'I don't know. I only saw two of them. They're wearing scarves over their mouths.' She reached out a hand to pluck at his sleeve, but he stepped back sharply as if she were leprous. 'They know you're James's solicitor.'

'Courtesy of you, presumably,' he said with an expression of distaste. 'You've whipped up half the countryside to believe I'm representing a murderer. There's no law against revealing my name, Mrs Bartlett, but there are laws of libel and slander and you've broken all of them in relation to my client. I hope you can afford to defend yourself . . . *and* pay damages when Colonel Lockyer-Fox wins—' he jerked his head in the direction of Shenstead House – 'otherwise your property will be forfeit.'

There was no agility of thought in Eleanor's mind. The pressing issue of the moment was the travellers in the Copse, and that was the question she addressed. '*I* didn't tell them,' she protested. 'How could I? I've never seen them before in my life. They said the land's *terra nullius* . . . I think that was the expression . . . something to do with Lockean theory . . . and they're claiming it by adverse possession. Is that legal?'

'Are you asking for my professional opinion?'

'Oh, for goodness sake!' she said impatiently, anxiety bringing sparks of colour back into her cheeks. 'Of course I am. It's James who's going to be affected by them. They're talking about building structures on the Copse.' She waved a hand up the road. 'Go and look for yourself if you don't believe me.'

'My fees are three hundred pounds per hour, Mrs Bartlett. I am prepared to negotiate a flat rate for advice on legislation re. adverse possession, but in view of the complexity of the issue, I would almost certainly have to consult counsel. His charges would be in addition to the agreed amount, and that could take the final figure well over five thousand. Do you still want to engage me?'

Eleanor, whose sense of humour excluded irony, interpreted this answer as deliberately obstructive.

Whose side was he on, she wondered, as she looked down the drive after Nancy's black-clad figure? Was this another of them? Was James conspiring with these people? 'Are you responsible for this?' she demanded angrily. 'Is that how they know so much about the village? Was it you who told them the land was unowned. They said you were in situ and knew something about this wretched *terra nullius* nonsense.'

Mark experienced a similar revulsion to Wolfie's. Ailsa always said Eleanor was older than she looked, and, close up, Mark could see she was right. Her roots needed seeing to and there were pinch marks round her mouth from bad-tempered pouting when she didn't get her own way. She wasn't even handsome, he thought in surprise, just tight-skinned and waspish. He put his hands on the gate and leaned forward, dislike narrowing his eyes.

'Would you care to explain the twisted logic that gave rise to those questions?' he said in a voice that grated with contempt, 'or is making false accusations a disease with you? This isn't normal behaviour, Mrs Bartlett. Normal people do not force themselves into private conversations and refuse to leave when asked . . . nor do they make wild allegations without some basis in fact.'

She quailed slightly. 'Then why are you treating this as a joke?'

'Treating what as a joke? An assertion by a deeply

disturbed woman that people in scarves are talking about me? Does that sound sane to you?' He smiled at her expression. 'I'm trying to be generous, Mrs Bartlett. My personal view is that you're mentally ill . . . and my judgement is based on the recordings I've listened to of your calls to James. It might interest you to know that your friend, Prue Weldon, has been more intelligent. She never speaks at all, just leaves a record of her phone number. It won't stop her being charged with making malicious telephone calls, but *your* calls—' he made a ring of his thumb and forefinger – 'we're going to have a field day with them. My best advice is that you see a doctor before you consult a solicitor. If your problems are as serious as I think they are, you might be able to plead mitigation when we play your tapes in open court.'

'That's ridiculous,' she hissed. 'Tell me one thing I've said that isn't true.'

'*Everything* you say is untrue,' he flashed back, 'and I'd like to know where you've been getting it from. Leo wouldn't speak to you. He's more of a snob than James and Ailsa have ever been, and a social climber wouldn't appeal at all—' he ran a scathing eye over her pastel outfit – 'particularly the mutton-dressed-as-lamb variety. And if you believe anything Elizabeth says, you're an idiot. She'll tell you anything you want to hear . . . as long as the gin keeps flowing.'

Eleanor gave a vicious little smile. 'If it's all lies, why hasn't James reported the calls to the police?'

'*Which* calls?' he slammed back aggressively.

There was a tiny hesitation. 'Mine and Prue's.'

Mark made a commendable attempt to look amused. 'Because he's a gentleman . . . and he's embarrassed on behalf of your husbands. You should listen to yourself occasionally.' He put the knife in where he thought it would hurt the most. 'The kindest interpretation of your rants against men and where they put their penises is that you're a closet lesbian who's never found the courage to declare herself. A more realistic interpretation is that you're a frustrated bully with obsessions about sex with strangers. Either way, it doesn't say much about your relationship with your husband. Isn't he interested any more, Mrs Bartlett?'

It was a throwaway line, designed to puncture her conceit, but he was surprised by the strength of her reaction. She stared at him, wild-eyed, then turned and fled down the road towards her house. Well, well, he thought with surprised satisfaction. Now *that* was a hit.

*

He found Nancy leaning against an oak tree to the right of the terrace with her face turned to the sun and her eyes closed. Beyond her, the long vista of the lawn, peppered with trees and shrubs, dipped towards the farmland and the distant sea. Wrong county, wrong period, but it might have been a painting by Constable: *Rural setting with boy in black.*

She could have been a boy, thought Mark, taking a good look at her as he approached. *Butch as hell!* Muscular, strong-jawed, barren of make-up, too tall for comfort. She wasn't his type, he told himself firmly. He liked them delicate, blue-eyed and blonde.

Like Elizabeth . . .?

Like Eleanor Bartlett . . .? Shit!

Even in relaxation and with her eyes closed, the stamp of James's genes was powerful. There was none of Ailsa's fine-boned, pale beauty which had passed to Elizabeth, only the dark, sculptured looks that had passed to Leo. It shouldn't have worked. It was unnatural. So much strength in a woman's face ought to have been a turn-off. Instead, Mark was riveted by it.

'How did you get on?' she murmured with her eyes still closed. 'Did you give her a bollocking?'

'How did you know it was me?'

'Who else could it be?'

'Your grandfather?'

She opened her eyes. 'Your boots don't fit,' she told him. 'Every tenth step you slide the soles along the grass to get a better grip with your toes.'

'God! Is that part of your training?'

She grinned at him. 'You shouldn't be so gullible,

Mr Ankerton. The reason I knew it wasn't James is because he's in the drawing room . . . assuming I've got my bearings right. He inspected me through his binoculars, then opened the French windows. I think he wants us to go in.'

'It's Mark,' he said, holding out his hand, 'and you're right, these boots don't fit. I found them in the scullery, because I don't have any of my own. There's not much call for wellingtons in London.'

'Nancy,' she said, solemnly shaking his hand. 'I noticed. You've been walking as if you had flippers on since we left the house.'

He held her gaze for a moment. 'Are you ready?'

Nancy wasn't sure. Her confidence had faltered as soon as she spotted the binoculars, and made out the figure behind them. *Would she ever be ready*? Her plan had gone awry from the moment Mark Ankerton opened the door. She had hoped for a private one-on-one conversation with the Colonel, which would follow an agenda set by her, but that was before she had seen his distress or realized how isolated he was. Naively she had believed she could keep an emotional distance – at least on a first meeting – but Mark's wavering had provoked her into championing the old man's cause, and this without even meeting him or knowing if the cause was a true one. She had a terrible fear suddenly that she wasn't going to like him.

Perhaps Mark read it in her eyes because he took her hat from his pocket and gave it to her. 'Usher only fell because there was no one like you around,' he said.

'You're a naive romantic.'

'I know. It sucks.'

She smiled. 'I think he's guessed who I am – probably from the Herefordshire cattle sticker on my windscreen – otherwise he wouldn't have opened the French windows. Unless I look like Elizabeth, of course, and he's mistaken me for her.'

'You don't,' said Mark, holding his arm behind her back to encourage her forward. 'Trust me . . . in a million years, no one would mistake you for Elizabeth.'

*

Eleanor began in Julian's dressing room, searching through his jacket pockets and turning out his chest of drawers. From there she moved to his study, rifling through his filing cabinet and ransacking his desk. Even before she switched on his computer and scrolled through his email correspondence – the man was too blasé even to use a password – the evidence of betrayal was colossal. He hadn't even bothered with the pretence of keeping the affair a secret. There was a mobile-phone number on a scrap of paper in one of his jackets, a silk scarf at the bottom of his handkerchief drawer, hotel and restaurant receipts in his desk, and dozens of emails filed under the initials 'GS'.

Darling J, What about Tuesday? I'm free from 6.00 . . .

Can you make the Newton point-to-point? I'm riding Monkey Business in the 3.30 . . .

Don't forget you promised me a grand towards MB's vets' bills . . .

Are you coming to the Hunt AGM . . .?

Do you really mean it about the new horsebox? I LOVE you to distraction . . .

Meet me on the bridleway at the back of the farm. I'll be there around 10.00 a.m. . . .

I'm sorry about Bouncer's leg. Give him a get-well kiss from his favourite lady . . .

With murder in her heart, Eleanor went into 'sent items', looking for Julian's messages to GS.

Thelma is taking Louise shopping on Friday. Usual place? Usual time . . .?

T and L are playing golf – Sept 19th . . .

T is off to London next week – Tues to Friday. 3 whole days of freedom! Any chance . . .?

T's an idiot. She'll believe anything . . .

Do you think T could have found herself a toy boy? Keep finding her on the phone. Hangs up immediately . . .

T's definitely up to something. Keeps whispering in the kitchen with L . . .

What are the odds on Dick and me being given the boot together? Do you think a miracle's happened and they've both found toy boys . . .?

The sudden ringing of the telephone on the desk caused Eleanor to give a guilty start. The raucous sound, a reminder that real life existed beyond the grubby secrets on the screen, set her nerves jangling in the silence of the room. She shrank back into her seat, heart thumping like a steam hammer, anger and fear colliding in her gut to produce nausea. Who was it? Who knew? People would laugh at her. People would crow. People would say she deserved it.

After four seconds the line switched to the answerphone and Prue's vexed voice came through the loudspeaker. 'Are you there, Ellie? You promised to call when you'd spoken to the solicitor. I don't understand why it's taking so long . . . plus Dick's refusing to answer his mobile so I don't know where he is or if he wants lunch.' She gave an angry sigh. 'It's so damn childish of him. I could have done with some help before Jack and Belinda arrive . . . and now he'll just sour the evening with one of his moods. Ring soon. I'd like to know what's going on before he comes back otherwise there'll be another row about James's bloody solicitor.'

Eleanor waited for the click as Prue hung up, then pressed the 'delete' button to erase the message. She took the scrap of paper with the mobile number on it out of her shirt pocket, stared at it for a moment, then lifted the receiver and dialled. There was no rationale to what she was doing. Perhaps the habit of accusing James – and his timid reactions – had taught her that this was the way to deal with transgressors. Nevertheless, it took two attempts to make a connection, because her fingers were shaking so much that they fumbled on the keys. There was no answer, just a few seconds of silence before the call was diverted to voicemail. She listened to the prompts to leave a message, then, with belated recognition that it might not be GS's phone, she rang off.

What would she have said, anyway? Screamed and yelled and demanded her husband back? Called the woman a slut? The awful pit of divorce opened in front of her. She couldn't be alone again, not at sixty. People would avoid her, just as they had when her first husband had left her for the woman who carried his child. Then she had worn her desperation blatantly, but at least she'd been younger and still employable. Julian had been the last throw of her dice, an office affair that had finally led to marriage. She couldn't go through it a second time. She'd lose the house, lose her status, be forced to start again somewhere else . . .

Carefully, so that Julian wouldn't know she'd found the emails, she exited Windows and shut down the computer before closing the desk drawers and repositioning the chair. *This was better. She was beginning to think straight.* As Scarlett O'Hara had said, 'tomorrow is another day'. Nothing was lost while GS remained secret. Julian hated commitment. The only reason Eleanor had been able to force his hand twenty years ago was because she'd made sure his first wife knew of her existence.

She was damned if she'd let GS do the same to her.

With renewed confidence, she went back upstairs and replaced everything neatly in Julian's dressing room, then sat in front of her mirror and worked on her face. For a woman of such shallow mind, the fact that she didn't like her husband and he didn't like her was irrelevant. The issue, rather like the issue of adverse possession at the Copse, was one of ownership.

What she didn't appreciate – because she didn't own a mobile telephone – was that she'd set a time bomb that was about to go off. A 'missed call' was logged on the display unit beside the number of the caller, and Gemma Squires, reining in Monkey Business beside Bouncer as the hunt was abandoned, was about to show Julian that his landline was showing on her handset with the call timed at just ten minutes previously.

*

The foundations of Prue Weldon's world also began to rock when her daughter-in-law phoned to say that she and Jack wouldn't be staying the night after all. They both had hangovers from their Christmas celebrations, Belinda told her, which meant they wouldn't be drinking that evening and could safely drive home after dinner. 'I didn't want you to make the beds unnecessarily,' she finished.

'I've already done it,' said Prue irritably. 'Why couldn't you have phoned earlier?'

'Sorry,' said the girl with a yawn. 'We only surfaced about half an hour ago. It's one of the few days in the year when we get a decent lie-in.'

'Yes, well, it's very inconsiderate of you. I do have other things to do, you know.'

'Sorry,' Belinda said again, 'but we didn't get back from my parents till after two. We left the car there and slogged across the fields. They're bringing it over in half an hour. Jack's cooking lunch for them.'

Prue's irritation grew. Eleanor hadn't called, she didn't know where Dick was, and at the back of her mind were growing worries about slander and nuisance calls. Also, her son's relationship with his in-laws was so much easier than hers with Belinda. 'It's

200

disappointing,' she said tightly. 'We hardly ever see you . . . and when we do you're always dashing to get away again.'

There was an exasperated sigh at the other end. 'Oh, come on, Prue, that's very unfair. We see Dick most days. He's always popping over to keep a check on things at this end of the business. I'm sure he keeps you posted.'

The sigh fuelled Prue's anger. 'It's hardly the same,' she snapped. 'Jack was never like this before he married. He loved coming home, particularly at Christmas. Is it too much to ask – that you'll allow my son to stay one night under his mother's roof?'

There was a short silence. 'Is that what you think this is? A competition to see who has more control over Jack?'

Prue wouldn't recognize a trap if it jumped up and bit her on the nose. 'Yes,' she snapped. 'Please put him on. I'd like to talk to him. I presume you've decided for him.'

Belinda gave a small laugh. 'Jack doesn't want to come at all, Prue, and if you speak to him that is what he'll tell you.'

'I don't believe you.'

'Then ask him this evening,' said her daughter-in-law coolly, 'because I've persuaded him that we *should* come – at least for Dick – on the basis that we won't stay long and we won't stay the night.'

The '*at least for Dick*' was the last straw. 'You've

turned my son against me. I know how much you resent the time I spend with Jenny. You're jealous because she has children, and you don't . . . but she *is* my daughter and *they* are my only grandchildren.'

'Oh, *please*!' said Belinda with equally scathing emphasis. 'We don't all share your petty values. Jenny's kids spend more time here than they do with you . . . which you'd know if you bothered to come and see us occasionally instead of fobbing us off because you'd rather be at the golf club.'

'I wouldn't have to go to the golf club if you made me feel welcome,' said Prue spitefully.

She listened to the nasal breathing at the other end as the girl struggled to calm herself. When Belinda spoke again, her voice was brittle. 'That's the pot calling the kettle black, wouldn't you say? Since when have you made *us* feel welcome? We flog over once a month for the same ridiculous ritual. Chicken casserole in dishwater because your time's too precious to cook properly . . . character assassination of Jack's dad . . . invective against the man at Shenstead Manor . . .' She drew a rasping breath. 'Jack's even more hacked off with it than I am, bearing in mind he adores his dad and we both have to get up at six every morning to keep the business afloat at this end. Poor old Dick's dead on his feet by nine o'clock because he's doing the same thing . . . while you sit there stuffing your face and slagging people off . . . and the rest of us are too damn knackered earning your bloody golfing fees to tell you what a bitch you are.'

The assault was so unexpected that Prue was stunned into silence. Her eyes were drawn to the casserole dish on the worktop while she listened to her son's voice in the background telling Belinda that his dad had just come through the kitchen door, and he wasn't looking happy.

'Jack will phone you later,' said Belinda curtly before ringing off.

Thirteen

ELEANOR BOLSTERED her courage with a neat whisky before she phoned Prue, knowing that her friend wasn't going to be happy about no solicitor, no police and no Bartlett involvement. Eleanor couldn't afford to alienate her husband further by signing him up for expensive legal fees, nor was she prepared to tell Prue why. Julian's preference for a thirty-something was humiliating enough without it becoming public knowledge.

Her relationship with Prue was based on their mutual certainty of their husbands, whom they tore to shreds for their own amusement. Dick was slow. Julian was boring. Both allowed their wives to rule the roost because they were too lazy or inept to make decisions themselves, and so helpless that if their women ever said enough is enough, they would be lost and rudderless like ships adrift. Such statements were funny when made from a position of strength, deeply unfunny with a blonde threatening in the background.

Prue answered at the first ring as if she'd been

waiting for the call. 'Jack?' Her voice sounded strained.

'No, it's Ellie. I've just come in. Are you all right? You sound cross.'

'Oh, hello.' She seemed to make an effort to inject some lightness into her tone. 'Yes, I'm fine. How did it go?'

'Not very well, I'm afraid. The situation's completely different from the way you described it,' said Eleanor in a slightly accusing tone. 'It's not just travellers stopping over, Prue, it's people who say they're going to stay there until someone produces deeds to show who owns it. They're claiming it by adverse possession.'

'What does that mean?'

'Fencing it in and building on it . . . effectively what you and Dick tried to do when you first came here. As far as I understand it, the only way to get rid of them is for either Dick or James to produce evidence that it's part of their estate.'

'But we don't have any evidence. That's why Dick gave up the attempt to enclose it.'

'I know.'

'What did your solicitor say?'

'Nothing. I haven't spoken to him.' Eleanor took a quiet sip of her whisky. 'There's no point, Prue. His advice will be that it's nothing to do with us . . . which, in fairness, it isn't – there's no way we can claim the Copse as part of our land – so our chap won't be able to access any of the deeds or give us a considered judgement. I know it's boring, but I actually think Dick was right to phone James's solicitor. Dick and James are the only ones with an interest, so they'll have to come to an agreement over who's going to fight it.'

Prue didn't answer.

'Are you still there?'

'Did you call the police?'

'Apparently Dick phoned them from the Copse. You should have talked it through with him. It was a complete waste of my time going up there.' She warmed to her grievance in order to put Prue on the back foot. 'And it was pretty damn frightening as well. They're wearing masks . . . and they're alarmingly well informed about everyone in the village. People's names . . . who owns what . . . that kind of thing.'

'Have you been talking to Dick?' demanded Prue. 'No.'

'Then how do you know he spoke to the police?'

'The man at the Copse told me.'

Prue's voice was scornful. 'Oh, *really*, Ellie! How can you be so gullible? You *promised* you'd phone the police. Why agree to it if you had no intention of following through? I could have done it myself two hours ago and saved us all a lot of trouble.'

Eleanor bridled immediately. 'Then why didn't you? If you'd listened to Dick instead of assuming he was running away from the problem, you and he could have dealt with this mess yourselves instead of expecting Julian and me to bail you out. We're hardly to blame if people move onto your land . . . and it's *certainly* not our responsibility to pay a solicitor to rescue you from it.'

If Prue was surprised by Eleanor's volte-face she didn't show it. Instead she said petulantly, 'It's not our land, not according to the deeds anyway, so why should we have to take responsibility?'

'Then it's James's . . . which is exactly what Dick was trying to tell you before you had your row. If you want my advice, you'll eat some humble pie before you have another go at him . . . either that or talk to these squatters yourself. At the moment they're cock-a-hoop because Dick and I are the only people who've bothered to turn up . . . they think the rest of the village doesn't care.'

'What about James's solicitor? Has he done anything?'

Eleanor hesitated before the lie. 'I don't know. I caught a glimpse of him outside the Manor, but he had someone with him. They seemed more interested in the state of the roof than what's going on at the Copse.'

'Who was it?'

'Someone who drives a green Discovery. It's parked in the drive.'

'Man? Woman?'

'I don't know,' said Eleanor again, rather more impatiently. 'I didn't hang around to find out. Look, I can't waste any more time on this . . . you need to talk it through with Dick.'

There was a silence, laden with suspicion, as if Prue were questioning the value of Ellie's friendship. 'I'll be very angry if I find out you've been speaking to him behind my back.'

'That's ridiculous! Don't blame me if you and he have fallen out. You should have listened to him in the first place.'

Prue's suspicions deepened. 'Why are you being so peculiar?'

'Oh, for goodness sake! I've just had a frightening encounter with some extremely unpleasant people. If you think you can do any better, *you* go and talk to them. See how far *you* get!'

*

Any fears Nancy might have had about meeting James Lockyer-Fox were allayed by the straightforward way he greeted her. There was no forced sentiment, no feigned affection. He met her on the terrace and took her hand briefly in both of his. 'You couldn't be more welcome, Nancy.' His eyes were a little watery, but his handshake was firm and Nancy applauded him for taking the embarrassment out of a potentially difficult situation.

To Mark, the observer, it was a moment of appalling tension. He held his breath, certain that James's confident demeanour would rapidly collapse. What if the phone rang? What if Darth Vader began a monologue on incest? Guilty or innocent, the old man was too frail and exhausted to remain detached for long. Mark doubted there was ever a right time or method to discuss DNA sampling, but he ran hot and cold at the thought of discussing it to Nancy's face.

'How did you know it was me?' Nancy asked James with a smile.

He stood aside to usher her through the French windows and into the drawing room. 'Because you're so like my mother,' he said simply, leading her towards a bureau in the corner where a wedding photograph stood in a silver frame. The man was in uniform, the woman in a plain, 1920s-style, low-waisted dress, with a train of lace curled about her feet. James picked it up and looked at it for a moment before handing it to Nancy. 'Do you see a resemblance?'

It surprised her that she could, but then she'd never known anyone to compare herself with. She had this woman's nose and jawline – neither of which, in Nancy's view, were anything to be pleased about – and the same dark colouring. She looked for beauty in the celluloid face but couldn't see it, any more than she could see it in her own. Instead, the woman wore a small frown above her eyes as if she were questioning the point of her history being recorded on camera. A similar frown creased Nancy's brow as she studied the photograph. 'She looks undecided,' she said. 'Did marriage make her happy?'

'No.' The old man smiled at her perspicacity. 'She was much brighter than my father. I think it suffocated her to be trapped in a subservient role. She was always champing at the bit to do something with her life.'

'Did she succeed?'

'Not by today's standards . . . but by the Dorset standards of the 1930s and 40s, I think she did. She started a racing stable here – trained some decent horses – mostly hurdlers – one of them came second in the Grand National.' He saw the flash of approval in Nancy's eyes, and gave a happy laugh. 'Oh, yes, that was a splendid day. She persuaded the school to let me and my brother take the train to Aintree and we won a lot of money on an each-way bet. My father took the credit, of course. Women weren't allowed to train professionally in those days, so he was the nominal licence holder in order to allow her to charge fees and make the enterprise pay for itself.'

'Did she mind?'

'About him taking the credit? No. Everyone knew she was the trainer. It was just a bit of gobbledegook to satisfy the Jockey Club.'

'What happened to the stables?'

'The war put paid to them,' he said regretfully.

'She couldn't train with my father away . . . and when he came back he had them converted into the garage block.'

Nancy replaced the photograph on the bureau. 'That must have annoyed her,' she said, with a teasing glint in her eyes. 'What did she do for revenge?'

Another chuckle. 'Joined the Labour party.'

'Wow! A bit of a rebel, then!' Nancy was genuinely impressed. 'Was she the only member in Dorset?'

'Certainly in the circle my parents moved in. She joined after the '45 election when they published their plans for a National Health Service. She worked as a nurse during the war and became very unhappy about the lack of medical care for the poor. My father was appalled, because he was a lifelong Conservative. He couldn't believe his wife would want Churchill overthrown in favour of Clement Attlee – very ungrateful, he called it – but it made for some spirited debates.'

She laughed. 'Whose side were you on?'

'Oh, I always took my father's side,' said James. 'He could never win an argument against my mother without assistance. She was too powerful a character.'

'What about your brother? Did he take her side?' She looked at a photograph of a young man in uniform. 'Is this him? Or is this you?'

'No, that's John. He died in the war, sadly, otherwise he would have inherited the estate. He was the older by two years.' He touched a gentle hand to Nancy's arm and steered her towards the sofa. 'My mother was devastated, of course – they were very close – but she wasn't the type to hide herself away because of it. She was a wonderful influence . . . taught me that a wife with an independent mind was a prize worth having.'

She sat down on the edge of the seat, turning towards James's armchair and placing her feet apart like a man with her elbows on her knees. 'Is that why you married Ailsa?' she asked, glancing past him towards Mark, surprised to see satisfaction in the younger man's face as if he were a schoolteacher showing off a prize pupil. Or was the commendation for James? Perhaps it was harder for a grandfather to meet the child he'd helped put up for adoption, than it was for the granddaughter to offer the possibility of a second chance.

James lowered himself into his own chair, bending towards Nancy like an old friend. There was a power-ful intimacy in the way they'd arranged themselves, though neither seemed aware of it. It was clear to Mark that Nancy had no idea of the impact she was making. She couldn't know that James rarely laughed – that even an hour ago he wouldn't have been able to lift a photograph without his hands trembling so much she'd have noticed it – or that the sparkle in the faded eyes was for her.

'Goodness me, yes,' said James. 'Ailsa was even

more of a rebel than my mother. When I first met her, she and her friends were trying to disrupt her father's shoot in Scotland by waving placards around. She didn't approve of killing animals for sport – thought it was cruel. It worked, too. The shoot was abandoned when the birds were frightened off. Mind you,' he said reflectively, 'all the young men were much more impressed by the way the girls' skirts rode up when they lifted their placards above their heads than they were by the cruelty-to-animals argument. It wasn't a fashionable cause in the fifties. The savagery of war seemed far worse.' His face became suddenly thoughtful.

Mark, fearing tears, stepped forward to draw attention to himself. 'How about a drink, James? Shall I do the honours?'

The old man nodded. 'That's a splendid idea. What time is it?'

'After one.'

'Good lord! Are you sure? What are we doing about lunch? This poor child must be starving.'

Nancy shook her head immediately. 'Please don't—'

'How does cold pheasant, pâté de foie gras and French bread sound?' Mark broke in. 'It's all in the kitchen . . . won't take a minute to do.' He smiled encouragingly. 'Drink's limited to what's in the cellar, I'm afraid, so it has to be red or white wine. Which do you prefer?'

213

'White?' she suggested. 'And not too much. I'm driving.'

'James?'

'The same. There's a decent Chablis at the far end. Ailsa's favourite. Open some of that.'

'Will do. I'll bring it in, then make the lunch.' He caught Nancy's eye and lifted his right thumb at hip level, out of James's sight, as much as to say 'well done'. She dropped him a wink in return, which he interpreted rightly as 'thank you'. Had he been a dog, his tail would have wagged. He needed to feel he was more than just an observer.

James waited until the door closed behind him. 'He's been a wonderful support,' he said. 'I was worried about dragging him away from his family at Christmas, but he was determined to come.'

'Is he married?'

'No. I believe he had a fiancée once, but it didn't gel for some reason. He comes from a large Anglo-Irish family . . . seven daughters and one son. They all get together at Christmas – it's an old family tradition, apparently – so it was very generous of him to come here instead.' He fell silent for a moment. 'I think he thought I'd do something silly if I was left on my own.'

Nancy eyed him curiously. 'Would you?'

The bluntness of the question reminded him of Ailsa who had always found tiptoeing around other people's sensibilities an irritating waste of time. 'I don't know,' he said honestly. 'I've never thought of myself as a quitter, but then I've never been into battle without my friends beside me . . . and which of us knows how brave he is until he stands alone?'

'First define bravery,' she commented. 'My sergeant would tell you it's a simple chemical reaction which pumps the heart with adrenalin when fear paralyses it. The poor bloody soldier, terrified out of his wits, experiences a massive rush and behaves like an automaton under the influence of hormonal overdose.'

'Does he say that to the men?'

She nodded. 'They love it. They practise self-induced adrenalin rushes to keep their glands in trim.'

James looked doubtful. 'Does it work?'

'More in the mind than the body, I suspect,' she said with a laugh, 'but it's good psychology whichever way you look at it. If bravery is a chemical then we all have access to it, and fear is easier to deal with if it's a recognizable part of the process. In simple terms, we have to be frightened before we can be brave, otherwise the adrenalin won't flow . . . and if we can be brave without being frightened first—' she lifted an amused eyebrow – 'then we're dead from the neck up. What we imagine is worse than what happens. Hence my sergeant's belief that a defence-less civilian, waiting day after day for the bombs to fall, is braver than a member of an armed unit.'

'He sounds quite a character.'

'The men like him,' she said with a dry edge to the words.

'Ah!'

'Mm!'

James chuckled again. 'What's he really like?'

Nancy pulled a wry face. 'A self-opinionated bully who doesn't believe there's a place for women in the army . . . certainly not in the Engineers . . . certainly not with an Oxford degree . . . and certainly not in command.'

'Oh dear!'

She gave a small shrug. 'It would be all right if it was amusing . . . but it isn't.'

She seemed such a confident young woman that he wondered if she was being kind, trading a weakness for advice in order to allow him to do the same. 'I never had to face that specific problem, of course,' he told her, 'but I do remember one particularly tough sergeant who made a habit of taking me on in front of the men. It was all very subtle, mostly in the tone of his voice . . . but nothing I could challenge him about without looking stupid. You can't take a man's stripe away because he repeats your orders in a patronizing way.'

'What did you do?'

'Swallowed my pride and asked for help. He was transferred out of the company within a month.

216

Apparently, I wasn't the only one having trouble with him.'

'Except my subalterns think the sun shines out of his backside. They let him get away with murder because the men respond to him. I feel I ought to be able to handle him. It's what I've been trained for, and I'm not convinced my CO's any more sympathetic to women in the army than my sergeant is. I'm fairly sure he'll tell me that if I can't take the heat I should get out of the kitchen—' she made an ironic correction – 'or, more likely, get *back* to it because it's where a woman belongs.' As James had guessed, she had chosen a subject to draw him out, but she hadn't intended to reveal so much. She told herself it was because James had been in the army and knew the power a sergeant could wield.

He watched her for a moment. 'What sort of bullying does this sergeant go in for?'

'Character assassination,' she said in a matter-of-fact tone that belied the very real difficulties it was causing her. 'There's a lot of whispering about slags and tarts behind my back and sniggers whenever I appear. Half of the men seem to think I'm a dyke who needs curing, the other half think I'm the platoon bicycle. It doesn't sound like much, but it's a drip-drip of poison that's starting to have an affect.'

'You must feel very isolated,' murmured James,

wondering how much Mark had told her about his situation.

'It's certainly getting that way.'

'Doesn't the fact that your subalterns kowtow to him suggest they're having problems as well. Have you asked them about it?'

She nodded. 'They deny that they are . . . says he responds to them exactly as a senior NCO should.' She shrugged. 'Judging by his smiles afterwards, I guessed the conversation went straight back to him.'

'How long's it been going on?'

'Five months. He was posted to the unit while I was on leave in August. I never had any trouble before, then – wham! – I get stuck with Jack the Ripper. I'm on a month's secondment to Bovington at the moment, but I'm dreading what I'll find when I get back. If I have any reputation left, it'll be a miracle. The trouble is, he's good at his job, he certainly gets the best out of the men.'

They both looked up as the door opened and Mark came in with a tray. 'Perhaps Mark has some ideas,' James suggested. 'The army's always had its share of bullies, but I confess I have no idea how you deal with a situation like this.'

'What?' asked Mark, handing Nancy a glass.

She wasn't sure she wanted him to know. 'Trouble at the office,' she said lightly.

James had no such qualms. 'A new sergeant, recently posted to the unit, is undermining Nancy's authority with her men,' he said, taking his glass. 'He derides women behind her back – calls them tarts or lesbians – presumably with the intention of making life so uncomfortable for Nancy that she'll leave. He's good at his job and popular with the men, and she's worried that if she reports him it'll reflect badly on her, even though she's never had any trouble exercising authority before. What should she do?'

'Report him,' said Mark promptly. 'Demand to be told what his average length of service is with any unit. If he moves regularly then you can be certain that similar accusations have been made against him in the past. If they have – indeed, even if they *haven't* – insist on full disciplinary charges rather than a quiet passing of the buck to someone else. Men like this get away with it because commanding officers would rather transfer them quietly than draw attention to the poor discipline in their ranks. It's a big problem in the police service. I sit on a committee that's producing guidelines on how to deal with it. The first rule is: don't pretend it isn't happening.'

James nodded. 'Sounds like good advice to me,' he said gently.

Nancy smiled slightly. 'I suppose you knew Mark was on this committee?'

He nodded.

'So what's to report?' she asked with a sigh. 'A good old guy swaps jokes with his men. Have you heard the one about the tart who joined the Engineers because she was looking for a screw? Or the dyke who poked her finger in the sump to check the lubrication levels?'

James looked helplessly towards Mark.

'Sounds like a rock and a hard place,' said Mark sympathetically. 'If you show an interest in a man, you're a tart . . . if you don't, you're a lesbian.'

'Right.'

'Then report him. Whichever way you look at it, it's sexual intimidation. The law's on your side, but it's powerless unless you exercise your rights.'

Nancy exchanged an amused glance with James. 'He'll be suggesting I take out injunctions next,' she said lightly.

Fourteen

'WHERE THE HELL are you going?' hissed Fox, grabbing Wolfie by his hair and swinging him round.

'Nowhere,' said the child.

He had moved as quietly as a shadow, but Fox was quieter. There had been nothing to alert Wolfie to his father's presence behind the tree, yet Fox had heard him. From the middle of the wood came the loud and persistent buzz of a chainsaw which drowned all other sounds, so how had Fox heard Wolfie's stealthy approach? Was he a magician?

Shrouded in his hood and scarf, Fox was staring across the lawn at the open French windows where the old man and the two people Wolfie had seen earlier were looking for the source of the noise. The woman – for there was no mistaking her gender without her hat or bulky fleece – stepped through the opening and raised a pair of binoculars to her eyes. 'Over there,' her lips said plainly, as she lowered the binoculars and pointed through the skeletal trees to where the chainsaw gang was operating.

Even Wolfie with his sharp sight could barely

make out the dark-coated figures against the black of the serried trunks, and he wondered if the lady, too, was a magician. His eyes widened as the old man came out to join her and scanned the line of trees where he and Fox were hiding. He felt Fox draw back into the lee of the trunk before his hand whipped Wolfie round and clamped his face against the rough serge of his coat. 'Keep still,' Fox muttered.

Wolfie would have done, in any case. There was no mistaking the bulk of the hammer in Fox's coat pocket. Whatever fears the razor held for him, the hammer held more, and he didn't know why. He'd never seen Fox use it – just knew it was there – but it held a multitude of terrors for him. He thought it was something he'd dreamed, but he couldn't remember when or what the dream was about. Carefully, so that Fox wouldn't notice, he held his breath and eased a space between himself and the coat.

The chainsaw coughed suddenly and fell silent, and the voices from the Manor terrace carried clearly across the grass. '. . . seemed to have fed Eleanor Bartlett a load of nonsense. She quoted *terra nullius* and Lockean theory at me like a sort of mantra. Presumably she got it from the travellers because they're unlikely terms for her to know. Rather archaic as a matter of fact.'

'No-man's-land?' asked the woman's voice. 'Does it apply?'

'I wouldn't think so. It's a concept of dominion. In simple terms, the first arrivals in an uninhabited area can lay claim to it on behalf of their sponsor, usually a king. I can't imagine it could be applied to disputed land in Britain in the twenty-first century. The obvious claimants are James or Dick Weldon . . . or the village, on the grounds of common usage.'

'What's Lockean theory?'

'A similar concept of private ownership. John Locke was a seventeenth-century philosopher who systematized ideas of possession. The first individual in a place acquired rights to it which could then be sold. The early American homesteaders used the principle to fence in land which hadn't been enclosed before, and the fact that it belonged to the indigenous people who didn't subscribe to the notion of enclosure was ignored.'

Another man spoke, a gentler, older voice. 'Akin to what these chaps are up to, then. Take what you can by ignoring the established practice of the settled community that already exists. It's interesting, isn't it? Particularly as they probably think of themselves as nomadic Indians in tune with the land rather than violent cowboys intent on exploiting it.'

'Do they have a case?' asked the woman.

'I don't see how,' said the older man. 'Ailsa nominated the Copse as a site of scientific interest when Dick Weldon tried to fence it in, so any attempt to cut down the trees will bring the police in quicker than if they'd camped on my lawn. She was afraid Dick would do what his predecessors did and demolish an ancient natural habitat in order to acquire an extra acre of arable land. When I was a child this wood stretched half a mile towards the west. It's hardly believable now.'

'James is right,' said the other man. 'Almost any-one in this village – even the holidaymakers – can demonstrate a history of usage long before this lot turned up. It might take a while to shift them so the nuisance levels will be fairly high . . . but in the short term we can certainly stop them felling the trees.'

'I don't think that's what they're doing,' said the woman. 'From what I can see, they're cutting the dead wood on the ground . . . or would be if the chainsaw hadn't packed up.' She paused. 'I wonder how they knew this place might be worth a shot. If the ownership of Hyde Park was in dispute then that would be newsworthy . . . but *Shenstead*? Who's even heard of the place?'

'We have a lot of holidaymakers here,' said the older man. 'Some of them come back year after year. Perhaps one of the travellers was brought here as a child.'

There was a period of silence before the first man spoke again. 'Eleanor Bartlett said they knew every-one's names . . . even mine, apparently. It suggests some fairly meticulous research or a helpful insider passing on knowledge. She was pretty worked up for

224

some reason, so I'm not sure how much to believe, but she was convinced they've been spying on the village.'

'It would make sense,' said the woman. 'You'd have to be an idiot not to recce a place before you invaded it. Have you seen anyone hanging around, James? That wood's perfect cover, particularly the elevation to the right. With a decent pair of binoculars you can probably see most of the village.'

Aware that Fox was concentrating on what was being said, Wolfie carefully twisted his head to make sure he wasn't missing anything. Some of the words were too complicated for him to understand, but he liked the voices. Even the murderer's. They sounded like actors, just as Fox did, but he took most pleasure from the lady's voice because there was a soft lilt in it that reminded him of his mother.

'You know, Nancy, I think I've been very foolish,' said the older man then. 'I thought my enemies were closer to home . . . but I wonder if you're right . . . I wonder if it's these people who've been mutilating Ailsa's foxes – such unbelievable cruelty. It's a sickness – muzzles smashed and brushes lopped off while the poor things are still al—'

For no reason that he understood, Wolfie's world suddenly exploded in a flurry of movement. Hands clapped against his ears, deafening him, before he was whisked upside down and thrown over Fox's shoulder. Disorientated, weeping with fear, he was run through the wood and thrown to the ground in front of the fire. Fox's mouth, pressed up against his face, grated words that he could only partially hear.

'Have . . . been watching? That woman . . . when . . . she get there? . . . heard what they say? Who's Nancy?'

Wolfie had no idea why Fox was so angry, but his eyes widened when he saw him reach for the razor in his pocket.

'What the hell are you doing?' demanded Bella angrily, barging Fox away and kneeling beside the terrified child. 'He's a kid, for Christ's sake. Look at him, he's scared out of his wits.'

'I caught him sneaking down to the Manor.'

'So?'

'I don't want him queering our pitch.'

'Jesus wept!' she growled. 'And you think frightening the life out of him is the way to do it. Come here, darlin',' she said taking Wolfie in her arms and standing up. 'He's skin and bone,' she accused Fox. 'You ain't feeding him right.'

'Blame his mother for abandoning him,' said Fox indifferently, taking a twenty-pound note from his pocket. '*You* feed him. I don't have time. That should keep him going for a while.' He stuffed the money between her arm and Wolfie's body.

Bella eyed him suspiciously. 'How come you're so flush all of a sudden?'

'None of your fucking business. As for you,' he

said, jabbing a finger under Wolfie's nose, 'if I catch you round that place again, you'll wish you'd never been born.'

'I didn't mean no harm,' the child wailed. 'I was only looking for Mum and li'l Cub. They's gotta be *somewhere*, Fox. They's gotta be *somewhere* . . .'

*

Bella hushed her own three children to silence as she put plates of spaghetti bolognese in front of them. 'I want to talk to Wolfie,' she said, sitting beside him and encouraging him to tuck in. Her children, all girls, eyed the stranger solemnly before bending obediently to their food. One looked older than Wolfie, but the other two were about his age, and it made him shy to be amongst them because he was acutely aware of how dirty he was.

'What happened to your mum?' asked Bella.

'Dunno,' he muttered, staring at his plate.

She picked up his spoon and fork and put them in his hands. 'Come on, eat up. This ain't charity, Wolfie. Fox has paid, don't forget, and he'll be mad as a hatter if he don't get his money's worth. Good lad,' she said approvingly. 'You've got a lot of growing to do. How old are you?'

'Ten.'

Bella was shocked. Her eldest daughter was nine and Wolfie's height and body weight were well below hers. On the last occasion when she'd seen him,

227

back in the summer at Barton Edge, Wolfie and his brother had rarely emerged from behind their mother's skirt. Bella had assumed their timidity was due to their age, placing Wolfie at six or seven, and his brother at three. Certainly the mother had been timid, though Bella couldn't remember what her name was now, assuming she'd ever known it.

She watched the child shovel food into his mouth as if he hadn't eaten in weeks. 'Is Cub your brother?'

'Yeah.'

'How old is he?'

'Six.'

Christ! She wanted to ask him if he'd ever been weighed, but she didn't want to alarm him. 'Did either of you ever go to school, Wolfie? Or get taught by the travelling teachers?'

He lowered his spoon and fork with a shake of his head. 'Fox said there was no point. Mum taught me and Cub to read and write. We went to libraries sometimes,' he offered. 'I like computers best. Mum showed me how to work the Net. I've learned lots off that.'

'What about the doctor? Did you ever go to the doctor?'

'No,' he said. 'Ain't never been ill.' He paused. 'Haven't never been ill,' he corrected himself.

Bella wondered if he had a birth certificate, if the authorities even knew of his existence. 'What's your mother's name?'

'Vixen.'

'Does she have another one?'

He spoke through a mouthful. 'You mean like Evil? I asked her once and she said only Fox is Evil.'

'Sort of. I meant a surname. Mine's Preston. That makes me Bella Preston. My girls are Tanny, Gabby, and Molly Preston. Did your mum have a second name?'

Wolfie shook his head.

'Did Fox ever call her anything except Vixen?'

Wolfie glanced at the girls. 'Only "bitch",' he said, before stuffing his mouth again.

Bella smiled, because she didn't want the children to know how disturbed she was. Fox was showing another character from Barton Edge, and she wasn't the only member of the group who thought he was following a different agenda from the one of adverse possession proposed five months ago. Then the emphasis had been on family.

'It's better odds than the fourteen million to one chance of buying a lottery ticket, and just as legal,' Fox had told them. 'At worst, you'll stay in the same place for as long as it takes interested parties to organize a case against you . . . time for your kids to log on with a GP and get some decent schooling . . . maybe six months . . . maybe longer. At best, you'll get a house. I'd say that's worth a gamble.'

No one really believed it would happen. Certainly not Bella. The most she could hope for was local-

229

council accommodation on some depressed estate, and that was less attractive to her than staying on the road. She wanted safety and freedom for her kids, not the corrupting influence of delinquent yobs in a pressure cooker of poverty and crime. But Fox was convincing enough to persuade some of them to take the chance. 'What have you got to lose?' he'd asked.

Bella had met him once again between Barton Edge and the convoy forming last night. All other arrangements had been made by phone or radio. No one had been told where the waste ground was – except that it was somewhere in the south-west – and the only other meeting had been to make a final decision on who would be included. By that time news of the project had spread and competition for places was intense. A maximum of six buses, Fox had said, and the choice of who went would be his. Only people with kids would be considered. Bella had asked what gave him the right to play God in this way, and he answered: 'Because I'm the one who knows where we're going.'

The single logic to his selection was that there were no existing alliances amongst the group, making his leadership unassailable. Bella had argued strongly against this. Her view was that a bonded group of friends would make a more successful unit than a disparate group of strangers, but given a blunt ultimatum – take it or leave it – she had capitulated.

Surely any dream – *even a pipe dream* – was worth pursuing?

'Is Fox your dad?' she asked Wolfie.

'I guess so. Mum said he was.'

Bella wondered about that. She remembered his mother saying that Wolfie took after his father, but she could see no resemblance between this child and Fox. 'Have you always lived with him?' she asked.

'Reckon so, 'cept when he went away.'

'Where did he go?'

'Dunno.'

Prison, Bella guessed. 'How long was he away?'

'Dunno.'

She mopped up the sauce in his plate with a piece of bread and handed it to him. 'Have you always been on the road?'

He crammed the bread into his mouth. 'Not rightly sure.'

She lifted the saucepan off the cooker and put it in front of him with more bread. 'You can wipe this out as well, darlin'. You've a powerful hunger, that's for sure.' She watched him set to, wondering when he'd last had a proper meal. 'So how long since your mum left?'

She expected another one word answer, instead she received a flood. 'Dunno. I don't have a watch, see, and Fox won't never tell me what day it is. He don't reckon it matters, but I do. She and Cub was gone one morning. Weeks, I reckon. Fox gets mad if I ask. He says it's me she abandoned but I don't reckon that's right, 'coz I was the one always looked out for her. It's more likely him. She was really frightened of him. He don't – *doesn't*—' he corrected himself – 'like it when people argue with him. You shouldn't say "ain't" and "don't" too much, neither,' he added gravely, dropping into an abrupt imitation of Fox. 'It's bad grammar and he doesn't like it.'

Bella smiled. 'Does your mum talk posh, too?'

'You mean like in the movies?'

'Yes.'

'Sometimes. She don't say much, though. It's always me talks to Fox 'coz she's too scared.'

Bella thought back to the selection meeting of four weeks ago. Had the woman been there then, she asked herself? It was hard to remember. Fox was so dominant that he tended to fill the mind. Had Bella cared if his 'wife' was around? *No.* Had she cared if the children were visible? *No.* For all her questioning of his right to lead, she found his certainty exciting. He was a man who could make things happen. A tough bastard, yes – not one she'd want to cross in a hurry – but a bastard with a vision . . .

'What does he do when people argue with him?' she asked Wolfie.

'Gets out his razor.'

*

Julian closed the doors on Bouncer, then went look-ing for Gemma, whose own horsebox was parked fifty yards away. She was the daughter of one of the tenant farmers in Shenstead Valley and Julian's passion for her was as intense as any sixty-year-old's for a willing young woman. He was enough of a realist to recog-nize that this had as much to do with her youthful body and uninhibited libido as it did with a desire for conversation but to a man of his age, married to a wife who had long since lost her attraction, the com-bination of sex and beauty was a powerful stimulus. He felt fitter and younger than he had for years.

Nevertheless, Gemma's alarm when she realized that Eleanor was her caller had surprised him. His own reaction had been relief that the cat was finally out of the bag – he was even fantasizing that Eleanor might have decamped by the time he reached home, preferably leaving a bitter little note to say what a bastard he'd been. Julian had always felt comfortable with guilt, perhaps because he had no experience of betrayal. Even so, a small voice kept reminding him that the reality would be tantrums. Did he care? No. In his non-committal, detached way – a 'man's thing' his first wife had always called it – he assumed that Eleanor was no keener to prolong a sexless marriage than he was.

He found Gemma beside her car with her hackles up. 'How could you be such dork?' she demanded, glaring at him.

'What do you mean?'

'Leaving my phone number lying around.'

'I didn't.' In a clumsy attempt to deflect her anger he slipped an arm around her waist. 'You know what she's like. She's probably been poking through my things.'

Gemma smacked his hand away. 'People are watching,' she warned, shrugging out of her jacket.

'Who cares?'

She folded the jacket and put it on the back seat of her black Volvo estate. 'I do,' she said tightly, walking round him to check the tow bar connection to her horsebox. 'In case you hadn't noticed, that bloody reporter's standing twenty yards away . . . and it's not going to help to have a picture of you groping me slapped all over tomorrow's paper. Eleanor would have to be *really* stupid not to put two and two together if she saw that.'

'It'll save time on explanations,' he said flippantly.

She fixed him with a withering gaze. 'Who to?'

'Eleanor.'

'And what about my dad? Have you any idea how angry he's going to be about this? I'm just hoping that bitch of a wife of yours hasn't phoned him already to tell him what a whore I am, seeing as how stirring's about the only thing she's good at.' She stamped her foot in exasperation. 'Are you *sure* there's nothing with my name on it in the house?'

234

'I'm sure.' Julian ran a hand up the back of his neck and glanced behind him. The reporter was looking the other way, more interested in the huntsman marshalling his pack than she was in them. 'Why are you so worried about what your father thinks?'

'You *know* why,' she snapped. 'I can't race Monkey Business without him. I can't even afford to *keep* a horse on a bloody secretary's wages. *Nobody* can. Dad pays for everything . . . even the bloody car . . . so unless you're offering to take over immediately then you'd bloody well better make sure Eleanor keeps her mouth shut.' She gave an irritated sigh at his suddenly beleaguered expression. 'Oh, for Christ's sake, grow up,' she hissed. 'Can't you see this is a fucking disaster? Dad's hoping for a son-in-law who'll help on the farm . . . not someone the same age as he is.'

He'd never seen her angry before, and in a horrible sort of way she reminded him of Eleanor. Blonde and pretty and only interested in money. They were both just clones of his first wife, who'd always been fonder of their children than she'd been of him. Julian was a man with few illusions. For whatever reason, desperate thirty-plus blondes appealed to him . . . and *he* appealed to them. It wasn't something he could explain, any more than he could explain why he became uninfatuated with them just as easily.

'It was going to come out sooner or later,' he muttered. 'What were you planning to tell your father then?'

'Yes, well, that's it, isn't it. It was *me* who was going to tell him. I hoped we could do it a little more tactfully . . . lead him in gently. You *know* all this,' she said impatiently. 'Why do you think I kept telling you to be careful?'

Julian hadn't given it much thought, merely looked to when and where the next sexual encounter would happen. The technicalities were immaterial as long as Gemma kept presenting her body for his pleasure. Any discretion he'd shown was on his own behalf. He'd been around long enough to know it wasn't worth showing his hand until the gamble looked solid, and he certainly didn't fancy being at Eleanor's mercy for the rest of his life if he dangled Gemma in front of her and Gemma took off.

'So what do you want me to do?' he asked lamely. Her mention of what Peter Squires was looking for in a son-in-law had unsettled him. Yes, he wanted freedom from Eleanor, but he also wanted to keep the status quo with Gemma. Stolen moments of sex between golfing and drinking that enlivened his life but brought no responsibility. He'd done marriage and he'd done babies, and neither appealed to him. A mistress, on the other hand, was infinitely appealing . . . until her demands became excessive.

'Jesus, I hate it when men do that! I'm not your

bloody nursemaid, Julian. *You* got us into this mess . . . *you* get us out. It's not me who left my sodding phone number lying around.' She flung herself into the driver's seat and started her engine. 'I'm not giving up Monkey Business . . . so if Dad gets to hear of it—' She broke off angrily, thrusting the Volvo into gear. 'We can keep Monkey in the stables at your place as long as Eleanor's not there.' She slammed the door closed. 'Your choice,' she mouthed through the window before driving off.

He watched her turn out onto the main road before thrusting his hands into his pockets and stomping back to his own car. To Debbie Fowler, who had witnessed the contretemps out of the corner of her eye, the body language said it all. An affair between a dirty old man using Grecian 2000 and a spoilt bimbo with her biological clock running out.

She turned to one of the hunt followers who was standing beside her. 'Do you know what that man's name is?' she asked, nodding at Julian's departing back. 'He gave it to me earlier when I did an interview with him but I seem to have lost the piece of paper.'

'Julian Bartlett,' said the woman obligingly. 'He plays golf with my husband.'

'Where does he live?'

'Shenstead.'

'He must be worth a bob or two.'

'Came from London.'

'That explains it, then,' said Debbie, locating the page in her notebook where she'd written 'gypsies, Shenstead' and jotted 'Julian Bartlett' underneath. 'Thanks,' she told the woman with a smile, 'you've been really helpful. So, in a nutshell, what you're saying is that it's kinder to kill vermin with dogs than by shooting or poisoning.'

'Yes. There's no argument. Dogs kill cleanly. Poison and shot pellets don't.'

'Does that apply to all vermin?'

'How do you mean?'

'Well, for example, is it kinder to set dogs on rabbits? Or grey squirrels . . . or rats . . . or badgers? They're all vermin, aren't they?'

'Some people would say so. Terriers were bred to go down burrows and setts.'

'Do you approve?'

The woman shrugged. 'Vermin is vermin,' she said. 'You have to control it somehow.'

*

Bella left Wolfie with her daughters and went back to the chainsaw gang. The machine was working again and a dozen posts of various widths and lengths had been hacked out of fallen timber. The idea, which had seemed feasible in the planning but appeared naive to Bella now, was to drive posts into the ground to create a stockade. It looked an impossible task. Placed upright, these dozen haphazardly shaped posts would neither stand straight nor enclose more than a couple of metres, not to mention the arduous task of digging them into the frozen earth.

The Copse had been flagged as a site of scientific interest, Fox had warned that morning, and a felled tree would be an excuse for eviction. There was enough on the ground to get them started. Why had he waited until now to tell them? Bella had asked angrily. Who was going to let them build on a protected site? It wasn't protected yet, he told her. They would lodge an objection while they established themselves. He spoke as if establishing themselves would be easy.

It didn't seem so now. Much of the dead wood was rotten and crumbling, with fungus growing out of the sodden bark. Impatience was beginning to set in and Ivo, angry and frustrated, already had his eye on the living wood. 'This is a waste of time,' he growled, kicking the end of a branch that crumbled to dust under his boot. 'Look at it. There's only about three feet that's usable. We'd do much better to take out one of these trees in the middle. Who's going to know?'

'Where's Fox?' asked Bella.

'Guarding the barrier.'

She shook her head. 'I've just been there. The two lads on it are getting bored.'

Ivo made a throat-cutting gesture to the guy on the chainsaw and waited for the noise to die down. 'Where's Fox?' he demanded.

'Search me. Last time I saw him he was heading for the Manor.'

Ivo looked enquiringly at the rest of the gang but they shook their heads. 'Jesus,' he said disgustedly, 'this fucker's got a nerve. Do this, do that. So what the hell's *he* doing? The rules as I remember them is that if we pull together we got a chance, but all he's done so far is play the ponce in front of a pissed-off farmer and a sad bitch in an anorak. Am I the only one with reservations?'

There were mutters of discontent. 'The farmer recognized his voice,' said Zadie, who was married to the chainsaw operator. She tugged off her scarf and balaclava and lit a roll-up. 'That's why he's got us wearing this shit. He doesn't want to be singled out as the only one trying to hide.'

'Is that what he said?'

'No . . . just guessing. The whole thing sucks. Me and Gray came here to try and get our kids a house . . . but now I'm figuring it's a set-up. We're the diversion. While everyone's looking at us, Fox is off doing his own thing.'

'He's mighty interested in this house,' said her man, lowering the chainsaw to the ground and jerking his head towards the Manor. 'Every time he vanishes it's in that direction.'

Ivo glanced thoughtfully through the trees. 'Who is he, anyway? Does anyone know him? Seen him around?'

They all shook their heads. 'He's a type you notice,' said Zadie, 'but the first time we saw him was Barton Edge. So where was he before . . . and where's he been holed up the last few months?'

Bella stirred. 'He had Wolfie's mother and brother with him then, but there's no sign of them now. Does anyone know what happened to them? The poor little kid's frantic . . . says they left weeks ago.'

The question was greeted with silence.

'It makes you wonder, doesn't it?' said Zadie.

Ivo took an abrupt decision. 'OK, let's shift back to the buses. There's no way I'm breaking my balls on this crap till I get some answers. If he thinks—' He broke off to look at Bella as she put a warning hand on his arm.

A twig snapped.

'Thinks what?' asked Fox, sliding out from behind a tree. 'That you'll follow orders?' He smiled unpleasantly. 'Sure, you will. You don't have the guts to take me on, Ivo.' He threw a scathing glance around the group. 'None of you does.'

Ivo lowered his head like a bull preparing to charge. 'Try me, you fucker!'

Bella saw the glint of a steel blade in Fox's right hand. *Ah, Jesus!* 'Let's eat before someone does

241

something stupid,' she said, grabbing Ivo's arm and turning him towards the campsite. 'I signed on for my kids' future . . . not to watch a couple of Neanderthals drag their knuckles along the ground.'

Fifteen

THEY ATE LUNCH in the kitchen with James presiding at the head of the table. The two men prepared the food – the elegant fare that Mark had brought from London – and Nancy was put in charge of finding plates. For some reason, James insisted on using the 'good' ones, and she was sent to the dining room to find them. She guessed it was an excuse to give the men a chance to talk, or a subtle way to introduce her to photographs of Ailsa, Elizabeth and Leo. Perhaps both.

From the way the dining room had been turned into a junk room for unwanted chairs and chests of drawers, it was apparent that it was a long time since it had been used. It was cold, and dust lay everywhere. There was the smell of the decay that Mark had mentioned earlier, although Nancy thought it was disuse and damp rather than rot. There were blisters in the paintwork above the skirting boards, and the plaster underneath was soft to the touch. It had obviously been Ailsa's domain, she thought, and she wondered if James avoided it as he avoided her garden.

A dark mahogany table stretched the length of one wall, covered in papers and with piles of cardboard boxes stacked at one end. Some of the boxes had 'RSPCA' inscribed in large letters across their fronts, others 'Barnardo's' or 'Child Soc'. The writing was strong and black, and Nancy guessed that this was Ailsa's filing system for her charities. Patches of mildew on the boxes suggested Ailsa's interests had died with her. A few were unmarked, and these lay on their side, with files spilling out across the table. Household bills. Garden receipts. Car insurance. Bank statements. Savings accounts. The stuff of everyday life.

There were no paintings, only photographs, although pale rectangular patches around some of the frames suggested paintings had hung there at one time. The photographs were everywhere. On the walls, on every available surface, in a stack of albums on the sideboard that held the dinner plates. Even if she'd wanted to, Nancy couldn't have ignored them. They were largely historical. A pictorial record of past generations, of Shenstead's lobster enterprise, landscapes of the Manor and the valley, shots of horses and dogs. A studio portrait of James's mother hung over the mantelpiece, and in the alcove to the right was a wedding photograph of a younger, unmistakable James and his bride.

Nancy felt like an eavesdropper, in search of secrets, as she stared at Ailsa. It was a pretty face, full of character, as different from James's square-jawed, black-haired mother as the north pole is from the south. Blonde and delicate, with bright blue, impish eyes like a knowing Siamese cat's. Nancy was astonished. She hadn't imagined Ailsa like this at all. In her mind, she had transposed her late adoptive grandmother – a tough, wrinkled farmer's wife with gnarled hands and spiky personality – onto her natural grandmother, turning her into a daunting woman with a quick tongue and little patience.

Her eyes were drawn to two more photographs which stood in a leather double-hander on the bureau beneath the wedding picture. In the left frame: James and Ailsa with a couple of toddlers; in the right: a studio portrait of a girl and a boy in their teens. They were dressed in white against a black background, a studied pose of profiled bodies, the boy behind the girl, his hand on her shoulder, their faces turned to the camera. '*Trust me,*' *Mark had said, 'in a million years no one would mistake you for Elizabeth.*' He was right. There was nothing in Nancy that recognized this made-up Barbie doll with petulant mouth and bored eyes. She was a clone of her mother, but with none of Ailsa's sparkle.

Nancy told herself it wasn't fair to judge a person by a photograph – particularly one that was so fake – except that Leo wore the same bored expression as his sister. She had to assume the whole set-up was their choice, for why would James and Ailsa want such a bizarre record of their children? Leo interested her. From her perspective of twenty-eight years his attempts to look sultry were amusing, but she was honest enough to admit that at fifteen she would probably have found him attractive. He had his grandmother's dark hair and a paler version of his mother's blue eyes. It made for an interesting combination, although it disturbed Nancy that she saw more of herself in him than she did in his sister.

She took against both of them, though she couldn't say whether her dislike was instinctive or a result of what Mark had told her. If they reminded her of anything – possibly because of the white clothes and Elizabeth's false eyelashes – it was Malcolm McDowell's deceptively innocent face in *A Clockwork Orange*, as he slashed and cut his victims in an orgy of violent self-expression. Was that their intention, she wondered? Was it a coded image of amorality that would amuse their friends and pass their parents by?

The dinner service stood on the sideboard, covered in dust, and she lifted the stack of plates to the table to retrieve clean ones from the bottom. You could read too much into a picture, she told herself, recalling the unsophisticated snapshots of herself, mostly taken by her father, that littered the farmhouse. What did such unimaginative portrayals say about her? That Nancy Smith was a genuine person who concealed nothing? If so, it wouldn't be true.

As she returned the plates to the sideboard, she noticed a small heart-shaped mark in the dust where they'd been standing. She wondered who or what had made it. It seemed a poignant symbol of love in that cold, dead room, and she gave a superstitious shiver. You could read too much into anything, she thought, as she took a last look at her grandparents' smiling faces on their wedding day.

*

Fox ordered Wolfie back to the bus, but Bella intervened. 'Let him stay,' she said, pulling the child into her side. 'The kid's worried about his mum and brother. He wants to know where they are, and I said I'd ask you.'

Wolfie's alarm was palpable. Bella could feel the tremors through her coat. He shook his head anxiously. 'It's o-k-kay,' he stuttered. 'F-fox can tell me later.'

Fox's pale eyes stared at his son. 'Do as I tell you,' he said coldly, jerking his head towards the bus. 'Wait for me there.'

Ivo put out a hand to stop the child moving. 'No. We've all got an interest in this. You chose families for this project, Fox ... let's build a community, you said ... so where's yours? You had a lady and another kid at Barton Edge. What happened to them?'

Fox's gaze travelled round the group. He must

have seen something in their collective expressions that persuaded him to answer, because he gave an abrupt shrug. 'She took off five weeks ago. I haven't seen her since. Satisfied?'

No one said anything.

Bella felt Wolfie's hand steal into hers. She ran her tongue round the inside of her mouth to stimulate some saliva. 'Who with?' she asked. 'Why didn't she take Wolfie with her?'

'You tell me,' Fox said dismissively. 'I had some business to see to and when I got back she and the kid were gone. It wasn't my choice she left Wolfie. He was stoned out of his head when I found him . . . but he can't remember why. Her stuff was gone and there were signs someone had been in the bus with her, so I'm guessing she put the kids to sleep in order to score. Probably for H. She couldn't go long without it.'

Wolfie's fingers squirmed inside Bella's hand, and she wished she knew what he was trying to tell her. 'Where was this? Were you on a site?'

'Devon. Torquay area. We were working the fair-grounds. She got desperate when the season ended and the clients dried up.' He lowered his gaze to Wolfie. 'Cub was easier to carry than this one, so I expect she salved her conscience by taking the small-est.' He watched tears limn the child's eyes, and his mouth thinned into a cynical smile. 'You should try living with a zombie, Bella. It fucks the brain when the only thing in it is obedience to a craving. Every-thing else can go to hell – kids, food, responsibilities, life – only the drug matters. Or maybe you've never thought about it like that ... maybe your own addictions make you feel sorry for them.'

Bella squeezed Wolfie's hand. 'My guy had a habit,' she said, 'so don't lecture *me* about zombies. I've been there, done that, got the sodding T-shirt. Sure, his brain was fucked, but I went looking for him every time till he OD'd. Did you do that, Fox? Did you go looking?' She stared him down. 'It don't make no difference how she got her fix ... she'd be on the streets again within half a second flat. So do me a favour. A lady with a kid in her arms? The cops and the social would have had her in safety before she even woke up. Did you go to them? Did you ask?'

Fox shrugged. 'I might have done if I'd thought that's where she was, but she's a whore. She's holed up in a squat somewhere with a pimp who'll put up with her as long as he has access to hits and she does the business. It's happened before. She had her first kid taken off her because of it ... made her so scared of cops and social workers she won't go near them now.'

'You can't just leave her,' Bella protested. 'What about Cub?'

'What about him?'

'He's your son, ain't he?'

249

He looked amused. ''Fraid not,' he said. 'That little bastard's some other fucker's responsibility.'

*

James wanted to discuss the travellers, for which Nancy was grateful. She wasn't keen to talk about herself or her impressions of photographs. On the various occasions that she and Mark exchanged glances across the table, she could see he was baffled by James's sudden curiosity about the squatters at the Copse, and she wondered what their conversation had been while she was in the dining room. The topic of mutilated foxes had been dropped very abruptly. 'I don't want to talk about it,' James had said.

*

'Make sure the table's clean, Mark. She's obviously a very well-brought-up young lady. I don't want her telling her mother I live in a pigsty.'

'It is clean.'

'I didn't shave this morning. Does it show?'

'You look fine.'

'I should have worn a suit.'

'You look fine.'

'I feel I'm a disappointment. I think she was expecting someone more impressive.'

'Not at all.'

'I'm such a boring old man these days. Do you think she'd be interested in the family diaries?'

'Not at the moment, no.'

'Perhaps I should ask her about the Smiths? I'm not sure what the etiquette is in these circumstances.'

'I don't think there is one. Just be yourself.'

'It's very difficult. I keep thinking about those terrible phone calls.'

'You're doing great. She likes you a lot, James.'

'Are you sure? You're not just being kind?'

*

James quizzed Mark on the law of adverse possession, land registry and what constituted habitation and usage. Finally, he pushed his plate aside and asked the younger man to repeat what both Dick Weldon and Eleanor Bartlett had said about them.

'How very odd,' he mused, when Mark mentioned the scarves over the mouths. 'Why should they be doing that?'

Mark shrugged. 'In case the police turn up?' he suggested. 'Their mugshots must be in most of the nicks in England.'

'I thought Dick said the police didn't want to be involved.'

'Yes, he did but—' He paused. 'Why so interested?'

James shook his head. 'We're bound to find out who they are eventually, so why hide their faces now?'

'The lot I saw through the binoculars were wearing scarves *and* balaclavas,' said Nancy. 'Pretty heavily muffled, in fact. Doesn't that make Mark right . . . they're worried about being recognized?'

James nodded. 'Yes,' he agreed, 'but by whom?'

'Certainly not Eleanor Bartlett,' said Mark. 'She was adamant that she'd never seen them before.'

'Mm.' He was silent for a moment before smiling from one to the other. 'Perhaps I'm the one they're afraid of. As my neighbours seem fond of pointing out, they *are* on my doorstep. Shall we go and talk to them? If we cross the ha-ha and approach through the wood we can surprise them from behind. The walk will do us good, don't you think?'

This was the man Mark knew of old – *Action Man* – and he smiled at him before looking enquiringly at Nancy.

'I'm game,' she said. 'As someone once said: "know your enemy". We wouldn't want to shoot the wrong people by mistake, now, would we?'

'They may not be the enemy,' Mark protested.

Her eyes teased him. 'Even better, then. Perhaps they're our enemy's enemy.'

*

Julian was brushing the dried mud off Bouncer's legs when he heard the sound of approaching footsteps. He turned suspiciously as Eleanor appeared at the stable door. It was so out of character that he assumed she'd come to tear strips off him. 'I'm not in the mood,' he said curtly. 'We'll discuss it when I've had a drink.'

Discuss what? Eleanor asked herself frantically. She felt as if she were skating blindfolded on thin ice. As far as Julian was concerned, there was nothing to discuss. Or was there? 'If you mean those wretched people at the Copse, I've already dealt with it,' she said brightly. 'Prue tried to pass the buck back to you but I told her she was being unreasonable. Do you want a drink, sweetheart? I'll fetch you one if you like.'

He tossed the grooming brush into a bucket and reached for Bouncer's blanket. '*Sweetheart . . .?*' 'What do you mean Prue tried to pass the buck?' he asked, spreading the blanket over Bouncer's back and stooping to buckle it under his belly.

Eleanor relaxed slightly. 'Dick couldn't get hold of his solicitor so she asked me to put Gareth onto it. I said I didn't think that was fair, bearing in mind we have no claim to the land and you'd be paying Gareth's fees.' She was unable to suppress her hectoring personality indefinitely. 'I thought it was a bloody cheek, actually. Dick and James's solicitor had a row about it . . . then Prue rowed with Dick . . . so you and I were expected to pick up the pieces. I said to Prue, why should Julian cover the costs? It's not as though we've anything to gain by it.'

Julian made what he could of this. 'Has anyone phoned the police?'

'Dick did.'

'And?'

'I only know what Prue said,' Eleanor lied. 'It's to do with ownership of land, so it's a matter for a solicitor.'

He frowned at her. 'So what's Dick doing about it?'

'I don't know. He went off in a huff and Prue doesn't know where he is.'

'You said something about James's solicitor.'

She pulled a face. 'Dick spoke to him and got blown out of the water for his pains – which is probably what put him in a bad mood – but I've no idea if the man's done anything about it.'

Julian kept his thoughts to himself while he filled the water pail and replenished the hay in Bouncer's trough. He gave the elderly hunter's neck a final pat, then picked up the grooming bucket and waited pointedly by the door until Eleanor moved. 'Why would Dick phone James's solicitor? How can he help? I thought he was in London.'

'He's staying with James. He arrived on Christmas Eve.'

Julian shot the bolt on the stable door. 'I thought the poor old boy was on his own.'

'It's not just Mr Ankerton. There's someone else there as well.'

Julian frowned at her. 'Who?'

I don't know. It looked like one of the travellers.'

Julian's frown deepened. 'Why would James have travellers visiting him?'

Eleanor smiled weakly. 'It's nothing to do with us.'

'Like hell it isn't,' he snapped. 'They're parked on the bloody Copse. How did the solicitor blow Dick out of the water?'

'Refused to discuss it with him.'

'Why?'

She hesitated. 'I suppose he resents what Prue said about James and Ailsa fighting.'

'Oh, come on!' said Julian impatiently. 'He might not like her for it – he might not like Dick either – but he's not going to refuse to discuss something that affects his client. You said they had a row. What was that about?'

'I don't know.'

He marched up the path to the house with Eleanor scurrying behind him. 'I'd better call him,' he said crossly. 'The whole thing sounds totally ridiculous to me. Solicitors don't row with people.' He pulled the back door open.

She caught his arm to hold him back. 'Who are you going to phone?'

'Dick,' he said, shaking her off as abruptly as Mark had done earlier. 'I want to know what the hell's been going on. Anyway, I said I'd call as soon as I got back.'

'He's not at the farm.'

'So?' He wedged his right heel into the bootjack to yank off his riding boot. 'I'll call him on his mobile.'

She eased round him into the kitchen. 'It's not our fight, sweetheart,' she called gaily over her shoulder, taking a whisky tumbler from a cupboard and unscrewing the bottle to top up her own and pour him a generous slug. 'I told you. Dick and Prue have already come to blows over it. Where's the sense in our getting caught in the middle?'

The 'sweethearts' were grating on his nerves, and he guessed it was her answer to Gemma. Did she think terms of endearment could win him back? Or perhaps she thought 'sweetheart' was a word he used as a matter of course with mistresses? *Had he used it with her when he was two-timing his first wife . . .?* God knew. It was so long ago he couldn't remember. 'OK,' he said, padding into the kitchen in stockinged feet. 'I'll call James.'

Eleanor handed him the tumbler of whisky. 'Oh, I don't think that's a good idea either,' she said rather too hastily. 'Not if he's got visitors. Why don't you wait till tomorrow? It'll probably have sorted itself by then. Have you eaten? I could make a turkey risotto or something? That would be nice, wouldn't it?'

Julian took in her flushed face, the half-empty whisky bottle and the signs of repaired make-up round her eyes, and wondered why she was so determined to stop him using the phone. He tipped the glass to her. 'Sounds good, Ellie,' he said with an artless smile. 'Give me a call when it's ready. I'll be in the shower.'

Upstairs in his dressing room he opened his wardrobe door and looked at the neatly spaced suits and sports jackets that he'd left pushed to one side in order to remove his hunting jacket, and he asked himself why his wife had suddenly decided to search his things. She had always behaved as if looking after a husband was a form of slavery, and he had long since learnt to pull his weight, particularly in the rooms he called his own. He even preferred it. Comfortable clutter was more in tune with his nature than the showy cleanliness in the rest of the house.

He set the shower running, then pulled out his mobile and scrolled down the menu for Dick's number. When the phone was answered at the other end, he quietly closed his dressing room door.

*

James and his two companions made no secret of their approach, although by mutual consent they didn't speak after they left the terrace and crossed the lawn to the ha-ha. There was no sign of the chainsaw gang, but Nancy pointed out the machine itself, which had been abandoned on a small pile of logs. They headed up to their right, skirting the thickly sprouting ash and hazel bushes which, once used for coppicing, created a natural sight screen between the Manor and the encampment.

In light of James's questions about recognition, Nancy wondered how deliberate the positioning of the vehicles had been. Any farther inside the wood and they would have been visible through the skeletal trees as the Copse dipped into the valley. Certainly James could have kept an easy eye on them through binoculars from the drawing-room windows. She turned her head to catch sounds, but there was nothing to hear. Wherever the travellers were, they were keeping as quiet as their visitors.

James guided them up to the path that led towards the entrance. Here the trees were thinner and they could see the encampment clearly. A couple of the buses were brightly coloured. One in yellow and lime green, the other painted purple with 'Bella' sprayed in pink along its side. By comparison, the rest were curiously drab – ex-coach-hire vehicles in greys and creams, with their logos obliterated.

They were parked in a rough semicircle arcing out from the entrance, and even from a hundred yards away Nancy could see that each bus was linked by rope to its neighbours, with more 'keep out' notices strung between the gaps. There was a beat-up Ford Cortina nosed in behind the lime green bus, and children's bicycles lying on the ground. Otherwise, the site appeared to be empty except for the fire in the middle and two distant hooded figures who sat on chairs at either end of the rope barrier facing the road. A couple of Alsatians lay tethered at their feet.

Mark jerked his chin towards the two figures, then pointed his forefingers at his ears to indicate headphones, and Nancy nodded as she watched one of the guardians mark time with his foot as he strummed an air guitar. She raised the binoculars to take a closer look. They weren't adults, she thought. Their immature shoulders were too narrow for their borrowed coats, and their skinny wrists and hands protruded from the bunched sleeves like tablespoons. Easy prey for anyone prepared to cut the rope and reclaim the Copse for the village. Too easy. The dogs were old and threadbare, but presumably their barks still worked. The parents and owners had to be within calling range.

She scanned across the windows of the various vehicles, but they all had cardboard obscuring visibility from this side. It was interesting, she thought. None of the engines was running so the interiors must be lit by natural light – unless the travellers were crazy enough to use batteries alone – yet the strong sunlight from the south had been blocked out. Why? Because the Manor lay in that direction?

She whispered her guesses into James's ear. 'The kids on the barricade are vulnerable,' she finished, 'so at least one of the buses has to have adults in it. Do you want me to find out which one?'

'Will it help?' he whispered back.

She made a rocking motion with her hand. 'It depends how aggressive they're likely to be and how many reinforcements they have. Bearding them in their den looks safer than being caught in the open.'

'It'll mean crossing one of the barriers between the coaches.'

'Mm,' she agreed.

'What about the dogs?'

'They're old, and probably too far away to hear us as long as we move quietly. They'll bark if the occupants kick up a ruckus, but we'll be inside by then.'

His eyes gleamed with amusement as he glanced towards Mark. 'You'll frighten our friend,' he warned, tilting his head fractionally in the lawyer's direction. 'I can't believe his rules of engagement allow for unlawful entry to other people's property.'

She grinned. 'And yours? What do they allow?'

'Action,' he said without hesitation. 'Find me a target and I'll follow your signal.'

She made a ring with her thumb and forefinger and slipped away among the trees.

'I hope you know what you're doing,' murmured Mark in his other ear.

The old man chuckled. 'Don't be such a killjoy,' he said. 'I haven't had such fun in months. She's *so* like Ailsa.'

'An hour ago you were saying she was like your mother.'

'I can see the two of them in her. It's the best of both worlds . . . she's got all the good genes, Mark, and none of the bad.'

Mark hoped he was right.

*

There were raised voices inside 'Bella' which became increasingly audible the closer Nancy came. She guessed the door was open on the other side for the sound to travel, but too many people were talking at once to follow the thread of individual arguments. It was all good. It meant the dogs were indifferent to altercation in the vehicles.

She knelt on one knee beside the off-side front wheel, which was as near to the door as she could safely go, confident that the cardboard blinds made her as invisible to those inside as they were to her. As she listened, she unhitched the rope barrier at 'Bella's' end and let it fall to the ground with the 'keep out' notice face down, then she searched the trees to the south and west for movement. The argument seemed to be about who should be in control of the enterprise, but the reasoning was largely negative.

'Nobody else knows anything about the law . . .' 'Only his word that he does . . .' 'He's a fucking psycho . . .' 'Sh-sh, the kids are listening . . .' 'OK, OK, but I'm not taking any more of his crap . . .' 'Wolfie says he carries a razor . . .'

She raised her eyes to search for chinks at the base of the cardboard blinds, hoping to get a glimpse of the interior and a rough count of heads. From the number of different voices, she suspected the whole encampment was in there, minus the one who was under discussion. The psycho. She would have been happier knowing where he was, but the absolute stillness beyond the buses meant he was either very patient or he wasn't there.

The last window she examined was the one above her head, and her heart missed a beat as she locked eyes with someone looking down at her through a tweaked-back edge of the cardboard. The eyes were too round and the nose too small to be anything but a child's, and, instinctively, she smiled and raised a finger to her lips. There was no reaction, just a quiet withdrawal as the board was pressed back into place. After two or three minutes, during which the rumble of conversation continued undisturbed, she stole back amongst the trees and signalled to James and Mark to join her.

*

Wolfie had sneaked into the driving seat of Bella's bus, which was partitioned off by a piece of curtain. He didn't want to be noticed, frightened that someone would say he should be with his father. He had curled into a ball on the floor between the dashboard and the seat, hiding as much from Fox on the outside as from Bella and the others inside. After half an hour, when the cold of the floor set his teeth chattering, he crawled onto the seat and peered over the steering wheel to see if he could spot Fox.

He was more frightened now than he'd ever been. If Cub wasn't Fox's, then perhaps that was why his mother had taken him away and left Wolfie behind. Perhaps Wolfie didn't belong to Vixen at all, but only to Fox. The thought terrified him. It meant Fox could do what he liked, whenever he liked, and there'd be no one to stop him. At the back of his mind, he knew it didn't make any difference. His mother had never been able to keep Fox from acting crazy, just holler and cry and say she wouldn't be bad again. He had never understood what the badness was, though he was beginning to wonder if the sleeps she made him and Cub take had something to do with it. A tiny knot of anger – a first understanding of maternal betrayal – wound like a noose about his heart.

He heard Bella say that if Fox was telling the truth about working the fairgrounds, it would explain why none of them had come across him on the circuit, and he wanted to call out: but he *isn't* telling the truth. There wasn't a single time that Wolfie could remember when the bus had been parked near other people except in the summer when the rave had happened. Most of the time Fox left them in the middle of nowhere, then vanished for days on end. Sometimes Wolfie followed to see where Fox went, but he was always picked up by a black car and driven away.

When his mother had been brave enough she'd walked him and Cub along the roads till they came to a town, but most of the time she was curled on the bed. He had believed it was because she was worried about do-gooders, but now he wondered if it had more to do with how much she slept. Perhaps it hadn't been bravery at all, but just a need to find whatever it was that made her feel better.

Wolfie tried to remember the time when Fox wasn't there. Sometimes it came to him in his dreams, memories of a house and a proper bedroom. He was sure it was real and not just a piece of fantasy engendered by movies . . . but he didn't know when it had happened. It was very confusing. *Why was Fox his father and not Cub's?* He wished he knew more about parents. His entire knowledge of them was based on the American flicks he'd seen – where moms said 'love you', the kids were called 'pumpkin' and telephone codes were 555 – and all of it was as fake as Wolfie's 'John Wayne' walk.

He stared hard at Fox's bus, but he could tell from the way the handle was tilted that it had been locked from the outside. Wolfie wondered where

Fox had gone and tweaked the edge of the cardboard in the side window to search the woodland towards the murderer's house. He saw Nancy long before she saw him, watched her slip out of the wood to crouch beside the wheel below where he was sitting, saw the rope barrier fall to the ground. He thought about calling out a warning to Bella, but Nancy raised her face and put a finger to her lips. He decided that her eyes were full of soul, so he pressed the cardboard back and dropped down between the seat and the dashboard again. He would like to have warned her that Fox was probably watching her too, but his habit of self-protection was too ingrained to draw attention to himself.

Instead, he sucked on his thumb and closed his eyes, and pretended he hadn't seen her. He'd done it before – closed his eyes and pretended he couldn't see – but he didn't remember why . . . and didn't want to . . .

*

The ringing of the telephone made Vera jump. It was a rare occurrence at the Lodge. She looked furtively towards the kitchen where Bob was listening to the radio, then picked up the receiver. A smile lit her faded eyes as she heard the voice at the other end. 'Of course I understand,' she said, stroking the fox's brush in her pocket. 'It's Bob who's stupid . . . not Vera.' As she replaced the receiver, something

stirred in her mind. A fleeting recollection that someone had wanted to talk to her husband. Her mouth
sucked and strained as she tried to remember who it
was, but the effort was too great. Only her long-
term memory worked these days and even that was
full of holes . . .

Sixteen

THIS TIME KEYS were unnecessary. Fox knew the Colonel's habits of old. He was obsessive about barring his front and back doors, but rarely remembered to lock the French windows when he left the house via the terrace. It was the work of seconds to sprint across the grass, after James and his visitors had disappeared into the wood, to let himself into the drawing room. He stood for a moment, listening to the heavy silence of the house, but the heat from the log fire was too intense after the cold outside, and he flung back his hood and loosened the scarf around his mouth as he felt himself start to burn up.

A hammer throbbed in his temple and he reached out a hand to steady himself against the old man's chair as sweat poured out of him. A sickness of the mind, the bitch had called it, but maybe the kid was right. Maybe the alopecia and the shakes had a physical cause. Whatever it was, it was getting worse. He gripped the leather chair, waiting for the faintness to pass. He was afraid of no man, but fear of cancer writhed like a snake through his gut.

*

Dick Weldon was in no mood to protect his wife. Plied with wine by his son – something he rarely drank – his belligerence had come to the fore, particularly after Belinda relayed the bullet points of her telephone conversation with Prue while Jack cooked lunch.

'I'm sorry, Dick,' she told him in genuine apology, 'I shouldn't have lost my rag, but it drives me mad when she accuses me of keeping Jack away from her. *He's* the one who doesn't want to see her. All I ever do is try to keep the peace . . . not very successfully.' She sighed. 'Look, I know this isn't something you want to hear, but the honest-to-God truth is that Prue and I loathe each other. It's a personality clash in spades. I can't stand her Lady-Muck routine, and she can't stand my everyone's-equal attitude. She wanted a daughter-in-law she could be proud of . . . not a country bumpkin who can't even make babies.'

Dick saw the glint of tears along her lashes and his anger with his wife intensified. 'It's only a matter of time,' he said gruffly, taking Belinda's hand in both of his and patting it clumsily. 'I had a couple of cows once when I was still doing the dairy lark. They took an age to do the business but they got there in the end. Told the vet he wasn't shoving the gizmo up far enough . . . worked a treat when he went in up to his elbow.'

Belinda gave a half-laugh, half-sob. 'Maybe that's where we're going wrong. Maybe Jack's been using the wrong gizmo.'

He gave a grunt of amusement. 'I always said the bull would have done it better. Nature has a way of getting things right . . . it's the short cuts that cause the problems.' He pulled her into a hug. 'If it's worth anything, pet, no one's prouder of you than I am. You've made more of our lad than we ever managed. I'd trust him with my life these days . . . and that's something I never thought I'd say. Did he tell you he burnt the barn down once because he took his friends in there for a smoke? I marched him up to the nick and made them give him a caution.' He chuckled. 'It didn't do much good but it made *me* feel better. Trust me, Lindy, he's come a long way since he married you. I wouldn't swap you for the world.'

She wept her heart out for half an hour and by the time Julian called, several glasses later, Dick was in no mood to keep dirty laundry under wraps.

'Don't believe anything Ellie tells you,' he said drunkenly. 'She's even more of an idiot than Prue is. Thick as two short planks, the pair of them, and vicious with it. I don't know why I married mine . . . skinny little thing with no tits thirty years ago . . . fat as a bloody carthorse now. Never liked her. Nag . . .

nag . . . nag. That's all she knows. I'll tell you this for nothing . . . if she thinks I'm paying the damn legal bills when she's done for slander and malicious phone calls then she's got another think coming. She can pay for them herself out of the divorce settlement.' There was a small hiatus as he knocked over his glass. 'If you've any sense you'll tell that bit of scrag-end you married the same bloody thing. According to Prue, she's been smoking James out.'

'What's that supposed to mean?'

'I'm buggered if I know,' said Dick with unconscious humour, 'but I bet James didn't enjoy it.'

*

In the library, Fox's curiosity led him to press 'play' on the tape recorder. A woman's voice came to life in the amplifier. He recognized it immediately as Eleanor Bartlett's. High pitched. Strident. Tell-tale vowels, exaggerated by electronics, which suggested a different background from the one she was claiming.

'. . . *I've met your daughter . . . seen for myself what your abuse has done to her. You disgusting man. I suppose you thought you'd got away with it . . . that no one would ever know because Elizabeth kept the secret for so long . . . Who would believe her, anyway? Was that your thinking? Well, they did, didn't they . . . ? Poor Ailsa. What a shock it must have been to find out that she wasn't your only victim . . . no wonder she called you mad . . . I hope you're frightened now. Who's going to believe you didn't kill her when the truth comes out? It can all be proved through the child . . . Is that why you demanded Elizabeth be aborted? Is that why you were so angry when the doctor said it was too late? It all made sense to Ailsa when she remembered the rows . . . how she must have hated you . . .'*

Fox let the tape run while he searched the desk drawers. Eleanor's message clicked to one of Darth Vader's, followed by another. He didn't bother to rewind after he pressed 'stop'. James had stopped listening when he took to guarding the terrace with his shotgun, and it was unlikely Mark Ankerton would notice the difference between one Darth Vader monologue and another. In a detached way, Fox recognized that the most powerful impact came, not from the endless repetition of fact, but from the five-second silences before Darth Vader announced himself. It was a waiting game that played on the listener's nerves . . .

And Fox, who had seen the old man's haggard face and trembling hands too often at the window, knew the game was working.

*

Julian's approach to his wife was rather more subtle than Dick's had been to Prue, but he had an advantage because of Eleanor's decision not to confront him about his infidelity. He recognized that

271

Eleanor's tactics were to bury her head in the sand and hope the problem would go away. It surprised him – Eleanor's nature was too aggressive to take a back seat – but his conversation with Dick suggested a reason. Eleanor couldn't afford to alienate her husband if James's solicitor made good his threat to sue. Eleanor understood the value of money, even if she didn't understand anything else.

The one theory that never occurred to him was that she feared loneliness. To his logical mind, a woman who was vulnerable would have reined in her determination to have her own way. But even if he'd guessed the truth, it wouldn't have made any difference. He wasn't a man who ever acted out of sympathy. He didn't expect it for himself, so why should others expect it from him? In any case, he was buggered if he'd pay to keep a wife who tired him out of the courts.

'I've just been talking to Dick,' he told Eleanor, returning to the kitchen and picking up the whisky bottle to examine the level inside. 'You're going at this a bit strong, aren't you?'

She turned her back on him to look in the fridge. 'Only a couple. I'm starving. I waited on lunch until you came home.'

'You don't usually. Usually I get my own. What's different about today?'

She kept her back to him by taking a bowl of yesterday's sprouts off a shelf and carrying it to the cooker. 'Nothing,' she said with a forced laugh. 'Can you stand sprouts again or shall we have peas?'

'Peas,' he said maliciously, helping himself to another glass and topping it up with water from the tap. 'Have you heard what that idiot Prue Weldon's been doing?'

Eleanor didn't answer.

'Only making dirty phone calls to James Lockyer-Fox,' he went on, dropping onto a chair and staring at her unresponsive back. 'The heavy-breathing variety, apparently. Doesn't say anything . . . just puffs and pants at the other end. It's pathetic, isn't it? Something to do with the menopause, presumably.' He chuckled, knowing the menopause was Eleanor's worst fear. He treated his own midlife crisis with young blondes. 'Like Dick says, she's fat as a carthorse so *he's* not interested any more. I mean, *who* would be? He's talking about divorce . . . says he's damned if he'll support her if she ends up in court.'

He watched Eleanor's hand shake as she took a lid off a saucepan.

'Did you know she was doing it? You're pretty good pals . . . always got your heads together when I come in.' He paused to give her time to answer, and when she didn't: 'You know those rows you mentioned,' he continued casually, 'between Dick and James's chap . . . and Dick and Prue . . . well, they were nothing to do with the travellers. Dick wasn't given a chance to talk about what's going on at the Copse, instead he was read the riot act about Prue's heavy breathing. He went straight off to bawl her out and she got all hoity-toity and said it was perfectly reasonable. She's so bloody thick, she thinks the fact that James hasn't challenged any of it is because he's guilty . . . calls it "smoking him out"—' another laugh, rather more scathing this time – 'or bollocks to that effect. You have to feel sorry for Dick. I mean, it's not something a moron like Prue would ever have come up with herself . . . so who's been feeding her the crap? *That's* the bastard should be done for slander. Prue's just the halfwit who repeated it.'

This time there was a long silence.

'Maybe Prue's right. Maybe James is guilty,' Eleanor managed at last.

'Of what? Being in bed when his wife died of natural causes?'

'Prue heard him hit Ailsa.'

'Oh, for God's sake!' Julian said impatiently. 'Prue *wanted* to hear him hit Ailsa. That's all *that* was about. Why are you so gullible, Ellie? Prue's a tedious social climber who was miffed because the Lockyer-Foxes didn't accept her dinner invitations. I wouldn't accept them myself if it wasn't for Dick. The poor bastard leads a dog's life and he's always asleep by the time the damn pudding arrives.'

'You should have said.'

'I have . . . numerous times . . . you never bother to listen. *You* think she's amusing, *I* don't. So what's new? I'd rather be in the pub than listen to a tipsy middle-aged frump trot out her fantasies.' He propped his feet on another chair, something he knew she hated. 'From the way Prue talks now, you'd think the Manor was her second home, but everyone knows it's a load of garbage. Ailsa was a private person . . . why would she choose the Dorset megaphone for a friend? It's a joke.'

It was a good two hours since Eleanor had realized she didn't know her husband as well as she thought she did. Now paranoia entered her psyche. *Why the emphasis on middle age . . . ? Why the emphasis on the menopause . . . ? Why the emphasis on divorce . . . ?* 'Prue's a nice person,' she said lamely.

'No, she isn't,' he retorted. 'She's a frustrated bitch with a chip on her shoulder. At least Ailsa had something in her life other than gossip, but Prue lives on the damn stuff. I told Dick he was doing the right thing. Get out quick, I said, before the writs roll in. It's hardly his responsibility if his wife embroiders the tag end of a conversation because she's so damn boring no one wants to listen to her.'

Eleanor was provoked into turning round. 'What makes you so convinced James has nothing to hide?'

He shrugged. 'I'm sure he has. He'd be a very unusual man if he didn't.'

275

He half expected her to say 'you should know', but she dropped her gaze and said lamely: 'Well then.'

'It doesn't pass the "so what" test, Ellie. Look at all the things you've been trying to hide since we moved down here . . . where we lived . . . what my salary was—' he laughed again – 'your age. I bet you haven't told Prue you're nearly sixty . . . I bet you've been pretending you're younger than she is.' Her mouth turned down in immediate anger, and he eyed her curiously for a moment. She was holding herself under enormous restraint. A remark like that yesterday would have brought a cutting response. 'If there was any evidence that James killed Ailsa, the police would have found it,' he said. 'Anyone who thinks differently needs their head examining.'

'You said he'd got away with murder. You went on and on about it.'

'I said if he *had* murdered her, it was the perfect crime. It was a joke, for Christ's sake. You should listen once in a while, instead of forcing everyone to listen to you.'

Eleanor turned back to the hob. '*You* never listen to me. You're always out or in your study.'

He drained his whisky. Here it comes, he thought. 'I'm all yours,' he invited her. 'What do you want to talk about?'

'Nothing. There's no point. You always take the man's side.'

'I'd certainly have taken James's if I'd realized what Prue was up to,' Julian said coolly. 'So would Dick. He's never had any illusions about being married to a bitch, but he didn't know she was venting her spleen on James. Poor old chap. It was bad enough Ailsa dying without having some twisted harpy plaguing him with the equivalent of poison-pen letters. It's a form of stalking . . . the kind of thing sex-starved spinsters do . . .'

Eleanor could feel his eyes boring between her shoulder blades.

'. . . or in Prue's case,' he finished brutally, 'women whose husbands don't fancy them any more.'

*

In Shenstead Farm kitchen, Prue was as worried as her friend. They were both deeply frightened. The men they had taken for granted had surprised them. 'Dad doesn't want to talk to you,' Prue's son had said curtly over the phone. 'He says if you don't stop calling his mobile, he'll have the number changed. We've told him he can stay here tonight.'

'Just put him on,' she snapped. 'He's being ridiculous.'

'I thought that was your province,' Jack flashed back. 'We're all trying to get our heads round the toe-curling embarrassment of your phone calls to that poor old man. What the hell did you think you were doing?'

'You don't know anything about it,' she said coldly. 'Neither does Dick.'

'That's exactly right. We don't . . . and never have done. Jesus wept, Mum! How could you *do* a thing like that? We all thought you were working the poison out of your system by slagging him off at home, but to plague him with calls and not even *say* anything . . . It's not as if anyone believes your version of what happened. You're *always* rewriting history to put yourself in a better light.'

'How dare you speak to me like that?' demanded Prue as if he were still a bolshie teenager. 'You've done nothing but criticize me since you married that girl.'

Jack gave an angry laugh. 'Point proved . . . *Mother*. You only ever remember what you want to remember, and the rest goes into a hole in your brain. If you have any sense you'll replay that conversation you say you heard, and try to recall the bits you've left out . . . it's damn bloody strange that the only person who believes you is that idiot Bartlett woman.' There was the sound of a voice in the background. 'I have to go. Lindy's parents are leaving.' He paused and when he spoke again his tone was final. 'You're on your own with this one, so just remember to tell the police and any solicitors who turn up that the rest of us were in the dark. We've all worked too hard to see the business go down the drain because you can't keep your mouth shut. Dad's already protected this end by transferring it to Lindy and me. Tomorrow he's going to ring-fence your end so we don't lose Shenstead in slander damages.' The line went dead as he hung up.

Prue's immediate reaction was a physical one. The saliva drained so drastically from her mouth that she couldn't swallow and with desperation she returned the receiver to its rest and filled a glass at the tap. She began by blaming everyone except herself. *Eleanor had done far worse than she had ... Dick was such a wet he'd been frightened off ... Belinda had poisoned Jack's mind against her from the start ... if anyone should know what James was like, it was Elizabeth ... all Prue had done was take the poor girl's side ... and, by default, Ailsa's ...*

In any case she knew what she'd heard. Of course, she did.

'*... you're always rewriting history ... you remember what you want to remember ...*'

Was Dick right? Had Ailsa been talking *about* James and not *to* him? She couldn't remember now. The truth was the one she had created during her drive home from the Copse when she'd filled in the gaps to make sense of what she'd heard, and at the back of her mind was the memory of a police officer suggesting exactly that.

'No one remembers anything with absolute accuracy, Mrs Weldon,' he had told her. 'You need to be very sure indeed that what you're saying is true, because you may have to stand up in court and swear to it. Are you that sure?'

'No,' she had answered. 'I am not.'

But Eleanor had persuaded her differently.

*

Fox knew a file must exist – James was too meticulous about his correspondence – but a search of the cabinets against the wall failed to produce it. In the end, he came across it by accident. It was at the bottom of one of the dusty desk drawers, with 'Miscellaneous' written in the top right-hand corner. He wouldn't have bothered with it except that it looked less battered than the rest and suggested a more recent collating of information than the files on Lockyer-Fox history which were stacked on top of it. More out of curiosity than with any recognition that he was about to strike the mother lode, he opened the cover and found James's correspondence with Nancy Smith on top of Mark Ankerton's reports on his progress in finding her. He took the entire file because there was no reason not to. Nothing would destroy the Colonel quicker than knowing his secret was out.

*

Nancy rapped lightly on the side of the bus before she mounted the steps and appeared in the open doorway. 'Hi,' she said cheerfully, 'mind if we come in?'

Nine adults were grouped around a table on the same side as the door. They sat the length of a U-shaped banquette in purple vinyl, three with their backs to Nancy, three facing her, and three in front of the unboarded window. On the other side of the narrow aisle was an elderly stove with a Calor gas bottle beside it, and a kitchen unit with an inset sink. Two of the coach's original bench seats remained in the area between the door and the banquette – presumably for the use of passengers while the vehicle was moving – and dazzling pink and purple curtaining hung from rails around the interior to provide partitioning for privacy. In a psychedelic way it reminded Nancy of the layout of the narrowboats her parents had hired for canal holidays when she was a child.

The occupants had been eating lunch. Dirty plates littered the table and the air was redolent with the smells of garlic and cigarette smoke. Her sudden entrance and the deceptive speed with which she advanced up the aisle in three long strides took them by surprise, and she was amused to see the comical expression on the face of the fat woman at the end of the banquette. Caught in the process of lighting a joint – perhaps fearing a raid – her black eyebrows shot like inverted V's towards her cropped, peroxided hair. For no reason at all – except that beauty was the least of her attributes and she was dressed in flowing purple – Nancy decided this was Bella.

She raised a friendly hand to a group of children who were clustered around a small battery-operated television behind a half-drawn curtain, then positioned herself between Bella and the sink, effectively pinning her to her seat. 'Nancy Smith,' she introduced herself before gesturing to the two men following close on her heels. 'Mark Ankerton and James Lockyer-Fox.'

Ivo, sitting with his back to the window, made an attempt to rise, but he was hampered by the table in front of him and the people wedged against him on either side. 'We do mind,' he snapped, jerking his head urgently at Zadie who still had freedom of movement opposite Bella.

He was too late. With James urging him forward, Mark found himself guarding the end of the table, while James became the stop that closed the exit at Zadie's end. 'The door was open,' Nancy said good-humouredly, 'and in these parts, that constitutes an invitation to enter.'

'There's a "keep out" notice on the rope,' Ivo told her aggressively. 'You gonna tell me you can't read?'

Nancy glanced from Mark to James. 'Did you see a "keep out" notice?' she asked in surprise.

'No,' said James honestly, 'I didn't see a rope either. Admittedly my eyesight's not as good as it was, but I think I'd have noticed if our way was barred.'

Mark shook his head. 'It's completely free entry from the Copse,' he assured Ivo courteously. 'Perhaps you'd like to check for yourself. Your vehicles are parked at an angle to each other so you should be able to see from the window whether the rope's there or not. I can guarantee it isn't.'

Ivo twisted round to peer along the length of the bus. 'It's fallen on the fucking ground,' he said angrily. 'Which of you idiots tied that one?'

No one volunteered.

'It was Fox,' said a child's nervous voice from behind James.

Ivo and Bella spoke in unison.

'Shut your mouth,' growled Ivo.

'Hush, darlin',' said Bella, trying to rise against the apparently casual pressure of Nancy's arm, resting on the banquette back.

Mark, as ever the observer, turned to look in the direction from which the voice had come. He was becoming obsessed with Lockyer-Fox genes, he thought, as he stared into Wolfie's startling blue eyes beneath the tangled thatch of platinum blond hair. Or perhaps the word 'fox' had created associations in his mind. He nodded to the boy. 'Hey, mate, what's happening?' he said, aping the style of his numerous nephews while wondering what the child had meant. Had a fox gnawed through the rope?

Wolfie's lower lip trembled. 'I dunno,' he muttered, his courage ebbing away as fast as it had come.

He had wanted to protect Nancy because he knew she'd untied the rope, but Ivo's angry reaction had frightened him. 'No one never tells me nothing.'

'So what's "fox"? A pet?'

Bella gave a sudden hard shove against Nancy to push her out of the way and came up against an immovable force. 'Look, lady, I wanna stand up,' she grunted. 'It's my sodding bus. You got no right to come in here and throw your weight around.'

'I'm just standing beside you, Bella,' said Nancy amiably. 'It's you who's throwing her weight around. We came for a chat, that's all . . . not to exchange blows.' She jerked a thumb at the unit behind her. 'If it's of any interest, my back's rammed up against your sink, and if you don't stop shoving your unit's going to collapse . . . which seems a shame, since you've obviously installed a tank and a pump, and the system will run dry if your pipes rupture.'

Bella assessed her for a moment, then relaxed her pressure. 'A bit of a wise-arse, eh? How do you know my name?'

Nancy lifted an amused eyebrow. 'It's written on your bus in large letters.'

'You a cop?'

'No. I'm a Captain in the Royal Engineers. James Lockyer-Fox is a retired Colonel from the Cavalry and Mark Ankerton is a solicitor.'

'*Shi-i-it!*' said Zadie ironically. 'It's the heavy brigade, folks. They've given up on the candyfloss and sent in the armoured division.' She sent a mischievous glance round the table. 'What do you reckon they're after? Surrender?'

Bella quelled her with a frown before assessing Nancy a second time. 'At least let the kid get by,' she said then. 'He's scared out of his wits, poor mite. He'll be better off with the others round the telly.'

'Sure,' Nancy agreed, nodding to James. 'We can pass him along in front of us.'

The old man shifted to make room, reaching out a hand to guide Wolfie forward, but the child dodged back. 'I ain't going,' he said.

'No one's gonna hurt you, darlin',' said Bella.

Wolfie backed further away, poised for flight. 'Fox said he was a murderer,' he muttered, staring at James, 'and I ain't going down that end of the bus in case it's true. There ain't no way out.'

There was an uncomfortable silence which was only broken when James laughed. 'You're a wise lad,' he said to the child. 'In your shoes I wouldn't go down that end of the bus either. Is it Fox who taught you about traps?'

Wolfie had never seen so many creases round anyone's eyes. 'I ain't saying I believe you'se a murderer,' he told him. 'I'se just saying I'se ready.'

James nodded. 'That shows you have good sense. My wife's dog walked into a trap not so long ago. There was no way out for him either.'

'What happened to him?'

'He died . . . rather painfully as a matter of fact. His leg was broken by the trap and his muzzle was crushed with a hammer. I'm afraid the man who caught him wasn't a nice person.'

Wolfie recoiled abruptly.

'How do you know it was a man?' asked Ivo.

'Because whoever killed him left him on my terrace,' said James, turning to look at him, 'and he was too big for a woman to carry – or so I've always thought.' His eyes came to rest thoughtfully on Bella.

'Don't look at me,' she said indignantly. 'I don't hold with cruelty. What sort of dog was he, anyway?'

James didn't answer.

'A Great Dane,' said Mark, wondering why James had told him the dog had died of old age. 'Elderly . . . half blind . . . with the sweetest nature on God's earth. Everyone adored him. He was called Henry.'

Bella gave a shrug of compassion. 'That's pretty sad. We had a dog called Frisbee that got run over by some bastard in a Porsche . . . took us months to get over it. The guy thought he was Michael Schumacher.'

A murmur of sympathy ran round the table. They all knew the pain of losing a pet. 'You should get another one,' said Zadie, who owned the Alsatians. 'It's the only way to stop the heartache.'

There were nods of approval.

'So who's Fox?' asked Nancy.

Their faces blanked immediately, all sympathy gone.

She glanced at Wolfie, recognizing the eyes and nose. 'How about you, friend? Are you going to tell me who Fox is?'

The child wriggled his shoulders. He liked being called 'friend', but he could feel the undercurrents that swirled about the bus. He didn't know what was causing them but he understood that it would be a great deal better if these people weren't here when Fox came back. 'He's my dad, 'n' he's going to be right mad 'bout you being here. Reckon you ought to leave before he gets back. He don't – *doesn't* – like strangers.'

James bent his head, searching Wolfie's eyes. 'Will it worry you if we stay?'

Wolfie leaned forward in unconscious mimicry. 'Reckon so. He's got a razor, see, and it won't be just you he gets mad with . . . it'll likely be Bella, too . . . and that ain't fair 'coz she's a nice lady.'

'Mm.' James straightened. 'In that case I think we should go.' He gave a small bow to Bella. 'Thank you for allowing us to talk to you, madam. It's been a most instructive experience. May I offer some advice?'

Bella stared at him for a moment, then gave an abrupt nod. 'OK.'

'Question why you're here. I fear you've been told only half the truth.'

'What's the whole truth?'

'I'm not entirely sure,' said James slowly, 'but I suspect that Clausewitz's dictum, "war is an extension of politics by other means", may be at the root of it.' He saw her puzzled frown. 'If I'm wrong, then no matter . . . if not, my door is usually open.' He gestured to Nancy and Mark to follow him.

Bella caught at Nancy's fleece. 'What's he talking about?' she asked.

Nancy glanced down at her. 'Clausewitz justified war by arguing that it had political direction . . . in other words, it's not just brutality or blood lust. These days, it's the favourite argument that terrorists put forward to validate what they do . . . politics by other means – i.e. terror – when legitimate politics fail.'

'What's that gotta do with us?'

Nancy shrugged. 'His wife's dead and someone killed her foxes and her dog,' she said, 'so I'm guessing he doesn't think you're here by accident.'

She released herself from Bella's grasp and followed the two men. As she joined them at the bottom of the steps, a car drew up in front of the barrier on the road and set the Alsatians barking. All three glanced at it briefly, but as none of them recognized the occupant, and the guardians and their leashed dogs moved to obscure the view, they turned towards the path through the Copse and headed back towards the Manor.

Debbie Fowler, in the process of reaching for her camera, cursed herself roundly for being too late. She had recognized James immediately from her coverage of his wife's inquest. Now, *that*, alongside her shot of Julian Bartlett, would have been a picture worth having, she thought. *Discord at the heart of village life: Colonel Lockyer-Fox, subject of a recent police investigation, drops in for a friendly chat with his new neighbours while Mr Julian Bartlett, vermin-hater and player, threatens to put the hounds on them.*

She opened her door and climbed out, pulling the camera after her. 'Local press,' she told the two masked figures. 'Do you want to tell me what's going on here?'

'The dogs'll have you if you come any closer,' warned a boy's voice.

She laughed as she clicked the shutter. 'Great quote,' she said. 'If I didn't know better, I'd think this whole script had been written in advance.'

Prepared copy for *Wessex Times*,
27 December 2001

DORSET DOG FIGHTING

West Dorset Hunt's Boxing Day meet was abandoned in chaos after well-organized saboteurs fooled the hounds into following false trails. 'We've had a 10-month layoff and the dogs are out of practice,' said huntsman Geoff Pemberton, as he tried to regain control of his pack. The fox, the alleged reason for this clash of ideologies, remained elusive.

Other hunt members accused saboteurs of deliberate attempts to unseat them. 'I was within my rights to protect myself and my mount,' said Julian Bartlett (pictured) after striking Jason Porritt, 15, with his crop. Porritt, nursing a bruised arm, denied any wrongdoing despite an attempt to grab Mr Bartlett's reins. 'I was nowhere near him. He rode at me because he was angry.'

As frustration mounted, so did the noise levels, with honours even in the obscenity department. Gentlemanly behaviour on horseback and the moral high ground of campaigning for animal welfare were

forgotten. This was turf warfare on the terraces during a lacklustre Arsenal v Spurs local derby, where sport was merely the excuse for a rumble.

Not that any of the huntsmen or their supporters defined what they were doing as sport. Most suggested it was a Health & Safety exercise, a quick and humane method of exterminating vermin. 'Vermin is vermin,' said farmer's wife Mrs Granger, 'you have to control it. Dogs kill cleanly.'

Saboteur Jane Filey disagreed. 'It's defined in the dictionary as sport,' she said. 'If it was just a question of exterminating a single verminous animal, why do they get so angry when the event is sabotaged? The chase and the kill are what it's all about. It's a cruel and uneven version of a dog fight with the riders getting a privileged view.'

This wasn't the only dog fight on offer in Dorset yesterday. Travellers have moved onto woodland in Shenstead Village and are guarding the roped-off site with German shepherds. Visitors should beware. 'Keep out' notices and warnings that 'the dogs will have you' if you breach the barrier are a clear indication of intent. 'We are claiming this land by adverse possession,' said a masked spokesman, 'and like all citizens we have a right to protect our boundary.'

Julian Bartlett of Shenstead House disagreed. 'They're thieves and vandals,' he said. 'We should set the pack on them.'

Dog fighting, it seems, is alive and well in our beautiful county.

Debbie Fowler

Seventeen

TIME WAS RUNNING out for Nancy. She had an hour to report to Bovington Camp, but when she tapped her watch and reminded Mark, he looked appalled. 'You can't go now,' he protested. 'James is behaving as if he's had a blood transfusion. You'll kill him off.'

They were in the kitchen, making tea, while James stoked the fire in the drawing room. James had been remarkably chatty since they left the campsite, but his conversation had been related to the wildlife that inhabited the Copse and not to the subject of the travellers or what had happened to Henry. He was as reticent about that as he had suddenly become about Ailsa's foxes before lunch, saying it wasn't a fit topic for Christmas.

Neither Mark nor Nancy had pressed him. Nancy didn't feel she knew him well enough, and Mark was reluctant to stray into any area that might raise more questions than it answered. Nevertheless, they were both curious, particularly about the name 'Fox'.

'It's a bit of a coincidence, don't you think?'

Nancy had murmured as they entered the kitchen. 'Mutilated foxes and a man called Fox on the doorstep. What do you suppose is going on?'

'I don't know,' said Mark truthfully, his mind obsessed with the coincidence of Fox and Lockyer-Fox.

Nancy didn't believe him but nor did she feel she had a right to demand explanations. Her grandfather both intrigued and intimidated her. She told herself it was the natural order of the army: captains looked up to colonels. It was also the natural order of society: youth looked up to age. But there was something else. A repressed aggression in James – despite his age and frailty – that broadcast 'keep out' as effectively as the travellers' notices. Even Mark trod carefully, she noticed, despite a relationship with his client that spoke of mutual respect.

'It would take more than my departure to kill him off,' she said now. 'You don't become a colonel by accident, Mark. Apart from anything else, he fought in the jungles of Korea . . . spent a year in a POW camp undergoing Chinese brainwashing . . . and was decorated for heroism. He's tougher than you or I will ever be.'

Mark stared at her. 'Is that true?'

'Yup.'

'Why didn't you tell me before?'

'I didn't realize I had to. You're his solicitor. I assumed you knew.'

'I didn't.'

She shrugged. 'You do now. He's quite something, your client. A bit of a legend in his regiment.'

'Where did you find out all this?'

She started to clear the lunch plates from the table. 'I told you . . . I looked him up. He's mentioned in several books. He was a major at the time and took over as senior officer of the British group in the POW compound when the previous SCO died. He was confined to solitary for three months because he refused to order a ban on religious gatherings. The roof over his cell was corrugated iron and when he came out he was so baked and dehydrated his skin had turned to leather. The first thing he did on release was conduct a lay service . . . his sermon was entitled "Freedom of Thought". After the service was over, he accepted a drink of water.'

'Jesus!'

Nancy laughed as she filled the sink. 'Some might say so. I'd say sheer bloody guts and bolshiness, myself. You shouldn't underestimate him. He's not the type to give in to propaganda. He wouldn't be quoting Clausewitz if he were. It was Clausewitz who coined the phrase "fog of war" when he saw how the clouds of smoke from the enemy's guns during the Napoleonic Wars deceived the eye into thinking the opposing army was larger than it actually was.'

Mark was busy opening cupboard doors. It was

she who was the romantic, he thought, jealousy of the old man's heroism gnawing away at his heart. 'Yes, well, I just wish he'd be a bit more forthcoming. How am I supposed to help him if he doesn't tell me what's going on? I had no idea Henry had been killed. James said he died of old age.'

She watched his fruitless search. 'There's a caddy on the worktop,' she said, nodding towards a tin box with the logo 'tea' on it. 'The teapot's beside it.'

'Actually, I was looking for mugs. James is too good a host. The only thing he's let me do since I arrived was today's lunch . . . and then only because he wanted to talk to you.' Too bloody afraid Mark would plug in the telephone jack and intercept a Darth Vader phone call, he thought.

She pointed a finger over his head. 'Hanging on hooks above the Aga,' she told him.

He raised his eyes. 'Oh, yes. Sorry about this.' He cast around the worktops for electric sockets. 'You can't see the kettle as well, can you?'

Nancy suppressed a laugh. 'I think you'll find it's that big round thing on the Aga. You don't plug it in, though. It's the old-fashioned method of heating water. Assuming the kettle's full, you just lift the chrome lid on the left and bring the water back up to the boil by putting the kettle on the hotplate.'

He did as instructed. 'I suppose your mother has one of these?'

'Mm. She leaves the back door open so that

everyone can help themselves whenever they want.'
She rolled up her sleeves and started on the washing-
up.

'Even strangers?'

'Dad and his workers usually, but the odd passer-
by comes in from time to time. She found a tramp in
the kitchen once, swigging tea like there was no
tomorrow.'

Mark spooned tea leaves into the teapot. 'What
did she do?'

'Made up a bed and let him stay for two weeks.
When he left he took half her silver with him, but
she still refers to him as "that funny old man with
the tea addiction".' She broke off as he reached for
the kettle. 'I wouldn't do that, if I were you. Those
handles get very hot. Try using the oven glove to
your right.'

He shifted his hand to the glove and pulled it on.
'I only know about machines that work off electricity,' he said. 'Give me a microwave and a processed meal and I'm in seventh heaven. This is all a
bit serious for me.'

She giggled. 'You really are a prime candidate for
a survival course. You'd have a whole new perspective
on life if you were marooned in the middle of a
jungle during a tropical storm with a fire that won't
light.'

'What do you do?'

'Eat your worms raw . . . or go without. It

depends how hungry you are and how strong your stomach is.'

'What do they taste like?'

'Disgusting,' she said, putting a plate in the rack. 'Rat's all right . . . except you don't get much on the bone.'

He wondered if she was teasing him because his life was so normal. 'I'd rather stick with the microwave,' he said mutinously.

She flicked him an amused glance. 'It's hardly living dangerously, though, is it? How will you know what you're capable of if you never test yourself?'

'Do I need to? Why can't I just face the problem when it comes?'

'Because you wouldn't advise a client to do that,' she said. 'At least I hope you wouldn't. Your advice would be the opposite . . . find out all the information you can in order to defend yourself against whatever's thrown at you. That way, you're less likely to underestimate the opposition.'

'What about *overestimating* the opposition?' he said tetchily. 'Isn't that just as dangerous?'

'I don't see how. The warier you are, the safer you are.'

She was back on the black and white answers, he thought. 'What if it's your own side? How do you know you're not overestimating James? You're assuming he's tough because of what he went through fifty years ago, but he's an old man now.

Yesterday, his hands were shaking so much he couldn't lift a glass.'

'I'm not talking about his physical toughness, I'm talking about his *mental* toughness.' She placed the last pieces of cutlery in the rack and pulled out the plug. 'No one's character changes just because they get old.' She reached for a towel. 'If anything, it becomes more exaggerated. My mother's mother was a virago all her life . . . and when she hit eighty she became a mega-virago. She couldn't walk because of rheumatoid arthritis but her tongue kept wagging. Old age is about rage and resentment, not about going tamely into oblivion . . . it's Dylan Thomas's cry to "burn and rave at close of day". Why should James be the exception? He's a fighter . . . that's his nature.'

Mark took the towel from her and hung it on the Aga rail to dry. 'Yours, too.'

She smiled. 'Perhaps it goes with the job.' He opened his mouth to say something, and she raised a finger to stop him. 'Don't quote my genes at me again,' she told him firmly. 'My entire individuality is in danger of being swamped by your obsessive need to explain me. I am the complex product of my circumstances . . . not the predictable, linear result of an accidental coupling twenty-eight years ago.'

They both knew they were too close. She saw it in the flash of awareness that sparked in his eyes. He saw it in the way her finger hovered within inches of his mouth. She dropped her hand. 'Don't even think about it,' she said, baring her teeth in a fox-like smile. 'I've enough trouble with my bloody sergeant without adding the family lawyer to my list of difficulties. You weren't supposed to be here, Mr Ankerton. I came to speak to James.'

Mark raised his palms in a gesture of surrender, jealousy spent. 'It's your fault, Smith. You shouldn't wear such provocative clothes.'

She gave a splutter of laughter. 'I specifically dressed butch.'

'I know,' he murmured, putting the mugs on a tray, 'and my imagination's in overdrive. I keep wondering about all the softness that's underneath the armour plating.'

*

Wolfie wondered why adults were so stupid. He tried to warn Bella that Fox would know they'd had visitors – Fox knew everything – but she hushed him and swore him to silence along with the rest. 'Let's just keep it to ourselves,' she said. 'There's no point getting him worked up over nothing. We'll tell him about the reporter . . . that's fair enough . . . we all knew the press would stick their noses in sooner or later.'

Wolfie shook his head at her naivety but didn't argue.

'It's not that I want you to lie to your dad,' she

told him, crouching down and giving him a hug, 'just don't tell him, eh? He'll be mad as a hatter if he finds out we let strangers into the camp. Can't do that, see, not if we want to build houses here.'

He touched a comforting hand to her cheek. 'OK.' She was like his mother, always hoping for the best even though the best never happened. She must know she would never have a house here, but she needed to dream, he thought. Just as he needed to dream about running away. 'Don't forget to tie the rope again,' he reminded her.

Jesus Christ! She *had* forgotten. But what kind of life had this little boy led that made him mindful of every little detail? She searched his face, saw wisdom and intelligence well beyond his physical immaturity and wondered how she'd missed them before. 'Is there anything else I should remember?'

'The door,' he said solemnly.

'What door?'

'Lucky Fox's door. He said it was usually open.' He shook his head at her baffled expression. 'It means you have a hiding place,' he told her.

*

The tremors came back into James's hand when Nancy told him she had to leave, but he made no attempt to dissuade her. The army was a hard task-master, was all he said, turning to stare out of the window. He didn't accompany her to the door, so she and Mark said their farewells alone on the doorstep.

'How long are you planning to stay?' she asked him, pulling on her hat and zipping up her fleece.

'Till tomorrow afternoon.' He handed her a card. 'If you're interested, that has my email, landline and mobile on it. If you're not, I'll look forward to seeing you the next time.'

She smiled. 'You're one of the good guys, Mark. There aren't many lawyers who'd spend Christmas with their clients.' She took a piece of paper from her pocket. 'That's my mobile . . . but you don't have to be interested . . . think of it more as "just in case".'

He gave her a teasing smile. 'Just in case of what?'

'Emergencies,' she said soberly. 'I'm sure he's not sitting on that terrace every night for fun . . . and I'm sure those travellers aren't there by accident. They were talking about a psycho when I was outside their bus, and, from the way the child behaved, they were referring to his father . . . this Fox character. It can't be a coincidence, Mark. With a name like that he has to be connected in some way. It would explain the scarves.'

'Yes,' he said slowly, thinking of Wolfie's blond hair and blue eyes. He folded the piece of paper and put it in his pocket. 'Much as I appreciate your offer,' he said, 'wouldn't it make more sense to phone the police in an emergency?'

She unlocked the Discovery door. 'Whatever . . . the offer's there if you want to take it up.' She hoisted herself behind the steering wheel. 'I should be able to come back tomorrow evening,' she said diffidently, bending forward to feed the key into the ignition so that he couldn't see her face. 'Could you ask James if that's OK, and text me the answer?'

Mark was surprised both by the question and the tentative way she put it. 'I don't need to. He's besotted with you.'

'He didn't say anything about me coming back, though.'

'You didn't either,' he pointed out.

'No,' she agreed, straightening. 'I guess meeting a grandfather isn't as easy as I thought it was going to be.' She gunned the engine to life and thrust the vehicle into gear.

'What made it difficult?' he asked, putting a hand on her arm to stop her closing the door.

She flashed him a wry smile. 'Genes,' she said. 'I thought he'd be a stranger and I wouldn't care very much . . . but I discovered he isn't and I do. Pretty naive, eh?' She didn't wait for an answer, just let out the clutch and slowly accelerated, forcing Mark to drop his hand, before she pulled the door closed and headed up the drive towards the gate.

*

James was sitting hunched in his armchair by the time Mark returned to the drawing room. He looked a forlorn and diminished figure again, as if the energy that had possessed him during the afternoon had indeed been the result of a brief transfusion of blood. There was certainly no sign of the tough SCO who had opted for solitary confinement rather than barter his religion to Communist atheism.

Assuming the cause of his depression was Nancy's departure, Mark took up a position in front of the fireplace and announced cheerfully: 'She's a bit of a star, isn't she? She'd like to come back tomorrow evening if that's all right with you.'

James didn't answer.

'I said I'd let her know,' Mark persisted.

The old man shook his head. 'Tell her I'd rather she didn't, will you? Put it as kindly as you can, but make it clear that I don't want to see her again.'

Mark felt as if his legs had been chopped out from underneath him. 'Why on earth not?'

'Because your advice was right. It was a mistake to go looking for her. She's a Smith, not a Lockyer-Fox.'

Mark's anger flared abruptly. 'Half an hour ago you were treating her like royalty, now you want to ditch her like a cheap tart,' he snapped. 'Why didn't you tell her to her face instead of expecting me to do it?'

James closed his eyes. 'It was you who warned Ailsa of the danger of resurrecting the past,' he murmured. 'A little belatedly, I'm agreeing with you.'

'Yes, well, I've changed my mind,' the younger man said curtly. 'Sod's law predicted that your granddaughter should have been a clone of Elizabeth because that's exactly what you *didn't* want. Instead – and for God knows what reason – you get a clone of yourself. Life isn't supposed to be like that, James. Life's supposed to be a complete and utter bummer where every step forward takes you two back.' He clenched his fists. 'For *Christ's* bloody sake, I told her you were besotted. Are you going to make me a liar?'

To his dismay, tears welled through the old man's lids and ran down his cheeks. Mark hadn't intended another breakdown. He was tired and confused himself, and he'd been seduced by Nancy's conviction that James was the tough soldier of her imagination and not the shadow Mark had witnessed for the previous two days. Perhaps the tough soldier had been the reality of James Lockyer-Fox for the few hours she'd been there, but this broken man, whose secrets were unravelling, was the one Mark recognized. All his suspicions gathered like a knot around his heart.

'Ah, *shit*!' he said in despair. 'Why couldn't you

have been honest with me? What the hell am I going to say to her? Sorry, Captain Smith, you didn't come up to expectations. You dress like a dyke ... the Colonel's a snob ... and you speak with a Herefordshire accent.' He took a shuddering breath. 'Or maybe I should tell her the truth?' he went on harshly. 'There's a question mark over your paternity ... and your grandfather intends to disown you a second time rather than put himself forward for a DNA test.'

James pressed a thumb and forefinger to the bridge of his nose. 'Tell her anything you like,' he managed, 'just so long as she never comes back.'

'Tell her yourself,' said Mark, taking his mobile from his pocket and programming in Nancy's number before dropping the piece of paper in James's lap. 'I'm going out to get drunk.'

*

It was a foolish ambition. He hadn't appreciated the difficulty of getting drunk on Boxing Day afternoon in the wilds of Dorset and drove in aimless circles, looking for a pub that was open. In the end, recognizing the futility of what he was doing, he parked on the Ridgeway above Ringstead Bay, and in the rapidly fading light watched the turbulent waves thrash the coast.

The wind had swung to the south-west quadrant

during the afternoon and clouds rode up the channel on the warmer air. It was a darkening wilderness of louring sky, angry sea and mighty cliffs, and the elemental beauty of it brought a return of perspective. After half an hour, when the spume was just a phosphorescent glow in the rising moonlight and Mark's teeth were chattering with cold, he switched on the engine and headed back to Shenstead.

Certain truths had become clear to him once the red mist had faded. Nancy had been right to say that James had changed his mind some time between his first and second letter to her. Prior to that, the pressure to locate his granddaughter had been intense, so much so that James had been prepared to forfeit damages by writing to her. By the end of November, the pressure was working the other way. '*You will under no circumstances feature in any legal documents relating to this family.*'

So what had happened? The phone calls? The mutilation of foxes? Henry's death? Were they linked? What was the order in which they'd happened? And why had James never mentioned any of it to Mark? Why write a fable to Nancy but refuse to discuss anything with his solicitor? Did he think Nancy might believe in Leo's guilt where Mark could not?

For all James's insistence that the man Prue Weldon had heard must have been his son – '*we sound alike . . . he was angry with his mother for changing*

her will . . . Ailsa blamed him for Elizabeth's problems'
– Mark knew it couldn't have been. While Ailsa was
dying in Dorset, Leo was shafting Mark's fiancée in
London, and, much as Mark now despised the air-
head he had once adored, he never doubted she was
telling the truth. At the time Becky had had no
regrets at being cited as Leo's alibi. She thought it
meant the affair – so much more passionate than
anything she'd experienced with Mark – was leading
somewhere. But Mark had listened to too many
hysterical pleas for a second chance since Leo had
unceremoniously dumped her to believe she
wouldn't retract a lie that had been coerced.

It had made sense nine months ago. Leo –
charismatic Leo – had taken an easy revenge on
the lawyer who'd dared to usurp his friend, and,
worse, refused to break his pledge of confidentiality
to his clients. It was hardly difficult. Mark's long
hours and disinclination to party night after night
had presented Leo with a peach, ripe for the pluck-
ing, but the idea that wrecking his imminent marriage was anything but a malicious game had never
occurred to Mark. Ailsa had even planted the idea in
his head. 'Do be careful of Leo,' she'd warned when
Mark mentioned the dinners he and Becky had had
with her son. 'He's so charming when he wants to
be, and so deeply unpleasant when he doesn't get his
own way.'

Unpleasant was hardly the word for what Leo had

done, he thought now. Sadistic – twisted – perverted – all were better descriptions of the callous way he had destroyed Mark and Becky's lives. It had left Mark rudderless for months. So much trust and hope invested in another person, two years of living together, the wedding booked for the summer, and the desperate shame of explanations. Never the truth, of course – *she was being laid behind my back by a dissolute gambler old enough to be her father*, only the lies – '*it didn't work out . . . we needed space . . . we realized we weren't ready for a long-term commitment.*'

At no point had he ever had time to step back and take stock. Within twenty-four hours of arriving in Dorset to support James through the police questioning, he had had a weeping Becky on his mobile, telling him she was sorry, she hadn't meant it to come out like this, but the police had asked her to confirm where she was the night before last. Not, as she'd told Mark, shepherding a group of Japanese businessmen round Birmingham in her role as PR to a development agency, but with Leo in his Knightsbridge flat. And, no, it wasn't a one-night stand. The affair had started three months before, and she'd been trying to tell Mark for weeks. Now that the secret was out, she was moving in with Leo. She'd be gone by the time Mark came home.

She was sorry . . . she was sorry . . . she was sorry . . .

He had struggled with his devastation in private. In public he had remained impassive. The pathologist's findings – *'no evidence of foul play . . . animal blood on the terrace'* – took the heat out of the investigation, and police interest in James promptly died. Where was the point then in telling his client that the reason his accusations against Leo had been dismissed as 'wild and unfounded' was because his solicitor's fiancée had exonerated him? He couldn't have said it even if he'd thought it necessary. His scars were too raw to be opened up to public inspection.

He wondered now if Leo had gambled on that. Had he guessed that Mark's pride would prevent him telling James the truth? Mark knew the moment Becky admitted to it that the affair had had nothing to do with Ailsa's death. He could salvage some self-esteem by calling it Leo's revenge – he even believed it at times – but the truth was more pedestrian. What had he done wrong? he asked Becky. Nothing, she said tearfully. That was the trouble. It had all been so *boring*.

There was no way back from that, not for Mark. For Becky it was different. Reconciliation was a way to salvage her own pride after Leo threw her out. Most of what she said was recorded on his answerphone. *'Leo was a mistake. All he wanted was sex on tap. Mark was the only man she'd ever really loved.'*

She begged and pleaded to be allowed home. Mark never returned her calls, and on the few occasions when she caught him in, he laid the receiver beside the telephone and walked away. His feelings swung from hatred and anger through self-pity to indifference, but he'd never once considered that Leo's motive had been anything other than spite.

He should have done. If the tapes in James's library proved anything it was that someone who knew him intimately was prepared to play a long game. Three months' worth? To provide a rock-solid alibi on a single night in March? Maybe. This was all about fighting demons alone, he thought ... the absurd British class psyche that said, keep a stiff upper lip and never show your tears. But what if he and James were fighting the same demon, and that demon was clever enough to exploit it?

'*Divide and rule ... fog of war ... propaganda is a powerful weapon ...*'

If he understood anything at the end of his cold vigil on that Dorset cliffside, it was that James would not have pressed so hard to find his granddaughter if there had been the remotest chance that he had fathered her. He didn't fear a DNA test for himself, he feared it for Nancy ...

... and had done since the calls began ...

... better she hate him for rejecting her a second time than drag her into a dirty war over allegations of incest ...

310

. . . particularly if he knew who her father really
was . . .

*

Message from Mark
I've picked a side. James is a good guy. If he's told you
different he's lying.

Eighteen

WOLFIE MARVELLED at how clever Fox was as he watched him pretend to Bella that he didn't know anyone had been in the camp. But Wolfie knew he knew. He knew it in the way Fox smiled when Bella told him everything was cool: Ivo had taken the chainsaw gang back to work and she and Zadie were about to relieve the guards on the rope. 'Oh, and a reporter came,' she added lightly. 'I explained about adverse possession and she left.'

He knew it in the way Fox praised her. 'Well done.'

Bella looked relieved. 'We'll get on then,' she said, nodding to Zadie.

Fox blocked her way. 'I'll need you to make a phone call later,' he told her. 'I'll give you a shout when I'm ready.'

She was too trusting, thought Wolfie, as her natural bullishness returned with the baldly stated order. 'Sod that,' she said crossly. 'I'm not your fucking secretary. Why can't you do it yourself?'

'I need the address of someone in the area, and I don't think a man will be able to get it. A woman might, though.'

'Whose address?'

'No one you know.' He held Bella's gaze. 'A woman. Goes by the name of Captain Nancy Smith of the Royal Engineers. It'll take one call to her parents to find out where she's staying. You wouldn't have a problem with that, would you, Bella?'

She gave an indifferent shrug, but Wolfie wished she hadn't dropped her gaze. It made her look guilty. 'What d'ya want with an army tart, Fox? Ain't you got enough excitement here?'

His lips spread in a slow smile. 'Are you offering?'

A flash of something Wolfie didn't understand passed between them, before Bella took a step to the side and walked past him. 'You're too deep for me, Fox,' she said. 'I wouldn't have a clue what I was signing on for if I took you to bed.'

*

Mark found the Colonel in the library, sitting behind his desk. He seemed absorbed in what he was doing, and didn't hear the younger man come in. 'Have you called her?' Mark asked urgently, leaning his hands on the wooden surface and nodding towards the phone.

Alarmed, the old man pushed his chair away from the desk, scrabbling his feet on the parquet floor in an attempt to gain some purchase. His face was grey and drawn, and he looked frightened.

'I'm sorry,' said Mark, backing away himself and holding up his hands in surrender. 'I just wanted to know if you'd phoned Nancy.'

James ran his tongue nervously across his lips but it was several seconds before he found his voice. 'You gave me a shock. I thought you were—' He broke off abruptly.

'Who? Leo?'

James waved the questions away with a tired hand. 'I've written you an official letter—' he nodded to a page on the desk – 'asking for a final account and a return of all documents relating to my affairs. I'll settle as promptly as I can, Mark, and afterwards you can be assured that your connection with this family is at an end. I have expressed my gratitude – warmly meant – for everything you've done for Ailsa and myself, and all I ask is that you continue to respect my confidence—' there was a painful pause – 'particularly where Nancy's concerned.'

'I would never betray your confidence.'

'Thank you.' He signed the letter in a shaking hand and made an attempt to fold it into an envelope. 'I'm sorry it had to end this way. I've much appreciated your kindness over the last two years.' He abandoned the envelope and offered the letter to Mark. 'I do understand how difficult this whole wretched business has been for you. I fear we've both missed Ailsa. She had a way of seeing things in their true light that, sadly, you and I seem unable to do.'

Mark wouldn't take the letter. Instead he dropped into a leather armchair beside the desk. 'This isn't to stop you sacking me, James – I'm a bloody useless lawyer so I think you probably should – but I'd like to apologize unreservedly for everything I said. There are no excuses for what I've been thinking except that you hit me with those tapes without warning or explanation. En masse they have a powerful effect – particularly as I know that some of the facts are true. The hardest thing to deal with has been Nancy herself. She *could* be your daughter. Her looks, her mannerisms, her personality – *everything* . . . it's like talking to a female version of you.' He shook his head. 'She's even got your eyes – *brown* – Elizabeth's are blue. I know there's a rule about that – Mendel's law, I think – which says she can't have a blue-eyed father, but that's no grounds for assuming the nearest brown-eyed man was responsible. What I'm trying to say is that I've let you down. This is the second time I've listened to unpalatable facts delivered by telephone and on both occasions I've believed them.' He paused. 'I should have been more professional.'

James examined him closely for a moment before putting the letter on the desk and clasping his hands on top of it. 'Leo always accused Ailsa of thinking the worst,' he mused pensively, as if a memory had been triggered. 'She said she wouldn't need to if just once or twice the worst hadn't happened. By the end she had such an abhorrence of self-fulfilling prophecies that she refused to comment on anything . . . which is why *this*—' he made an all-encompassing gesture to include the terrace and the stack of tapes – 'has come as such a shock. She was obviously keeping something from me, but I've no idea what it was . . . possibly these terrible allegations. The only thing that comforts me in the cold hours of the night is that she wouldn't have believed them.'

'No,' agreed Mark. 'She knew you too well.'

The old man gave a faint smile. 'I presume Leo's behind it . . . and I presume it's about money – but in that case why doesn't he say what he wants? I've agonized over it, Mark, and I can't understand what this endless repetition of lies is supposed to achieve. Is it blackmail? Does he believe what he's saying?'

The younger man gave a doubtful shrug. 'If he does, then it's Elizabeth who's persuaded him.' He reflected for a moment. 'Don't you think it more likely Leo's fed the idea to her and she's busy repeating it as fact? She's very suggestible, particularly if it means she can blame someone else for her problems. A false memory of abuse would be right up her street.'

'Yes,' said James with a small sigh – *of relief*? –

'which is why Mrs Bartlett is so convinced. She mentions several times that she's met Elizabeth.'

Mark nodded.

'But if Leo knows it to be untrue, then he also knows that I merely have to produce Nancy to discredit what he and Elizabeth are saying. So why attempt to ruin my reputation like this?'

Mark propped his chin in his hands. He didn't know any better than James, but at least he'd started to think laterally. 'Isn't the whole point of the exercise that Nancy doesn't exist for Leo or Elizabeth? They don't even know what name she was given. She's just a question mark on an adoption form twenty years ago – and as long as she remains a question mark, they can accuse you of anything they like. If it's any help, I spent the last hour working backwards from effect to cause. Maybe you should do the same. Ask yourself what the result of these phone calls has been and then decide if that's the result that was intended. It might give you an idea of what he's after.'

James thought about it. 'I've been forced onto the defensive,' he admitted slowly, explaining it in military terms, 'fighting a rearguard action and waiting for someone to show himself.'

'It looks more like isolation to me,' said Mark brutally. 'He's turned you into a recluse, cut you off from anyone who might support you . . . neighbours

. . . police—' he took a breath through his nose – '*solicitor* . . . even your grandchild. Do you really think he doesn't know that you'd rather leave her as a question mark than put her through the nightmare of a DNA test?'

'He can't be sure of that.'

Mark shook his head with a smile. 'Of course he can. You're a gentleman, James, and your responses are predictable. At least recognize that your son's a better psychologist than you are. He knows damn well you'd suffer in silence rather than let an innocent girl think she's the product of incest.'

James conceded the point with a sigh. 'Then what does he want? These lies to stand? He's already made it clear he and Elizabeth will bring claims under the family-provision legislation if I try to cut them out altogether, but all he's doing by accusing me of incest is giving this alleged child of mine a reason to bring a claim as well.' He shook his head in bafflement. 'Surely a third claimant would reduce his share? I can't believe that's what he wants.'

'No,' said Mark thoughtfully, 'but Nancy wouldn't have a case anyway. She's never been financially dependent on you in the way that Leo and Elizabeth have. It's the catch-22 I told you about when you first consulted me . . . if you'd refused to support your children through their difficulties, they wouldn't have a claim. Because you've helped them, they've a right to expect reasonable provision for

318

their future . . . particularly Elizabeth who would be left effectively destitute if you abandoned her.'

'Through her own fault. She's squandered everything she's ever been given. All a legacy will do is maintain her various addictions until they kill her.'

Which had been Ailsa's point, thought Mark. But they'd been over it numerous times and he'd persuaded James that it was better to leave Elizabeth an equitable maintenance allowance than open the door to a claim for a larger share after his death. Under family-provision legislation a testator's moral responsibility to provide for his dependants had become a legal obligation in 1938. Gone were the Victorian days when the right to dispose of property freely was inviolable, and wives and children could be cut off without a penny if they displeased their husbands or fathers. The social justice favoured by twentieth century parliaments, both in divorce and the bequeathing of property, had imposed a duty of fairness, although children had no automatic rights to inherit unless they could prove dependency.

Leo's case was less clear-cut as he had no history of dependence, and Mark's view was that he would have a hard time proving an entitlement to a share of the assets after James drew a line in the sand following Leo's theft from the bank. Nevertheless, Mark had advised him to make the same maintenance provision for Leo as he had for Elizabeth, particularly as Ailsa had reduced the size of her bequest to her children from the promised half of everything she owned to a token amount of fifty thousand, with the rest passing to her husband. It was hardly tax efficient, but it allowed for the second chance that Ailsa wanted.

The difficulty was – and always had been – how to dispose of the bulk of the estate, specifically the house, its contents, and the land, all of which had a long connection with the Lockyer-Fox family. In the end, as so often happened in these cases, neither James nor Ailsa was willing to see it broken up and sold off piecemeal, with family papers and photographs destroyed by strangers uninterested in and ignorant of the generations that had gone before. Hence the search for Nancy.

The irony was that it had produced so perfect a result. She fitted the bill in every respect, although, as Mark had suggested to James after the first time he met her, her attraction, both as an heir and a long-lost granddaughter, was greatly enhanced by her indifference. Like a femme fatale, she seduced through coolness.

He linked his hands behind his head and stared at the ceiling. He had never discussed any of his clients with Becky, but he was beginning to wonder if she'd been through his briefcase. 'Did Leo know you were looking for your granddaughter?' he asked.

'Not unless you told him. Ailsa and I were the only other ones who knew.'

'Would Ailsa have mentioned it to him?'

'No.'

'To Elizabeth?'

The old man shook his head.

'OK.' He hunched forward again. 'Well, I'm pretty sure he does know, James, and it may be my fault. If not, he's taken a gamble that it was your most likely course of action. I think this is about removing the only other heir from the equation in order to force you to reinstate your previous will.'

'But Nancy's been out of the equation for months.'

'Mm. Leo doesn't know that, though . . . wouldn't even guess. *We* didn't. It's as I said earlier, we thought she'd be a clone of Elizabeth . . . and I can't believe Leo's expectations were any different. You base your judgements on what you know, and by the law of averages Elizabeth's child should have jumped at the chance to inherit a fortune.'

'So what are you suggesting? That these calls will stop if I make it clear she's not my heir?'

Mark shook his head. 'I think they might get worse.'

'Why?'

'Because Leo wants the money and he doesn't much care how he gets it. The sooner you die of exhaustion or depression the better.'

'What can he do if the main beneficiaries are charities? Ruining my reputation won't prevent them from accepting the legacies. It's written in stone now that the estate will be broken up. There's nothing he can do about it.'

'But you haven't signed the will, James,' Mark reminded him, 'and if Leo knows that, then he knows your previous will, leaving the bulk of the estate to him, still stands.'

'How can he know that?'

'Vera?' Mark suggested.

'She's completely senile. In any case, I lock the library door now every time she comes into the house.'

Mark shrugged. 'It doesn't make any difference. Even if you *had* signed, the will can be torn up and revoked at any time . . . as can enduring power of attorney.' He leaned forward urgently and tapped the answerphone. 'You've been saying these calls are a form of blackmail . . . but a better description would be coercion. You're dancing to his tune . . . isolating yourself . . . becoming depressed . . . blocking people out. His greatest success is bullying you into doing what you've just done – erecting a barrier between yourself and Nancy. He certainly won't know what he's achieved, but the effect on you is the same. More depression . . . more isolation.'

James didn't deny it. 'I was isolated once before and it didn't make me change my mind,' he said. 'It won't this time either.'

'You're talking about the POW camp in Korea?'

'Yes,' he said in surprise. 'How did you know?'

'Nancy told me. She looked you up . . . says you're a bit of a legend.'

A smile of pleasure lit the old man's face. 'How extraordinary! I thought that war was long forgotten.'

'Apparently not.'

The return of self-esteem was almost palpable. 'Well, at least you know that I'm not easily defeated . . . certainly not by bullies.'

Mark shook his head apologetically. 'That was a different kind of isolation, James. You were defending a principle . . . your men supported you . . . and you emerged a hero. This isn't the same at all. Don't you see how friendless your position is? You're refusing to go to the police because you're afraid of involving Nancy.' He jerked a thumb towards the window. 'For the same reason, you've no idea what anyone out there is thinking because you won't go out and challenge them. *Plus*—' he turned his thumb to jab it at the letter on the desk – 'you're ready to sack me because you're worried about my commitment . . . and the *reason* my commitment wavered was because you didn't tell me a damn thing.'

James sighed. 'I hoped it would stop if I didn't react.'

'That's probably what Ailsa thought – and look what happened to her.'

The old man pulled a handkerchief from his pocket and held it to his eyes.

323

'Oh, lord!' said Mark contritely. 'Listen, I really don't want to upset you again, but at least consider that Ailsa felt as isolated as you do. You talked about her being afraid of self-fulfilling prophecies . . . so don't you think she was subjected to these lies as well? That Bartlett cow goes on and on about how she must have felt when she found out. Whoever fed Mrs Bartlett the information almost certainly knew that Ailsa was shattered by it. It's easy to say she should have told you – I expect she was trying to protect you just as you're protecting Nancy – but the *effect* is the same. The more you try to keep something secret, the harder it is to bring it out into the open.' He leaned forward again and his tone became more insistent. 'You really *can't* let these accusations stand, James. You *must* challenge them.'

He crumpled the handkerchief between his fingers. 'How?' he asked tiredly. 'Nothing's changed.'

'Oh, but you couldn't be more wrong. *Everything's* changed. Nancy isn't a figment of your imagination any more . . . she's *real*, James . . . and a real person can disprove everything Leo's saying.'

'She's always been real.'

'Yes, but she didn't want to be involved. Now she does. She wouldn't have come here otherwise, and she certainly wouldn't have asked for an invitation back if she wasn't prepared to support you. Trust her, please. Explain to her what's been going on, let her listen to the tapes, then ask her if she'll agree to a DNA test. You may be able to do it on blood groups alone. Whichever . . . it doesn't matter . . . I'll lay my last cent on her saying yes, and then you'll have evidence of menace and coercion that you can take to the police. Don't you see how much stronger your position is since she turned up this morning? You have an honest-to-God champion at last. I'll talk on your behalf if you won't do it yourself.' He grinned. 'Apart from anything else, it'll allow you to take Pokeweed and Staggerbush to the cleaners. Ailsa would approve.'

He shouldn't have mentioned Ailsa. The handker-chief rushed to James's eyes again. 'All her foxes are dead, you know,' he said in quiet despair. 'He catches them in traps and crushes their muzzles before he throws them on to the terrace. I've had to shoot them to put them out of their misery. He did the same to Henry . . . left him where Ailsa died with a broken leg and a shattered mouth. The dear old thing growled at me as I approached, and when I put the barrel to his head I knew he thought I was responsible for hurting him. There's a terrible mad-ness behind it. I'm sure Ailsa was subjected to it. I think she was made to watch while some poor creature's skull was smashed, and I believe Prue Weldon heard it happen. I'm sure it's what killed the poor old girl. She couldn't bear cruelty. If the creature was still alive, she'd have sat beside it while it died.'

It would explain a lot, thought Mark. The blood-stains near her body. Ailsa's accusations of madness. The sound of a punch. 'You should have reported it,' he said inadequately.

'I tried. The first time, anyway. No one was interested in a dead fox on my terrace.'

'What about the evidence of cruelty?'

James sighed and squeezed the handkerchief into his fist again. 'Have you any idea of the damage a shotgun blast does to an animal's head? Perhaps I should have left it to die in agony while I waited for a policeman to turn up? Assuming, of course, they'd be remotely interested in a flea-ridden animal that gets hunted and poisoned every day of the year . . . which they weren't, of course. They told me to phone the RSPCA.'

'And?'

'Sympathetic but impotent where vermin's concerned. They thought it was the work of a poacher who took out his venom when he trapped a fox instead of a deer.'

'Is this why you sit on the terrace every night? Are you hoping to catch him?'

The old man gave another faint smile as if he found the question amusing.

'You should be careful, James. Reasonable force is all you're allowed in the protection of your property. If you do anything that smacks of vigilantism, you'll go to prison. The courts are very hard on people who take the law into their own hands.' He might not have spoken for all the reaction he got. 'I'm not blaming you,' he went on. 'In your position I'd feel exactly the same. I'm just asking you to consider the consequences before you do something you'll regret.'

'I consider little else,' said James harshly. 'Perhaps it's time you listened to your own advice . . . or is it true that a man who has himself for a lawyer has a fool for a client?'

Mark pulled a wry face. 'I'm sure I deserve that, but I don't understand it.'

James tore the letter into pieces and dropped them into the bin beside his desk. 'Think twice before you persuade Nancy to reveal her connection with me,' he said coldly. 'I have lost my wife to a madman . . . I have no intention of losing my granddaughter as well.'

*

Wolfie slipped through the trees in the wake of his father, drawn by a terrified curiosity to find out what was happening. He didn't know the term 'knowledge is power' but he understood the imperative. How else could he find his mother? He felt braver than he had for weeks, and he knew it had something to do with Bella's kindness and the conspiratorial finger that Nancy had put to her lips. They spoke to him of a future. Alone with Fox, he thought only of death.

The night was so black that he couldn't see anything, but he trod lightly and bit his tongue against the assault of branches and brambles. As the minutes passed, his eyes adjusted to the niggardly moonlight, and he could always hear the sound of twigs snapping as Fox's heavier tread broke through the woodland floor. Every so often he paused, having learned from his capture earlier not to walk blindly into a trap, but Fox kept moving towards the Manor. With the cunning of his namesake, Wolfie recognized that the man was returning to his territory – the same tree – his favourite vantage point – and, eyes and ears alert to obstacles, the child moved off at a tangent to establish a territory of his own.

Nothing happened for several minutes, then, to Wolfie's alarm, Fox began to speak. The child shrank down, assuming there was someone with him, but when no answer came he guessed Fox was talking into his mobile. Few of the words were distinguishable, but the inflections in Fox's voice reminded Wolfie of Lucky Fox . . . and that seemed strange when the old man was visible to him in one of the downstairs windows of the house.

*

'. . . *I have the letters and I have her name . . . Nancy Smith . . . Captain, Royal Engineers. You must be proud to have another soldier in the family. She even looks like you when you were younger. Tall and dark . . . the perfect clone . . . It's a pity she won't do what she's told. Nothing can be gained by involving you, you*

*said . . . but here she is. So what price DNA now? Does
she know who her father is . . .? Are you going to tell
her before someone else does . . .?'*

*

Mark replayed the recording several times. 'If this is
Leo then he really believes you're Nancy's father.'

'He knows I'm not,' said James, dropping files
to the floor as he looked for the one marked
'Miscellaneous'.

'Then it isn't Leo,' said Mark grimly. 'We've been
looking in the wrong direction.'

With resignation, James abandoned his search and
folded his hands in front of his face. 'Of course it's
Leo,' he said with surprising firmness. 'You really
must understand that, Mark. You're a godsend to him
because your reactions are so predictable. You panic
every time he shifts his position, instead of holding
your nerve and forcing him to declare himself.'

Mark stared at the window and the darkness outside, and his face in reflection had the same hunted
look that James had worn for two days. Whoever this
man was he had been in the house and knew what
Nancy looked like, was probably watching them
now. 'Perhaps it's you who're the godsend, James,'
he murmured. 'At least consider that your reaction
to your son is also entirely predictable.'

'Meaning what?'

'Leo is the first person you accuse in any situation.'

Nineteen

PRUE'S FACE, TOO, looked hunted when she answered the hammering on her front door. A peek through her curtains had shown her the gleam of a pale car in the drive, and she assumed immediately that the police had come for her. She would have pretended she wasn't at home if a voice hadn't shouted: 'Come on, Mrs Weldon. We know you're in there.'

She attached the chain and opened the door a couple of inches, peering at the two shadowy figures standing on the doorstep. 'Who are you? What do you want?' she asked in a terrified voice.

'It's James Lockyer-Fox and Mark Ankerton,' said Mark, jamming his shoe into the gap. 'Switch on your porch light and you'll be able to see us.'

She pressed her finger to the button, and a little courage returned with recognition. 'If this is about serving a writ, I'm not going to accept it. I'm not accepting *anything* from you,' she said rather wildly.

Mark gave an angry snort. 'You certainly will.

You'll accept the truth. Now let us in, please. We want to talk to you.'

'No.' She put her shoulder to the door and tried to close it.

'I'm not taking my foot away until you agree, Mrs Weldon. Where's your husband? This will go a lot faster if we can talk to him as well.' He raised his voice. 'Mr Weldon! Will you come to the door, please! James Lockyer-Fox would like to speak with you!'

'He's not here,' hissed Prue, leaning her considerable weight against the insubstantial leather of Mark's loafer. 'I'm on my own and you're frightening me. I'm going to give you one chance to take your foot away, and if you don't I'll slam the door so hard it'll really hurt you.'

She relaxed the pressure briefly and watched the shoe vanish. 'Now, *go away*!' she shouted, shoving against the panels and turning the mortise lock. 'I'll call the police if you don't.'

'Good idea,' said Mark's voice from the other side. 'We'll be calling them ourselves if you refuse to speak to us. What do you think your husband will feel about that? He was pretty unhappy when I spoke to him this morning. As far as I could make out, he didn't know about your malicious calls . . . the whole idea shocked him rigid.'

She was breathing heavily from fear and exertion. 'The police will be on my side,' she panted, bending forward to bring her heaving chest under control. 'You're not allowed to terrorize people like this.'

'Yes, well, it's a pity you didn't remember that when you started your campaign against James. Or perhaps you think the law doesn't apply to you?' His voice took on a conversational tone. 'Tell me . . . would you have been so vindictive if Ailsa hadn't run away every time she saw you? Isn't that what this is about? You wanted to boast about your chum at the Manor . . . and Ailsa made it plain she couldn't stand your poisonous tongue.' He gave a small laugh. 'No, I'm putting the cart before the horse. You were *always* poisonous . . . you can't help yourself . . . you'd have made these calls eventually whether Ailsa lived or died – if only to get your own back for being called Staggerbush behind your back—'

He broke off when he heard Prue's squeal of shock, immediately followed by the rattle of the chain and the mortise turning. 'I think I've given her a heart attack,' said James, opening the door. 'Look at the silly creature. She'll break that chair if she's not careful.'

Mark stepped inside and looked critically at Prue who was gasping for air on a delicate wicker seat. 'What did you do?' He kicked the door closed with his heel and handed his briefcase to James.

'Touched her on the shoulder. I've never see anyone jump so high.'

Mark stooped to put a hand under her elbow.

'Come on, Mrs Weldon,' he said, heaving her to her feet and supporting her with his other arm round her back. 'Let's get you onto something more solid. Where's your sitting room?'

'This looks like it,' said James, entering a room on the left. 'Do you want to put her on the sofa, and I'll see if I can find some brandy?'

'Water might be better.' He lowered her onto the padded seat while James returned to the kitchen in search of a glass. 'You shouldn't leave your back door unlocked,' he told her unsympathetically, hiding his relief as colour came into her cheeks. 'In these parts it's an invitation to enter.'

She tried to say something but her mouth was too dry. Instead she took a swipe at him. She was a long way from dying, he thought, as he stepped out of reach. 'You're allowed to use reasonable force only, Mrs Weldon. You've already broken my foot because you're so damn fat. If you hurt me anywhere else I might just decide to prosecute.'

She glared at him before taking the glass James handed her and drinking the water greedily. 'Dick'll be so angry about this,' she said, as soon as her tongue was loosened. 'He'll . . . he'll . . .' Her vocabulary deserted her.

'What?'

'Sue you!'

'Is that right?' said Mark. 'Let's find out. Does he have a mobile? Can we call him?'

'I'm not telling you.'

'His son's number will be in the book,' said James, lowering himself into an armchair. 'I believe his name's Jack. As far as I recall, the other arm of the business is based in Compton Newton, and the house is on site. He'll know Dick's mobile.'

Prue snatched up the phone beside the sofa and smothered it with her arms. 'You're not ringing from here.'

'Well, I am . . . but at my expense,' said Mark, taking his mobile from his pocket and dialling Directory Enquiries. 'Yes, please. Compton Newton . . . surname Weldon . . . initial J . . . thank you.' He cut the line and redialled.

Prue took another slash at him, trying to knock the phone from his hand.

Grinning, Mark moved farther away. 'Yes . . . hello. Is that Mrs Weldon? I'm sorry . . . Belinda. Totally understood . . . Mrs Weldon is your mother-in-law—' he lifted an eyebrow at Prue – 'and you don't want to be confused with her. I wouldn't either. Yes, my name's Mark Ankerton. I'm a solicitor, representing Colonel Lockyer-Fox. I need to contact your father-in-law as a matter of urgency. Would you know where he is . . . or if he has a mobile number?' He watched Prue with amusement. 'He's with you. Excellent. May I speak to him? Yes, tell him it relates to what we discussed this morning. The Colonel and I are in his house . . . we came to speak to Mrs Weldon . . . but she assures us that her husband will take action if we don't leave. I'd appreciate confirmation of that as it will affect our decision on whether to involve the police.'

He tapped his foot on the carpet while he waited. A second or two later he held the phone away from his ear as Dick's voice roared down the line. He made one or two attempts to halt the angry tirade, but it was only when Dick ran out of steam that he was able to jump in. 'Thank you, Mr Weldon. I think I got the gist all right . . . no, I'd rather you told your wife yourself. Do you want to speak to her now? Right . . . goodbye.' He touched 'end' and dropped the mobile into his pocket. 'Dear, dear, dear! You seem to have upset everyone, Mrs Weldon. There's not much support there, I'm afraid.'

'It's none of your business.'

'Apparently Mrs Bartlett's husband is equally angry . . . neither of them knew what the pair of you were up to. If they had, they'd have stopped it.'

Prue didn't say anything.

'James guessed as much, which is why he hasn't taken any action to date . . . he didn't want to embarrass Dick or Julian. He hoped if he didn't react you'd lose interest or your husbands would start questioning what you were doing. It's gone too far for that now, though. The threats in these calls are too dangerous to be ignored any longer.'

'I've never made any threats,' she protested. 'I've

never said anything. It's Eleanor you should be talking to. She's the one who started it.'

'So it was Mrs Bartlett's idea?'

Prue stared at her hands. After all, what loyalty did she owe her friend? She'd called Shenstead House twice in the last hour and each time Julian had told her that Ellie was 'unavailable'. The word alone implied that the woman was there and refusing to speak to her, but the amused tone of Julian's voice confirmed it. Prue had excused her on the grounds that she didn't want to speak in front of Julian, but she suspected now that Ellie was busy blaming her in order to keep in his good books.

Prue's resentment against everyone grew. She was the least at fault yet she was the most accused. 'It certainly wasn't my idea,' she muttered. 'I'm not the type to make abusive calls . . . which is why I never said anything.'

'Why make them at all then?'

'Eleanor called it natural justice,' she said, refusing to look at either man. 'No one seemed interested in how Ailsa died except us.'

'I see,' said Mark sarcastically. 'So despite a police investigation, a post-mortem and a coroner's inquest, you decided no one was interested. That's a very bizarre conclusion, Mrs Weldon. How did you reach it, exactly?'

'I heard James and Ailsa arguing. You can't just put a thing like that out of your mind.'

Mark watched her for a moment. 'That's it?' he asked in disbelief. 'You appointed yourself judge, jury and executioner on the basis of a single argument between two people you couldn't see or even hear properly? There was no other evidence?'

She wriggled her shoulders uncomfortably. How could she possibly repeat in front of James what Eleanor knew? 'I know what I heard,' she said, falling back on the only argument she'd ever really had. Stubborn certainty.

'I doubt that very much.' Mark propped his briefcase on his knee and brought out the tape recorder. 'I want you to listen to these messages, Mrs Weldon.' He located a socket beside the armchair in which James was sitting and plugged in the machine, handing it to James to operate. 'At the end I'd like you to tell me what you think you've heard.'

*

There was nothing in the allegations of child abuse to shock Prue – she knew them all – but the relentless repetition did shock her. She felt dirty just listening to the continuously stated details of child rape, as if she were a willing party to their telling. She argued to herself that the calls hadn't come en bloc like this, but the cumulative effect was disturbing. She wanted to say, stop, I've heard enough, but she knew what the reaction would be. James hadn't been given that choice.

Every so often Eleanor's high-pitched rants and Darth Vader's distorted monologues were punctuated by periods of silence in which the sound of stealthy breathing – *her* breathing – was audible on the tape. She could hear the pauses as she turned away from the mouthpiece, afraid that Dick had woken up and come downstairs to discover what she was doing. She could hear her trembling excitement as fear of exposure and a sense of power collided in her chest to produce sibilant little hisses on inhalation.

She tried to persuade herself that Eleanor's strident hectoring was worse but she didn't succeed. Speech – whatever it said – had the merit of honesty; breathing – *heavy* breathing – the coward's furtive choice – sounded lewd. Prue *should* have spoken. Why hadn't she?

Because she hadn't believed what Eleanor had told her . . .

She remembered whispers of gossip from Vera Dawson about how Ailsa had had to return early from a two-year posting in Africa when Elizabeth contracted glandular fever at school. Of course no one was fooled. The girl was known to be wild, and she truanted too often – particularly at night – for a swollen belly to be anything but an unwanted pregnancy. Rumour had it that James didn't learn about the baby until he returned at the end of the posting, several months after it had been adopted, and his fury had been so intense that Ailsa had allowed Elizabeth to sweep another mistake under the carpet.

Eleanor said it proved nothing except that James was capable of anger. A foreign posting allowed for holidays just like any other job, and if Elizabeth said he was in England at the time the baby was conceived then that was good enough for her. Elizabeth was the most damaged woman she'd ever met, she told Prue forcefully, and that sort of personality disorder didn't happen by accident. Whoever forced the adoption had pushed an already vulnerable girl into a spiral of depression and, if anyone doubted it, they should speak to Elizabeth. As Eleanor had done.

The dreadful procession of messages clicked through with one of Prue's to every two of Eleanor's and five of Darth Vader's, and it dawned on Prue that she'd been conned. Everyone was doing it, Eleanor had told her. People were livid that James had got away with murder. The 'girls' were making at least one call a day, preferably at night to wake him. It was the only way Ailsa would ever receive justice.

Prue raised her head as James pressed the 'stop' button and silence fell in the room. It was a long time since she'd looked the Colonel in the face, and a flush of shame spread up her neck. He had aged so much, she thought. She remembered him as an upright, handsome man with weather-beaten cheeks and clear eyes. Now he was stooped and gaunt, and his clothes were too big for him.

'Well?' asked Mark.

She chewed at her lip. 'There were only three people. Eleanor, myself and the man. Are there any other tapes?'

'Several,' he said, nodding to his open briefcase on the floor, 'but they're all just you, Mrs Bartlett and our friend who's too frightened to use his real voice. You started to flag recently, but you were calling in regular as clockwork every night for the first four weeks. Do you want me to prove it? Choose any tape you like and we'll play it for you.'

She shook her head but didn't say anything.

'You don't seem very interested in the content of the messages,' said Mark after a moment. 'Does a catalogue of child rape and incest not disturb you? I've listened to these tapes for hours and I'm appalled by them. I'm appalled that a child's pain should be so callously exploited in this way. I'm appalled that I've had to listen to the details. Was that the intention? To humiliate the listener?'

She ran a nervous tongue around her mouth. 'I . . . er . . . Eleanor wanted James to know we knew.'

'Knew what? And please don't refer to Colonel Lockyer-Fox by his Christian name again, Mrs Weldon. If you ever had the right to use it, you forfeited that the first time you picked up the telephone in menace.'

Her face burned with embarrassment. She waved a despairing hand towards the recorder. 'Knew about . . . *that*. We didn't think he should be allowed to get away with it.'

'Then why didn't you report him to the police? There are cases of child abuse in the courts at the moment that go back thirty years. The Colonel would face a lengthy prison sentence if these allegations were true. It would also support your contention that he beat Ailsa if you can demonstrate a history of brutality against his daughter.' He paused. 'Perhaps I'm being stupid, but I don't understand the logic behind these calls. They were done in such secrecy – even your husband didn't know you were doing it – so what exactly were they supposed to achieve? Is it blackmail? Were you expecting money in return for silence?'

Prue panicked. 'It's not my fault,' she blurted out. 'Ask Eleanor. I told her it wasn't true . . . but she kept talking about a campaign for justice. She said all the girls from the golf club were phoning in . . . I thought there'd be dozens of calls . . . I wouldn't have done it otherwise.'

'Why only women?' asked Mark. 'Why weren't men involved?'

'Because they sided with Ja—, the Colonel.' She

glanced guiltily towards the old man. 'I never felt comfortable,' she pleaded. 'You can tell that by the way I never say anything . . .' She petered into silence.

James stirred in his chair. 'There were one or two calls at the beginning before I installed the answerphone,' he told her. 'They were much like yours – long silences – but I didn't recognize the numbers. I presume they were friends of yours who felt a single call discharged their duty. You should have asked them. People rarely do as they're told unless they take pleasure from it.'

Shame turned to humiliation. It had been a delicious secret between the clique that she and Eleanor had formed around themselves. Nods and winks. Stories about near misses when Dick got up for a pee in the middle of the night and almost caught her crouched over the telephone in the dark. What a fool she must have seemed, trotting out her poodle-like obedience to Eleanor, while the rest of their friends were secretly keeping their hands clean. After all, who would ever know? If Eleanor's plan to 'smoke James out' had worked, then they would take credit. If it didn't, Eleanor and Prue would have no idea how two-faced they'd been.

Memories of what Jack had said beat against her brain. '. . . *the toe-curling embarrassment of your phone calls to that poor old man . . . the only person who believes you is that idiot Bartlett woman . . .*' Was that how her friends perceived it, too? Were they as disgusted and disbelieving of her as her family was? She knew the answer, of course, and the last remnants of her self-esteem ran in tears down her fat cheeks. 'It wasn't pleasure,' she managed. 'I never really wanted to do it . . . I was always frightened.'

James lifted a concerned hand as if to absolve her, but Mark overrode him. 'You loved every minute of it,' he accused her harshly, 'and if I have my way, the Colonel will take you to court – either with the help of the police or without. You've slandered his good name . . . slandered his wife's memory . . . weakened his health with malicious calls . . . aided and abetted the killing of his animals and the burglary of his house . . . placed his life and the life of his granddaughter in danger.' He took an angry breath. 'Who put you up to it, Mrs Weldon?'

She hugged herself frantically, his doom-laden words whirling in her mind. *Blackmail . . . slander . . . malice . . . killing . . . burglary . . .* 'I don't know anything about burglary,' she whimpered.

'But you knew that Henry had been killed?'

'Not killed,' she protested, 'only dead. Eleanor told me.'

'How did she say he died?'

She looked scared. 'I can't remember. No . . . *truly* . . . I can't remember. I know she was pleased about it. She said the chickens were coming home to roost.' She pressed her hands to her mouth. 'Oh, that sounds so callous. I'm sorry. He was such a sweet dog. Was he really killed?'

'His leg and muzzle were smashed before he was dumped on the Colonel's terrace to die, and we think the same man mutilated a *fox* in front of Ailsa the night she died. We believe you heard him do it. What you described as a punch was the sound of a fox's head being crushed, which is why Ailsa accused him of insanity. That's the man you've been helping, Mrs Weldon. So who is he?'

Her eyes widened. 'I don't know,' she whispered, playing the sound of the 'punch' through her mind and remembering, with sudden clarity, the order in which events had happened. 'Oh, God, I was wrong. He said "bitch" *afterwards*.'

Mark exchanged an enquiring glance with James.

The old man gave a rare smile. 'She was wearing wellingtons,' he said. 'I expect she kicked him. She couldn't abide cruelty of any sort.'

Mark smiled in return before shifting his attention back to Prue. 'I need a name, Mrs Weldon. Who told you to do this?'

'No one . . . just Eleanor.'

'Your friend's been reading from a script. There's no way she could know so many details about the family. Who gave them to her?'

Prue flapped her hands against her mouth in a desperate attempt to find the answers he wanted.

'Elizabeth,' she wailed. 'She went up to London to meet her.'

*

Mark turned left out of the farm drive and headed up towards the Dorchester to Wareham Road. 'Where are you going?' asked James.

'Bovington. You have to tell Nancy the truth, James.' He rubbed his hand up the back of his head where his headache of the morning had come back in force. 'Do you agree?'

'I suppose so,' the Colonel said with a sigh, 'but she's in no immediate danger, Mark. The only addresses on file are her parents in Hereford and her regimental HQ. There's no reference to Bovington.'

'Shit!' Mark swore violently as he slammed on the brakes, slewed the steering wheel to the left and bumped to a halt on the grass verge. He tugged his mobile from his pocket and punched in 192. 'Smith . . . initial J . . . Lower Croft, Coomb Farm, Herefordshire.' He switched on the overhead light. 'Just pray God they've been out all day,' he said as he dialled. 'Is that Mrs Smith? Hi, it's Mark Ankerton. Do you remember? Colonel Lockyer-Fox's solicitor . . .? Indeed, yes . . . I saw her too . . . I'm spending Christmas with him. A real thrill. The best present he could have had . . . no, no, I have her mobile number. I'm phoning on her behalf as a matter of fact . . . there's a man who's been pestering her . . . yes, one of her sergeants . . . the point is, if he calls she'd rather you didn't tell him she was at Bovington . . . I see . . . a woman . . . no, that's fine . . . you, too, Mrs Smith.'

Twenty

BELLA WONDERED HOW long the child had been standing beside her. It was freezing cold and she was huddled in her coat and scarf, listening to *Madame Butterfly* on her walkman. Zadie had taken the dogs back to her coach to feed them, and half the world could have crossed the rope barrier without Bella noticing. 'Un bel di vedremo' swelled in her head as Butterfly sang of Pinkerton's ship appearing on the horizon and her beloved husband climbing the hill to their house to claim her. It was a fantasy. A hopeless, wrong-headed vision. The truth, as Butterfly would learn, was abandonment. The truth for women was *always* abandonment, thought Bella sadly.

She had looked up with a sigh to find Wolfie shivering in his thin jumper and jeans at her elbow. 'Oh, for fuck's sake,' she said roundly, tugging out the earphones, 'you'll freeze to death, you silly kid. Here. Get inside my coat. You're one weird bugger, Wolfie. What's with all this sneaking around, eh? It

347

ain't bloody natural. Why don't you never draw attention to yerself?'

He allowed her to wrap him inside the flap of her army greatcoat, snuggling up to her big squashy body. It was the most wonderful feeling he'd ever known. Warmth. Security. Softness. He felt safe with Bella in a way he had never felt safe with his mother. He kissed her neck and cheeks, and rested his arms along her breasts.

She put a finger under his chin and lifted his face to the moonlight. 'You sure you're only ten?' she asked teasingly.

'Reckon so,' he said sleepily.

'Why aren't you in bed?'

'Can't get in the bus. Fox's locked it.'

'Jesus wept!' she growled crossly. 'Where's he gone?'

'Dunno.' He pointed towards Shenstead Farm. 'He took off that way through the wood. Reckon he's gone for a lift.'

'Who with?'

'Dunno. He makes a call and someone picks him up. I used to follow him when Mum was around. Don't bother no more.'

Bella eased him onto her lap inside the voluminous coat and rested her chin on his head. 'You know what, darlin', I don't much like what's going on here. I'd take me and my girls away tomorrow . . . 'cept I'm worried about you. If I knew what your dad was up to . . .' She lapsed into a brief, thoughtful silence. 'How 'bout I drive you to the coppers tomorrow and you tell 'em about your mum? It'll mean you'll probably be fostered for a while – but it'll get you away from Fox – 'n' back to your mum 'n' Cub in the end. What d'you reckon?'

Wolfie shook his head violently. 'Na. I'm scared of coppers.'

'Why?'

'They look for bruises, 'n' if they find them they take you away.'

'Are they gonna find them on you?' she asked.

'Reckon so. Then you get sent to hell.'

His skinny body shivered, and Bella wondered angrily why he had been fed such crap. 'Why would you go to hell for having bruises, darlin'? It ain't your fault. It's Fox's fault!"

'It's against the rules,' he told her. 'Doctors get right angry when they find bruises on kids. You don't wanna be around when that happens.'

Godalmighty! It was a twisted mind that had come up with that disgusting piece of logic. Bella pulled him closer. 'Trust me, darlin', you ain't got nothin' to worry about. You have to do somethin' really bad for doctors and coppers to get angry, 'n' you ain't done nothin' bad.'

'*You* have,' said Wolfie, who had listened to Bella's phone call from his hiding place under the blankets. 'You didn't oughta tell Fox where Nancy is. All she ever did was untie the rope so she could make friends with you.' He looked up at Bella's moon face. 'You reckon he's gonna cut her with the razor?' he asked sadly.

'No chance, darlin',' she said comfortably, resting her chin on his head again. 'I told him she was doing night ops on Salisbury Plain. It was crawling with soldiers three days ago – training for Afghanistan, I guess – so it'll be like looking for a needle in a haystack . . . 'ssuming the needle was ever there, of course.'

*

Message from Mark
Emergency. Phone me ASAP

*

Mark had one last try to get through, then thrust his mobile into James's hand and spun the wheel to take the Lexus back onto the road. 'Do you know how these things work?'

James looked at the tiny machine in his palm. The buttons glowed for a second or two in the darkness, then went out. 'I'm afraid not,' he confessed. 'The only mobile telephone I ever used was the size of a shoe box.'

'No problem. Give it back to me when it rings.' Mark floored the accelerator and drove at high speed up the narrow lane, scraping the bank with his tyres.

James braced himself against the dashboard. 'Would you mind if I give you a few facts of army life?' he said.

'Go ahead.'

'Apart from the problem of IRA terrorism – which is an ongoing alert – there is now the threat of al-Qaida terrorism. Both these factors mean military camps are no-go areas to anyone without documents and authority . . . and that includes army personnel.' He flinched as the hedgerow loomed dangerously close in the headlights. 'The best you and I, as civilians, can hope for is that we can persuade the sergeant of the guard to phone through and ask Nancy to come to the gate. He will almost certainly refuse and suggest we apply through proper channels tomorrow. Under *no* circumstances will we be allowed to wander around the camp, looking for her. Our friend on the telephone will be subject to the same restrictions.'

They screamed round a bend. 'Are you saying there's no point going?'

'I'm certainly questioning the wisdom of dying in the attempt,' the old man said dryly. 'Even if we do decide to proceed, an extra fifteen minutes will make no difference to Nancy's safety.'

'Sorry.' Mark slowed to a manageable speed. 'I just think she needs to know what's going on.'

'We don't know ourselves.'

'Warn her, then.'

'You've already done that with your message.' The old man's tone was apologetic. 'We're not going to find out anything by running away, Mark. Headlong flight smacks of panic under fire. Standing our ground will at least tell us who and what we're up against.'

'You've been doing that for weeks,' Mark pointed out impatiently, 'and it's got you precisely nowhere. Also, I don't see why you're suddenly so laid back about him knowing her name and address. It's you who keeps describing him as a madman.'

'Which is why I'd like to keep him in my sights,' said James calmly. 'If we know anything in this present situation, it's that he's at our door. Almost certainly with the travellers. He's obviously been watching us . . . may even have followed us to Mrs Weldon's . . . and if he did, then he'll have seen which way we turned out of her drive. At the moment, the Manor is undefended and that may have been what his last call was intended to achieve.'

Mark's headlights picked up a break in the hedge-row a hundred yards ahead where a gate led into a field. He drew into it and was preparing to do a three-point turn when James laid a gentle hand on his arm.

'You'll never make a soldier, my boy,' he said with a smile in his voice, 'not unless you learn to think before you act. We need to decide on some tactics before we roar back the other way. I'm no more inclined to walk into a trap than that little boy this afternoon.'

Wearily, Mark killed his engine and switched off his headlamps. 'I'd be happier if we went to the police,' he said. 'You keep talking as if you're in a private little war that has no bearing on anyone else, but too many innocent people are being dragged into it. That woman – Bella – and the little boy. You said yourself they were probably being used, so what makes you think they aren't in danger as well?'

'Leo's not interested in them,' said James. 'They're just his excuse for being here.'

'So Leo's this Fox character?'

'Not unless he had a child he's never told me about . . . or the child isn't his.' He handed Mark the mobile. 'The police won't be interested until somebody gets hurt,' he said cynically. 'These days you have to be dead or dying to get any attention, and then it's lip service only. Talk to Elizabeth. She won't pick up the receiver – calls go straight to her answer machine – but I'm fairly sure she listens. It's pointless my speaking . . . she hasn't answered since Ailsa died . . . but she might talk to you.'

'What do I say to her?'

'Anything that will persuade her to give us infor-mation,' said James harshly. 'Find out where Leo is. You're the wordsmith. Think of something. There must be some trigger point that will persuade my only daughter to behave decently for the first time in her life. Ask her about this meeting with Mrs Bart-lett. Ask her why she's been telling lies?'

Mark switched on the overhead light again, and reached into the back for his briefcase. 'Is that the sort of tone you use to Elizabeth?' he asked without emphasis, pushing back his seat and opening the case on his lap. He retrieved his laptop and balanced it on the lid, booting up the screen.

'I never speak to her. She won't pick up.'

'But you leave messages?'

James gave an irritable nod.

'Mm.' Mark waited for the icons to appear, then brought up Elizabeth's file. 'Right,' he said, casting an eye over the details, most of which related to her monthly allowance. 'I suggest we bribe her with another five hundred a month, and tell her it's your Christmas present to her.'

The old man was outraged. 'Absolutely not,' he spluttered. 'I shouldn't be paying anything. I certainly won't increase it. It's only a few months since she had fifty thousand from her mother's will.'

Mark smiled slightly. 'But that wasn't your gift, James, it was Ailsa's.'

'So?'

'It's *you* who wants a favour. Look, I know the whole subject drives you mad – and I know we've debated it endlessly – but the fact remains, you did set up a fund for her after her marriage failed.'

'Only because we thought she'd been badly treated. We wouldn't have done it if we'd known the details of the divorce. She was little better than a whore . . . touting herself round the clubs and selling herself to anyone who'd buy her drink.'

'Yes, well, unfortunately the result was the same.' Mark raised a calming hand. 'I know . . . I know . . . but if you want information, then you must give me some leverage . . . and, frankly, beating her about the head isn't going to produce anything. You've tried that before. The promise of an extra five hundred will make her more amenable.'

'And if it doesn't?'

'It will,' Mark said bluntly. '*However* . . . as I'm planning to be pleasant to her, you either get out of the car now or you give me a sworn guarantee that you'll keep your mouth shut.'

James lowered his window and felt the cold night pinch at his cheeks. 'I'll keep my mouth shut.'

*

There was no answer. As James had predicted, the call went straight to the answerphone. Mark talked until the time ran out, mentioning money and his regret that, as he hadn't been able to reach Elizabeth in person, payment would inevitably be delayed. He redialled a couple of times, stressing the urgency of the matter and asking her to pick up if she was listening, but if she was there she wasn't biting. He left his mobile number and asked her to call him that evening if she was interested.

'When did you last to speak to her?' he asked.

'I can't remember. The last time I *saw* her was at the funeral, but she came and went without saying a word.'

'I remember,' said Mark. He scrolled down the screen. 'Her bank's acknowledging receipt of the cheques. Presumably they'd inform us if nothing was being drawn against the account?'

'What are you suggesting?'

The younger man shrugged. 'Nothing really . . . just wondering why the long silence.' He pointed at an item, dated the end of November. 'According to this, I wrote to her a month ago with the annual reminder to review her house and contents insurance. She hasn't replied.'

'Does she usually?'

Mark nodded. 'She does, as a matter of fact, particularly when it's a cost that you've agreed to shoulder. The premium doesn't have to be paid until the end of next month, but I'd have expected to hear from her by now. I always threaten her with a visit if she doesn't provide me with an up-to-date valuation. The house and contents are nominally your property still, so it's a way of stopping her flogging them off.' He clicked through to his diary.

'I've given myself a reminder to chase her up at the end of next week.'

James pondered for a moment. 'Didn't Mrs Weldon say Mrs Bartlett had seen her?'

'Mm, and I'm wondering how she got hold of her. I can't imagine Elizabeth returning a call from Pokeweed.' He was busy bringing up his email address book.

'Then perhaps we should be talking to Mrs Bartlett?'

Mark looked at Becky's contact numbers on the screen and wondered if he'd left them there on purpose. He'd torn up everything else that would give him access to her – deliberately cleared his memory of the mobile number that had once been as familiar as his own – but perhaps a part of him couldn't bear to erase her entirely from his life. 'Let me try this person first,' he said, retrieving his mobile. 'It's a long shot – she probably won't answer either – but it's worth a try.'

'Who is it?'

'An ex-girlfriend of Leo's,' he said. 'I think she'll talk to me. We were pretty close for a while.'

'How do you know her?'

Mark tapped in Becky's number. 'We were due to get married in June,' he said in a deadpan voice. 'On March 7 she gave Leo an alibi for the night Ailsa died, and by the time I got home she was gone.

They'd been having an affair for three months.' He flicked James an apologetic smile as he raised the phone to his ear. 'It's why I've always accepted that Leo wasn't in Shenstead that night. I should have told you . . . I'm sorry I didn't. Pride's a terrible thing. If I could put the clock back and do it differently, I would.'

The old man sighed. 'So would we all, my boy . . . so would we all.'

*

Becky couldn't stop talking. Every sentence ended with 'darling'. Was it really him? How *was* he? Had he been thinking of her? She just *knew* he'd phone eventually. Where was he? Could she come home? She loved him so much. It was all a terrible mistake. Darling . . . darling . . . darling . . .

'*It's a term of endearment that means very little . . . if someone said it to me, I'd stick my fingers down my throat . . .*'

Mark caught his grim reflection in the windscreen and abruptly killed the overhead light to blot it out. He questioned why he had ever allowed Becky's departure to upset him. He might have been listening to a stranger for all the emotion she stirred in him. 'I'm sitting in my car in the middle of Dorset with Colonel Lockyer-Fox,' he broke in, choosing to answer the question of where he was. 'I'm calling on my mobile and the battery's likely to go at any minute. We need to get hold of Elizabeth as a matter of urgency but she's not answering her phone. I was wondering if you knew where she was.'

There was a short silence. 'Is the Colonel listening?'

'Yes.'

'Does he know about—?'

'I've just told him.'

'Oh God, I'm sorry, darling. I never meant to embarrass you. Believe me if I could—'

Mark cut in again. 'About Elizabeth, Rebecca. Have you seen her recently?'

He never called her Rebecca, and there was another silence. 'You're angry.'

If James hadn't been listening, he would have said he was bored. Give him a woman with intelligence, he thought, who knew when to walk away without asking questions. 'We can talk when I get back to the flat,' he said by way of an inducement. 'For the moment, tell me about Elizabeth. When did you last see her?'

Her voice warmed again. 'July. She came to Leo's flat about a week before I left. The pair of them went out . . . and I haven't seen her since.'

'What did she want?'

'I don't know. She kept saying she needed to speak to Leo in private. She was paralytic so I didn't bother to ask why. You know what she's like.'

'Did Leo talk about it afterwards?'

'Not really. He just said her mind was going and he'd taken her home.' She paused. 'It happened once before. The police phoned to say they had a woman in their waiting room . . . it was all a bit weird . . . they said she couldn't remember where she lived but was able to give them Leo's number.' Another pause. 'I expect the time in July was something similar. She was always haunting the flat.'

There were too many hesitations, and he wondered how truthful she was being. 'What was wrong with her?'

Her tone grew spiteful. 'Drink. I doubt she's got any brain cells left. I told Leo she needed treatment, but he wouldn't do anything about it. It flattered his pathetic little ego to have his plaything around him.'

'What does that mean?'

'What do you think it means? They didn't have the sort of relationship you have with *your* sisters, you know. Haven't you ever wondered why Elizabeth's brain-dead and Leo's never married?'

It was Mark's turn to be silent.

'Are you still there?'

'Yes.'

'Well, for Christ's sake, watch what you say in front of the Colonel. No one'll get any money if his father—' She broke off abruptly. 'Look, forget I said that. Leo scares the shit out of me. He's a really sick bastard, Mark. He's got this thing about his Dad . . . something to do with the Colonel being tortured during the war. Don't ask me why because I don't understand it . . . but Leo really hates him for it. I know it sounds crazy – oh, God, he *is* crazy – but all he ever thinks about is how to bring the old man to his knees. It's a kind of crusade with him.'

Mark ran through his very limited psychological vocabulary, acquired through briefing barristers on defendants' psychiatric reports. *Transference . . . compensation . . . displacement . . . depersonalization . . .* He took it a step at a time. 'OK, let's start with this relationship you mentioned – are we talking fact or guesswork?'

'Oh, for Christ's sake!' Becky said angrily. 'I told you to watch what you say. You're so damn thoughtless, Mark. As long as you're all right, you couldn't give a shit about anybody else.'

That sounded more like the Becky he knew. 'You're doing all the talking . . . *darling*,' he said coolly. 'Anything I say is purely incidental. Fact or guesswork?'

'Guesswork,' she admitted. 'She was always sitting on his lap. I never actually *saw* anything but I'm sure it happened. I was at work all day, don't forget, earning the bloody mon—' She checked herself again. 'They could have been doing anything. Elizabeth *definitely* wanted it. She used to trail after Leo as if he were God.'

Mark glanced at James and saw that his eyes were closed. But he knew he was listening. 'Leo's an attractive man,' he murmured. 'A lot of people gravitate towards him. You thought he was God for a while . . . or have you forgotten?'

'Oh, please don't do that,' she begged. 'What will the Colonel think?'

'More or less what he thinks now, I should imagine. Why does it matter? You're never likely to meet him.'

She didn't say anything.

'You were the one with illusions,' he went on, wondering if she still had hopes of Leo. 'For everyone else the charm had run a bit thin.'

'Yes, and I found that out the hard way,' she said harshly. 'I've been trying to tell you for ages, but you wouldn't listen. It's just an act. He uses people then throws them aside.'

Mark decided it would be counterproductive to say: I told you so. 'How did he use you?'

She didn't answer.

'Was the alibi a lie?'

There was a long hesitation as if she were considering her options. 'No,' she said finally.

'Are you sure?'

There was the sound of a stifled sob. 'He's such a bastard, Mark. He took all my money and then got me to borrow off my parents and my sisters. They're all so angry with me . . . and I don't know what to do. They've told me to get it back, but I'm so scared of him. I was hoping you'd . . . being his father's

solicitor and everything . . . I thought he might . . .'
She petered into silence.

Mark took a deep breath to hide his irritation.
'What?'

'You know . . .'

'Reimburse you?'

Her relief was so strong he could feel it through
the phone. 'Will he?'

'I shouldn't think so . . . but I'll discuss it with
him if you give me some honest answers. Did you go
through my briefcase? Did you tell Leo the Colonel
was looking for his grandchild?'

'Only once,' she said. 'I saw a draft of a will that
mentioned a granddaughter. That's all I told him.
There was no name or anything. I didn't mean any
harm, honestly I didn't . . . the only thing he was
interested in was how much he and Lizzie were
going to get.'

A car approached down the narrow lane, blinding
him with its headlights. It was travelling too fast and
the rush of wind as it passed the Lexus buffeted
against the sides. It was too close for comfort and
it set Mark's nerves jangling. '*Christ!*' he swore,
switching on his headlights.

'Don't be cross with me,' Becky pleaded at the
other end. 'I know I shouldn't have done it . . . but
I was so frightened. He's really horrible when he
doesn't get his own way.'

'What does he do?'

But she wouldn't or couldn't say. Whatever terrors Leo held for her – real or imagined – she was not about to share them with Mark. Instead she became coy in an attempt to discover if her 'terrors' would persuade Mark to recover her parents' money.

He rang off, saying his battery was on the blink.

A year ago he would have trusted her implicitly . . .

. . . now he didn't believe a word she said . . .

Twenty-One

PRUE'S SENSE OF isolation was becoming unbearable. She was too ashamed to phone any of her friends, and there was no answer from her daughter. Loneliness led her to imagine that Jenny, too, had gone to Jack and Belinda's house, and her resentment against Eleanor grew. She pictured her at home with Julian, using her wiles to bind him to her, while Prue stared into an abyss of rejection and divorce.

The focus of her dislike was her so-called friend. Darth Vader existed only on the periphery of her thinking. Her mind was too trammelled in misery to give any thought to who he was or what sort of relationship he had with her friend. It was with a thrill of terror, then, that she looked up to see a man's face at the window. It was a momentary glimpse, a flash of white skin and dark eye sockets, but a scream rocketed from her mouth.

This time she did call the police. She was incoherent with fear, but managed to give her address. The police had been expecting trouble since the arrival of the travellers, and a car was dispatched immediately to investigate. Meanwhile, the female officer at the centre kept Prue on the line to calm her. Could Mrs Weldon give a description of this man? Had she recognized him? Prue delivered what sounded like a stereotypical description of a burglar or a mugger. 'White face ... staring eyes ...' It wasn't James Lockyer-Fox or Mark Ankerton, she kept repeating.

The policewoman asked her why Colonel Lockyer-Fox and Mr Ankerton should even be considered, and was rewarded with a garbled account of forced entry, intimidation, incest, nuisance calls, tape recordings, Darth Vader, the murder of a dog and Prue's innocence of any wrongdoing. 'It's Eleanor Bartlett at Shenstead House you should be talking to,' Prue insisted, as if the police had called her and not the other way round. 'She's the one who started all this.'

The woman relayed the information to a colleague who had worked on the Ailsa Lockyer-Fox investigation. This might interest him, she said. A Mrs Weldon was suggesting some bizarre skeletons in the Lockyer-Fox closet.

*

It was self-pity that persuaded Prue to talk so freely. She had been starved of kindness all day and the calming voice on the end of the phone, followed by the arrival of two solid-looking uniformed men to search the house and yard for an intruder, won her allegiance in a way that badgering never could. Tears bloomed in her eyes as one of the constables pressed a cup of tea into her hand and told her there was nothing to worry about. Whoever the peeping Tom was, he was no longer there.

By the time Detective Sergeant Monroe arrived half an hour later she was falling over herself to assist the police in any way she could. Better informed since James and Mark's visit, she gave a rambling exposition of events, finishing with a description of the nuisance caller who used a voice distorter, the 'murder' of James's dog, and Mark's mention of a burglary at the Manor.

Monroe frowned. 'Who is this caller? Do you know?'

'No, but I'm sure Eleanor Bartlett does,' she said eagerly. 'I thought the information came from Elizabeth . . . that's what Eleanor told me, anyway . . . but Mr Ankerton said Eleanor was reading from a script, and I think he's right. When you listen to both of them – her and the man – you notice how many repetitions there are.'

'Meaning what exactly? That this man wrote the script?'

'Well, yes, I suppose so.'

'So you're saying that Mrs Bartlett's conspiring with him to blackmail Colonel Lockyer-Fox?'

Such an idea had never occurred to Prue. 'Oh, no . . . it was to shame James into confessing.'

367

'To what?'

'Ailsa's murder.'

'Mrs Lockyer-Fox died of natural causes.'

Prue waved a despairing hand. 'That was the coroner's verdict . . . but no one believed it.'

It was a sweeping statement which the sergeant chose to discount. He flicked back through his notes. 'And you're assuming the Colonel killed her because the day before her death Mrs Lockyer-Fox was told by her daughter that the baby was his? Do you know for a fact that Mrs Lockyer-Fox saw her daughter that day?'

'She went to London.'

'London's a big place, Mrs Weldon, and our information was that she attended a committee meeting of one of her charities. Also, both Elizabeth and Leo Lockyer-Fox said they hadn't seen their mother for six months. That doesn't square with what you're alleging.'

'Not me,' she said, 'I've never alleged anything. I kept quiet in my calls.'

Monroe's frown deepened. 'But you knew your friend was alleging it, so who put the idea of the meeting into her mind?'

'It must have been Elizabeth,' said Prue uncomfortably.

'Why would she do that if she told us she hadn't seen her mother in six months?'

'I don't know.' She chewed her lip anxiously.

'This is the first time I've heard that you even knew Ailsa had gone to London. Eleanor always says James never told you.'

The sergeant smiled slightly. 'You don't have a very high opinion of the Dorset police, do you?'

'Oh, no,' she assured him, 'I think you're wonderful.'

His smile, a cynical one, vanished immediately. 'Then why assume we wouldn't check Mrs Lockyer-Fox's movements in the days prior to her death? There was a question mark over how she died until the pathologist delivered his post-mortem findings. For two days we talked to everyone who might have been in contact with her.'

Prue fanned herself as a hot flush spread up her neck. 'Eleanor said you were all Freemasons . . . and so was the pathologist.'

Monroe eyed her thoughtfully. 'Your friend is either misinformed, malicious or ignorant,' he said, before consulting his notes again. 'You claim you were convinced the story of the meeting was true because of this row you overheard when Mrs Lockyer-Fox accused her husband of destroying Elizabeth's life . . .'

'It seemed so logical . . .'

He ignored her. '. . . but now you're not sure if it was the Colonel she was talking to. Also, you think you may have put the events in the wrong sequence, and that Mr Ankerton was right when he said the

369

subsequent killing of the Colonel's dog was connected in some way with the sound of the punch you heard. He believes Mrs Lockyer-Fox may have witnessed the deliberate mutilation of a fox.'

'It was so long ago. At the time I really did think . . . it was all very shocking, particularly as Ailsa was dead the next morning . . . I couldn't see who else it could have been except James.'

He didn't speak for a moment, but mulled over some bullet points he'd made. 'The Colonel reported a mutilated fox on his terrace at the beginning of the summer,' he said suddenly. 'Did you know about that one? Or if there've been any others since?'

She shook her head.

'Could your friend Mrs Bartlett have been responsible?'

'God, no!' she protested, deeply shocked. 'Eleanor *likes* animals.'

'But eats them for lunch, presumably?'

'That's not fair.'

'Very little is, I find,' Monroe said dispassionately. 'Let me put this another way. It's quite a catalogue of brutality that's been aimed at Colonel Lockyer-Fox in the wake of his wife's death. You keep telling me the nuisance campaign was your friend's idea, so why balk at the suggestion that she was prepared to kill his dog?'

'Because she's afraid of dogs,' she said lamely, 'particularly Henry. He was a Great Dane.' She shook her head in bewilderment, as much in the dark as he was. 'It's so cruel . . . I can't bear to think about it.'

'But you don't think it's cruel to accuse an old man of incest?'

'Ellie said he'd come out fighting if none of it was true, but he's never said a word . . . just stayed in his house and pretended it wasn't happening.'

Monroe was unimpressed. 'Would you have believed him if he'd said he hadn't done it? In the absence of the child, it was his word against his daughter's and you and your friend had already made up your minds that the daughter was telling the truth.'

'Why would she lie about it?'

'Have you met her?'

Prue shook her head.

'Well, I have, Mrs Weldon, and the only reason I accepted her statement that her mother did not visit her the day before she died was because I double-checked with her neighbours who deal with her on a daily basis. Did your friend do that?'

'I don't know.'

'No,' he agreed. 'For a self-styled judge you really are remarkably ignorant . . . and frighteningly willing to change your viewpoint when someone challenges it. You said earlier that you told Mrs Bartlett you didn't believe the child could be the Colonel's, yet you tamely went along with the hate campaign. Why?

Did Mrs Bartlett promise you money if you con-spired to destroy the Colonel? Will *she* benefit if he's driven from his home?'

Prue's hands flew to her blazing cheeks. 'Of *course* not,' she cried. 'That's an *outrageous* suggestion.'

'Why?'

The bluntness of the question sent her grasping miserably at straws. 'It all seems so obvious now . . . but it wasn't at the time. Eleanor was so convinced . . . and I *had* heard that awful row. Ailsa *did* say Elizabeth's life was destroyed, and I know I'm remembering that correctly.'

The sergeant gave a disbelieving smile. He'd sat through too many trials to believe that memory was accurate. 'Then why did none of your friends go along with it? You told me you were shocked to find you were the only one who'd signed up. You felt you'd been conned.' He paused and, when she didn't say anything, went on: 'Assuming Mrs Bartlett is as gullible as you – which I doubt – then the instigator is this man with the Darth Vader voice. So who is he?'

Prue showed the same anxiety that she'd shown when asked the same question by Mark. 'I've no idea,' she muttered wretchedly. 'I didn't even know he existed until this evening. Eleanor never men-tioned him, just said it was the girls who were phoning—' She stopped abruptly as her mind groped through the fog of confused shame that had been clouding it since James's visit. 'How stupid of me,' she said with sudden clarity. 'She's been lying about everything.'

*

A police car drew up in front of the rope barrier and two burly constables climbed out, leaving the head-lights on full beam to illuminate the camp. Blinded, Bella eased Wolfie off her lap and stood up, shelter-ing him inside the flap of her coat. 'Good evening, gents,' she said, pulling her scarf over her mouth. 'Can I help you?'

'A lady up the road reported an intruder on her property,' said the younger of the two, pulling on his cap as he approached. He gestured to his right. 'Has anyone from here set off in that direction in the last hour or two?'

Bella felt Wolfie tremble. 'I didn't see anyone, darlin',' she told the policeman cheerfully, 'but I've been facin' towards the road . . . so I wouldn't, would I?' She was cursing Fox roundly inside her head. Why make a rule that no one should leave the site after dark, then break it himself? Unless, of course, the only reason for the rule was to give himself free run of the village. The idea that he was a common thief appealed to her. It brought him down to a manageable size in a way that Wolfie's constant references to the cut-throat razor did not.

The other officer chuckled as he moved into the

light. 'That has to be Bella Preston,' he said. 'It'd take more than a scarf and a bulky coat to disguise that shape and voice. What are you up to this time, girl? Not organizing another rave, I hope. We're still recovering from the last one.'

Bella recognized him immediately as a police negotiator from the Barton Edge rave. Martin Barker. One of the good guys. Tall, brown-eyed, forty-plus, and a heart pleaser. She lowered the scarf with a smile. 'Nn-nn. It's all above board and legal, Mr Barker. This land don't belong to anyone, so we're claiming it through adverse possession.'

Another chuckle. 'You've been reading too much fiction, Bella.'

'Maybe, but we're planning to stay until someone produces deeds, proving it's theirs. We're entitled to have a go – *anyone's* entitled – we just happened to think of it first.'

'No chance, darlin',' he said, aping her manner of speech. 'If you're lucky you'll get a delay on the usual seven days' notice, but if you're still here in two weeks I'll eat my hat. How's that for an offer?'

'Should be amusing. Why so confident?'

'What makes you think this land isn't owned?'

'It's not on anyone's deeds.'

'How do you know?'

It was a good question, thought Bella. They'd taken Fox's word for it, just as they'd taken his word on everything else. 'Put it this way,' she answered, 'it don't look like anyone in the village wants to take us on. A couple of them have blustered a bit and threatened us with lawyers, but the only lawyer that's turned up wasn't interested in talking about squatters on his client's doorstep.'

'I wouldn't pin your hopes on it,' Martin Barker warned kindly. 'They'll get round to it as soon as the holiday's over. There's too much money invested in this place to let travellers bring down the price of the houses. You know the rules as well as I do, Bella. The rich get richer, the poor get poorer, and there's damn all the likes of you and me can do about it.' He put his hand on the rope. 'Are you going to let us in? It would be useful to confirm that no one here was involved.'

Bella jerked her head in invitation. They would come in whatever she said – on suspicion of breach of peace if nothing else – but she appreciated Martin's courtesy in asking. 'Sure. We didn't come here to cause trouble, so the sooner you count us out the better.' She was prepared to play 'keeper' to Fox's son but not to Fox himself. Let the bastard make his own explanations, she thought, as she eased Wolfie from under her coat. 'This is Wolfie. He's stopping with me 'n' the girls while his mum's away.'

Wolfie shook with alarm as he stared at the constables' faces, his trust in Bella running like sawdust from his knees. Hadn't he told her Fox wasn't there? What would these men do when they found the bus empty? Bella should never have let them in . . . should never have mentioned his mother . . . they'd search for bruises and take him away . . .

Martin saw the fear in his face and squatted on his haunches to bring himself to the child's level. 'Hi, Wolfie. Do you want to hear a joke?'

Wolfie shrank against Bella's legs.

'What do you call two rows of cabbages?'

No response.

'A dual cabbageway.' Martin studied Wolfie's unsmiling face. 'Heard it before, eh?'

The child shook his head.

'You don't think it's funny?'

A tiny nod.

Martin held his gaze for a moment, then dropped him a wink and stood up. The boy's fear was palpable, although whether he was afraid of policemen per se or of what a search of the camp might find, it was difficult to say. One thing was certain. If Bella had been looking after him for any length of time, he wouldn't be dressed in such inadequate clothing for a winter's night and he wouldn't be looking half-starved.

'Right,' he said, 'do you want to introduce us to your friends, Bella? My colleague here is PC Sean Wyatt, and you might like to make it clear that we're not interested in anything except the intruder at Shenstead Farm.'

She nodded, taking Wolfie's hand firmly in hers.

'Far as I know, there's nothing to find, Mr Barker,' she said with as much conviction as she could muster. 'We're all families and we started this project the way we mean to go on . . . doing it by the book so the people round about wouldn't have nothing to complain about. There's the odd bit of dope stashed away, but nothing worse.'

He stood aside for her to lead the way, noticing that she chose to start with the bus to the right of the semicircle – the most distant – where light leaked from cracks around the window blinds. He, of course, was more interested in the bus to the left which drew Wolfie's eyes like magnets and appeared to be in total darkness.

*

DS Monroe passed the campsite on his way to Shenstead House and saw figures milling in front of the buses, thrown into relief by the headlamps of his colleagues' parked car. It was a reasonable assumption that the face at the window belonged to a newly arrived traveller, but he intended to exploit Mrs Weldon's insistence that her friend had turned 'peculiar' since she visited the site. It was an excuse of sorts to interview Mrs Bartlett because there was nothing else to investigate. No complaint had been made against her, and the file on Mrs Lockyer-Fox had been closed for months.

Nevertheless, Monroe was curious. Ailsa's death

continued to play on his mind, despite the coroner's verdict. He had been the first on the scene and the impact of the sad little body, propped against the sundial, wearing a thin nightdress, a man's threadbare dressing-gown, and a pair of wellington boots had been powerful. Whatever the final conclusion, it had always felt like murder to Monroe. The bloodstains a yard from the body, the incongruity of insubstantial nightclothes and solid wellingtons, the inevitable conclusion that something had disturbed her sleep and she had ventured outside to investigate.

He had played down Prue's hysterical conclusion that Eleanor's 'peculiarity' meant the face at the window was Darth Vader's – '*You have a habit of putting two and two together and making five, Mrs Weldon*' – but he was interested in the coincidence of the travellers' arrival and the falling-out between the women. He was too experienced to assume a connection without evidence, but the possibility that one existed remained at the back of his mind.

He drew to a halt at the entrance to Shenstead Manor, still undecided about whether to talk to Colonel Lockyer-Fox before he spoke to Mrs Bartlett. It would help to know exactly what the woman had been saying, but if the Colonel refused to cooperate then Monroe's already limited excuses for questioning the woman would vanish. He needed an official complaint, a fact that the Colonel's solicitor would certainly point out, assuming he was the one advising reticence.

It was this reticence that really intrigued Monroe. The idea that lodged in his mind – strengthened both by the need for a voice distorter and the lawyer's remark to Mrs Weldon that her friend's knowledge of the family was very detailed – was that Darth Vader was closely related to the Colonel.

And he kept remembering that, in the hours following his wife's death, the Colonel had accused his son of murdering her . . .

*

It was Julian who answered the bell. He looked at Monroe's warrant, listened to his request for an interview with Mrs Bartlett, then shrugged and pulled the door wide. 'She's in here.' He ushered him into a sitting room. 'The police want to talk to you,' he said indifferently. 'I'm going to my study.'

Monroe saw the alarm on the woman's face change rapidly to relief as her husband announced his attention of leaving. He moved to bar Julian's exit. 'I'd rather you didn't, sir. What I have to say involves everyone in this house.'

'Not me it doesn't,' Julian retorted coolly.

'How do you know, sir?'

'Because I only learnt about these damn phone calls this afternoon.' He stared at the sergeant's unresponsive face. 'That's why you're here, isn't it?'

Monroe glanced at Eleanor. 'Not precisely, no. Mrs Weldon reported an intruder at Shenstead Farm and she seems to think your wife knows who it might have been. It happened shortly after Colonel Lockyer-Fox and his solicitor played some tapes to her of Mrs Bartlett and a man making identical allegations against the Colonel, and Mrs Weldon believes that this man was her intruder. I'm hoping Mrs Bartlett can throw some light on the situation.'

Eleanor looked as if she'd been sandbagged. 'I don't know what you're talking about,' she managed.

'I'm sorry. I obviously didn't explain myself very well. Mrs Weldon believes her intruder to be the man who's behind a hate campaign against Colonel Lockyer-Fox. She further believes him to be one of the travellers, camped in the wood above the village . . . and says you must have spoken to him this morning as you've been acting very strangely ever since. He uses a voice distorter to disguise his voice, but she says you know who he is.'

Eleanor's mouth turned down in an unattractive horseshoe. 'That's ridiculous,' she snapped. 'Prue's a fantasist . . . always has been. Personally, I think you should question whether an intruder ever existed because she's not above inventing one to get a little attention. I suppose you know she's had a row with her husband and he's talking about divorcing her?'

Monroe didn't, but he wasn't about to admit it.

'She's frightened,' he said. 'According to her, this man mutilated the Colonel's dog and left him outside for the Colonel to find.'

Her eyes darted nervously towards her husband. 'I don't know anything about that.'

'You knew the dog was dead, Mrs Bartlett. Mrs Weldon says you were pleased about it—' he paused for emphasis – 'something to do with chickens coming home to roost.'

'That's not true.'

Julian's reaction was to throw her to the wolves. 'It sounds like you,' he said. 'You never liked poor old Henry.' He turned to Monroe. 'Sit down, sergeant,' he invited, pointing to an armchair and taking another for himself. 'I hadn't realized there was any more to this—' he made a gesture of distaste – 'humiliating story than my wife and Prue Weldon making phone calls. It seems I was wrong. What exactly has been going on?'

Monroe watched Eleanor's face as he took the other chair. She was a different animal from her plump friend – stronger and tougher – but catastrophe was showing in her eyes just as clearly as it had been in Prue's.

Twenty-Two

A SIMILAR THOUGHT was running through Martin Barker's head as Bella tried to pretend that the reason there was no bed for Wolfie in her bus was because he preferred to curl up in a sleeping bag on the banquette seat. 'He's a bit of a nomad is Wolfie,' she said with feigned confidence while worry created wrinkles on her brow. 'Don't go much for beds, do you, darlin'?'

The child's eyes widened yet further. Terror seemed to be his constant companion, stalking him relentlessly the closer they came to the darkened bus. Bella had made various attempts to leave him behind in the other vehicles, but he clung to her coat tails and refused to be parted from her. Barker pretended not to notice, but he was seriously interested in the boy's connection with the bus.

Bella put a despairing arm around Wolfie's shoulders and turned him towards her. Lighten up, kid, she begged inside her head. If you shake any more, you're gonna collapse. It was like dragging a neon sign behind her, flashing: *sure we've got some-*

thing to hide. We're the brain-dead decoys while the fucker who brought us here is out casing the village.

Her anger with Fox was intense, and not just because he'd brought the police down on their heads. No one should make a child so afraid that the mere sight of uniforms struck him dumb. She wanted to take Mr Barker aside and blurt out her concerns – the mother's vanished, the brother's vanished, the child says he has bruises – but what was the good if Wolfie denied it? She knew he would. His fear of authority was far greater than his fear of Fox. In any child's mind a bad parent was better than no parent at all.

At the back of her mind, too, was a worry that she only had Wolfie's word for it that Fox had ever left the camp. Supposing he was wrong? Or supposing Fox had slipped back through the woods and was watching from his bus? What then? Wouldn't the child's situation be a hundred times worse? And wasn't that what he was really afraid of? That Bella would do or say something to make Fox angry?

'He don't know what "nomad" means,' she explained to Barker. 'He reckons it's something bad.' She gave the child a comforting squeeze. 'Why don't you stay with the girls, darlin', while I take these gentlemen to the last bus? Fox said he'd man the barrier tonight, remember, so he's likely asleep. He'll be that mad at being woken . . . and there ain't no reason for you to hear him cursin' and swearin' just because he's in a bad temper.'

Barker's curiosity intensified. *Fox?* What were the odds on a relationship between a Fox and a Wolfie in a community as small as this one? He ruffled Wolfie's hair. 'Your dad?' he asked amiably, raising an enquiring eyebrow at Bella.

No answer.

Bella gave a small nod. 'Fox ain't much of a cook . . . so the poor kid ain't getting proper meals.' She was staring at Barker as if she were trying to tell him something. 'That's why he's stopping with me for a while.'

Barker nodded. 'So where's his mum?'

'Wolfie ain't too—'

Abruptly, the child pulled away from Bella's supporting arm. He had shadowed her from the moment she'd said his mother was away, because he knew the policeman would ask that question. 'She's in Devon,' he said in a rush.

Barker chuckled. 'So you do have a voice!'

Wolfie stared at the floor, distrusting the way this man looked at people as if he could read their thoughts. He spoke in staccato sentences. 'My mother's on holiday with my brother. They're staying with friends. I said I'd rather be with my father. He's very busy because he's the organizer of this project. That's why Bella's cooking for me. It's not charity. My Dad's paying her. Mum and Cub will be joining us in a few days. Fox likes families. That's why he's chosen them to build this community.'

It was arguable who was the more taken aback. Martin Barker because of the sophistication of Wolfie's speech when he finally opened his mouth – like Bella he had assumed the child was younger than he was – or Bella because he chose to ape his father's classy accent. She smiled weakly as the policeman frowned. *They'd be accusing her of kidnap next . . .*

'He watches too much telly.' She plucked a film out of the air. 'Probably thinks he's– whatsisname – Mark Lester in *Oliver!*' She ruffled Wolfie's blond hair. 'He's got the looks for it, even if he's more of an Artful Dodger at heart.'

Barker raised amused eyebrows. 'Which makes you Nancy, I suppose? The tart with the heart in Fagin's den of thieves?'

Bella grinned in response. ''Cept I'm no tart, this ain't no den of thieves, 'n' I sure as hell don't plan to get done in by Bill Sikes.'

'Mm. So who's Bill Sikes?'

'Oliver Reed,' she said firmly, wishing she'd chosen her film more wisely. 'The sodding film's full of Olivers.'

Barker bent down to look through her windscreen at the last bus. 'How about Fox?'

'No chance,' she said, squeezing past him to lead the way outside and feeling the tug on her coat as Wolfie followed. '*Oliver!* was a random pick so don't go reading Freud into it. The kid copies voices. I might just as well have said *Little Lord Fauntleroy.*'

'Or *Greystoke . . . the Legend of Tarzan,*' he suggested.

'Sure. Why not? He's a good imitator.'

Barker thumped heavily to the ground behind her. 'They're all films about orphaned boys being rescued by their grandfathers, Bella.'

'So?'

He glanced past Wolfie's blond head, searching for the lights of Shenstead Manor through the trees. 'Just curious about the coincidence.'

*

James shook his head when Mark started to explain about Leo's alibi. 'No need for details,' he murmured gently. 'I do understand. I've always wondered why you sided with the police when I accused Leo. Now I know. It can't have been easy for you.' He paused. 'Is his alibi still watertight?'

Mark thought of Becky's hesitation. He spread his hand, palm down, and made a rocking motion.

'I've always thought it must have been Leo that Mrs Weldon heard that night,' said James apologetically. 'People often confused us over the telephone.'

The younger man pondered for a moment. 'Becky said Elizabeth's brain was shot the last time she saw her . . . some story about Leo having to rescue her from a police station because she'd forgotten where she lived.'

James took the change of tack in his stride. 'It was always on the cards. Ailsa's father went the same way – drank himself into dementia by the age of seventy.'

'She must be in a pretty bad way, though, if she can't remember her address. She's only mid-forties.' He scrolled down Elizabeth's file again, looking for correspondence details. 'As far as I can make out, I haven't heard from her since June when she acknow-ledged receipt of Ailsa's fifty thousand . . . and the last time Becky saw her was July when she described her as paralytic. How many times have you phoned her?'

'Ten . . . twelve. I gave up when she didn't return my calls.'

'When was that?'

'Soon after the nuisance calls began. It seemed pointless going on when I assumed she was a party to them.'

'The middle of November, then?'

'More or less.'

'But she hadn't answered any calls since March?'

'No.'

'And you were always able to leave a message? You didn't get blocked out because the voicemail was full?'

James shook his head.

'Well, at least we know someone was deleting them. What about Leo? When did you last speak to him?'

There was a small pause. 'Last week.'

Mark glanced at him in surprise. 'And?'

The old man gave a hollow laugh. 'I spoke . . . he listened . . . he hung up. It was a one-sided conversation.'

'What did you say?'

'Nothing very much. I lost my temper when he started laughing.'

'Did you accuse him of being Darth Vader?'

'Among other things.'

'And he didn't say anything?'

'No, just laughed.'

'How many times had you spoken to him prior to that?'

'You mean since Ailsa died? Just once . . . the night of her funeral.' There were slight breaks in his voice, as if his emotions weren't as well under control as he was pretending. 'He . . . phoned at about eleven o'clock to tell me what a bastard I was for giving his name to the police. He said I deserved everything I got . . . and hoped someone would find a way to pin her death on me. It was very unpleasant.'

Mark eyed him curiously. 'Did he mention Ailsa?'

'No. He was only interested in lambasting me. It

was the usual raking over of history where I'm always at fault . . . and he never is.'

Mark thought back to James's two days of interrogation. 'How did he know it was you who named him?'

'I imagine the police told him.'

'I wouldn't think so. It was a concern I raised at the time – you were there when I did it – and we were given assurances that neither Leo nor Elizabeth would be told where the suggestion came from. The way Sergeant Monroe put it, close relatives are questioned as a matter of course when death is suspicious, so the issue wouldn't arise.'

James hesitated. 'Obviously the promises weren't honoured.'

'Then why didn't Leo call you after the police first visited him? It sounds as if somebody at the funeral said something, and he worked himself into a rage on his way home.'

James frowned. 'He didn't talk to anyone. He and Elizabeth stormed in and stormed out. That's what set the tongues wagging.'

Mark scrolled through his address book again. 'I'm going to phone him, James, and I'm applying the same rules as before. You either get out of the car or you keep your mouth shut. Agreed?'

The old man's chin jutted angrily. 'Not if you offer him money, no.'

'I may have to . . . so you'd better decide now how badly you want to know who Darth Vader is.'

'It's a waste of time,' he said stubbornly. 'He won't admit to it.'

Mark gave an impatient sigh. 'All right. Explain some logistics to me. For a kick-off, how did Mrs Bartlett get in touch with Elizabeth? Even if she had her phone number, which I doubt since Elizabeth's ex-directory, why would Elizabeth answer when she's not answering anyone else? Does she know who the woman is? Did she ever meet her? I can't imagine Ailsa introducing them. She loathed Mrs Bartlett, and she certainly wouldn't have wanted a gossip finding out about Elizabeth's dirty laundry for fear of it being spread all over the countryside. Did *you* introduce them?'

James stared out of the window. 'No.'

'OK. Well, all the same arguments apply to Leo. As far as I know, he hasn't been back to Shenstead since you paid off his debt – the nearest he's come was Dorchester for the funeral – so how did he meet Mrs Bartlett? He's also ex-directory, so how did she get hold of his number? How could she write to him if she doesn't know his address?'

'You said he spoke to someone at the funeral.'

'I meant it more loosely . . . on the *day* of the funeral. It doesn't make sense, James,' Mark went on slowly, sorting ideas in his head. 'If Leo's Darth Vader, how did he know Mrs Bartlett was the one to approach? You can't just cold-call people and ask them if they're interested in a hate campaign. Mrs Weldon was a more obvious choice. At least she's on record as giving evidence against you . . . but, if she's telling the truth, then she was never even approached . . .' He fell silent.

'Well?'

Mark picked up his phone again and punched in Leo's mobile number. 'I don't know,' he said irritably, 'except that you're a bloody idiot for letting this go as far as it has. Half of me wonders if this hate campaign is just a fog to get you looking in the wrong direction.' He jabbed an aggressive finger at his client. 'You're as bad as Leo. You both want total capitulation – but it takes two to fight a war, James, and two to reach an honourable peace.'

*

Message from Nancy
Your phone engaged. Am at the Manor. Where R U?

*

Bob Dawson's hackles rose as his wife sidled into the kitchen and disturbed his radio listening. It was the only room he could call his own because it was the one Vera usually avoided. Dementia had persuaded her that the kitchen was linked to drudgery, and she only visited it when hunger drove her to abandon the television.

She glared at him as she came through the door, her pinched mouth muttering imprecations that he couldn't hear.

'What's that?' he demanded crossly.

'Where's my tea?'

'Make it yourself,' he said, laying down his knife and fork and pushing his empty plate aside. 'I'm not your damn slave.'

Theirs was a hate-filled relationship. Two solitary people, under a single roof, who could only communicate through aggression. It had always been so. Bob controlled through physical beating, Vera through spite. Her eyes glinted evilly as she noticed an echo of her own oft-repeated martyrdom. 'You've been stealing again,' she hissed, clicking onto another well-worn track. 'Where's my money? What have you done with it?'

'Wherever you hid it, you stupid bitch.'

Her mouth twisted and turned in an effort to translate chaotic thought into speech. 'It's not where it should be. You give it back, you hear.'

Bob, never a patient man at the best of times, clenched a fist and shook it at her. 'Don't you come in here accusing me of stealing. You're the thief in the family. Always have been, always will be.'

'It wasn't me,' she said obstinately, as if a lie repeated often enough acquired the stamp of truth.

His responses were as predictable as hers. 'If you've been at it again since the missus died, I'll fling you out,' he threatened. 'I don't care how senile you are, I'm not losing my home because you can't keep your fingers to yourself.'

'Wouldn't need to worry if we owned it, would we? A real man would have bought his own place.'

He thumped his fist on the table. 'Watch your mouth.'

'Half a man, that's all you are, Bob Dawson. Tough as iron in public. Limp as jelly in bed.'

'Shut up.'

'Won't.'

'Do you want the back of my hand?' he demanded angrily.

He expected her to cower away as usual, but instead a sly smile crept into her eyes.

Oh, good God! He should have known threats alone wouldn't work. He surged to his feet, sending his chair crashing to the floor. 'I warned you,' he shouted. 'Keep away from him, I said. Where is he? Is he here? Is that why we've got gypsies in the Copse?'

'None of your business,' she spat. 'You can't tell me who I can talk to. I've got rights.'

He slapped her hard across the face. '*Where is he?*' he snarled.

She hunched away from him, hate and malice blazing in her eyes. 'He'll get you first. You see if he doesn't. You're an old man. He's not afraid of you. He's not afraid of anyone.'

Bob reached for his jacket on a hook beside the sink. 'More fool him,' was all he said, before going out and slamming the door behind him.

*

They were fine words, but the reality of the night made a mockery of them. The westerly wind had covered the moon with cloud, and without a torch Bob was virtually blind. He turned towards the Manor, intending to use the drawing-room lights as a guide, and he had time to be surprised that the Manor was in darkness before a hammer hit his skull and the black night engulfed him.

Twenty-Three

DS MONROE WAS tired of middle-aged women pleading ignorance. He crossed his legs and stared around the room, listening to Eleanor Bartlett huff and puff her outrage at his suggestion that she knew anything about an intruder at Prue's. The village was full of travellers, and everyone knew that travellers were thieves. As for a hate campaign, that was a gross misrepresentation of one or two phone calls advising the Colonel that his secrets were out. Presumably the police knew the nature of the accusations?

It was a rhetorical question. She didn't wait for an answer but listed James's crimes against his daughter in salacious detail, as much for Julian's benefit, Monroe decided, as for his own. She was seeking to justify herself by creating a monster out of the Colonel, and it seemed to be working if Julian's thoughtful expression was anything to go by. 'Also, Henry wasn't James's dog,' she finished heatedly, 'he was *Ailsa's* dog . . . and if anyone killed him, it was probably James himself. He's a very cruel man.'

Monroe brought his attention back to her. 'Can you prove any of these allegations?'

'Of course I can. They were told to me by Elizabeth. Are you suggesting she'd lie about a thing like that?'

'Someone seems to be lying. According to Mrs Weldon, Colonel Lockyer-Fox was abroad when the baby was conceived.'

More huffing and puffing. It was a piece of gossip that Prue had picked up – half heard and certainly wrongly reported. If the sergeant knew Prue as well as Eleanor did, he'd know that she never got anything right, and, in any case, Prue had changed her mind as soon as Eleanor relayed the details of what Elizabeth had said. 'You should be questioning James about murder and child abuse,' she snapped, 'not intimidating me because I've been doing your job for you.' She drew breath. 'Of course we all know why you're *not* . . . you're hand in glove with him.'

The sergeant stared her down. 'I won't dignify that with a response, Mrs Bartlett.'

Her mouth curled disdainfully. 'But it's true. You never investigated Ailsa's death properly. It was swept under the carpet to avoid scandal for James.'

He shrugged. 'If you believe that, you'll believe anything, and I shall have to assume that nothing you say can be relied on . . . including these allegations against the Colonel.'

She launched into further justification. Of course they could be relied on. If not, why had James allowed them to continue? It wasn't as if Eleanor had hidden her identity, unlike Prue who was a coward. If James had bothered to come round and explain his side of the story, Eleanor would have listened. The truth was the only thing she was interested in. Ailsa was her friend, and there was no doubt that both James's children believed him guilty of murdering her. It had traumatized Eleanor to think of Ailsa suffering at the hands of a violent husband . . . particularly after hearing what Elizabeth claimed had happened to *her* as a child. If the police had asked the right questions, they would have discovered all this for themselves.

Monroe let her run on, more interested in comparing her 'sitting room' with the dilapidated 'drawing room' at the Manor. Everything in Eleanor's room was new and spotless. Cream furniture on a luscious shag-pile carpet. Chocolate walls to add vibrancy. Pastel curtains, draped in Austrian style, to lend a 'romantic' feel to the high-ceilinged Victorian room.

It was very 'designer' and very expensive, and it said nothing at all about the people who lived there. Except that they were flashy and wealthy. There were no paintings on the walls, no heirlooms, no homely litter that spoke of the inhabitants feeling comfortable in their surroundings. Give him the Manor drawing room any day, he thought, where the tastes of different centuries vied for attention, and a hundred personalities, and generations of dogs, had left their marks on the scuffed leather sofas and threadbare Persian rugs.

Every so often his eyes came to rest on the woman's sharp face. She made him think of an ageing American film star who showed too much teeth because the last facelift was a facelift too far in the desperate attempt to cling to youth. He wondered who Eleanor's competition was – certainly not Mrs Weldon – and he suspected it was the husband, with his dyed hair and tight-fitting jeans. What sort of relationship did they have where image was more important than comfort? Or was each afraid of losing the other?

He let a silence develop when she came to a halt, refusing to give her a moral victory by defending police actions in the matter of Ailsa's death. 'When did you move here?' he asked Julian.

The man was staring at his wife as if she'd grown horns. 'Four years ago from London.'

'Before the housing boom, then?'

Eleanor looked irritated as if missing the boom by a whisker still rankled. 'It didn't really affect us,' she said grandly. 'We lived in Chelsea. Property there has always been expensive.'

Monroe nodded. 'I was in the Met until a year and a half ago,' he said in a conversational tone. 'The value of our house went up by twenty per cent in twelve months.'

Julian shrugged. 'It's the only time inflation will work in your favour. The London economy is booming, the West Country's isn't. Simple as that. You won't be able to afford to go back to London if Dorset starts to pall.'

Monroe smiled slightly. 'You neither, I suppose?'

Julian steepled his fingers under his chin and continued to stare at Eleanor. 'Not unless we're prepared to trade down. We certainly wouldn't get a Shenstead House in Chelsea . . . probably not even a 1970s box on the outskirts any more. Unfortunately, my wife doesn't seem to have considered the financial implications of one-way inflation.'

The 'any more' wasn't lost on Monroe. 'What brought you down here?'

'Redun—'

Eleanor broke in sharply. 'My husband was a director in a construction company,' she said. 'He was offered a generous retirement package, and we decided to take it. It's always been our ambition to live in the country.'

'Which company?' asked Monroe, taking out his notebook.

There was a silence.

'Lacey's,' said Julian with a small laugh, 'and I wasn't a director, I was a senior manager. London inflation also extends to impressing the new neighbours, I'm afraid. And, for the record, we lived at 12 Croydon Road, which had a Chelsea postcode by virtue of the boundary running past the back of our garden.' He smiled unpleasantly. 'I think your chickens are coming home to roost, Ellie.'

She looked rather more alarmed than the exposure of a few white lies appeared to warrant. 'You're being silly,' she snapped.

He gave a contemptuous snort. 'My God, that's rich! What's sillier than fouling your own nest? How are we are supposed to go on living here now that you've managed to alienate every damn neighbour we have? Who are you going to go shopping with? Who are you going to play golf with? You'll be stuck in the house again, whining and moaning about how lonely you are. Have you any idea what that's like for me? How do you suppose your ridiculous behaviour is going to impact on my friendships? You're so bloody selfish, Ellie . . . always have been.'

Eleanor made a clumsy attempt to divert attention back to Monroe. 'The sergeant didn't come here to listen to a row. I'm sure he realizes it's a stressful situation for both of us . . . but there's no need to lose our tempers.'

Angry colour flared in Julian's face. 'If I want to lose my temper, I bloody well will,' he said furiously. 'Why the hell can't you tell the truth for once? This afternoon you swore you weren't involved in this nonsense, now you hit me with a load of crap about James being a child abuser. And who's this man with a voice distorter? What's all that about?'

'Please don't swear,' she said primly. 'It's rude and unnecessary.'

She wasn't very bright, thought Monroe, watching her husband's cheeks turn purple. 'Well, Mrs Bartlett?' he prompted. 'It's a fair question. Who is this man?'

She turned to him gratefully as Julian's fury threatened to explode. 'I've no idea,' she said. 'Prue's obviously been filling your head with nonsense. It's true that I spoke to some of the travellers to try to find out what was going on up there – at *Prue's* request as a matter of fact – but I can't imagine why she thinks I *know* any of them.' She gave a shudder of distaste. 'As if I would. They were *horrible* people.'

It sounded convincing, but Monroe reminded himself that she'd had a good twenty minutes since his arrival to manufacture excuses. 'The man I'm interested in is the one who speaks through a voice distorter.'

She looked genuinely puzzled. 'I'm afraid I don't understand.'

'I'm asking for a name, Mrs Bartlett. You've already committed a criminal offence by making nuisance calls. I'm sure you don't want to make your situation worse by withholding information.'

She shook her head nervously. 'But I don't know what you're talking about, sergeant. I've never heard anyone speak through a distorter.'

Perhaps she was cleverer than he thought. 'He may not use the distorter when talking to you, so let me put it another way. Who's been telling you what to say? Who wrote your script for you?'

'No one,' she protested. 'I've just been repeating the things Elizabeth told me.' She seemed to gather strength from somewhere. 'It's all very well to have a go at me, but I *believed* her . . . and so would you if you'd heard her. She's sure her father murdered her mother . . . and she described the most terrible things . . . it was awful listening to her. She's a very damaged woman . . . a very *sad* woman . . . the rest of us can only imagine what it's like to have a child born in such dreadful circumstances . . . and then removed.'

Monroe was watching her closely as she spoke. 'Who contacted who?' he asked bluntly.

She looked worried. 'You mean, did I phone Elizabeth?'

'Yes.'

'No. Leo wrote and invited me to meet him in London.' She raised uneasy eyes to Julian's, as if she knew he wouldn't approve. 'It was completely inno-cent,' she said. 'The letter came out of the blue. I'd never spoken to him before. He introduced me to

402

Elizabeth. We met in Hyde Park. There were thousands of witnesses.'

Julian's disapproval had nothing to do with the 'innocence' or otherwise of the meeting. 'Good God!' he groaned. 'Why would you want to meet Leo Lockyer-Fox? He and his father loathe each other.' He watched her lips thin to a stubborn line. 'That's *why*, I suppose,' he said sarcastically. 'It was a little bit of stirring to pay James and Ailsa back for their snubs? Or maybe you thought you'd get a hoist up the social ladder when Leo came into the Manor?' He rubbed his thumb and forefinger together. 'Perhaps you hoped he'd be grateful if you dragged his father through the mire?'

One or all were true, thought Monroe, as spots of tell-tale colour blotched Eleanor's face. 'Don't be so vulgar,' she snapped.

Julian's eyes glittered angrily. 'Why didn't you ask me about him? I could have told you what Leo Lockyer-Fox's gratitude was worth.' He turned the thumb and finger into a circle and jabbed it at her. 'Zero. Zilch. He's a loser . . . so is his sister. They're a couple of parasites, living on their father's charity. She's a dipso and he's a gambler, and if James is stupid enough to leave the Manor to them, they'll sell it before he's even in his grave.'

Monroe, who had interviewed both of Ailsa's children, thought it an accurate description. 'You seem to be better acquainted with them than your wife is,' he remarked. 'How is that?'

Julian turned to look at him. 'Only through what I've heard. James's tenant farmers have known them for years, and they haven't a good word to say for either of them. Spoilt rotten as children and gone to the bad as adults seems to be the consensus view. According to Paul Squires, they were due to inherit Ailsa's money when she died . . . but she changed her will last year after James sacked his previous solicitor and took on Mark Ankerton. It's why there was so much ill feeling at the funeral. They'd been expecting half a million each . . . and got nothing.'

Monroe knew that to be untrue. The children had been left fifty thousand each, but perhaps in comparison with half a million it did rank as 'nothing'. 'Were you at the funeral?'

Julian nodded. 'At the back. We couldn't see much except rows of heads . . . but it didn't make any difference. Everyone could feel the animosity. James and Mark sat on one side and Leo and Elizabeth on the other. They stormed out at the end without even saying goodbye to poor old James . . . blamed him for persuading Ailsa to change her will, presumably.' He flicked an accusing glance at his wife. 'It set the women's tongues wagging, of course. Fathers are guilty . . . children are innocent . . . all that crap.' He gave a sour laugh. 'Most of the men just felt glad they weren't in James's shoes. Poor bugger. He should have taken a rod to his kids years ago.'

Monroe could feel an accumulating frustration boil unpleasantly below the surface of this relationship. Too many cards were being placed on the table at one sitting, he thought. Now Eleanor was staring at her husband as if he'd grown horns.

'I suppose Paul Squires is one of your drinking buddies,' she said acidly. 'How's his daughter? The blonde who rides horses.'

Julian shrugged. 'Search me.'

'Gemma . . . Gemma Squires. She's in your hunt. I think she has a horse called Monkey Business.'

Her husband looked amused. 'It's a big hunt, Ellie. Off the top of my head I can think of twenty blondes who belong to it. You should come as a follower one day. I'll even blood you, if you like. You could do with some colour in your cheeks.' He laughed at her expression. 'My wife doesn't approve of hunting,' he told the sergeant. 'She thinks it's cruel.'

Monroe was wondering about the blonde and her aptly named horse. 'I agree with Mrs Bartlett,' he said mildly. 'It's hardly an equal contest . . . one frightened little animal, driven to exhaustion by the cavalry, then chewed to death by dog bites. It's neither brave nor honourable – and anyone who takes pleasure from it is a sadist.' He smiled again. 'It's a personal opinion, of course. I don't know what the official view is, except that the taxpayer would be horrified if they knew what it cost to keep hunters and saboteurs apart.'

'Oh lord!' Julian held up his hands in amiable surrender. 'Each to his own, eh? No need to come to blows over it.'

Monroe smiled. 'That's not very sporting of you, sir. I'm sure the fox says the same thing every time the dogs sniff him out. Live and let live, that's all he wants to do. The trouble is he's outnumbered. Just as you are at the moment—' he glanced at Eleanor – 'and the Colonel's been in the matter of these nuisance calls. I understand you told Mrs Weldon to make them at night, Mrs Bartlett. Why was that? It looks to me like a deliberate attempt to wear him down.'

'I . . .' she ran her tongue over her lips. 'It was the most likely time for him to be there.'

Monroe shook his head. 'That's not an answer. According to Mrs Weldon, all the calls were recorded, so whether he was there or not was immaterial. She also said he's become a recluse. Do you want to explain that to me? Because I don't understand why you think it's cruel to back a fox into a corner from exhaustion . . . but not an old man in his eighties? What were you trying to achieve?'

More silence. This entire evening had been punctuated by silences, he thought, while spiteful women worked out how to justify themselves.

'We were giving James some of his own medicine,' she muttered, refusing to look at him.

'I see,' he said slowly. 'Entirely on the word of someone you describe as "damaged".' It was a statement, not a question. 'Why do we have trials, Mrs Bartlett? Why do you think the defence and prosecution stories are so rigorously examined by a judge and jury before verdict and sentence can be passed? Where was reasonable doubt in the Colonel's favour?'

She didn't say anything.

'Whose idea was it to cloak malice as justice?'

She found her voice. 'It wasn't malice.'

'Then it was worse,' he said bluntly. 'You will be looking at charges of coercion and blackmail if the Colonel's tapes demonstrate you made demands of him.'

She licked her lips nervously. 'I never did.'

'Demanding that he confess is coercion, Mrs Bartlett. Even if he's guilty of what you accuse him, it is a criminal offence to use the telephone to threaten him. If you asked for money in return for silence—' he looked pointedly about the room – 'or accepted money from a third party to make life so unbearable for him that he would comply with that person's demands, you will be charged with a number of offences ... the most serious being conspiracy to defraud.'

'I didn't,' she insisted, turning to her husband.

407

Julian shook his head abruptly. 'Don't look to me for help,' he warned. 'You and Prue are on your own with this one. I'm following Dick's lead.' He air-washed his hands. 'Find some other mug to bail you out.'

Eleanor's pent-up anger burst its constraints. 'That would suit you, wouldn't it? A free run with the little bitch . . . and all *my* fault. How much have you spent on her so far? Vet's fees . . . a horsebox . . .' She took a shuddering breath. 'I suppose you thought you could carry on indefinitely as long as you gave me the odd sop—' she kicked at the carpet – 'like this. Do you make *her* wait? No, of course not. Even you aren't stupid enough to think a thirty-year-old tart would want you for your body.'

Julian gave a small laugh. 'You're so predictable, Ellie. Yack . . . yack . . . yack . . .' He worked his hand like a mouth. 'You can't leave it alone, can you? You have to be at someone's throat. But I'm not the bad guy here – *you* are – along with your fat little clone.' He gave a derisory snort. 'Tell me this, have you and Prue ever drawn breath long enough to ask yourselves if you're *right*? A moron could feed you a story and you'd believe it, as long as it confirmed one of your vicious little grievances.'

'*You* said James had got away with murder,' she shot back angrily. 'Jammy bastard, you called him . . . committed the perfect murder . . . locked Ailsa out in the cold and took barbiturates so he wouldn't have to listen to her whining away on the terrace.'

'Don't be an idiot,' he said. 'She could have walked down to the Lodge if she really couldn't get back in. Bob and Vera have keys.' His eyes narrowed. 'You need to worry about your brain, Ellie. Vera's the only person in this village with more resentments than you, and she's completely senile.' He examined her face for a moment, then gave a grunt of disbelief. 'I hope to God you haven't been getting your information from her, you silly bitch. She's had it in for James since he accused her of stealing. She was guilty as sin, but it hasn't stopped her bad-mouthing him. If you've been relying on anything she says, you really do need your head examined.'

Monroe watched catastrophe move a step closer in the woman's painted face. She dropped her eyes to her hands. 'I—' she broke off. 'How do you *know* so much?' she asked suddenly. 'Does the little tart tell you?'

Twenty-Four

LEO ANSWERED AT the first ring. 'Lizzie?' he whispered softly, as if he were in a public place and didn't want to be overheard.

Leo's mobile wouldn't have recognized Mark's, but it was an odd leap to associate an unknown number with his sister. 'No, it's Mark Ankerton.' He strained to hear noise in the background, but there was none. 'Why did you think it was Lizzie?'

'None of your business,' said the other man aggressively, immediately raising his voice. 'What do you want?'

'How about, Happy Christmas, Mark? How's my father getting on?'

'Fuck that.'

'Where are you?'

A small laugh. '*Wouldn't* you like to know?'

'Not particularly. It's Lizzie I'm after, as a matter of fact. I've been trying to raise her on her phone, but she isn't answering. Do you know where she is and if she's all right?'

'Fat lot you care.'

'I wouldn't be calling if I didn't.' He flicked a sidelong glance at James. 'Your father's decided to raise her allowance. He's also considering your position. He's not happy about the row you had the other day . . . but he wants to be fair.' He put a warning hand on James's arm as he felt the old man bristle with indignation.

Leo gave an angry laugh. 'You mean the row *he* had. I never said a word. He's completely senile, shouldn't be in control of anything.' He paused as if he expected Mark to answer. 'You're down there as usual, I suppose, pulling his blasted strings. You'd better know I've put a solicitor onto challenging the wills. The old man's obviously been shot for years – Ma, too, probably – and you drew up new ones without ever questioning their competence.'

Mark ignored the rant. 'I'm down here, yes. I didn't want him spending Christmas alone.' He tried again. 'Where are *you*?'

Another angry laugh. 'God, you're a patronizing bastard! *You* didn't want him to be alone. Do you know how sickening that sounds? Bloody Mark this . . . bloody Mark that . . . You *damn* well influenced my mother. Dad's dangled the estate over our heads since time immemorial, but Ma was always going to leave her money to us.'

Mark allowed his own anger to surface. 'If that's the kind of bullshit you're giving another solicitor you won't get far. You and Elizabeth were both shown copies of Ailsa's will. She wanted her money put to a useful purpose, and she didn't believe that giving it to you and Elizabeth would serve any purpose at all, except your rapid dissolution.'

'And who put the idea into her head?'

'You did when you sent Lizzie down to retrieve the Monets.'

'They're hers.'

'No, they're not. James's mother entrusted them to him until his death. Only then do they become Lizzie's. Ailsa was furious with you. She knew you'd take them and sell them . . . and it caused yet another screaming match with Lizzie. Frankly, you should be grateful Ailsa didn't close the door on you entirely by handing her fortune straight to charity. At least by passing it to your father, she gave you a second chance to prove yourselves.'

'*He's* never going to leave it to us. Becky said it was all going to Lizzie's love child.' A snort of derision. 'How is she? I presume you took her back . . . she said you would.'

Mark was caught off balance. 'Becky?'

'Of course Becky. How many exes do you have? You're welcome to her, by the way . . . and you can tell her I said so. She's a two-faced bitch—' another laugh – 'but you know that already. It served you right. All that Mandrake crap . . . you *owed* me one.'

Mark ran a thoughtful hand around his jawline. 'I haven't seen Becky since she left me for you. And, just for the record, I'd slit my throat before I took one of your cast-offs. Damaged goods don't interest me.'

'Fuck you!'

'Also for the record,' Mark went on, 'your mother wouldn't have left you a damn farthing if I *hadn't* influenced her. So how about thanking me for the fifty thousand?'

'I'd slit *my* throat first. So where *are* the Monets?'

Odd question. 'Where they always were.'

'No, they're not.'

'How do you know?'

'None of your business. Where are they?'

'Safe,' said Mark succinctly. 'Your mother didn't trust you not to have another go.'

'You mean *you* didn't trust me . . . Ma would never have thought of it herself.' Another pause. 'Have you really not seen her? She said she only had to crook her little finger and you'd come running.'

'Who?'

'Becky. I assumed you'd been mug enough to cover her debts. It put me in a good humour, as a matter of fact. I liked the idea of you being fleeced. She's got the bug something chronic.'

'What bug?'

'Work it out for yourself. Is Dad serious about upping Lizzie's allowance?'

Gambling . . .? 'Yes.'

'How much?'

'Five hundred a month.'

'Jesus!' Leo said disgustedly. 'It's a pittance. He hasn't put it up in two years. Couldn't you have pressed for a grand?'

'What's it to you? You won't get your hands on it.'

'I don't expect to.'

It would be a first, then, thought Mark cynically. 'It's better than nothing. If she's already blown her mother's fifty thousand, then it's a guaranteed fifty bottles of gin a month . . . but James won't give it to her unless she talks to him.'

'What about me?'

'I'm still negotiating.'

'Well, don't expect gratitude. Far as I'm concerned the best place for you is six feet under.'

'Fuck you!'

This time the laugh was amused. 'It's my only option at the moment.'

Mark smiled rather grudgingly at his end. 'Tell me about it,' he said dryly.

There was a second of mutual understanding. 'You've obviously twisted Dad's arm for some reason,' Leo said then. 'In normal circumstances he'd cut it off before he gave us any more money, so what's this call really about?'

'Do you know Eleanor Bartlett? Lives at Shenstead House.'

No answer.

'Have you ever spoken to her? Did you introduce her to Elizabeth?'

'Why do you want to know?'

Mark tossed a mental coin in his head, and opted for honesty. What did he have to lose? If Leo was involved, he already knew what was being said. *If he wasn't* . . . 'She's accusing James of incest – says he's the father of Lizzie's child – and she's claiming Lizzie gave her the information. She's been using the telephone to threaten him, which makes it a criminal offence, and I'm advising James to go to the police. Before we do that, we want to know if Eleanor Bartlett's telling the truth about hearing the slander from Lizzie.'

Leo's grin sounded in his voice. 'What makes you think it's slander?'

'Are you saying it isn't?'

'It depends what it's worth.'

'Nothing.'

'Wrong answer, my friend. Dad's reputation matters to him. Reopen negotiations on that basis and find out how much he's prepared to pay to protect it.'

Mark didn't reply immediately. 'What about your reputation, Leo? How much is yours worth?'

'I'm not the one with the problem.'

'You will be if I repeat this conversation to the police, plus the various allegations that Becky's making against you.'

415

'You mean the garbage about me forcing her to borrow money?' Leo said scathingly. 'It won't hold water. She's in hock up to her eyeballs on her own damn account.' A suspicious pause. 'You said you hadn't spoken to her.'

'I said I hadn't *seen* her. I rang her about half an hour ago. She was very forthcoming . . . none of it complimentary. She's accusing you of abuse . . . says she's frightened of you—'

'What the hell are you talking about?' Leo broke in angrily. 'I never laid a finger on the bitch.'

Mark glanced at James. 'Wrong victim. Try again.'

'What's that supposed to mean?'

'Work it out for yourself. You thought it was funny when it didn't apply to you, even suggested you could make money out of it.'

There was a long silence. 'Do you want to put that into words of one syllable?'

'In the circumstances, I wouldn't advise it.'

'Is Dad listening?'

'Yes.'

The line went dead immediately.

*

Nancy had received three conflicting messages in two hours. One from James in a deeply troubled voice saying that, much as he had enjoyed meeting her, he didn't feel it was appropriate in the circumstances for her to visit him again. A text from Mark, saying that James was lying, followed by another, talking about an emergency. Every attempt she'd made to call Mark's mobile had been diverted to voicemail, and her message to him had gone unanswered.

She had been concerned enough to abandon her unpacking and make the fifteen-minute drive from Bovington. Now she felt foolish. What circumstances? What emergency? Shenstead Manor was in darkness, and there was no response to her ringing of the bell. A fitful moon shone intermittent light on the facade but there was no sign of life anywhere. She peered through the glass panes of the library, looking for light under the closed door to the hall, but all she could see was her own reflection.

She felt uncomfortable. What would James think if he came back and found her peering through his windows? Worse, what was he thinking if he was watching her from the darkness inside? Whatever the circumstances he had referred to, presumably they still existed, and his message couldn't have been clearer. He didn't want to see her again. She remembered his tears of the morning, and her own embarrassment. She shouldn't have come.

She walked back to the Discovery and swung herself onto the driver's seat. She tried to convince herself they'd gone to the pub – it's what her parents would have done – but she wasn't persuaded. In the circumstances – *were these the circumstances?* – the arguments were all against them abandoning the house. Mark's messages. James's reclusive nature. His isolation. The proximity of the travellers. The trap set for James's dog. It didn't feel right.

With a sigh, she took a torch from the dashboard pocket and jumped to the ground again. She was going to regret this. She would put money on them sitting in the drawing room, pretending to be out; even more on seeing a terrible politeness cross their faces when she showed herself at the window. She walked round the side of the house and along the terrace.

The drawing-room lights were out, with the French windows bolted on the inside. She tested them, but they held firmly. She cupped her hand over her eyes to search the interior, but the muted glow of burning embers in the hearth showed the room to be empty. As a last lip service to duty, she stepped back to look at the rooms above, and a bad feeling prickled up her spine as she realized she was standing on or near the spot where Ailsa had died.

This was crazy, she thought angrily. A wild-goose chase, engineered by Mark bloody Ankerton, and ripples of superstitious fear because of a woman she'd never even met. But she could feel the weight of someone's gaze on the back of her neck . . . could even hear their breathing . . .

She whirled around, scything the torch beam in a wavering arc . . .

*

The older policeman hammered on the door of Fox's bus and showed little surprise when no one answered. He tested the handle to see if it was locked, then looked curiously towards Wolfie. Bella gave an irritated sigh. 'Stupid fucker,' she muttered under her breath, before gluing a smile to her face.

'Do you know where he is?' Barker asked.

She shook her head. 'I thought he was asleep. Like I said, he's doing the night shift on the barrier . . . that's why I started at the other end . . . didn't want to wake him earlier than I needed to.'

Barker switched his attention to Wolfie. 'What about you, son? Do you know where your dad is?'

The child shook his head.

'Does he always lock the bus when he goes away?'

A nod.

'Does he tell you when he's going?'

A frightened shake.

'So what are you supposed to do? Freeze to death? What happens if there's no one like Bella around?' He was angry, and it showed. 'What's in the bus that's more important than his kid?' he demanded of Bella. 'I think it's time we had a chat with this mysterious friend of yours. Where is he? What's he up to?'

Bella felt a rush of movement beside her. 'Oh,

great!' she said crossly, watching Wolfie take off into the wood as if the hounds of hell were behind him. 'Well done, Mr Barker. *Now* what are we gonna do? 'Coz you're right about one thing, darlin', his dad won't care if he freezes to death . . . and neither will anyone else.' She poked a finger at Barker's chest. 'And d'you wanna know *why*? I don't reckon he's been registered, so the poor little tyke don't *fucking* exist.'

*

Nancy's message came through as soon as Mark disconnected, and this time there was no discussion. He punched 999 into his mobile before lodging the handset into the car rest. 'Police,' he said curtly into the overhead microphone, before slamming the Lexus into a three-point turn.

*

It was dog-eat-dog, thought Monroe, as the Bartletts tore into each other. He had no sympathy for Eleanor, but Julian's sneering grated on his nerves. The dynamics of their relationship were relentlessly aggressive, and he began to wonder if some of Eleanor's problems could be laid at her husband's door. For all his urbanity, the man was a bully.

'You're making an idiot of yourself, Ellie. Someone's obviously fed you a piece of gossip, and now you're trying to manufacture a war out of it. Where did all this rubbish about a tart come from?'

She was too fired-up to think through her answers. 'The people at the Copse,' she snapped. 'They've been watching us.'

He gave a surprised laugh. 'The gyppos?'

'It's not funny. They know a lot about us . . . my name . . . what car you drive.'

'So? It's hardly secret information. They probably got it off a weekender. You need to cut down on the HRT and Botox injections, girl. They're frying your brain.'

She stamped her foot. 'I looked in your computer, Julian. It's all there. Emails to GS.'

Not any more, thought Monroe, as Julian gave an amused shrug. It was too easy for him. He was a step ahead of her every time. Monroe's mobile started to vibrate in his breast pocket. He retrieved it and listened to the request to attend an incident at the Manor. 'Will do. Three minutes.' He stood up. 'I shall want to talk to you again,' he told Eleanor. 'You, too, Mr Bartlett.'

Julian frowned. 'Why me? I'm not answerable for my wife's actions.'

'No, but you're answerable for your own, sir,' said Monroe, heading for the door.

*

421

The sound of tyres on gravel reached Nancy on the terrace, and, with relief, she turned her head towards it. Her sergeant was right. Imagination was a terrible thing. The shrubs and trees on the lawn made too many shadows, and each one resembled a dark, crouching figure. She recalled James's words of earlier. '*Which of us knows how brave he is until he stands alone?*' Well, now she knew.

She had remained rooted to the same spot for what seemed like hours, her back to the windows, torch beam flicking to and fro, unable to persuade herself to move. It was highly irrational. Her training and experience told her to return to her car, protecting her rear by hugging the contours of the house, but she couldn't bring herself to do it.

The climber-clad walls of the house held as many alarms for her as the garden. A thickly-growing, unpruned pyracantha, lethal with thorns, belled out between the drawing room and the library. Reason told her there was no one behind it. She had walked past it on her way to the French windows and would have seen a lurker in its shadow, but every time she held her breath she could hear breathing.

'Who's there?' she asked at one point.

The only answer was silence.

In periods of darkness when the moon was hidden by cloud she saw the glow of light behind the hazel clumps in the Copse. Once or twice, she heard laughter and muted conversation. She thought about calling out, but the wind was in the wrong direction. Any sound she made would be swallowed by the house behind her. She couldn't have done it, anyway. Like an ostrich with its head in the sand, fear had persuaded her that inertia was safer than provoking confrontation.

*

Fox raised his head, and the girl felt him do it. His senses, so much better attuned than hers, caught the reaction. A flash of agonizing awareness as something – a vibration in the air, perhaps – heightened her fear. She had no idea where he was but she knew her danger had increased. Like her grandmother, whose pleas to be let back inside had fallen on deaf ears but who had been too afraid to move because she believed death would come from the hammer and not from the insidious cold of the night.

He could smell fear . . .

. . . like a fox in a chicken run . . .

Twenty-Five

MARTIN BARKER acknowledged the radio message while his colleague retrieved a couple of torches from the boot. He propped one foot on the door sill and watched coated figures emerge from buses as Bella rousted everyone to look for Wolfie. 'Yes, I've got that . . . intruder, Shenstead Manor . . . mm . . . it's a fair bet . . . the farm's less than half a mile away. Yes, we've one traveller unaccounted for . . . I'd say so . . . same guy . . . Nancy Smith? No . . . Hang on.' He beckoned to Bella to join him. 'What's Fox's full name?'

She pulled a wry face as she approached. 'Fox Evil.'

'*Real* name, Bella.'

She shook her head. 'Sorry, Mr Barker. That's all he gave us. Even Wolfie don't know. I asked him.'

'Has he ever mentioned a Nancy Smith to you?'

She looked troubled. 'Yeah, he got me to phone her parents to find out where she was. I didn't tell him, though. I said she was up on Salisbury Plain. Who is she? What's his beef with her? She came to the bus earlier, but Fox don't know that.'

Barker shook his head, narrowing his eyes to focus on Fox's bus. 'He's driving an IVECO coach,' he said into the radio, 'cream and grey . . . battered condition . . . logo obscured . . . registration number: L324 UZP . . . Will do. We were heading there anyway. His kid took off in that direction about five minutes ago. Apparently the Colonel leaves his door open, so there's a possibility he's inside . . . Right. Tell Monroe we're on our way. Hang on,' he said again, as Bella laid an urgent hand on his arm.

'You wanna tell your blokes to be a bit wary, Mr Barker. He carries a cut-throat razor. Wolfie's shit-scared of him. His mum and brother vanished a while back, and the rest of us are pretty worried about it.'

'The kid said they were in Torquay.'

'Only 'coz he's frightened of you. He heard Fox tell us she went off with a pimp after they worked the fairgrounds in Devon. But Wolfie don't believe it and neither do we. Why would she take one kid and leave the other?'

Zadie came up behind her. 'Fox's been acting weird ever since we arrived. He sure as hell knows Shenstead. I reckon he's lived here.' She jerked her head at the Manor. 'That's the draw. Heads off towards it every time our backs are turned.'

Barker spoke into the radio. 'How much of that did you get . . .? Yes, cut-throat razor. Query, lived in Shenstead . . . query, missing woman and child . . . possibly Devon. Names?' he asked Bella, holding the radio towards her. 'Descriptions?'

'Vixen and Cub,' she said. 'Clones of Wolfie, both of them. Blond, blue-eyed, skinny. Sorry, Mr Barker, it's the best I can do. I only saw them the once. The mother was stoned and the kid looked about three though Wolfie says he's six.'

Barker put the radio to his ear again. 'I agree. Tell Monroe we'll meet him at the front.' He switched off and dropped the radio into its rest. 'OK, this is how we're going to play it. Forget the search for Wolfie, I want you all in Bella's bus with the door locked. If Fox comes back, don't approach him and don't try to stop him leaving.' He jotted a number into his notebook and tore off the sheet. 'Presumably you still have your mobile, Bella? Good. This is the quickest way to get hold of me.'

'What about Wolfie?'

'The sooner we flush out Fox, the sooner we can find him.'

'What if Fox comes back, and he's got the kid with him?'

'Same instructions. Avoid confrontation.' He put a hand on Bella's shoulder. 'I'm relying on you. Keep everyone away from him. It won't help Wolfie if his father thinks there's no way out.'

*

Wolfie crept towards Fox's tree, his eyes straining through the darkness in search of his father. In the first heat of flight, his one confused idea had been to find Fox and tell him to make the policemen go away, but second thoughts had prevailed when his stampeding feet set twigs snapping like gunshots. Fox would lash out with his razor if Wolfie's wild approach alerted people to where he was.

The child exerted tremendous will power to slow his panicky heart, then circled round with the stealth of a cat to come at Fox from the slope where the hazel coppices grew. His father would be looking towards the Manor, and wouldn't know Wolfie was there until he put his hand in his. It was a good plan, he thought. Fox couldn't take out the razor if Wolfie had hold of his hand, and he couldn't be cross if Wolfie didn't make a noise. He shied away from thoughts of the hammer. If he didn't think about it, it didn't exist.

But Fox wasn't by his tree, and fear gripped the child's heart anew. For all his father's failings, he had trusted him to keep the police away. What should Wolfie do now? Where could he go where he wouldn't be found? The cold was biting at his bones, and he had enough intelligence to know he couldn't stay outside. He thought about Lucky Fox, thought about his smiley face and his promise that his door was always open, thought about the size of the house and how easy it would be to hide in it. With nowhere else to go, he slid into the ha-ha and crawled up the other side onto the Manor lawn.

The darkness of the building didn't trouble him. Time meant nothing without a watch, and he assumed the old man and his friends were asleep. More concerned about the police than about what lay ahead of him, he scampered on all fours, negotiating his way via the shrubs and trees that dotted the park and keeping a watchful eye over his shoulder. Every so often, when he peeked at the terrace to take a bearing, a light winked in one of the downstairs windows. He thought it was inside the house and paid it no attention.

His shock was enormous then, when, fifty feet from the terrace, the clouds began to thin and he saw that it was a torch in the hand of a person. He could make out the bulk of a black-clad figure against the French windows, and the pale gleam of a face. He shrank into a trembling huddle behind a tree. He knew it wasn't Fox. He could always tell Fox's shape by his coat. Was it a policeman, put there to catch him?

The cold dampness of the ground seeped through his thin clothes, and a dreadful lethargy stole over him. If he went to sleep, he might never wake up. The thought appealed to him. It was better than being frightened all the time. He clung to the belief that, if his mother hadn't gone away, she would save him. But she *had* gone away, and his new, tiny voice of cynicism told him why. She cared more about herself and Cub than she did about Wolfie. He rested his head on his knees as tears spilled in hot streams down his frozen cheeks.

'Who's there?'

He recognized Nancy's voice and heard the fear in it, but he thought she was talking to someone else and didn't answer. Like her, he held his breath and waited for something to happen. The silence stretched interminably until nervous curiosity drove him to see if she was still there. He lay on his belly and squirmed around the base of the tree, and this time he saw his father.

Fox stood a few yards to Nancy's left, his head bent to stop the moonlight catching his face, the silhouette of his hooded coat unmistakable against the stone wall of the Manor. The only movement either of them made was Nancy's switching of the torch beam to and fro. With his infinite capacity to understand fear, Wolfie knew that she was aware of Fox's presence but couldn't see him. Every time the light flicked in his direction, it lit a bush on the front of the house and failed to show the shadow behind it.

Wolfie fixed his father with an intense gaze, trying to make out if he held his razor. He decided not. Nothing of Fox showed except the black shadow of his long hooded coat. There was no flash of blade, and the child relaxed slightly. Even if Fox was stroking it in his pocket, he was only truly dangerous when he held it in his hand. He didn't bother to question why his father should be stalking Nancy, guessing that her visit to the campsite had something to do with it. No one invaded Fox's territory without facing the consequences.

His sharp little ears picked up the sound of tyres on gravel, and he sensed Nancy's relief as she lowered the torch to light the flagstones at her feet. She shouldn't have done that, he thought, when Fox's only escape was to run past her to the back of the house. Panic-stricken, his eyes returned to his father, and he watched in alarm as Fox's hand slid from his pocket.

*

Monroe drew in beside Nancy's Discovery and left his motor running as he climbed out to look through her windows. The driver's door was unlocked and he hoisted himself onto the seat, leaning across to retrieve a canvas bag from the floor in front of the passenger seat. He thumb-punched numbers into his mobile, while he flicked through the contents. 'I've found a car,' he said. 'No sign of the owner but there's a wallet here – Visa in the name of Nancy Smith. The keys are in the ignition but I'd say the engine's been off for a while. There's precious little heat in here.' He peered through the windscreen. 'This side's certainly in darkness . . . no, the Colonel

430

sits in the room overlooking the terrace.' He frowned. 'Out? So who reported it? The solicitor?' He frowned. 'It sounds a bit flaky to me. How does the solicitor know this woman's in danger if he's halfway to Bovington? Who is she, anyway? Why the panic?' He was taken aback by the answer. 'The Colonel's *granddaughter*? My God!' He glanced back up the drive as he heard the sound of an approaching car. 'No, mate, I've no idea what's going on . . .'

*

'You shouldn't have told them who Nancy was,' said James angrily. 'Have you no sense? It'll be all over the newspapers tomorrow.'

Mark ignored him. 'Leo called her Lizzie's love child,' he said, accelerating to ninety on a straight piece of road. 'Is that how he usually refers to her? I'd have thought "bastard" was more in his line.'

James closed his eyes as they approached the bend before Shenstead Farm at high speed. 'He never refers to her as anything. It's not something we discuss. Never have done. I wish you'd concentrate on your driving.'

Again Mark ignored him. 'Whose idea was that?'

'Nobody's,' said James irritably. 'At the time it seemed no different from an abortion . . . and you don't revisit abortions over the lunch table.'

'I thought you and Ailsa had a row about it.'

'All the more reason for the matter to be closed. The adoption had happened. Nothing I said or did could reverse the decision.' He braced his hands against the dashboard as the hedgerow slapped the side of the car.

'Why did you feel so strongly about it?'

'Because I wouldn't give a dog away to a total stranger, Mark. Certainly not a child. She was a Lockyer-Fox. We had a responsibility to her. You really are going much too fast.'

'Stop bellyaching. So why did Ailsa give her away?'

James sighed. 'Because she couldn't think what else to do. She knew Elizabeth would neglect the baby if she forced her to acknowledge it, and Ailsa could hardly pass it off as her own.'

'What other option was there?'

'Admit our daughter had made a mistake and take responsibility ourselves. Of course, it's easy to be wise with hindsight. I don't blame Ailsa. I blame myself. She thought my views were so rigid that it wasn't worth consulting me.' Another sigh. 'We all wish we'd acted differently, Mark. Ailsa assumed Elizabeth would have other children – Leo, too. It was a terrible shock when they didn't.'

Mark slowed as a car's headlamps shone out from the Copse. He glanced in briefly as they passed, but couldn't see beyond the lights. 'Did Lizzie ever say who the father was?'

432

'No,' said the old man dryly. 'I don't think she knew herself.'

'Are you sure Leo's never had any kids?'

'Absolutely sure.'

Mark dropped down a gear as they approached the Manor drive, watching the lights of the other car swing out behind him. 'Why? He's been with a lot of women, James. By the law of averages he should have had at least one mistake.'

'We'd have heard about it,' said the old man even more dryly. 'He'd have enjoyed parading his bastards about the house, particularly after Ailsa took up the cause of child welfare. He'd have used them as leverage to get money out of her.'

Mark swung through the gate. 'That's pretty sad, then,' he said. 'It sounds to me as if the poor guy's firing blanks.'

*

Monroe reached through his window to kill his engine as the two cars drew to a halt beside him. He opened the passenger door of the Lexus and leaned forward to look into the interior. 'Colonel Lockyer-Fox, Mr Ankerton,' he said, 'we've met before. DS Monroe.'

Mark switched off his ignition and climbed out the other side. 'I remember. Have you found her? Is she all right?'

'I've only just arrived myself, sir,' said Monroe, putting a hand under James's elbow to help him to stand. 'She must be close. She's left her bag and keys behind.'

Silence fell abruptly as Barker's engine stilled.

*

Wolfie's first reaction was to cover his eyes with his hands. What he didn't see, he couldn't worry about. None of this was his fault. It was *Bella's* fault. *She* had done something bad by making the phone call for Fox. *She* had let the police onto the campsite. *She* had shown them Fox wasn't there.

But he liked Bella, and in his heart he knew that the only reason he wanted to blame her was to feel better about himself. Somewhere in his mind, in fragments of memory that he couldn't retain, he thought he knew what had happened to his mother and Cub. He couldn't explain it. Sometimes it seemed like bits of a dream. Other times a half-forgotten movie. But he was afraid it was real, and it consumed him with guilt because he knew he should have done something to help, and hadn't.

It was the same now.

*

Nancy toyed with crying out. The car had stopped, but she could still hear the purr of its motor. It had to be James and Mark – *who else could it be?* –

434

but why hadn't they come into the house and turned on the lights? She kept telling herself to keep calm, but paranoia was jumbling all sense in her head. Supposing it wasn't James and Mark? Supposing her screams provoked a reaction? Supposing no one came? Supposing . . .

Oh God!

*

Fox was cursing her in his head for remaining motionless. He might *feel* her, but he couldn't see her any more than she could see him, and if he moved first it was she who would hold the advantage. Was she brave enough – *or frightened enough* – to strike out? The reflected torchlight on the flagstones told him nothing except that the hand that held it was steady. And that worried him.

It suggested a stronger adversary than he was used to . . .

*

All three of them heard the sound of more cars arriving. They drove in at speed, churning the gravel as they slewed to a halt. With a sob of fear, knowing his father wouldn't wait any longer, Wolfie pushed himself to his feet and raced towards the terrace with all his turmoil and anguish for his lost mother pouring out in a high-pitched '*NO-O-O!*'

Twenty-Six

AFTERWARDS, WHEN SHE had time to think about it, Nancy wondered how many adrenalin rushes a person could tolerate before their legs gave way. She felt she was bathing in the stuff, but when the child started screaming her glands went into over-drive.

The whole incident remained sharp in her memory, as if the stimulus of Wolfie's cry cleared her brain for action. She remembered feeling calm, remembered waiting for the other person to react first, remembered switching off her torch because she didn't need it any more. She knew where he was now because he swore under his breath as the wailed 'No' reached him, and in the fraction of a second that it took him to move, she sorted and computed enough information to predict what he would do.

More than one car suggested police. Someone had alerted them. There were lights at the encampment. The cry was a child's. Only one child had been scared. The psycho's son. This was the psycho. Fox. He carried a razor. His only route to safety was towards the parkland and the valley beyond. Without wheels he'd be trapped between Shenstead and the sea. He needed a guarantee of free passage. The only guarantee was a hostage.

She began to move as soon as he did, cutting off his angled run towards the child's voice. With a shorter distance to cover – almost as if it were preordained – she caught him by Ailsa's last resting place in front of the sundial. His left side was towards her and she scanned for the flash of a blade in his hand. It looked empty and she gambled that he was right-handed. With a backhand swing of her torch, she chopped at his throat before bringing her left hand down in a slamming slice on his right forearm as he turned towards her. Something metal clattered to the flagstones.

'Bitch,' he snarled, backing away.

She flicked on the torch, blinding him. 'You touch the kid and I'll fucking cripple you,' she snarled back, locating the razor with her foot and sweeping it behind her against the sundial plinth. She raised her voice. 'Stay away, friend, and stay quiet!' she called to the child. 'I don't want you hurt. I'll give your dad a chance to get away as long as you don't come any closer.'

Something like amusement flickered briefly in Fox's eyes as Wolfie fell silent. 'Get over here, Wolfie. Now!'

No answer.

'You hear me? *Now!* Do you want me to smash the bitch's face?'

Wolfie's terrified voice stuttered out from a few yards away. 'He k-keeps a hammer in his p-pocket. He h-hit m-my m-mum with it.'

The warning came too late. Nancy saw only a blur of movement as the hammer, already in his hand, came scything from behind his back in an upward curve towards her jaw.

*

The despairing high-pitched 'No-o-o' stopped almost as soon as it began, giving the men at the front no time to register where it came from. 'Which way?' Monroe demanded.

Barker switched on his torch. 'The side nearest the Copse,' he said. 'It sounded like a kid.'

'The terrace,' said James. 'It's his killing ground.'

Mark made straight for the Discovery. 'Let's see him outrun this bastard,' he said, firing the engine and roaring backwards.

*

Nancy could only turn away and raise her right arm to take the impact. The force of the blow caught her below the elbow, sending pain shooting to the top of her skull. She staggered backwards against the sundial, losing her footing as the plinth unbalanced her. She twisted sideways to avoid being spread-eagled across the dial, and the torch slid from her numbed fingers, dropping to the flagstones and skittering away from her. As she hit the ground with a jarring thump and rolled frantically to avoid another hammer blow, she caught sight of the child's white-blond hair, lit up like a homing beacon against the black backdrop of the parkland. *Ah, shit!* What cruel fate had pointed the torch in that direction?

She scrabbled behind the sundial, and heaved herself into a crouch. *Keep his attention . . . keep him talking . . .* 'Do you know who I am?' she asked, as Fox dropped into a similar crouch, transferring the hammer to his right hand.

'Lizzie's little bastard.'

With her left hand, she felt round the plinth for the razor. 'Think again, Fox. I'm your worst nightmare. A woman who fights back.' Her straining fingers found the bone handle and folded it into her palm. 'Let's see how you do against a soldier.'

He brought the hammer round in a pile-driving smash, but it was a predictable move and she was ready for it. She flicked the razor up and slashed at his forearm as she thrust to her right to keep the sundial between herself and him. 'That was for my grandmother, fucker.' He gave a grunt of pain and shook the hood off his face as if it were stifling him. In the backwash of the torchlight, she saw that his face was glistening with sweat. 'You're not used to this, are you? Is that why you pick on kids and old ladies?' He took another wild swipe, and this time she sliced at his wrist. 'That was for Wolfie's mum. What did you do to her? Why's he so scared?'

He dropped the hammer and clutched at his wrist, and from the front of the house they heard the Discovery's engine roar to life. She saw a momentary indecision in his pale eyes before he went berserk, charging her down like a maddened bull. She reacted instinctively, flinging the razor away, and curling into a tight ball to present the smallest possible target. It was brief and violent – an orgy of kicking – with Nancy the writhing, squirming punchbag as Fox's boots hit their target every time.

He spoke in breathy grunts. 'Ask who I am next time . . . think I cared about your grandmother? . . . the bitch owed me . . .'

She would have surrendered if her Discovery's headlights hadn't split the night and sent Fox running for cover.

*

She lay on her back on the ground, staring at the wispy moonlight, thinking that every bone in her body was broken. Little fingers felt her face. 'Are you dead?' asked Wolfie, kneeling beside her.

'Absolutely not.' She smiled up at him, seeing him clearly in the Discovery's headlamps. 'You're a brave kid, Wolfie. How's it going with you, friend?'

'Not so good,' he said, his mouth wobbling. 'I

ain't dead, but I reckon my mum is 'n' I dunno what to do. What's gonna happen to me?'

They heard a car door slam and running feet. Mark loomed over them in the Discovery headlamps. 'Oh, *shit*! Are you all right?'

'Fine. Just having a little lie-down.' Nancy flexed her left hand and put it gingerly round Wolfie's waist. 'It's the cavalry,' she told him. 'They're always the last to arrive. *No*,' she said firmly as Mark reached down to lift the child away from her. 'Leave us be for the moment.' She listened to more feet pounding down the terrace. 'I *mean* it, Mark. Do *not* interfere, and don't let anyone else interfere until I'm ready.'

'You're bleeding.'

'Not my blood, I'm just winded.' She stared up into his anxious eyes. 'I need to talk to Wolfie in private. *Please*,' she said. 'I walked away when you asked. Do the same for me.'

He nodded immediately and strode up to meet the policemen, waving his arms to slow them down. Inside the house the lights came on as James moved from room to room.

Nancy drew Wolfie closer, feeling his bones through his inadequate clothing. She had absolutely no idea what to say to him. She didn't know if Fox was his father or stepfather, if his mother was dead or if he just thought she was dead, where he came from, if he had relatives. Indeed, she had no better idea than he what would happen to him, although

she guessed he would be taken into care and processed through the foster system while his circumstances were investigated. She didn't think it would
help to tell him that, however. What comfort was
there for anyone in abstract ideas?

'I'll tell you how it works in the army,' she
said. 'Everyone looks after everyone else. We call it
watching each other's backs. Do you know that
expression?'

Wolfie nodded.

'Right, well, when someone watches your back so
well that they save your life, then it becomes a debt,
and you have to do the same for them. Do you
understand?'

'Like the black geezer in *Robin Hood: Prince of
Thieves*?'

She smiled. 'That's it. You're Robin Hood, and
I'm the black geezer. You saved my life, so now I
have to save yours.'

He shook his head anxiously. 'But that ain't what
I'm scared of. I don't reckon the cops're gonna
kill me. I just reckon they're gonna be real angry
about my Mum and Cub . . . 'n' *everything*.' He
took a shuddering breath. ' 'N' they'll send me to
strangers . . . 'n' I'll be all alone.'

She squeezed his waist. 'I know. It's pretty frightening. I'd be afraid, too. So why don't I pay off my
debt by making sure the police don't do anything

until you tell me you feel safe? Does that count as saving your life?'

The child thought about it. 'I guess. How you gonna do it?'

'First I'm going to wriggle a bit to find out if everything's still working—' her legs seemed to be, but her right arm was numb from the elbow down – 'then you're going to grab this hand—' she squeezed his waist again – 'and keep holding it till you reckon it's OK to let go. How does that sound?'

Like all children, he was logical. 'What happens if I never let go?'

'We'll have to get married,' she said with a small laugh, wincing as pain ripped up her side. The bastard had broken a rib.

*

Ivo was trying to persuade the others to leave. 'Wise up,' he said. 'None of us knows what's been going on, but you can bet your lives the cops won't believe that. If we're lucky, we'll spend twenty-four hours at the flaming nick while they hit us with every unsolved crime in Dorset . . . if we're not, they'll take our kids off us and bang us up for being accessories to whatever Fox has done. We should take off now. Leave the bastard to face the firing squad alone.'

'What do you think?' Zadie asked Bella.

The big woman twisted a roll-up between her

stubby fingers and licked the paper. 'I think we should stay put and follow Mr Barker's instructions.'

Ivo surged to his feet. 'It's not your call,' he said aggressively. 'You made that deal without asking the rest of us. I say we go . . . pack up now before we end up in deeper shit than we're in already. I'm a hundred per cent sure the cops didn't take anyone's registration except Fox's, so, barring Bella, who he knows from before, he's only got vague descriptions to go on.'

'What about Bella?' asked Gray.

'She can talk her way out of it when they catch up with her . . . say she was scared for her kids and didn't need the aggro. It's the truth. None of us needs the fucking aggro.'

They all looked at Bella. 'Well?' Zadie asked.

'Can't see the point,' she said mildly, taking some heat from the argument. 'For a kick-off, we've all got stuff outside that needs bringing in – my kids' bikes for one – and I don't fancy being caught in the open if Fox comes back.'

'Safety in numbers,' said Ivo, pacing restlessly in the aisle. 'If we're all in the open, there'll be too many targets. But we need to move now. The longer we wait, the worse our chances.' He jerked his chin at Gray. 'You know damn well what's gonna happen. We'll have the busies on our backs for days. It'll be the kids taking the brunt of it, and who needs that?'

Gray looked uncertainly towards his wife. 'What do you think?'

'Maybe,' said Zadie, with an apologetic shrug for Bella.

'Maybe nothing,' she said bluntly, lighting her cigarette and taking a satisfying inhalation. 'I told Mr Barker I'd keep you in, and that's what I'm gonna do.' She eyed Ivo thoughtfully through the smoke. 'Looks to me like you're the one brought the fuzz down on our heads, and now you're trying to stampede the rest of us to get yourself off the hook.'

'How do you make that out?'

She narrowed her eyes. 'I ain't got nothing to hide . . . 'n' I'm fucked if I'm leaving till I know Wolfie's OK. Fox don't worry me, long as I'm in my bus . . . Mr Barker don't worry me neither. *You* fucking do, though. What're you running from, 'n' what's this "crimes in Dorset" crap, eh? Far as I'm concerned, Fox is a murdering bastard – probably a thief to boot – but he ain't stupid. I gave him more than enough time to get back to his bus – but all the time in the world wouldn't've helped if he didn't know he needed to. Reckon it was you up at the farm after bits of machinery to nick. It's what you do, ain't it? You've got enough equipment in your luggage compartment to start a fucking garden centre, mate. I've seen it.'

'That's bullshit.'

445

She blew a stream of smoke towards the ceiling. 'Don't think so. Maybe you was planning to give this project a whirl when you joined, but you sure as hell gave up on it by lunchtime. You was always gonna scarper tomorrow . . . so I reckon you went on the prowl looking to compensate yourself for wasted time—' she shrugged – ''n' now you're wetting yourself in case Fox comes back and beats the shit out of you for fouling his patch. Whatever he's up to, he ain't gonna be pleased to have cops crawling all over the place.'

'You're in the same boat. You told your copper friend about Vixen and Cub. You think Fox is going to be any more pleased about that?'

'Wouldn't think so.'

'Then use some sense and get out while the going's good. The police won't find him. He'll go to ground somewhere, then come after us.'

'He won't take us on in here – assuming he can break the door down, which I doubt.' She smiled slightly. 'It won't help *you*, mind. Either way, some-one's gonna do you. If it ain't Fox, it'll be Mr Barker when people start reporting their hedge trimmers stolen . . . but that's *your* problem, mate. One thing's for sure, I don't plan to get my throat slit 'coz you're too scared to go outside on your own. You wanna save your arse, save it yourself, but don't try 'n' pretend you're doing the rest of us a favour. 'N' don't take your kids and your lady out there, neither,' she added, glancing at the introvert woman who claimed to be Ivo's wife. 'She can't handle Fox on her own if you decide to leg it.'

He launched a frustrated kick at one of her seats. 'Maybe Fox isn't the only one who wants to slit your throat, you fat bitch. You're too fucking friendly with the cops. Who's to say it wasn't you brought them out here? You've been carrying on about Wolfie's mum most of the day. It wouldn't surprise me if you decided to do something about it.'

She shook her head. 'Not me . . .'n' I wouldn't be pointing the finger at someone else if had.' She jabbed her cigarette at him. 'I ain't scared of Fox. He's no different from any other two-bit con artist . . . throws his weight around, hoping to get his own way . . . and when it all goes pear-shaped looks for someone else to blame . . . usually a woman. Remind you of anyone, you little fucker?'

'You've got a big mouth, Bella. Someone should have slapped you down a long time ago.'

'Yeah . . . right. You wanna try?' She shook her head disdainfully. 'Nah. Didn't think so. Maybe it's a good thing this project's dead in the water. I'd go mad with a pathetic little weasel like you for a neighbour.'

*

Fox's trail went cold at the end of the terrace. Barker and Wyatt cast around for footprints on the lawn but, even after James had switched on the outside lights, few of which were working, there was nothing to indicate which direction he'd taken. Spots of blood showed here and there on the flagstones but if they continued on the grass they were black on black in the dark. Reluctant to confuse the trail with their own footprints, they abandoned the search and returned to the French windows.

There was a heated debate going on inside the drawing room between Monroe and Mark Ankerton, with Mark Ankerton backed up against the door to the hall and both men wielding their forefingers like clubs. 'No, I'm sorry, sergeant. Captain Smith has made it abundantly clear that she does not wish to go to hospital, nor is she ready at the moment to answer questions about the incident on Colonel Lockyer-Fox's terrace. As her lawyer, I insist that her views are respected.'

'For Christ's sake, man,' Monroe protested, 'she's got blood all over her face, and her arm's obviously broken. It's more than my job's worth to have Dorset police sued because I refused to call an ambulance.'

Mark ignored him. 'In addition, as Wolfie's lawyer, I am advising him that he should, under no circumstances, answer questions until the legal guidelines regarding the interrogation of children are implemented – principally, a full understanding of

what he's being questioned about, absence of pressure, unalarming surroundings and the presence of an
adult he knows and trusts.'

'I object to the language you're using, sir. There's
no question of interrogation. I merely want to satisfy
myself that he's all right.'

Martin stepped through the window. 'What's
going on?' he demanded.

Monroe gave an angry sigh. 'The girl and the boy
have disappeared with the Colonel, and Mr Ankerton's refusing to let me call an ambulance or give me
access to them.'

'It'll be the kid,' said Barker, reaching for the
telephone on the bureau. 'He's terrified of the police.
That's why he took off earlier when we were searching the campsite. I'd leave them to it, if I were you.
We don't want him vanishing again with his father
roaming around outside.' He nodded to Ankerton.
'May I use the phone?'

'It's disconnected. I'll plug it in if Mr Monroe
agrees to stay away from my clients.'

Barker yanked at the lead. 'Do it,' he ordered
Monroe, 'or it'll be you carrying the can if this
bastard goes to ground in someone's house and takes
hostages.' He tossed his mobile to him. 'If that rings,
answer it. It'll be a woman called Bella Preston. As
for you, sir,' he told Mark, as the younger man went
down on all fours to push in the jack plug, 'I suggest

449

you lock the Colonel and your clients into a bedroom until I give you the all-clear. I don't trust this man not to come back.'

*

In view of the darkness, the fact that the valley was unlit and there were too many natural hiding places to justify calling out the police helicopter, a decision was taken to abandon the search for Fox until daybreak. Instead, roadblocks were erected on either side of Shenstead Valley and the occupants of the village and the three outlying farms were given the choice of whether they wished to remain inside their homes or be escorted to temporary accommodation elsewhere.

The tenant farmers and their families chose to remain on site with shotguns levelled at their front doors. The Woodgates and their children went to Stephen's mother in Dorchester, while the banker's twin sons and their girlfriends, bored with household chores, happily accepted hotel rooms for the night. The two commercial rents returned hotfoot to London with demands for compensation ringing in police ears. It was a disgrace. They hadn't come to Dorset on holiday to be terrorized by maniacs.

Prue Weldon threw a fit and refused to leave or be left alone, clinging to Martin Barker's hand like a limpet and begging him to make her husband come home. This he succeeded in doing by impressing on

Dick that the police did not have the manpower to protect unoccupied buildings. Drunk as a skunk, he was driven back to Shenstead by Jack and Belinda who decided to stay after he loaded his shotgun and fired it at Prue's chicken casserole.

Surprisingly, the Bartletts were unanimous in their decision to stay, both insisting that there was too much of value in their house to leave it undefended. Eleanor was convinced her rooms would be vandalized – 'people like that defecate on the carpets and urinate on the walls' – and Julian feared for his cellar – 'there's a fortune in wine down there.' They were advised to go upstairs and stay in one room with the door barricaded, but from the way Julian started prowling the hall it seemed doubtful they would take the advice.

As for Vera Dawson, she agreed to be taken up to the Manor House to wait with the Colonel and Mr Ankerton. Bob was away fishing, she told the two young policemen, as she sucked and mumbled her way into an overcoat before locking the front door. They assured her he'd be stopped at one of the roadblocks when he came back and brought to the Manor to join her. She tapped their hands flirtatiously. Bob would like that, she told them with a happy little smile. He worried about his old lady. She still had her marbles, of course, but her memory wasn't as good as it used to be.

The problem of what to do with the travellers was

a difficult one. Police activity around Fox's bus was intense, and the travellers weren't inclined to stand idly by while the vehicle was searched. The Alsatians barked non-stop, and the children kept escaping their parents' clutches. There were also persistent demands to be allowed to leave on the basis that Bella was the only one who knew anything about Fox. Unimpressed, the police decided to escort them in convoy to a site outside Dorchester where they could be questioned the following day.

This rapidly became impossible after one of their number refused to wait his turn or follow instructions, and jammed the exit when his coach became bogged down in the softening ground. Furious, Barker ordered him and his family back to Bella's bus while he worked out another strategy for ensuring the safety of nine adults and fourteen children without a vehicle large enough to take them out of the valley.

Twenty-Seven

BELLA, MAGNIFICENT IN purple, shepherded her three daughters through the front door and stuck out a hand towards James. 'Ta, mister,' she said. 'I've told 'em all to keep their fingers to themselves so you won't get no trouble.' She flicked a sideways glance at Ivo. 'That's right, ain't it, Ivo?'

'Shut your mouth, Bella.'

She ignored him. 'Mr Barker tells me you've got Wolfie,' she went on, squeezing James's fingers like sausages. 'How's he doing?'

Overwhelmed, James patted her hand. 'He's fine, my dear. At the moment we can't prize him away from my granddaughter. They're upstairs in one of the bedrooms. I believe she's reading him *Aesop's Fables*.'

'Poor little bleeder. He's got this thing about cops . . . took off like a fucking rocket when Mr Barker asked him questions. I kept telling him not to be worried, but it didn't do no good. Can I see him? Him and me are friends. Might make him feel better if he knows I ain't abandoned him.'

James looked to his solicitor for rescue. 'What do you think, Mark? Will Wolfie swap Nancy for Bella? It might persuade Nancy to go to hospital.'

But Mark was under assault from the threadbare Alsatians that were sniffing around his trouser legs. 'Perhaps we could put them in the scullery,' he suggested.

'They'll bark non-stop,' Zadie warned. 'They don't like being away from the kids. Here,' she said giving the leads to one of her sons. 'Watch they don't lift their legs anywhere, and keep 'em off the sofas. And *you*,' she said, cuffing another son round the back of his head, 'don't go breaking things.'

Martin Barker, coming in behind her, suppressed a smile. 'This is very good of you, sir,' he told James. 'I'm leaving Sean Wyatt in charge. If everyone stays in the same room, it'll be easier to keep track.'

'Where do you suggest?'

'The kitchen?'

James looked at the sea of faces. 'But the children look so tired. Wouldn't it be better to put them to bed? We have enough rooms in all conscience.'

Martin Barker looked at Mark, tilted his chin towards the pieces of silver on a Chippendale table by the door, and gave a small shake of his head. 'The *kitchen*, James,' Mark said firmly. 'There's food in the freezer. Let's eat first and see how things go, eh? I don't know about anyone else, but I'm starving. How's Vera on the cooking front?'

'Terrible.'

'I'll do it,' said Bella, pushing her girls between Ivo and the Chippendale table as his fingers strayed towards a cigarette case. 'My friend here can peel the potatoes.' She gripped James firmly by the arm and drew him along with her. 'What's wrong with Nancy then? Did that fucker Fox hurt her?'

*

Wolfie pinched Nancy frantically as Vera Dawson peered through the gap in the door. 'She's back . . . she's back,' he whispered into her ear.

Nancy broke off from 'Androcles and the Lion' with a whistle of pain. 'Hoo-oosh!' She was sitting in an armchair in Mark's bedroom with Wolfie on her lap and, every time the child moved her rib moved with him, setting off sympathetic tremors in her right arm. She'd had a vain hope that if she read to him, he'd fall asleep, but the old woman wouldn't leave them alone, and Wolfie wriggled in panic every time he saw her.

Nancy assumed it was Mrs Dawson's mumbling and muttering that frightened him, otherwise it was a bizarre reaction to someone he didn't know. His alarm was so powerful that she could feel him trembling. She eased him on her lap, and frowned at the old woman. What on earth was the silly old thing's problem? Nancy had asked her several times to go downstairs, but she seemed drawn to stare at them as if they were freaks in the circus, and Nancy was beginning to feel the same aversion towards her as the child did.

'She won't hurt you,' she whispered in Wolfie's ear. 'She's old, that's all.'

But he shook his head and clung to her in desperation.

Mystified, Nancy abandoned courtesy and issued an order. 'Shut the door and go away, Mrs Dawson,' she said sharply. 'If you don't, I'll phone Mr Ankerton and tell him you're annoying us.'

The old woman came into the room. 'There's no telephone in here, miss.'

Oh, for God's sake! 'Let go for a moment,' she told Wolfie. 'I need to get at my mobile.' She felt in her fleece pocket, breathing shallowly as Wolfie pressed against her. 'OK, back as we were. Do you know how to work one of these? Good man. The code to unlock it is 5378. Now scroll through the numbers till you come to Mark Ankerton then press call and hold it to my mouth.'

She raised a booted foot as Vera came within striking range. 'I'm perfectly serious about wanting you to leave, Mrs Dawson. You're frightening the child. Please do not come any closer.'

'You won't hit an old woman. It's only Bob hits old women.'

'I don't need to hit you, Mrs Dawson, I only need to push you over. I don't particularly want to, but I will if you force me. Do you understand what I'm saying?'

Vera kept her distance. 'I'm not stupid,' she muttered. 'I've still got my marbles.'

'It's ringing,' said Wolfie, pressing the mobile to Nancy's mouth.

She heard it click through to voicemail. *Jesus wept!* Did the bastard *ever* answer his sodding phone? *Ah, well!* 'Mark!' she said peremptorily. 'Get your arse up here, mate. Mrs Dawson's frightening Wolfie, and I can't get her to go away.' She bared her teeth at the old woman. 'Yes, by force if necessary. She seems to be caught in a mental loop that makes her forget she's supposed to be downstairs with you and James. I'll tell her now.' She switched off. 'Colonel Lockyer-Fox wants you in the drawing room immediately, Mrs Dawson. Mr Ankerton says he's angry that you're not there already.'

The old woman tittered. 'He's always angry . . . got a bad temper has the Colonel. Just like my Bob. But don't you worry, they all get their comeuppance in the end.' She moved to the bedside table and picked up a book that Mark was reading. 'Do you like Mr Ankerton, Miss?'

Nancy lowered her foot, but didn't answer.

'You shouldn't. He's stolen your mother's money . . . your uncle's, too. And all because your grandma was so taken with him . . . fawned all over him every time he came to the house . . . called him Mandrake and flirted with him like a silly little girl. She'd have left it all to him if she hadn't died.'

It was a fluent piece of speech and Nancy wondered how demented she really was. 'That's nonsense, Mrs Dawson. Mrs Lockyer-Fox changed her will months before she died, and the main beneficiary was her husband. It was in the newspapers.'

Contradiction seemed to upset her. She looked lost for a moment, as if something she relied on had been knocked away. 'I know what I know.'

'Then you don't know very much. Now, will you please leave this room?'

'You can't tell me what to do. This isn't your house.' She dropped the book onto the bed. 'You're like the Colonel and the missus . . . Do this . . . do that. You're a servant, Vera. Don't go poking your nose in where it isn't wanted. I've been a drudge and a slave all my life—' she stamped her foot – 'not for much longer, though, not if my boy has his way. Is that why you've come? To take the house from your Ma and your Uncle Leo?'

Nancy wondered who 'her boy' was and how she'd guessed who Nancy was when James had made a point of introducing her only as a friend of Mark's. 'You're confusing me with someone else, Mrs Dawson. My mother lives in Herefordshire and I don't have an uncle. The only reason I'm here is because I'm a friend of Mr Ankerton's.'

The woman wagged a gnarled finger. 'I know who you are. I was here when you were born. You're Lizzie's little bastard.'

It was an echo of what Fox had called her, and Nancy felt the flesh creep on the back of her neck. 'We're going downstairs,' she told Wolfie abruptly. 'Hop off, and give me a tug out of the chair. OK?'

He shifted slightly as if he were going to do it, but Vera scuttled towards the door, slamming it closed, and he shrank back against Nancy again. 'He's not yours to take,' she hissed. 'Be a good girl, now, and give him to his gran. His daddy's waiting for him.'

Oh Christ! She felt Wolfie's arms slide round her neck in a strangulation hold. 'It's OK, sweetheart,' she told him urgently. '*Trust* me, Wolfie. I said I'd look after you and I will . . . but you must give me room to breathe.' She took a lungful of air as his arms relaxed and raised her boot again. 'Don't tempt me, Mrs Dawson. I'll kick the shit out of you the minute you come within range. Do you have enough marbles left to understand *that*, you senile old bitch?'

'You're like the missus. Think you can say what you like to poor old Vera.'

Nancy lowered her foot again and exerted all her strength to move forward in the chair. 'Poor old Vera, my arse,' she snapped. 'What did you do to Wolfie? Why is he so frightened of you?'

'Taught him some manners when he was littl'un.'
A strange little smile hovered on her lips. 'He had
pretty little brown curls then, just like his daddy.'

'I didn't! I didn't!' cried Wolfie hysterically, clinging to Nancy. 'I ain't never had brown hair. My
mum said I'se always like this.'

Vera's mouth started working furiously. 'Don't
you disobey your gran. You do as you're told. Vera
knows what's what. Vera's still got her marbles.'

'She ain't my gran,' Wolfie whispered urgently to
Nancy. 'I ain't never seen her before . . . I'se only
scared of nasty people . . .'n' she's nasty 'coz her
smiley lines are upside down.'

Nancy examined the old woman's face. Wolfie was
right, she thought in surprise. Every line turned
downwards, as if resentment had dragged trenches in
the skin. 'It's OK,' she soothed, 'I'm not going to
let her take you.' She raised her voice. 'You're very
confused, Mrs Dawson. This isn't your grandson.'

The old woman smacked her lips. 'I know what's
what.'

*No, you don't, you stupid bitch . . . you're round the
fucking twist . . .* 'Then tell me your grandson's
name. Tell me your son's name.'

It was computer overload. 'You're just like *her* . . .
but I have rights . . . though you wouldn't think it
the way I'm treated. Do this . . . do that . . . Who
cares about poor old Vera except her darling boy?
You put your feet up, Ma, he says. *I'll* see you

right.' She pointed an angry finger at Nancy. 'But look what precious Lizzie did. She was a whore and a thief . . . and everything forgiven and forgotten because she was a Lockyer-Fox. What about Vera's baby? Was he forgiven? No.' She turned her hands into fists and smacked them impotently against each other. 'What about Vera? Was she forgiven? Oh, no! Bob had to know *Vera* was a thief. Is that right?'

Even if Nancy had known what she was talking about, she recognized that there was nothing to be gained by agreeing. Far better to keep her off balance by taunting her than show an ounce of sympathy for her problems, whatever they were. At least while she talked, she was keeping her distance. 'You really *are* senile,' she said contemptuously. 'Why should a thief be forgiven? You should be in prison along with your murderous son – assuming Fox is your son, which I doubt, as you can't even give me his name.'

'*He* didn't murder her,' she hissed, 'never touched her. Didn't need to when she brought it on herself with her vicious tongue . . . accusing *me* of ruining her daughter. More like her daughter ruined my boy . . . *that's* nearer the truth . . . taking him to bed and making him think she cared. *Lizzie* was the whore, everyone knew that . . . but it was Vera was treated like one.'

Nancy ran her tongue round the inside of her mouth. '*I am the complex product of my circumstances . . . not the predictable, linear result of an accidental*

461

coupling twenty-eight years ago.' Dear God! How absurdly arrogant that statement seemed now. 'I don't know what you're talking about,' she said flatly, steeling herself to make another move forward.

'Oh, yes, you do.' A sly intelligence gleamed in the old eyes. 'It frightens you, doesn't it? It frightened the missus. It's one thing to go looking for Lizzie's little bastard . . . not so much fun to find Fox's. That wouldn't do at all. She tried to push past me to tell the Colonel . . . but my boy wouldn't have it. You go inside, Ma, he said, and leave her to me.' She patted her pocket and set some keys jangling. '*That's* what stopped her heart. I saw it in her face. She didn't think *Vera* would lock her out. Oh, no! Not when she'd shown Vera so much *kindness . . .'*

*

Bella was unimpressed by the level of cleanliness in James's house. 'What's wrong with his cleaner, then?' she asked as Mark took her into the scullery to show her the chest freezer. She stared with disgust at the filth in the sink and the cobwebs all over the windows. 'Gawd, will you look at this? It's a miracle the poor old bloke isn't in hospital with tetanus and food poisoning. If I was him, I'd give her the sack.'

'Me, too,' Mark agreed, 'but it's not that easy. There's no one else to do it, unfortunately. Shenstead's effectively a ghost village with most of the properties let out as holiday homes.'

'Yeah, Fox told us.' She lifted the lid of the freezer and snorted at the layers of frost on the food. 'When was this last opened?'

'Apart from when I checked it on Christmas Eve, not since the Colonel's wife died in March, I wouldn't think. Vera wouldn't go near it. She was lazy enough when Ailsa was alive, but she doesn't do a blind bloody thing these days . . . just takes her wages and runs.'

Bella pulled a face. 'You mean she gets *paid* to leave things in this state?' she asked incredulously. '*Shit!* Talk about money for old rope.'

'And gets a rent-free cottage.'

Bella was astonished. 'You gotta be joking. I'd give my right arm for a deal like that . . . and I wouldn't take advantage of it, neither.'

Mark smiled at her expression. 'In fairness, she probably oughtn't to be working at all. She's virtually senile, poor old thing. But you're right, she does take advantage. The trouble is James has been very—' he sought for a suitable word – '*depressed* these last few weeks so he hasn't been keeping an eye on her . . . or anything else for that matter.' His mobile started to ring. 'Excuse me,' he said, retrieving it from his pocket and frowning at the number displayed. He raised the handset to his mouth. 'What do you want, Leo?' he asked coolly.

*

Every doubt Nancy had ever had about discovering her biological history screamed for the old woman to be quiet, but she refused to give Vera the satisfaction of saying it aloud. Had she been alone, she would have denied any relationship with Fox or his mother, but she was conscious that Wolfie was listening to every word being said. She had no idea how much he understood, but she couldn't bring herself to deny a relationship with him.

'What did you do it for?' she asked the old woman. 'Money? Were you blackmailing Ailsa?'

Vera gave a grunt of laughter. 'Why not? The missus could afford it. It was such a little amount to keep quiet about your daddy. She said she'd rather die, silly woman.' She seemed to wander suddenly. 'Everyone dies. Bob'll die. My boy gets angry when people annoy him. Not Vera, though. Vera does what she's told ... do this ... do that ... Is that right?'

Nancy didn't say anything because she didn't know what to say. Was it better to sympathize? Or was it better to tie the old woman's brain in knots by arguing? She wanted to believe that Vera was so confused that nothing she said was true, but she had a terrible fear that the pieces relating to her were accurate. Hadn't she feared it all her life? Wasn't that why she had closed her mind to her heritage? It was truly said that 'what the heart didn't know, it couldn't grieve over'.

'The missus called my boy "vermin",' the old woman went on, her lips smacking ferociously, 'so he showed her what happens to real vermin. She didn't like that . . . one of her foxes with its brains on the ground . . . said it was cruel.'

Nancy screwed her eyes in pain as she inched forward. *She had to keep her talking* . . . 'It *was* cruel,' she said flatly. 'It was even crueller to kill Henry. What did a poor old dog ever do to your rotten son?'

'It wasn't my boy did that. It was the other one.'

Nancy took a breath, her nerve endings protesting at every movement. 'What other one?'

'Never you mind. Common as muck, sniffing around petticoats. Vera's seen it . . . Vera sees everything. You get out the house, Ma, says my boy, and let me do the talking. But *I* saw him . . . *and* the flighty little piece he had in tow. She was always a problem . . . made her parents' life hell with her flirting and her whoring.'

Elizabeth . . .? 'Stop blaming other people,' she said sharply. 'Blame yourself and your boy.'

'He's a good boy.'

'*Bullshit!*' she spat. 'He *kills* people.'

More lip smacking. 'He didn't want to,' Vera whined. 'The missus brought it on herself. What's more cruel than giving money to save foxes and refusing to help him? It wasn't enough to put him out of his house, she wanted him sent to jail as well.'

She smacked her fists together again. 'It was her own fault.'

'No, it wasn't,' countered Nancy angrily. 'It was *your* fault.'

Vera cowered against the wall. 'I didn't do it. It was the cold.' Her voice went into a croon. 'Vera saw her . . . all white and frozen with next to nothing on and her mouth open. She'd have been so ashamed. She was a proud lady. Never told anyone about Lizzie and my boy . . . never told the *Colonel*. He'd have been *very* angry. Got a bad temper has the Colonel.'

Nancy shifted forward another inch. 'Then he'll carve you into little pieces when I tell him you helped your son kill his wife,' she snarled through gritted teeth.

Vera tapped in agony at her mouth. 'He's a good boy. You put your feet up, Ma, he says. You've been a drudge and a slave all your life. What's Bob ever done for you? What's the Colonel ever done for you? What did the missus ever do except take the baby away because you weren't good enough?' Her mouth writhed. 'He'd have gone away if she'd given him what he asked.'

Wolfie seemed to grasp suddenly that Nancy was trying to work her way to the edge of the seat because he wedged his elbows onto the chair arm behind him and took his weight off her lap. 'Of *course* he wouldn't have gone away,' she said loudly, to keep Vera's attention. 'He'd have gone on bleeding Ailsa till there was nothing left. Thieving and killing're all he knows, Mrs Dawson.'

'She didn't bleed,' Vera countered triumphantly. 'My boy was cleverer than that. Only the fox bled.'

'Then there's a nice symmetry to this whole wretched story because it isn't my blood on this jacket, it's your darling boy's. So if you know where he is – and if you care for him at all – you should be persuading him to go to hospital instead of gibbering like a senile ape.'

Vera's mouth puckered into uncontrollable movement again. 'Don't you call me an ape . . . I've got rights. You're all the same. Do this . . . do that . . . Vera's been a drudge and a slave all her life—' she tapped the side of her head – 'but Vera knows what's what . . . Vera's still got her marbles.'

Nancy reached the edge of the seat. 'No, you haven't.'

The blunt contradiction was too much for the old woman's fragile hold on reality. 'You're just like *her*,' she spat. 'Making judgements . . . telling Vera she's senile. But he *is* my boy. Do you think I don't know my own baby when I see him?'

*

'OK, Mark, this is the deal. Take it or leave it. Lizzie and I will get Dad off the hook as long as he agrees to reinstate the previous will. We don't have a problem with everything going to Lizzie's kid in the long run but, in the short term, we want—'

'No deal,' said Mark, breaking in as he moved into the corridor.

'It's not your decision to make.'

'Right. So phone your father on the landline and put the offer to him. If you give me five minutes I'll make sure he answers.'

'He won't listen to me.'

'Congratulations!' Mark muttered sardonically. 'That's the second time you've got something right in under a minute.'

'Christ! You really are a patronizing bastard. Do you want our cooperation, or not?'

Mark stared at the corridor wall. 'I don't view a demand for reinstatement as cooperation, Leo, and neither will your father. Nor am I prepared to test him on it because you and Lizzie will be dead in the water from the moment I open my mouth.' He stroked his jaw. 'Here's why. Your niece – Lizzie's daughter – has been in this house since ten o'clock this morning. Your father would give her the entire estate tomorrow if she'd agree to accept it . . . but she won't. She has an Oxford degree, she's a captain in the army, and she's due to inherit her family's two-thousand-acre farm in Herefordshire. The reason she's here is because your father wrote to her in a moment of depression, and she cared enough to follow it up. She expects nothing from him . . . wants nothing from him. She came with no ulterior motive except to be kind . . . and your father's besotted with her as a result.'

'And showing it, I suppose,' the other man said with a trace of bitterness. 'So how would she be doing if he was treating her like a criminal? Not so well, I'll bet. It's easy to be nice to the old man when he treats you like royalty . . . bloody hard when you get the bum's rush.'

Mark might have said, 'You brought it on yourself', but he didn't. 'Have you ever thought he might feel the same? Someone has to call a truce.'

'Have you told him that?'

'Yes.'

'And?'

'A little help in the present situation would go a long way.'

'Why does it always have to be me who makes the first move?' There was a muted laugh at the other end. 'Do you know why he called me the other day? To rant about my thieving. I got the whole catalogue from the time I was seventeen to the present day. And from that he deduced that I killed my mother in anger, then embarked on a campaign of vilification to blackmail him into handing over the estate. There's no forgiveness in my father's nature. He took a view of my character while I was still at school, and he refuses to change it.' Another laugh. 'I came to the conclusion long ago that I might as well be hung for a sheep as for a lamb.'

'You could try surprising him,' suggested Mark.

'You mean like the squeaky-clean granddaughter? Are you sure you've found the right girl? She doesn't sound like any Lockyer-Fox I've ever met.'

'Your father thinks she's a cross between your grandmother and your mother.'

'Point made then. They were only Lockyer-Foxes by marriage. Is she pretty? Does she look like Lizzie?'

'No. Tall and dark – more like you as a matter of fact, but with brown eyes. You should be grateful for that. If she had blue eyes I might have believed Becky.'

Another laugh. 'And if it had been anyone but Becky who'd said it, I might have let you . . . just for the amusement factor. She's a jealous little bitch . . . had it in for Lizzie from the start. I blame you, as a matter of fact. You made Becky think she was important. Bad mistake. Treat 'em mean, keep 'em keen. It's the only way if you don't want to ruin them for the next man that comes along.'

'I'm not into revolving doors, Leo. I'd rather have a wife and kids.'

There was a brief hesitation. 'Then you'd better forget anything you learnt at school, my friend. It's a myth that blue-eyed parents can't produce brown-eyed children. Ma was an expert on genetic throw-backs. It made her feel better about herself to blame her children's addictions and her father's alcoholism on some distant ancestor who belonged to the Hell-fire Club.' Another pause to see if Mark would bite, and when he didn't: 'Don't worry. I can guarantee that Lizzie's baby was nothing to do with me. Apart from anything else, I never fancied her enough to sleep with her . . . not after she started going with riff-raff, anyway.'

This time Mark did bite. 'What riff-raff?'

'Irish tinkers that Peter Squires brought in to mend his fences. He had them camping in a field over one summer. It was pretty funny, actually. Ma made a tit of herself by taking the children's edu-cation in hand, then went ballistic when she dis-covered Lizzie was being shafted by one of them.'

'When was this?'

'What's it worth?'

'Nothing. I'll ask your father.'

'He won't know. He was away at the time . . . and Ma never told him. The whole thing was kept very hush-hush in case the neighbours found out. Even I didn't know till later. I was in France for four weeks, and by the time I got back Ma had put Lizzie under lock and key. It was a mistake. She should have let it run its natural course.'

'Why?'

'First love,' said Leo cynically. 'No one was ever as good again. It was the beginning of the slippery slope for my poor sister.'

*

Nancy put all her effort into her thigh muscles and, with an unsteady lurch, rose to her feet with Wolfie sitting on her left hip. It would take a feather to knock her down again, but she prayed the old woman wouldn't realise that. 'Move away from the door, please, Mrs Dawson. Wolfie and I are going downstairs now.'

Vera shook her head. 'Fox wants his boy.'

'No.'

Negatives disturbed her. She began smacking her fists together again. 'He belongs to Fox.'

'No,' said Nancy even more forcefully. 'If Fox ever had any rights as a parent, he forfeited them when he took Wolfie from his mother. Parenthood isn't about ownership, it's about duty of care, and Fox has failed to show this child any care at all. You, too, Mrs Dawson. Where were you when Wolfie and his mother needed help?'

Wolfie pressed his lips to her ear. 'Cub, too,' he whispered urgently. 'Don't forget li'l Cub.'

She had no idea who or what Cub was, but she didn't want to take her attention from Vera. 'Cub, too,' she repeated. 'Where were you for little Cub, Mrs Dawson?'

But Vera didn't seem to know who Cub was either and, like Prue Weldon, fell back on what she knew. 'He's a good boy. You put your feet up, Ma, he says. What's Bob ever done for you except treat you like a skivvy? He'll get his comeuppance, don't you worry.'

Nancy frowned. 'Does that mean Fox isn't Bob's son?'

The old woman's confusion intensified. 'He's *my* boy.'

Nancy gave the half-smile that was so reminiscent of James's. It would have been a warning to the old woman if she'd been capable of interpreting it. 'So people were right to call you a whore?'

'It's Lizzie was the whore,' she hissed. 'She lay with other men.'

'Good,' said Nancy, hoisting Wolfie higher on her hip. 'Because I couldn't give a damn how many men she slept with – just so long as Fox isn't my father . . . and *you* aren't my grandmother. Now, will you *move* . . . because there is *no way* I am going to allow a murdering old bitch to take Wolfie from me. You aren't fit to look after anything, let alone a child.'

Vera almost danced with frustration. 'You're so high and mighty . . . just like *her*. She's the one took babies away. All puffed up with her good works . . . making out she knew more than Vera did. You're not a suitable mother, she said. I can't allow it. Is that fair? Doesn't Vera have rights, too?' Up came the finger. 'Do this . . . do that . . . Who cares about Vera's feelings?'

It was like listening to a stylus jump tracks on a worn record to produce unrelated bursts of sound. The theme was recognizable but the pieces lacked cohesion and continuity. Who was she talking about now? Nancy wondered. Ailsa? Had Ailsa made a decision about Vera's fitness as a mother? It seemed unlikely – *on whose authority could she do it*? – but it might explain Vera's bizarre remark about 'knowing her baby when she saw it'.

Perhaps Vera saw the indecision in her face because the gnarled finger jabbed in her direction again. 'See,' she said jubilantly. 'I said it wasn't right, but she wouldn't listen. It won't work, she said, better to give it to strangers. So much heartache . . . and all for nothing when she had to go looking for it in the end.'

'If you're talking about me,' Nancy said coldly, 'then Ailsa was right. You're the last person in the world anyone should give a baby to. Look at the damage you did to your own child.' She started to walk forward. 'Are you going to move or will I have to make you?'

Tears welled in Vera's eyes. 'It wasn't my fault. It was Bob's fault. He told them to get rid of it. I wasn't even allowed to see it.'

But Nancy wasn't interested. Telling Wolfie to turn the handle, she backed into the old woman, forcing her aside, and with a sigh of relief hooked the door open with her foot and hurried into the corridor.

*

Leo's voice took on an amused drawl. 'When Dad got back, about two or three months later, he discovered his mother's rings had been nicked, along with bits of silver from the various display cabinets on the ground floor. Everything else had been shifted around to fill the gaps, so Ma didn't notice, of course – she was far too interested in her charity work – but *Dad* did. Spotted it within twenty-four hours of walking through the door. That's how acquisitive he is.' He paused to see if Mark would rise to the barb this time. 'Well, you know the rest. He lammed into poor old Vera like there was no tomorrow . . . and Ma never said a word.'

'About what?'

'Lizzie's shenanigans.'

'What did they have to do with it?'

'Who do you think stole the flaming stuff?'

'I thought you owned up to it.'

'I did,' Leo said with a grunt of laughter. 'Bad mistake.'

'Who, then? The boyfriend?'

'Christ, no! I wouldn't have taken the blame for him. No, it was Lizzie. She came to me, shaking like a leaf, and told me what had been going on. Her bloke persuaded her he'd marry her if she could get some money together to elope to Gretna Green. Silly cow. She was a pathetic romantic. Got comprehensively screwed by a waster . . . and still looks back on him as the best thing that ever happened to her.'

Mark took to staring at the wall again. Which was the lie? That Leo *had* stolen from his father . . . or that he *hadn't*? He could feel the tug of the man's charm again, but he wasn't so gullible these days. The single thing he could be sure of was that Leo was playing a gamble. 'Did Vera know about it?'

'Of course she did. She was part of the problem. She adored the toerag because he took the trouble to soften her up. He was a bit of a charmer, by all accounts. Vera told lies for Lizzie so Ma wouldn't know what was going on.'

'Why didn't she say something when your father accused her of stealing?'

'She would have done if she'd been given time. That's why Lizzie came howling to me.'

'Then why did your mother believe you? She must have guessed that Lizzie had something to do with it.'

'It made life easier for her. Dad would have given her hell for letting Lizzie run out of control. In any case, I'm a convincing liar. I told her I'd blown the lot in a casino in Deauville. She had no trouble believing that.'

Probably because it was true, thought Mark cynically. Or partially true. Ailsa had always said that what Leo did, Lizzie did six months later. *Nevertheless* . . . 'Will Lizzie vouch for you if I tell your father this?'

'Yes. So will Vera if she hasn't gone completely doolally.'

'Is Lizzie with you? Can I speak to her?'

'No, on both counts. I can ask her to ring you if you like.'

'Where is she?'

'Not your business. If she wants you to know, she'll tell you herself.'

Mark placed a palm against the wall and looked at the floor. *Pick a side* . . . 'It might be better not to mention that her daughter's here. I don't want her thinking she's going to meet the girl.' He heard Leo's indrawn breath. 'And before you blame your father for that, it's the girl herself who's not interested. She has a brilliant adoptive family, and she doesn't want her life complicated with the emotional baggage of a second. Also – and this is strictly between you and me – Lizzie is the one who will be hurt. There's no way she can measure up . . . either to the daughter or the daughter's adoptive mother.'

'It sounds as if Dad isn't the only one who's besotted,' said Leo sarcastically. 'Is this your way into the family fortune, Mark? Marry the heiress and scoop the jackpot? A bit old fashioned, isn't it?'

Mark bared his teeth into the receiver. 'It's time

you stopped judging the rest of us by your own standards. We're not all middle-aged pricks with self-esteem problems who think their fathers owe them a living.'

The grin came back into the other man's voice to have finally got a rise. 'There's nothing wrong with my self-esteem.'

'Good. Then I'll give you the name of a friend of mine who's a specialist in male fertility problems.'

'Fuck you!' said Leo angrily, hanging up.

Twenty-Eight

BY THE TIME Martin Barker returned to the campsite, the search of Fox's bus had produced as much
as it was going to. Doors, luggage compartments,
bonnet had all been opened, but there was little to
show for the search team's trouble. A table had been
set up under arc lights with some items of little value
across its surface – electric power tools, binoculars, a
battery-operated radio – which may or may not have
been stolen. Otherwise the only finds of interest
were the hammer and razor that had been retrieved
from the terrace and a metal cash box that had been
under one of the beds.

'It's small beer,' Monroe told Barker. 'This is
effectively it, and he doesn't even bother to keep it
locked. There's a couple of hundred quid, a driver's
licence in the name of John Peters with an address in
Lincolnshire, a few letters . . . and damn all else.'

'Is the licence kosher?'

'Nicked or bought. The John Peters at that
address is sitting with his feet up in front of a Bond

movie . . . deeply incensed to have had his identity stolen.'

It was a common enough story. 'Licence plates?'

'False.'

'Engine number? Chassis number?'

The sergeant shook his head. 'Filed off.'

'Fingerprints?'

'That's about the only thing I'm optimistic about. The steering wheel and gear stick are covered in them. We should know who he is by tomorrow, assuming he has a record.'

'What about Vixen and Cub? Anything to show where they are?'

'Nothing. Can't even tell if there was a woman and a second kid living there. It's a pigsty, but there's no female clothing, and barely any children's.' Monroe pushed the box away, and started on a small pile of papers. 'Jesus!' he said disgustedly. 'The guy's a joker. There's a letter here from the Chief Constable, assuring Mr Peters that the Dorset Constabulary is scrupulous in its dealings with travellers.'

Barker took the letter and inspected the address. 'He's using a PO box in Bristol.'

'Among others.' The other man shuffled through the remaining letters. 'They're all official responses to queries about travellers' rights, and all to different PO box numbers and areas.'

Barker leaned over to look at them. 'What's the point? Is he trying to prove he's a bona fide traveller?'

'I shouldn't think so. It looks more like a paper trail. If he's arrested he wants us to waste our time trying to track his movements round the country. He probably hasn't been to any of these places. The Bristol police could spend months looking for a trace of him while he was in Manchester all the time.' He put the letters back into the box. 'It's smoke and mirrors, Martin, rather like this flaming bus, as a matter of fact. It looks promising, but there's nothing in it—' he shook his head – 'and that makes me seriously interested in what our friend is up to. If he's thieving where does he keep his stash?'

'What about blood?' asked Barker. 'Bella's pretty convinced he's got rid of the woman and the younger kid.'

Monroe shook his head. 'Nothing obvious.'

'Forensics might find something.'

'I can't see them getting the chance. On this evidence—' he nudged the box – 'we're more likely to be on the receiving end of a solicitor's complaint. If some bodies turn up, then maybe . . . but that's not going to happen tomorrow.'

'What about traces on the hammer?'

'It won't help us without some DNA or a blood group to compare it against.'

'We can hold him for the assault on Captain Smith. He beat her up pretty thoroughly.'

'Yes, but not in the vehicle . . . and he'll probably claim self-defence, anyway.' He glanced at the bag

481

with the razor in it. 'If that's his blood then he might be worse off than she is. What was he doing at the Manor? Does anyone know? Did you find any evidence of a break-in?'

'No.'

The sergeant sighed. 'It's bloody odd. What's his connection with this place? Why attack the Colonel's granddaughter? What's he after?'

Barker shrugged. 'The best we can do is stake out the bus and wait for him to come back.'

'Well, don't hold your breath, mate. At the moment I can't see there's anything for him to come back for.'

*

Nancy lowered Wolfie to the floor and closed the door behind them. She gave him her hand. 'You're too heavy,' she told him apologetically. 'My bones are beginning to creak.'

'That's OK,' he said. 'My mum couldn't carry me, neither.' He looked nervously along the corridor. 'Are we lost?'

'No. We just have to walk down here, and the stairs are round the corner at the end.'

'There's a lot of doors, Nancy.'

'It's a big house,' she agreed. 'But we're OK. I'm a soldier, remember, and soldiers can always find their way around.' She gave his hand a small tug. 'Come on. Best foot forward, eh?'

He held back.

'What's the matter?'

'I can see Fox,' he said, as the corridor light went out.

*

Mark's phone rang again immediately with Nancy's message. He looked into the scullery. 'I'm going upstairs,' he told Bella. 'Apparently Mrs Dawson's upsetting Wolfie.'

She dropped the freezer lid. 'Then I'm coming with you, mate,' she said forcefully. 'This woman's getting on my tits something chronic. I've just watched a fucking rat poke its head out of the skirting board.'

*

With every instinct urging 'retreat', Nancy didn't bother to find out if Wolfie was right. She let go his hand and opened the door into the bedroom again, briefly flooding the corridor with light as she shoved him back inside. She didn't waste time looking behind her, instead she slammed the door and leaned her weight against it, feeling with her left hand for a key. Too late. Fox was stronger and heavier than she was, and all she could do was take the key to prevent him locking it against help.

'We're going to run into the far corner,' she urged Wolfie. '*Now!*'

Vera hadn't moved from where Nancy had pushed her, but she did nothing to impede their dash. She even looked frightened when the door gave way and Fox erupted into the room, as if the sudden flurry of activity was alarming her. She drew back against the wall as he fell to his knees under the impetus of his forward momentum.

There was a brief hiatus when nothing happened except that Fox whipped out a fist to slam the door, then stared up at Nancy, breathing heavily, as she put herself between him and his son. It was a strange few seconds during which they were able to see and take stock of each other for the first time. She would never know what he saw, but she saw a man with blood on his hands who reminded her of the picture of Leo in the dining room. He smiled at the shock in her face, as if he'd been looking for it, then lumbered to his feet. 'Give me the boy,' he said.

She shook her head, mouth too dry to speak.

'Lock the door, Ma,' he ordered Vera. 'I don't want Wolfie making a run for it while I sort this bitch out.' But Vera didn't move and he rounded on her angrily. 'Do what you're told!'

Nancy took the moment to press the key into Wolfie's hand behind her back, hoping he'd have the sense to throw it out of the window the minute he had the chance. At the same time she shuffled him towards a chest of drawers to their right which had some heavy bookends on it. It was the wrong side for her – she'd have to turn away from Fox in order to grab the nearest one – but it was a weapon of sorts. She had no illusions about her chances. In army terminology, she was fucked . . . unless a miracle happened.

'Go away,' Vera cried, beating at the air in front of Fox with her fists. 'You're *not* my baby. My baby's dead.'

Fox slammed his fingers round her throat and pinned her to the wall. 'Shut up, you stupid old fool. I don't have time for this. Are you going do what you're told or am I going to hurt you?'

Nancy felt Wolfie slip out behind her and reach for the bookend. 'He's not my dad neither,' he muttered fiercely, putting the heavy ornament into her good hand. 'I reckon my dad was somebody else.'

'Yes,' said Nancy, turning the bookend against her thigh to give herself a better grip in fingers that were slippery with sweat. 'Me, too, friend.'

*

In the great scheme of things, it hardly ranked as heroism. There was no time for thought, no weighing of danger, merely a gut response to a stimulus. It wasn't even a sensible thing to do with a policeman downstairs, but it brought a glow to Mark's heart whenever he thought about it. Coming round the corner from the top of the stairs he and Bella saw a man silhouetted against a shaft of light from a bedroom before the door slammed and the corridor was plunged into darkness again. 'What the hell—?' he exclaimed in surprise.

'Fox,' said Bella.

It was like a red rag to a bull. Ignoring Bella's restraining arm, Mark charged down the corridor and burst through the door.

*

Bella, with a stronger sense of self-preservation, paused long enough to yell down the stairs for help, then she, too, took off, exerting herself in a way she hadn't for years.

*

Mark was past Fox and into the room before he saw Nancy in the corner. 'Here!' She threw the bookend towards him. 'Behind you to your left.'

He caught the heavy weight like a rugby ball and spun on his heel just as Fox abandoned Vera to face him. For Mark, too, the likeness to Leo was extraordinary, but it was a fleeting impression that vanished as soon as he looked into the man's eyes. As Bella's cry for help reverberated down the corridor, he raised the bookend in his left hand and advanced on the man.

'Do you want to try someone your own size?' he invited.

Fox shook his head, but kept a wary eye on the bookend. 'You're not going to hit me with that, Mr Ankerton,' he said confidently, edging towards the door. 'You'll break my skull.'

He even sounded like Leo. 'Self-defence,' said Mark, moving to block his exit.

'I'm unarmed.'

'I know,' said Mark, feinting a clubbing blow with his left, while powering his right in a swinging uppercut to Fox's jaw. He danced away, grinning rather manically as the man's knees began to buckle. 'You can thank my dad for this,' he said, stepping in again to land a rabbit punch on the back of Fox's neck as he went down. 'He said a gentleman should appreciate the art of boxing.'

'Nice one, mate,' said Bella breathlessly from the doorway. 'Shall I sit on him? I could do with a bloody rest.'

Twenty-Nine

AN HOUR LATER Fox was escorted downstairs in handcuffs. He dismissed any suggestion that he was suffering from concussion, but Monroe, who didn't like his pallor or the welts on his arms where Nancy had cut him with the razor, telephoned ahead for a secure room at the county hospital to have him checked. They lived in a compensation culture, he told Mark sourly, and he didn't plan to give Fox any room to sue the Dorset Constabulary. For the same reason, he offered Nancy a ride, but again she refused. She knew what A&E was like on Bank Holidays when the drunks started rolling in, she said, and she was damned if she'd give Fox the pleasure of seeing her wait in line while he took precedence.

A preliminary search had produced several items of interest in the capacious pockets of Fox's coat, notably a matching set of keys to those Vera held, a roll of twenty-pound notes, a mobile telephone with a distorter attachment, and, alarmingly for both Mark and Nancy, a sawn-off shotgun in a canvas lining under his left arm. Bella looked extremely thoughtful when Barker told them about it. 'I thought he was wriggling a bit,' she said. 'Next time I'll sit on his head and make sure he doesn't come round.'

From the evidence of the keys in Fox's possession, his presence in the house, and Nancy's report that Vera had claimed him as her son, it seemed likely that Fox had had a free run of Shenstead Manor for some time. As he refused to say anything, however, the issue of what he had been doing there was temporarily put on hold. James was asked to make a thorough check of the premises in advance of a police search the following morning, and a small team was sent down to check out Manor Lodge.

Mark took Monroe aside to ask him what had been in Fox's bus. He was particularly interested in the file on Nancy that Fox had taken from the Colonel's desk that afternoon. It contained privileged information, he said, which neither the Colonel nor Captain Smith wanted made public. Monroe shook his head. No such file had been found, he said. He in turn picked Mark's brains about the telephone calls, explaining that he had interviewed both Mrs Weldon and Mrs Bartlett.

'They both say the information came from the Colonel's daughter, Mr Ankerton. Could there be a connection between her and this man?'

'I don't know,' said Mark honestly.

Monroe eyed him thoughtfully. 'The voice distorter certainly suggests it. Mrs Bartlett claims she was told about the incest some time in October when Leo introduced her to Elizabeth, but she denies any knowledge of the Darth Vader messages. And I believed her. So how is Fox involved?'

'I don't know,' said Mark again. 'I'm almost as new to this as you are, sergeant. The Colonel told me about the calls late on Christmas Eve, and I've been trying to make sense of them ever since. The allegations aren't true, of course, but we didn't learn until this evening that Elizabeth was the alleged informant.'

'Have you spoken to her?'

Mark shook his head. 'I've been trying to contact her for a couple of hours.' He glanced towards the drawing room, where Vera was sitting. 'The Colonel recorded the messages on tape, and they include details which were known only to the family. The obvious conclusion was that one or both of the Colonel's children were involved – which is why he didn't report it – but of course the other person who was privy to the family's secrets was Vera.'

'According to Captain Smith, Mrs Dawson said she locked Mrs Lockyer-Fox out in the cold on her son's instructions. Does that sound likely to you?'

'God knows,' said Mark with a sigh. 'She's completely batty.'

Vera couldn't help them at all. Questions about Fox were greeted with incomprehension and fear, and she sat in a pathetic huddle in the drawing room, whimpering to herself. James asked her where Bob was, suggesting the police should try to contact him, but that only seemed to unhinge her further. As yet, James had not seen Fox who was under restraint in the bedroom. However, he was able to say categorically that Vera had never had a child. He believed Ailsa had mentioned a still-birth on one occasion, which had devastated the poor woman, but unfortunately, being a man, he had not paid much attention.

For her part, Nancy repeated most of what Vera had said – the part she played in Ailsa's death, her mention of someone else being reponsible for Henry's mutilation, the woman's obvious confusion about her relationship with Wolfie. 'I don't think anything she said can be relied on,' she told Monroe. 'She repeats the same phrases over and over again, like a learnt mantra, and it's difficult to know if any of it's true.'

'What sort of phrases?'

'About being taken for granted . . . do this . . . do that . . . no one cares.' Nancy shrugged. 'She's very confused about children. She said she taught Wolfie manners when he was younger, and that he had brown curly hair. But he can't have done. Blond hair can darken as children get older but dark hair doesn't turn ash blond. I think she's mistaking him for another child.'

'What other child?'

'I've no idea. One from the village, perhaps.' She shook her head. 'I'm not sure it matters. She's got holes in her brain. She remembers a dark-haired child from somewhere and she's persuaded herself that that was Wolfie.'

'Or been persuaded by somebody else?'

'It wouldn't be difficult. Anyone who sympathized with her would get a hearing. She seems to feel the whole world's against her—' she pulled a cynical expression – 'except her darling boy, of course.'

She remained reticent about what the old woman had said on the subject of her parentage. She told herself she was protecting Wolfie, but it wasn't true. The child had agreed to go to the kitchen with Bella, and Nancy was free to speak as openly as she wanted. Instead, she remained tight-lipped, unwilling to tempt fate. The spectre of Vera as a grandmother seemed to have been removed, but it gave her no confidence that Fox was out of the picture. Deep in her stomach was a continuous flutter of foreboding that, in that respect at least, Vera had been telling the truth. And she cursed herself for ever coming to this house.

It made her brusque and sharp-tongued in response to James's solicitous queries about her welfare. She was fine, she told him. In fact, she didn't even think her arm was broken, so she was planning to drive back to Bovington to have it looked at there. She wished everyone would stop fussing and leave her alone. James retired, crushed, but Mark, with an intuition learnt through growing up with seven sisters, took himself off to the kitchen for a quiet word with Wolfie. With a little coaxing from Bella, and some filling in of gaps – '*she said she didn't want Fox to be her dad or the nasty lady to be her gran*' . . . '*me and her both reckoned our dads were somebody else*' – Mark guessed what the trouble was. And he, too, cursed himself for helping to unlock a biological history that Nancy had never wanted to know.

*

Monroe was interested enough in the vanishing file to send Barker back to Fox's bus. 'The solicitor says it's bulky, so where the hell has he hidden it? Take another look and see if you can spot something I've missed.' He handed over Fox's keys. 'We can't move the damn thing while the Welshman's blocking the exit, but if you power it up you can run the lights inside. They might help.'

'What am I looking for?'

'A compartment of some sort. There has to be one, Martin. Otherwise we'd have found the file.'

*

Mark took himself into the garden with his mobile telephone. 'I'll make you a promise,' he told Leo, well out of earshot of anyone in the house. 'Deal with me straight over the next five minutes, and

I'll try to persuade your father to reinstate you. Interested?'

'Maybe,' said the other with amusement. 'Is this about the granddaughter?'

'Just answer the questions,' said Mark grimly. 'Do you know a man who calls himself Fox Evil?'

'No. Good name, though . . . I might adopt it myself. Who is he? What's he done?'

'Vera claims he's her son and that she helped him murder your mother. But she's gone off the rails completely, so it may not be true.'

'Good God!' said Leo in genuine surprise. There was a short pause. 'Look, it *can't* be true, Mark. She's obviously confused. I know she saw Ma's body on the terrace, and was pretty shaken by it, because I rang her after the funeral to say I was sorry I hadn't spoken to her. She kept telling me how cold Ma must have been. She's probably convinced herself it was her fault.'

'What about this man being her son?'

'It's rubbish. She doesn't have a son. Dad knows that. *I* was her blue-eyed boy. She'd have jumped over the moon if I'd asked her to.'

Mark stared towards the house, brow furrowed in thought. 'OK, well, Fox Evil's just been arrested for breaking into the Manor, and he had a voice distorter in his possession. Did your father tell you that most of the incest allegations were made by someone who spoke like Darth Vader?'

'I thought he was barking,' said Leo sourly.

'Far from it. This guy's a psychopath. He's already attacked your niece with a hammer, and when he was arrested he was carrying a sawn-off shotgun.'

'Shit! Is she okay?'

It sounded genuine. 'Broken arm and broken rib, but still alive. The trouble is, you and Lizzie are implicated through the voice distorter. Mrs Bartlett has told the police that it was you who contacted her some time in October so that Lizzie could give her chapter and verse on your father's abuse. As Darth Vader's been saying identical things to Mrs Bartlett, the obvious conclusion – which the police are already drawing – is that you and Lizzie set this bastard on your father.'

'That's ridiculous,' said Leo angrily. 'The obvious conclusion is that the Bartlett woman's behind it.'

'Why?'

'What do you mean, why? She's lying through her teeth.'

'What does she have to gain by it? You and Lizzie are the only ones with a motive for destroying your father and Lizzie's child.'

'*Jesus!*' said Leo disgustedly. 'You're as bad as the old man. Give a dog a bad name and every sod on the planet can have a go at hanging him. That's what Becky's up to in case you're interested . . . and I'm hacked off with it.'

For the second time that evening, Mark ignored

the rant. 'What about Lizzie? Could she have been persuaded to get involved in something like this without your knowledge?'

'Don't be an idiot.'

'What's so idiotic about it? If Lizzie's as shot as Becky says, it's conceivable a con artist persuaded her to go along with it . . . though I don't understand why, unless he can get access to the money when she inherits.' He mentally crossed his fingers. 'You said she never got over her first love. Perhaps he came back for another go?'

'No chance. He was a craven little sod. Took the money and ran. That was half the problem. If he'd come back, she'd have seen him for what he was, instead of remembering him as an Irish charmer.'

'What did he look like?'

'I don't know. I never saw him. He was gone by the time I got back from France.'

'How well did your mother know him? Would she have recognized him again?'

'I've no idea.'

'I thought you said Ailsa took his education in hand.'

'He wasn't one of the children, you jerk. He'd fathered most of them. That's why Ma went ballistic. This bozo knew more about sex than Don Juan, which is why Lizzie fell for him so heavily.'

'Are you sure about that?'

'It's what Lizzie told me.'

'Then there's only a fifty-fifty chance it was the truth,' said Mark sarcastically.

Perhaps Leo agreed because, for once, he didn't react. 'Look, for what it's worth, I can prove Mrs Bartlett never spoke to Lizzie . . . not in October anyway. Or, if she did, she'd have been talking to her in the Intensive Care Unit at St Thomas' hospital. Did this woman mention drips and monitors to the police? Did she say Lizzie's in such a bad way she can't even stand up any more?'

Mark was taken aback. 'What's wrong with her?'

'Her liver packed up at the end of September and she's been in and out of Tommy's ever since. In between whiles, she lives with me. At the moment she's in a hospice for a couple of weeks' respite care, but the prognosis is pretty dire.'

Mark was truly shocked. 'I'm sorry.'

'Yes.'

'You should have told your father.'

'Why?'

'Oh, come on, Leo. He'll be devastated.'

The other man's voice took on an amused note again as if irony were a means of coping. 'That's what Lizzie's worried about. She feels ill enough without Dad weeping all over her.'

'What's the real reason?'

'I gave her a promise I wouldn't tell anyone. I wouldn't have told *you* except that I'm buggered if I'll let a fat cow tell lies about her.'

'It's Mrs Weldon who's fat,' said Mark. 'Why doesn't Lizzie want anyone to know?'

There was a long silence, and when Leo spoke again his voice wasn't entirely steady. 'She'd rather die quietly than find out that no one cares.'

*

When Fox was finally brought downstairs, James was asked to wait in the hall to see if he recognized him. He was given the option of standing in shadow but he chose instead to place himself in full view, with DS Monroe on one side and his solicitor on the other. Mark tried to persuade Nancy to join them, but she refused, preferring instead to take Bella's suggestion of positioning herself in the kitchen corridor to block any accidental view Wolfie might have of Fox being taken away in handcuffs.

'Take your time, sir,' Monroe told James when Fox appeared between two policemen on the landing above. 'There's no hurry.'

But James knew him immediately. 'Liam Sullivan,' he said, as the man was marched down the stairs, 'though I never believed that was his real name.'

'Who is he?' asked Monroe. 'How do you know him?'

'He's a thief who took my wife's charity and threw it in her face.' He stepped forward and forced the two constables to bring Fox to a halt. 'Why?' he asked simply.

A rare smile lit Fox's eyes. 'You're like Everest, Colonel,' he said in perfect mimicry of the old man's baritone. 'You're there.'

'What were you hoping to achieve?'

'You'll have to ask Leo and Lizzie that. I'm just the hired help. They want your money and they don't much care how they get it—' his gaze flickered towards the corridor as if he knew Nancy was there – 'or who gets hurt in the process.'

'You're lying,' said James angrily. 'I know Vera filled your head with nonsense about your similarity to Leo, but that's as far as your connection with this family went.'

Fox's smile widened. 'Did your wife never tell you about Lizzie and me? No, I can see she didn't. She was a great one for sweeping the family scandals under the carpet.' His voice dropped into Irish brogue. 'Your daughter liked her men rough, Colonel. Better still if it was Irish rough.'

'I don't know what you're talking about.'

Fox glanced at Mark. 'Mr Ankerton does,' he said with certainty.

James turned to his solicitor. 'I don't understand.'

Mark shrugged. 'I don't think Mr Sullivan does either,' he said. 'I suspect Vera's fed him a piece of gossip and he's busy trying to use it to his own advantage.'

Fox look amused. 'Why do you think Ailsa paid my bills? It wasn't charity. She was trying to keep the sordid details of Lizzie's love life under wraps . . . particularly her passion for men who reminded her of her brother.'

Monroe intervened before James or Mark could say anything. 'How do you know him, sir?'

James steadied himself against the newel post. He looked devastated, as if Fox had supplied some missing pieces in a jigsaw. 'He claimed squatters' rights over the companion cottage to the Lodge during the summer of '98. My wife took pity on him because he had a woman and two small children with him—' He broke off clearly questioning the basis of Ailsa's sympathy.

'Go on,' Monroe prompted.

'Ailsa persuaded me to let the family stay while she tried to find affordable housing for them. Meanwhile this *creature*—' he gestured towards Fox – 'exploited a passing resemblance to my son to charge goods to the Manor accounts. My wife paid the bills, and by the time it came to my attention he'd vanished with his family, leaving debts she was unable to clear. I had to sell the cottage to honour them.'

Monroe eyed Fox curiously. He'd spoken to Leo at the time of his mother's death, but he didn't remember him well enough to say if the resemblance was a strong one. 'Was Wolfie one of these children?'

'I don't believe I ever saw them, but I know it worried my wife intensely that three such vulnerable people should be under the influence of this man.'

'Did you inform the police?'

'Of course.'

'What names did you give?'

'I don't remember now. My wife passed all the papers on the housing application to your people, so the names will be there. She may have kept copies. If so, they'll be in the dining room.' With a sudden movement he stepped forward and slapped Fox across his face. 'How *dare* you come back? What lies did you tell my wife this time?'

Fox straightened his head with a malevolent smile. 'I told her the truth,' he said. 'I told her who fathered Lizzie's little bastard.'

Monroe caught James's hand as he lifted it again. 'Best not, sir.'

'Ailsa wouldn't have believed you,' said the old man angrily. 'She knew perfectly well that nothing as disgusting as you've suggested ever happened.'

'Oh, she believed me, Colonel, but I didn't say *you* were the father. That was Lizzie's idea – she didn't think Mrs Bartlett would get worked up over anything less.'

James turned helplessly to Mark.

'Who did you say was the father?' Mark asked.

Fox stared him down. 'I've been watching you all day – you could hardly keep your hands off her. She does me credit, don't you think, Mr Ankerton?'

Mark shook his head. 'Wrong eye colour, my friend. Elizabeth's are blue . . . as are yours . . . and

Mendel's law says it's impossible for two blue-eyed parents to produce a brown-eyed child.' *Gotcha, you bastard!* Either Leo had been lying for the fun of it, or this ignorant sap knew as much about genes as he did. 'You shouldn't have relied on Vera for information, Fox. She never could get her head around dates. The Irish tinker came and went two years before Elizabeth's pregnancy—' he levelled a finger at Fox's heart – 'which is why Ailsa wouldn't have believed you either. Whatever she died from . . . *however* she died . . . she knew there was no connection between her granddaughter and you.'

Fox shook his head. 'She knew me both times, Mr Ankerton . . . paid me off the first time . . . would have paid me off the second time if she hadn't died. She didn't want her husband knowing how many skeletons there were in the family closet.'

'Did you kill her?' asked Mark bluntly.

'No. I wasn't here that night.'

Nancy moved out from the corridor. 'Vera said he was trying to blackmail Ailsa. She seemed quite lucid. Apparently Ailsa said she'd rather die than give him money . . . so he made Vera lock the door and leave Ailsa to him.'

Fox's gaze flickered briefly in her direction. 'Mrs Dawson confuses me with Leo. Perhaps you should be putting these questions to the Colonel's son, Mr Ankerton.'

Mark smiled slightly. 'If you weren't here, where were you?'

'Probably Kent. We spent most of the spring in the south-east.'

'We?' Mark watched a bead of sweat drip down the side of the man's forehead. He was only frightening in the dark, he thought. In the light, and under restraint, he looked diminished. Nor was he clever. Cunning, possibly . . . but not clever. 'Where are Vixen and Cub?' he asked, when Fox didn't reply. 'Presumably Vixen will support the Kent alibi if you tell the police where she is?'

Fox shifted his attention to Monroe. 'Are you going to do your job, sergeant, or are you are going to allow the Colonel's solicitor to question me?'

Monroe shrugged. 'You've been cautioned. You have a right to silence, just like anyone else. Go on, sir,' he invited Mark. 'I'm interested in what you have to say.'

'I can give you the facts I know, sergeant.' He marshalled his thoughts. 'First fact. Elizabeth did have a brief liaison at the age of fifteen with an Irish traveller. He persuaded her to steal for him, and her brother took the blame to protect her. Vera certainly knew about the liaison, because she told lies for Elizabeth whenever Elizabeth went out. The whole episode caused a catastrophic breach of trust between all members of the household which was never repaired. Vera, in particular, felt badly treated because the Colonel accused her of the theft . . . and I doubt Mrs Lockyer-Fox behaved towards her in the same way again. I'm sure she felt Vera encouraged Elizabeth to act as she did.'

He put a hand on James's arm to keep the old man silent. 'Second fact. Elizabeth had a baby when she was seventeen which was put up for adoption. She was very promiscuous as a teenager and didn't know herself who the father was. Vera, of course, was privy to the birth and the adoption. However, I suspect she's confused the two episodes in her mind, which is why this man thinks the Irish traveller was the father.' He watched Fox's face. 'The only person left alive who can identify the traveller – apart from Vera whose testimony is flawed – is Elizabeth herself . . . and she describes him as a much older man who was father to most of the children in his entourage.'

'She's lying,' said Fox.

'Then it's your word against hers. If she fails to identify you, the police will draw their own conclusions about the truthfulness of everything you've said . . . including the death of Mrs Lockyer-Fox.'

He was rewarded with a flicker of indecision in the pale eyes.

'Third fact. Vera's resentment against her husband and the Lockyer-Foxes has grown exponentially since her dementia became noticeable in '97. The date is documented because it was at that time that a decision was taken to allow her and Bob to have the Lodge rent-free until their deaths. The Colonel has just said that Vera filled this man's head with nonsense about looking like Leo. I suspect it was the other way round. He used his likeness to Leo to fill Vera's head with nonsense. I don't pretend to understand why, except that he found out how easy it was to make money the first time and thought he'd have another go.' He paused. 'Finally, and most importantly, neither Leo nor Elizabeth has ever met or spoken to Mrs Bartlett. So whatever scam this man is operating, it has nothing to do with the Colonel's children.'

'Mrs Bartlett seemed very certain,' said Monroe.

'Then she's lying or she's been conned herself,' said Mark flatly. 'I suggest you put Fox into an identity parade to see if she recognizes him. Also Wolfie's mother when and if you find her. He and a blue-eyed blonde could probably pass muster quite successfully to someone who's only ever seen Leo and Elizabeth from a distance.'

'Can you prove they weren't involved?'

'Yes.' He put a hand under James's elbow to support him. 'The Colonel's daughter is dying. She's been in and out of hospital since September with incurable liver disease. Had she met Mrs Bartlett in October, it would have been within the confines of St Thomas' Hospital.'

*

It was a clever piece of welding, a false back to the forward luggage compartment, but it was sussed by a sharp-eyed female colleague of Barker's who questioned why a small strip of paint – the width of a chisel – had rubbed off midway down one panel. It wouldn't have been visible in daylight, but in the gleam of her torch the sliver of exposed metal winked against the grey paintwork.

'Neat,' said Barker admiringly, as minimal pressure from a knife released a spring catch that allowed the entire panel to be eased away from the lip that anchored it on the other side. He levelled his torch into the foot-deep, metre-square space that was revealed. 'Looks like he's been raiding half the stately homes of England.'

The policewoman climbed inside the compartment to squint behind the left-hand panel. 'There's more in here,' she said, feeling inside and releasing a second catch at floor level. She pulled the panel towards her and lowered it flat. 'How much of this belongs to the Colonel, do you reckon?'

Barker ran his torch over the paintings and bits of silverware that filled the cavity. 'No idea . . . but you'd think the old boy would have noticed if things were going missing.' He moved to the next compartment. 'If the depths of these two were the same when the bus was built, then I'd say there's a false back here as well. Do you want to give it a try?'

The WPC crawled obligingly into the luggage

space and fiddled with the knife again. She gave a grunt of satisfaction as the panel sprang open. 'Jesus!' she said, looking at what was revealed. 'What the hell does he want to do? Rob the World Bank?'

Barker lit a line of sawn-off shotguns and pistols that were attached by clamps to the rear wall. 'Trade,' he said dryly. 'This is good currency. No wonder he's been haunting the Manor. The Colonel's family built up the largest collection of guns and rifles in Dorset. I imagine that's what Fox has been looking for.'

'Then I don't have much sympathy for the Colonel,' said the policewoman, releasing the second panel and laying it flat. 'He's asking to be robbed.'

'Except it's not on the premises any more,' said Barker. 'The old boy donated the entire collection to the Imperial War Museum after his wife died. I guess no one bothered to tell Fox.'

Thirty

THE EVENTUAL FALLOUT from Fox's arrest spread a great deal farther than Shenstead when the bus was systematically taken apart and a genuine trail of evidence was uncovered. He was careless in what he had chosen to carry with him. A second mobile with a store of numbers and a trail of calls that allowed the police to track his movements. Keys to a lock-up that were painstakingly traced through the manufacturers to give a location. Passports. Driving licences – some in the names of women. Most worryingly, as far as the police were concerned, items of blood-stained clothing that seemed to be trophies, all hidden in a recess in the floor.

*

For the inhabitants of Shenstead, the fallout was more immediate and concentrated after the police went house to house late on Boxing Day evening to inform them that a man had been taken into custody following the murder of Bob Dawson. The news was greeted with shock by everyone. They pressed for

508

more information – '*What man . . .?*' '*Was anyone else hurt . . .?*' '*Was it connected with Ailsa's death . . .?*' '*What about Vera . . .?*' – but the officers were reticent, merely asking all householders to make themselves available for interview the following day.

The story spread beyond the boundaries of the valley as soon as the press got hold of it. Journalists stalked the hospital in the early hours, searching for information on the arrested suspect and a woman called 'Nancy' whose arm had been broken in a hammer attack. The police would only confirm the name of the murdered man and the fact that the suspect was a traveller from the site at Shenstead. However, word leaked out – via Ivo and his mobile when he spotted an opportunity to make money through chequebook journalism – that 'Nancy' was Colonel Lockyer-Fox's illegitimate granddaughter, and parallels were drawn between the attack on her and Ailsa's death in March. Why was the Colonel's family being targeted?

The issue of illegitimacy added spice to the story and the search was on to find her biological mother and her adoptive mother. Fortunately, Ivo remained coy about her rank and surname, recognizing that he wouldn't be paid for information over a telephone line, which gave Bella time to take him apart before he could sneak out and make contact with a reporter. She confiscated his mobile and suggested the Colonel lock him in the cellar for the night, but, in the absence of Mark, who had driven Nancy to the hospital, James chose instead to match the money offered by the newspaper.

'You are no different from your friend Fox,' he told Ivo as he wrote a cheque to 'cash' with an accompanying letter to his bank. 'You both believe in destroying lives to benefit yourselves. However, I would have given Fox everything I have in exchange for my wife, and I consider this a small price to pay for my granddaughter's peace of mind.'

'Each to his own,' said Ivo, tucking the cheque and the letter into his pocket and grinning maliciously at Bella who was leaning against the library wall, 'but you'd better approve this if the bank phones. You offered it fair and square so there's no going back.'

James smiled. 'I always honour my promises, Ivo. You'll have no trouble at the bank as long as you honour yours.'

'It's a deal, then.'

'Yes.' The old man stood up behind his desk. 'Now will you please leave my house?'

'You've gotta be joking. It's two o'clock in the morning. My wife and kids are asleep upstairs.'

'They're welcome to stay. You are not, however.' He nodded to Bella. 'Will you ask Sean Wyatt to come in here, my dear?'

'Why do you want the copper?' demanded Ivo.

'To have you arrested if you don't leave immediately. You have exploited my distress over my wife's murder, my gardener's murder and the attempted murder of my granddaughter to coerce blood money out of me. You either leave now and cash that cheque as soon as the bank opens, or you spend the night with your friend at the police station. Whichever way, once you've left this house, you will not come back into it.'

Ivo's eyes darted nervously towards Bella. 'You'd better not make out I had anything to do with Fox. I didn't know him from Adam before the selection meeting.'

'Maybe not,' she said, easing herself away from the wall and opening the door into the hall, 'but the Colonel's right. There ain't much difference between you and him. You both reckon you're more import- ant than anyone else. Now, come on, shift your arse before I decide to tell the coppers about the nicked stuff in your bus.'

'What about my wife and kids?' he complained, as James rounded the desk and forced him to walk backwards. 'I need to tell them what's going on.'

'No.'

'How am I supposed to get hold of them without a bloody phone?'

James looked amused. 'Perhaps you should have thought of that first.'

'Shit!' He allowed himself to be shepherded into the hall. 'This is a fucking kangaroo court.'

'Will you stop with the whinging!' said Bella disgustedly, pulling the bolts on the front door and dragging it open. 'You've got your thirty pieces of silver. Now beat it before I change my mind about dropping you in it.'

'I need my coat,' he said as a blast of cold air blew in.

'Fuck that!' She manhandled him through the opening and pushed the door closed again with a massive shoulder. 'The cops won't let him back on the campsite,' she said, 'so he's gonna freeze his arse off unless he wants to explain why you've thrown him out.' She chuckled at James's expression. 'But I guess you'd worked that out already.'

He took her arm. 'Let's have a brandy, my dear. I think we've earned it, don't you?'

*

The valley itself came under siege as soon as the road-blocks were removed at daybreak on the twenty-seventh, and any hope anyone had had of keeping a low profile evaporated. The Manor and the Copse remained under police guard but the tenant farmers, the Bartletts and the Weldons found themselves at the mercy of the press and the broadcasting media. Shenstead House attracted the most attention because of Julian's remarks on travellers in the local newspaper. A copy was posted through the door, and his phone rang continuously until he disconnected it. Photographers hung around outside his windows, waiting for pictures while reporters shouted questions.

'*Do you feel responsible because it's a traveller who did it?*' . . . '*Did you set the dogs on them? Is that what started this?*' . . . '*Did you call them thieves to their faces?*' . . . '*Do you know who this man is? Has he been to Shenstead before?*' . . . '*What's his interest in the Manor? Why did he kill the gardener?*' . . . '*Why did he attack the Colonel's granddaughter?*' . . . '*Do you think he was responsible for Mrs Lockyer-Fox's death?*'

Inside the house, Eleanor sat in huddled, grey misery in the kitchen while Julian, looking little better, paced his study behind closed curtains. Every attempt he'd made to contact Gemma on her mobile had been diverted to voicemail, as had his attempts to raise Dick Weldon. Both mobiles were switched off, and the landlines to Shenstead Farm and the Squires's farm were permanently engaged, suggesting they, too, had been disconnected. His only email contact with Gemma was at her office, which was closed until after the New Year, and his frustration grew with his inability to find out what was going on.

There was no one else to phone except the police, and in the end that's what Julian did, asking to speak to DS Monroe. 'We need help,' he told him. 'I'm worried sick that these bastards are going to learn about my wife's phone calls, and then what are we going to do?'

'There's no reason why they should.'

'Are you expecting me to take your word for that?' demanded Julian. 'No one's telling us what's going on. Who's this man you've arrested? What's he saying?'

Monroe broke off to talk to someone in the background. 'I'll be coming out to talk to you later, sir, but in the meantime I suggest you and Mrs Bartlett stay out of sight. Now, if you'll excuse—'

'You can't just leave it at that,' Julian broke in angrily.

'What else do you want to know, sir?'

Julian ran an irritable hand up the back of his neck. 'These reporters are saying the Colonel's granddaughter was attacked as well. Is that true?' There were more voices at the other end, and it stoked his ire to be relegated to second place. 'Are you listening?' he barked.

'Sorry, sir. Yes, her arm was broken, I'm afraid, but she's on the mend now. Look, my best advice is to keep your head down and stay quiet.'

'Bugger that!' said Julian aggressively. 'We're effectively imprisoned by these bastards. They're trying to photograph us through the windows.'

'Everyone's in the same boat, sir. You'll have to be patient.'

'I'm not prepared to be patient,' he snapped. 'I want this scum removed from my doorstep and I want to know what's going on. All we were told last night was that a man had been arrested . . . but from the questions being shouted through the letterbox, he's one of the travellers.'

'That's correct. We've already confirmed it with the press.'

'Then why didn't you tell *us*?'

'I would have done when I came out to see you. Why is it so important?'

'Oh, for God's sake! You said last night that Prue thought Darth Vader was one of the travellers. Can't you see how vulnerable it makes us if Ellie's connection with this man gets out?'

There was another break for muted conversation. 'I'm sorry, sir,' Monroe said again, 'we're very busy here, as you can appreciate. What makes you think the murder of Robert Dawson has anything to do with your wife's phone calls to the Colonel?'

'I *don't*,' Julian countered crossly, 'but you seemed convinced of a connection between Ellie and the travellers when you were questioning her.'

'I was repeating what Mrs Weldon said . . . but it wasn't a serious suggestion, sir. Mrs Weldon was hysterical about the intruder at Shenstead Farm. It led her to some rather bizarre conclusions. At the moment we have no reason to link the events of last night with the nuisance calls that your wife has been making.'

'*Right*,' Julian growled, 'then perhaps you'd like to send a car to deal with these reporters outside my window. I'm an innocent party to all of this and I'm being treated like a criminal.'

'We're very stretched, sir,' said Monroe apologetically. 'If it's any consolation, Captain Smith's having a far worse time of it.'

'It's no consolation,' he snapped. 'I'm sorry the girl was hurt, but it's not my fault if she was in the wrong place at the wrong time. Now are you going to send a car or do I have to cause a breach of peace to get some attention?'

'I'll send a car, sir.'

'Do that,' said Julian, slamming the phone onto its rest, then removing it again when it started to ring. He raised two fingers at the curtains. 'Bastards,' he mouthed.

*

Monroe replaced the receiver with a thoughtful smile for his Inspector. 'I told you he'd phone before long,' he said. 'He's shitting bricks . . . wants to know what Fox is saying.'

'What are you going to do?'

'Let him stew a bit longer. He's a control freak . . . it drove him mad to think I wasn't giving him my full attention.' He pondered for a moment. 'The longer we leave him to the mercy of the photographers, the more het up he's going to be. He wants to leave that house rather badly, but whether to do a runner or get rid of evidence, I don't know. Probably both.'

'Do you seriously believe he's behind it?'

Monroe shrugged. 'I certainly believe he set up his wife to make the phone calls. He was far too relaxed last night. I was watching him. He was playing her like a patsy. It's interesting. She obviously sees herself as a forceful character – Mrs Weldon certainly does – but compared with the husband she's a lump of jelly.'

'He may just have taken a pay-off to get her involved.'

Monroe narrowed his eyes towards the window. 'Possibly, but he's carrying a lot of expenses . . . the wife's demands . . . the girlfriend's demands . . . the horse . . . the hunt . . . the cellar. There were two sets of golf clubs in the hall . . . his and hers . . . not to mention the BMW, the Range Rover, the designer rooms and designer clothes. According to Mark Ankerton, this is his second marriage. He was divorced twenty years ago and has a couple of grown-up children. We're talking about a guy who only ever made senior-management level . . . had to give half his wealth to his first wife . . . supported children . . . sold his house before the boom . . . then took early retirement at fifty-five to live like a lord.' He shook his head. 'It doesn't add up.'

'Fox is making him out to be the biggest arms' dealer in Europe. How likely is that?'

'On a scale of one to ten? Zero,' Monroe admitted. 'I'm guessing he was into a share of the silver and the paintings, and he'll have a heart attack when he hears about the guns. I think Fox was telling the truth about giving him the file, though. Bartlett certainly knew who Captain Smith was. As to whose idea it was—' he made a rocking motion with his hand – 'six of one and half a dozen of the other. The timing suggests Fox. The Colonel's never been one for socializing, but he didn't leave the house after his wife's death. I'm betting Fox became bored with using Vera to steal for him and wanted to get inside himself. The method – driving the old boy into an exhausted defence of his terrace while Fox went in the back – suggests Bartlett. He's a nasty piece of work. I can easily believe he killed the Colonel's dog to up the ante.'

'Mark Ankerton quoted "fog of war" at me. Something to do with confusing the Colonel about where, who and how powerful the opposition was.'

'I prefer hunting metaphors,' said Monroe. 'Fox and Bartlett are two of a kind. They both enjoy terrorizing dumb animals.'

The inspector chuckled. 'The Colonel's not a dumb animal.'

'Might as well be when he's accused of raping his daughter. How do you argue against a thing like that?'

'Mm.' The inspector eased himself off the edge

of the sergeant's desk. 'There's something very personal about Fox's pursuit of that family. Do you
think he's telling the truth about the affair with the
daughter? The psychiatrists will have a field day if he
is. Pampered little rich girl. Boy from the wrong side
of the tracks.'

'We'll be asking for confirmation as soon as we
have access to Elizabeth.'

'She'll deny it for Captain Smith's sake.'

'I hope she does,' said Monroe. 'The man's an
animal. If he really believed the girl was his daughter,
why did he attack her?'

The inspector moved to the window. 'Because he
doesn't see her as an individual . . . just as a member
of a family he's obsessed with. It's bloody odd,
frankly. The Colonel and his son have jumped in
with offers of DNA to prove there's no relationship
between themselves and Fox.'

Monroe nodded. 'I know. I spoke to Ankerton.
His argument is that any similiarity to Leo is coinci-
dental, but it's the similarity that led Fox to plague
the family. He spouted a load of gobbledegook
about transference and depersonalization . . . something to do with bringing the Colonel down to size
in order to feel superior.'

'Mm. But Captain Smith is refusing a DNA
comparison?'

'On Ankerton's advice.' Monroe pressed his
thumb and forefinger to the bridge of his nose. 'Give

her a break, guv. She's a decent girl, and there's no compulsion to force her to find out who fathered her. It won't affect the case.'

The inspector nodded. 'Has Fox said how he and Bartlett hooked up again? That's the key to who planned it. They would certainly have overlapped in '97, but Bartlett wouldn't have known how to find Fox once he vanished. Common sense suggests it was Fox who made the initial contact.'

'Says it was a chance meeting in the Copse, and Bartlett threatened to turn him in for impersonating Leo if he didn't cut him in on this deal.'

'What was Fox doing in the Copse?'

'Sussing out the Manor. Says he read about Ailsa's death and wanted to know how the land lay. He doesn't deny that he was there to rob the place, but he does deny the wholesale stripping of the contents that he claims Bartlett wanted. According to him, Bartlett said the Colonel was a sitting duck. The trick was to make him so reclusive that it would be weeks before anyone else realized the place had been emptied.'

'The Colonel would have to be dead for that.'

'Which is what Fox says Bartlett ordered. Along with Robert and Vera Dawson. They were lonely people. No one spoke to them. By the time anyone bothered to investigate – probably Mark Ankerton – there'd have been no witnesses, the travellers would have been long gone and we'd have concentrated our efforts on them.'

'Do you buy that?'

The sergeant shrugged. 'It's undoubtedly what Fox was planning, but I can't see Bartlett going for it. The coats and balaclavas are the key. My guess is the plan was to concentrate everyone's attention on the travellers during the holiday while Bartlett and Fox went into the Manor, tied the Colonel up, stripped the place and left him to be found by Bob or Vera when they bothered to turn up for work. Assuming he was still alive, he would have told us the travellers were responsible.'

The inspector folded his arms. 'Or accused his son because of the nuisance calls.'

'It's quite neat, guv. Fox said they were planning to take the tapes so we wouldn't know the calls had happened. That's why I think he was intending to kill the old boy.'

'Then Mark Ankerton and Nancy Smith turned up.'

'Right.'

'What did Fox have to say about that?'

'That Bartlett ordered the go-ahead anyway.'

'How?'

'Through Vera.'

The inspector gave a grunt of amusement. 'That woman's very useful to him. He blames her for everything.'

'He certainly knows how to use women. Look at Mrs Bartlett and Mrs Weldon.'

'A coven of bloody witches,' said the inspector morosely, staring out of the window. 'That's what happens when rich bastards export their inflation to the countryside. Communities die and the scum floats to the surface.'

'You having a go at me, guv?'

'Why not? Your house is twice the size of mine, and I'm a sodding inspector.'

'Luck of the draw.'

'Bollocks! There should be a tax on people like you and Bartlett using your megabucks to deprive country people of homes. That way you'd both have stayed in London, and I wouldn't have a psychopath in my cells.'

Monroe grinned. 'He'd have come anyway . . . and you wouldn't have had my expertise.'

Another grunt of amusement. 'So what about the wife and Mrs Weldon? Any ideas? Ankerton's after their blood, but the Colonel's refusing to prosecute because he doesn't want the incest allegations in the public domain. He says – and I *agree* with him – that it doesn't matter how powerful the DNA evidence, mud will stick.'

Monroe stroked his jaw. 'Arrest and caution? It would be water off a duck's back to a fifteen-year-old, but it may just terrify the living daylights out of a couple of middle-aged harpies.'

'I wouldn't bet on it,' said the inspector. 'They'll be back in each other's pockets before the week's out, blaming Bartlett for their problems. They've no other friends. You could argue the Colonel brought his problems on his own head. If he'd been more welcoming to newcomers, the women wouldn't have behaved the way they did.'

'I hope you didn't tell Mark Ankerton that.'

'I didn't need to. The Colonel seems to have realized it for himself.'

*

Nancy and Bella stood side by side at the drawing-room window, watching James and Wolfie in the garden. Wolfie looked like Michelin man in some oversize cast-offs that Mark had discovered at the bottom of a chest in Leo's old bedroom, while James had decided to sport his great-grandfather's tatty ulster. The pair of them stood with their backs to the house, gazing out over the valley and the sea beyond and, from the way James was gesturing, it looked as if he were giving Wolfie a brief history of Shenstead.

'What's gonna happen to the poor little tyke?' asked Bella. 'It don't seem right to let him be swallowed by the system. Boys of his age never get adopted. He'll just be parcelled around from foster mum to foster mum till he starts to get stroppy in adolescence, then they'll bung him in a home.'

Nancy shook her head. 'I don't know, Bella.

Mark's going through Ailsa's files at the moment to see if he can locate a copy of this housing application she made. If he can find a name . . . if Wolfie was one of the children . . . if Vera was right about teaching him manners . . . if there are relatives . . .' She broke off. 'Too many "ifs",' she said sadly, 'and the trouble is, James thinks Fox or Vera has already done a similar search. According to him, Ailsa's boxes were neatly stacked the last time he went into the dining room . . . now they're all over the place.'

'Martin Barker ain't holding out much hope. He was the community policeman at the time of the squat, and he reckons it was a woman with daughters.' She touched a comforting hand to Nancy's shoulder. 'Better you hear it now, darlin'. The other thing he told me was they've found kids' and women's clothing in a hidey-hole in Fox's bus. They think they're trophies, like the fox brushes he hung.'

Tears sprang into Nancy's exhausted eyes. 'Does Wolfie know?'

'It ain't just one kid and one woman, Nance. Martin says there's ten distinct pieces – all different sizes. They're doing tests to see how many DNA prints they come up with. Looks at the moment like Fox has been murdering wholesale.'

'Why?' asked Nancy helplessly.

'Dunno, darlin'. Martin says people would've accepted him easier if he had a woman and kids with him . . . so he'd take on some spares till he got bored with the crying . . . then, wham, he'd hit 'em with a hammer.' She lifted her shoulders in a heavy sigh. 'Me, I'd say the fucker probably enjoyed it. I expect it gave him a sense of power to get rid of people no one else gave a shit about. Scares me rigid, to be honest. I keep wondering what would have happened to me and the girls if I'd been stupid enough to fall for the sod.'

'Were you tempted?'

Bella pulled a face. 'For a couple of hours when I was stoned. Didn't trust him much, but I liked the way he made things happen. Put it this way, I can understand why poor old Vera fell for him. Maybe your grandma, too. He could turn on the charm when he wanted, that's for sure. They always say psychos are good at manipulating people . . . 'n' you can't do that without charisma.'

'I suppose not,' said Nancy, watching James kneel down to put an arm round Wolfie's waist. 'Why do you think he left Wolfie alive?'

'If you believe Martin: 'coz he needed a kid to make himself look respectable for this adverse possession lark. I don't buy that, though. He could have picked up a junkie and her babes the last place he was at. I mean he wasn't gonna hang around long, so it didn't matter who he brought with him. I only spoke to Wolfie's mum once 'n' I wouldn't have been remotely surprised if he'd changed her for a different model.' She gave another sigh. 'It makes me feel bad. Maybe I could've saved her if I'd taken a bit more interest . . . but you don't *think*, do you?'

It was Nancy's turn to offer a comforting hand. 'Not your fault. So what's your theory on Wolfie?'

'I know it sounds crazy, but I reckon Fox liked him. He's a brave little bastard . . . been telling me about his "John Wayne" walk, so Fox wouldn't think he was scared . . . 'n' talking posh so Fox'd think he was clever. Maybe he's the one kid the fucker took a shine to. The way Wolfie describes it, Fox doped him up to the eyeballs before he took the hammer to Vixen 'n' Cub . . . and the only reason Wolfie saw it is because he woke up when his brother started calling for him. It makes your heart bleed, it really does. There ain't a kid in the world should have to go through something like that . . . but you gotta reckon Fox put him out so he wouldn't have to kill him.'

'Will Wolfie work that out for himself?'

'I hope not, darlin'. He's gonna have enough trauma in his life without building Fox into a sodding icon.'

They turned as they heard Mark come into the room. 'It's hopeless,' he said despondently. 'If Ailsa ever kept a copy, it definitely isn't there now. We'll just have to keep our fingers crossed that the police locate theirs.' He joined them at the window and put an arm round both of them. 'How are they doing?'

'I think James must be telling him about the lobster industry,' said Nancy. 'I'm not sure the ulster's going to last much longer, though. It seems to be splitting at the seams.'

'Good thing, too. It needs throwing out. He says he's been looking to the past too much.' It was his turn to sigh. 'I'm afraid the police are pressing for Wolfie to be handed over to social services. They want you both to persuade him to go.'

'Oh, God!' said Nancy. 'I promised him he wouldn't have to do anything until he was ready.'

'I know, but I think it's important. They have experts to deal with children like him, and the sooner they can start the process the better. It's what Bella just said. He needs to put Fox into perspective and he can only do that with professional guidance.'

'It don't make sense that he can't remember who he is or where he came from,' said Bella. 'I mean, he's ten years old and he's a bright kid. Yesterday lunchtime he told me he'd always been with Fox – today he's saying he thinks he lived in a house one time. But he ain't got no idea when. He just says it was when Fox wasn't there . . . but he don't know if it's 'coz Fox went away . . . or if it was before Fox. Do you reckon fear can do that?'

'I don't know,' said Mark. 'Put it this way, I shouldn't think drugs and permanent malnutrition helped.'

'*I* know,' said Nancy with feeling. 'I've never been

so scared in my life as I was last night. My brain stopped working completely. I'm twenty-eight years old, I have a degree, I'm a professional soldier and I can't remember having a single thought for the whole time that I stood in front of these windows. I don't even know how long I was there. Imagine what it must have been like for a child to put up with that level of terror day in, day out for months on end. The miracle is he isn't a complete vegetable. *I* would have been.'

'Yeah,' said Bella thoughtfully. 'No question Vixen and Cub were vegetables. Vera, too, if it comes to that. What's gonna happen to *her*, then?'

'I've managed to find a nursing home in Dorchester that will take her,' said Mark.

'Who's gonna pay?'

'James,' said Mark wryly. 'He wants her off the estate as fast as possible and says he doesn't mind how much it costs if it'll keep him from killing her.'

Bella chuckled. 'The old guy's pretty hot on this blood money lark. Me and Nancy have been watching Ivo skulking in the wood, trying to wave to his woman. It's pretty funny. All she's done so far is give him the finger.'

'She'll have to go soon. That's the other thing the police are pressing me on. They want the buses moved to a secure site. It's going to be a bit of a gauntlet-run, I'm afraid, because the press are lining the road, but you'll have a police escort the whole way.'

Bella nodded. 'How long?'

'Half an hour,' said Mark apologetically. 'I asked for longer, but they're using up too much manpower guarding the site. Also they want the house cleared so that James can make an inventory of anything that's missing. It looks as if the dining room's lost most of its silver.'

The big woman sighed. 'It's always the same. Just as you start getting comfortable the flaming cops turn up and move you on. Never mind, eh?'

'Will you talk to Wolfie first?'

'You bet,' she said roundly. 'Gotta tell him how to find me if he needs me.'

Thirty-One

THE PHOTOGRAPHERS weren't pleased that under sub judice rules none of their shots of Julian Bartlett resisting a search warrant could be used until after his trial. The police arrived in force at Shenstead House, and the man's fury when DS Monroe served him with the warrant was dramatic. He tried to slam the door and, when that didn't work, he seized a riding crop from the hall table and whipped at Monroe's face. Monroe, younger and fitter, caught his wrist in mid air and twisted his arm up behind his back before frogmarching him towards the kitchen. His words were inaudible to anyone outside, but the reporters all wrote with confidence: 'Mr Julian Bartlett of Shenstead House was arrested for assault at 11.43'.

Eleanor sat in a state of shock while Julian was handcuffed and cautioned in front of her before being taken to another room while the search of the house began. She seemed unable to grasp that the focus of police attention was her husband, not herself, and kept tapping her chest as if to say mea culpa, the blame is mine. It was only when Monroe put a series of photographs in front of her and asked her if she recognized any of them that she finally opened her mouth.

'That one,' she whispered, pointing to Fox.

'Could you name him for me, Mrs Bartlett?'

'Leo Lockyer-Fox.'

'Could you explain how you know him?'

'I told you last night.'

'Again, please.'

She licked her lips. 'He wrote to me. I met him in London with his sister. I don't remember his hair being like this – it was much shorter – but I remember his face very well.'

'Do you recognize any of the other photographs? Take as long as you like. Look at them closely.'

She seemed to feel it was an order and picked up each one in shaking fingers and stared at it for several seconds. 'No,' she said at last.

Monroe isolated a picture from the middle and pushed it towards her. '*That* is Leo Lockyer-Fox, Mrs Bartlett. Are you sure he wasn't the man you met?'

What little colour she had left drained from her cheeks. She shook her head.

Monroe laid another series of photographs on the table. 'Do you recognize any of these women?'

She hunched forward, staring at the faces. 'No,' she said.

'Are you absolutely certain?'

She nodded.

Again he isolated one. '*That* is Elizabeth Lockyer-Fox, Mrs Bartlett. Are you sure she wasn't the woman you spoke to?'

'Yes.' She stared up at him with tears in her eyes. 'I don't understand, sergeant. The woman I saw was so convincing. No one could *pretend* to be that damaged, could they? She was shaking the whole time she talked to me. I *believed* her.'

Monroe pulled out a chair on the other side of the table. Time enough to put the fear of God into her when he had her husband in the bag; for the moment he wanted cooperation. 'Probably because she was afraid of the man who was calling himself Leo,' he said, sitting down. 'Also, she may have been telling you the truth, Mrs Bartlett . . . but it would have been her own story and not Elizabeth Lockyer-Fox's. Sadly, we believe the woman you met is now dead, although there's a chance we've found her passport. In a day or two I'll ask you to look at some more photographs. If you recognize any of those faces then we may be able to put a name to her and find out something about her history.'

'But I don't understand. Why did she do it?' She looked at Fox's picture. 'Who's this person? Why did *he* do it?'

Monroe rested his chin on his hands. 'You tell me, Mrs Bartlett. Two strangers weren't likely to know that you'd be interested in a fabricated story about Colonel Lockyer-Fox. How did they know you'd believe it? How did they know you had a close friend in Mrs Weldon who would support a campaign of nuisance calls? How did they know you both thought the Colonel had murdered his wife?' He gave a sympathetic shrug. 'Someone very close to you must have given them your name, don't you think?'

She really was deeply unintelligent. 'Somone who doesn't like James?' she suggested. 'Otherwise, what was the point?'

'You were a decoy. Your phone calls were designed to make the Colonel think there was no one he could trust . . . not even his son or daughter. Your role—' he smiled slightly – 'which you performed extremely well – was to drive a defenceless old man to confusion and exhaustion. While he was concentrating on you – and by default his children because of what you were alleging – he was being robbed.' He raised enquiring eyebrows. 'Who knew you well enough to set you up like that? Who knew you resented the Lockyer-Foxes? Who thought it would be amusing to let you do his dirty work?'

*

As Monroe told his inspector afterwards, it might be true that hell hath no fury like a woman scorned, but hell broke loose in Shenstead House when a scorned woman found she'd been framed. Once started,

Eleanor couldn't stop. She had an absolute memory of their finances at the time of the move, the approximate value of Julian's portfolio, the amount of his early-retirement package and the minimal pension he was receiving until he turned sixty-five. She leapt at the chance to construct a list of her own expenditure since moving to Dorset, including the cost of every home improvement. The list she made of Julian's known expenses ran to two pages, with the gifts mentioned in the GS emails scored into the paper at the end.

Even Eleanor could see that expenditure far outweighed income so, unless Julian had sold every share they possessed, there was money coming from somewhere else. She disproved the sale of shares by taking Monroe to Julian's study and locating the stockbroker file in one of his cabinets. She then assisted the police further by going through all his other files and isolating anything she didn't recognize. She grew more and more confident as evidence of her husband's guilt became apparent – bank and investment accounts that he'd never mentioned, receipts for goods sold that had never belonged to them, even correspondence with a previous mistress – and it was obvious to Monroe that she was rapidly beginning to see herself as the victim.

He had requested specifically that she look for a file containing letters from Colonel Lockyer-Fox to a Captain Nancy Smith, and when she finally unearthed it at the bottom of a rubbish bag which she remembered Julian taking outside that morning – '*he's never so obliging usually*' – she handed it over with a triumphant flourish. She was even more triumphant when one of the officers dug further into the coffee grounds and sprouts and produced a Darth Vader voice distorter. 'I told you it wasn't my fault,' she said stridently.

Monroe, who had assumed a second voice distorter because of the number of calls Darth Vader had made, held open a polythene bag to take it. 'Perhaps this is why he was so keen to go out,' the other officer remarked as he dropped it in. 'He was hoping to chuck them into a hedge somewhere on the other side of Dorchester.'

Monroe glanced at Eleanor while he sealed the bag. 'He'll deny all knowledge of them,' he said matter-of-factly, 'unless his wife can prove she's never set eyes on them before. There are two people living in this house and there's no evidence at the moment to say which one was responsible.'

The woman gobbled like a turkey as all her fears resurfaced. It was a satisfying reaction. In Monroe's view, she was as much at fault as her husband. Her degree of involvement might have been less, but he'd heard some of her messages on tape and the pleasure she'd taken from bullying an old man had turned his stomach.

Death of a Fox

It was reported yesterday that 'Fox Evil', the suspect at the centre of one of the biggest murder investigations of the last 10 years, has died of an inoperable brain tumour in a London hospital. He was transferred there 10 days ago from the hospital wing of HMP Belmarsh where he was awaiting trial.

Brian Wells, 45, aka 'Liam Sullivan', aka 'Fox Evil', remained an enigma to the end. His refusal to cooperate in the murder investigation led to a 'missing persons' search involving 23 police forces. Described by some as a charmer and by others as a terrifying night stalker, Wells's arrest last year caused huge public concern when police revealed he was suspected of the slaughter of three women and seven children, none of whose bodies have been recovered.

'We believe his victims were squatters or travellers,' said a police spokesperson. 'Either single mothers or mothers persuaded to leave their partners. Sadly, these are people whose whereabouts are seldom known to their extended families and their disappearances go unreported.'

Police suspicions were aroused after Wells was taken into custody on 26 December last year. Camped with other travellers on waste ground in the tiny Dorset village of Shenstead, he was charged with a hammer attack on Nancy Smith, 28, an army officer, and the murder of Robert Dawson, 72, a gardener. Guns and stolen property were found in his vehicle and police began a search for underworld contacts.

The scope of the investigation widened after a witness reported seeing Wells murder a woman and child. Within hours bloodstained clothing belonging to seven toddlers and three women was found in a concealed compartment beneath the floor of the bus. Police feared they were looking at a sick murderer's 'trophies'.

Confirmation came earlier this year that two of the victims, a woman and her six-year-old son, had been identified. Their names were given only as 'Vixen' and 'Cub' to protect surviving family members. It is believed that DNA testing of the woman's relatives has shown genetic links to a woman's dress and a toddler's T-shirt. Police refused to comment further, saying only that the investigation was ongoing and travellers should not be afraid to come forward.

'All information will be treated in confidence,' said a female detective. 'We understand that some people may not want to give their real names but we ask them to trust us. Our only interest is to identify those who are genuinely missing.'

The horror, particularly the brutal slaying of seven innocent children, touched a chord in the public psyche. As newspaper headlines emphasized, who cares if they never see a traveller again? 'Not in my backyard,' screamed one. 'Out of sight out of mind,' said another. 'The invisible tribe.' It was a shocking reminder of the vulnerability of people who live on the margins.

Wells himself could be said to be a man from 'the margins'. Born into a cradle of poverty in south-east London, he was the only child of a drug-addicted single parent. Described by teachers at his primary school as 'gifted' and 'sweet-natured', he was thought to have a future beyond the sink estate where he grew up. By secondary level this had all changed. Known to the police as an out-of-control teen, he had a string of cautions for petty theft, drug use and drug dealing.

One of his teachers blames his altered personality on a fractured skull at 12. 'His mother hooked up with some travellers. She said the bus was involved in an accident. Brian became very angry afterwards.' Others attribute it to his high IQ, which allowed him to exploit those around him.

Whatever the truth, his reputation for being a dangerous man to cross grew with the years. 'Everyone was frightened of him,' said an ex-girlfriend. 'The smallest thing made him lose his temper.' From 18 to 37, Wells spent a total of 12 years behind bars. Following his release in 1994 after a five-year term for illegal possession of a firearm and assault, he informed fellow inmates that he wouldn't be going back to jail.

'He said staying on the move was the only way to drop out of circulation,' said a former friend. 'He must have done it because we never saw him again. Probation and police are blaming each other for losing track of him, but at the time they were pleased to be rid of him. He was full of hate.'

Tracking Wells's movements between 1994 and his arrest last year has proved difficult. Despite interviewing hundreds of travellers, police have been unable to establish where he was for long periods of that time. His *modus operandi* was to move in on vacant property and exploit whatever possibilities arose.

'We've tied him to three squats,' said a Scotland Yard detective in July. 'On two occasions he accepted money to evict his fellow squatters. We are now concerned about what happened to these people. One owner remembers a woman and three children. We've found no trace of them and we don't know their names.'

According to travellers who shared Wells's campsite in Shenstead, he was a chameleon. 'He could mimic voices,' said Bella Preston, 36. 'Most of the time he talked as if he'd been to public school. I was surprised to hear he came from south London.' Zadie Farrel, 32: 'He'd be standing a couple of metres away and we wouldn't know he was there. I think he liked watching people to see what made them tick.'

The two women still remember 'Fox Evil' with shudders of fear. 'We were naive,' said Bella. 'It never occurred to us that one of our own was bad.' 'He wouldn't let strangers see his face,' said Zadie. 'It was a terrible shock when the police found guns in his bus. I realized he could have killed us all, and no one would have known who'd done it.'

Wells's arrest followed an unsuccessful attempt to rob a Shenstead farmhouse. Farmer's wife Mrs Prue Weldon spotted an intruder in her yard and alerted local police. A routine search of neighbouring properties disturbed Wells's assault on Captain Nancy Smith in the grounds of Shenstead Manor. Granddaughter of the owner, Colonel Lockyer-Fox, she fought off her assailant, suffering a broken arm and ribs in the assault. Police have commended her for her bravery.

Wells's motives for murdering Robert Dawson and attacking Nancy Smith remain as puzzling as the man himself. He is known to have squatted in a cottage tied to the Manor for three months in 1997 with a woman and two small children. He is also known to have obtained goods fraudulently by impersonating the son of the owner, Leo Lockyer-Fox, whom he was said to resemble. Police have speculated that the presence of Dawson and Smith in the grounds of the Manor on Boxing Day night foiled Wells's attempt to burgle the house, and this led to the attacks.

Psychological profiler William Hayes offers a different interpretation. 'Wells's alias "Fox Evil", implies a fantasy relationship with this family. He knew a great deal about them before he moved into their property in '97, possibly from traveller families who had visited the area before. His original intention may simply have been to exploit a likeness to the owner's son, but something seeded in his mind that became obsessional.

'He was treated with generosity when he first arrived, particularly by the owner's wife who was concerned for the woman and toddlers in his care. Her kindness may have given him a false sense of belonging, but those feelings would have turned to anger very quickly when he discovered she was interested only in helping his partner break away from his influence. It is probable that this unknown woman and her children were his first victims. If so, his subsequent killings would have been strongly linked in his mind with the Lockyer-Fox family.

'The evidence suggests that Wells's pattern of behaviour moved from highly organized in 1997 to highly disorganized by 26 December 2001. Whatever his motives for acquiring "families", they seemed to serve a purpose until boredom and/or lust for killing led him to attack them. Within weeks of slaughtering two members of his travelling fantasy family in a hammer attack, he was using the same hammer on the gardener and granddaughter of his extended fantasy family.

'His disintegration may have been due in part to the growing tumour in his brain, but it's not unusual for serial murderers to spiral out of control. It's conceivable that he knew what was happening to him. He allowed a witness of the November attack to live, and he committed his final, frenzied killing spree against people who would recognize him. The inevitable conclusion is that he wanted to be caught and stopped.'

Bella Preston disagrees. 'Fox Evil was well named. He used women and children until he lost interest in them, then he killed them. He was the worst kind of predator. He killed for pleasure.'

Anne Cattrell

HOCKLEY & SPICER, SOLICITORS

OLD COMPTON HOUSE, BRIDPORT ROAD, DORCHESTER

Julian Bartlett, Esq.
Flat 3
32 Hardy Avenue
Dorchester
Dorset

18 September 2002

Dear Julian

Following your telephone call of this morning, I can confirm
that the death of Brian Wells will have no bearing on your
case. As you know, the only statement he made to police was
the one concerning his alleged dealings with you. While we
can and will challenge that statement, I should remind you
that most of what he claimed has been substantiated by police
searches, witness statements and forensic evidence.

I realize how frustrated you are, particularly in respect of your
bail conditions, but, unfortunately, the prosecution has always
believed that the charges against you can be successfully
proved without further testimony from Wells. Of course, you
are entitled to change your solicitor at any time. However,
solicitors can only work with the facts they've been given. As
a friend, I would urge you to consider the following before
you look for someone 'who believes you'.

As I have explained previously, it was not in your interests to
push for early trial. The more damning the case against Brian
Wells, the easier the jury would have accepted your proposed
defence that you were a victim of violent intimidation.
However I feel obliged to point out, as I have done several
times before, that you undermined that defence in advance
when, during police questioning, you accused your wife of
bearing sole responsibility.

If we take the saliva evidence from the voice distorter alone, it
is clear that you were the only person who used it. Nor was
Eleanor a signatory to the bank accounts you opened. In
addition, Ms Gemma Squires's evidence relating to your
sudden interest in Leo and Elizabeth Lockyer-Fox in July, and
in any secrets Vera Dawson would have known about the
family, suggests you were complicit long before Eleanor
became involved towards the end of October.

I would not be doing my duty if I did not remind you that
Courts impose stiffer penalties when a plea of 'not guilty' is
found to be unsustainable. The charges you face have been
considerably reduced since police and prosecution accepted
your assurance that you had no knowledge of the guns in
Wells's bus or of his murderous intent. However, again, I
must point out that your ignorance of these facts undermines
your proposed defence of intimidation.

If you had no idea that Wells was the sort of man who went
armed and was prepared to attack anyone who thwarted him,
then your defence looks unconvincing. If you knew he was

armed, then you may be in danger of having charges reinstated, namely those relating to Wells's possession of illegal weaponry. I do urge you to give a thorough consideration to these conflicting positions in the next few days, particularly as you have no satisfactory explanation for how amounts to the value of £75,000 came to be in your bank account.

Your stockbroker has no knowledge of the shares you claim to have sold, nor have you been able to supply documentary proof that you ever owned them. The situation is further complicated by allegations from your former employer that you were offered early retirement after an 'expenses' fraud pertaining to a 10-year period was uncovered in your department. While you denied, and continue to deny, involvement in this fraud, it is nevertheless naive to close your eyes to the implications of a police investigation into your activities there. A true accounting of funds is necessary if you are not to face additional charges.

Had you chosen to remain silent during questioning instead of allowing yourself to be provoked, then a change of solicitor might indeed bring 'an unbiased eye' to your case. However, I am bound to tell you that I do not think silence would have helped you. The evidence against you is forensic as well as circumstantial and any solicitor would advise you to reconsider your defence in light of it.

The prosecution can produce witness evidence that you met Brian Wells in a pub on 23 July, although they will have difficulty proving design rather than accident. Vera Dawson's evidence is inadmissible because of her senile dementia; therefore Wells's claim that you met several times subsequently at Manor Lodge is unproven. However, Ms Squires's assertion that she accompanied you there on 26 July and saw Brian Wells through the window is damaging, as is your 24 October email to her describing your wife as 'an idiot. She'll believe anything of L-F because she hates him so much.' Inferences will certainly be drawn, as Eleanor's meeting with Brian Wells and 'Vixen' took place on 23 October.

On 27 December 2001 you denied being shown any Monet sketches by Colonel or Mrs Lockyer-Fox, a fact attested to by the Colonel. Yet fingerprint evidence shows that both you and Wells handled one of the Monet sketches, stored in the Colonel's strong room for the last two years, which substantiates Wells's claim that he delivered it to you and you told him to replace it because it was too 'well authenticated' to sell. Further, you have been unable to explain why your fingerprints were found on several items of silverware in Brian Wells's bus. There is witness evidence to prove you sold items of jewellery in Bournemouth that have since been identified as belonging to Ailsa Lockyer-Fox. Most damagingly, the envelope containing the letter to your wife and purporting to come from Leo Lockyer-Fox carries your DNA in the saliva residue on the stamp.

With respect, you have offered no plausible rebuttal to this evidence except to say that Ms Squires is 'a desperate bitch who'll say anything because she fancies DS Monroe' and 'the fingerprint evidence is a plant'. This will not wash with a judge and jury, and I ask you to recognize that my efforts to have your charges reduced will result in a moderate sentence if Colonel Lockyer-Fox and his family are spared any more pain and distress. By the same token, the Court will give you little sympathy if you force the Colonel's granddaughter to listen to accusations of incest which are evidentially untrue.

In conclusion, I should like to remind you that solicitors, too, have a right of dismissal. While I understand your numerous frustrations, particularly in relation to divorce proceedings, loss of friends and inability to move away, I am not obliged to put up with the sort of language you used this morning. Should it happen again, I will certainly insist that you consult another partnership.

Yours sincerely,

Gareth Hockley.

Gareth Hockley

Thirty-Two

Early November 2002

NANCY PARKED BY the Lodge and walked up through the vegetable garden. It was very different from the last time she'd been there, nearly a year ago, when Bovington had released her to recuperate at home in Herefordshire. She had expected to return in the summer, but it hadn't happened. Instead she had been posted back to Kosovo.

The beds had been dug and a polytunnel was sheltering winter greens from frost and wind. She opened the gate into Ailsa's Italian courtyard. The tubs had been planted with chrysanthemums, Michaelmas daisies and everlasting pansies, and someone had swept the cobbled ground and painted the scullery door and windows. Children's bicycles leaned against the wall and she could hear music coming from the kitchen.

She opened the door into the impeccable scullery and tiptoed through to where Bella was setting out trays of glasses and canapés. She looked no different from the last time Nancy had seen her, still swathed in purple, still as wide as a house, still with cropped peroxided hair. 'Hello, Bella,' she said from the doorway.

The woman gave a whoop of pleasure and ran forward to clasp her arms around Nancy's waist in a massive bear hug. 'I knew you'd come. Mark thought you'd duck it at the last minute but I said, no chance.'

Nancy laughed. 'I might have done if you hadn't clogged my phone with messages.' She allowed herself to be drawn into the kitchen. 'Wow!' she said, staring about the newly decorated walls. 'It looks great, Bella . . . smells good, too.'

'It's a labour of love, darlin'. Poor old Manor. It never did no one no harm, but it's sure seen some trials and tribulations. I've got most of the downstairs rooms up and running . . . new decor . . . *bloody* tasteful. The Colonel reckons it's an improvement . . . wouldn't let me use purple, though.' She cupped Nancy's face in her hands. 'What's with coming to the back? You're the guest of honour. I oiled the front door specially so it wouldn't squeak.'

Nancy smiled. 'I thought it'd be easier to sneak down the corridor and mingle a bit before anyone noticed me.'

'Fat chance! Mark's been mooching around like a bear with a sore head, and the Colonel's been watching the clock since yesterday afternoon.' Bella turned away to fill a glass with champagne. 'Here, have a little Dutch courage. You look great, darlin'. Didn't know you had legs.'

Nancy smoothed her skirt self-consciously. 'How's James?'

'Good. Has the odd down day, but he perks up again when your letters arrive. He worries about you. Keeps scouring the newspapers to make sure there's been no enemy action in your sector. He's always on the blower to your mum 'n' dad, wanting news. Did they tell you they came down for a visit?'

She nodded. 'I gather my mother gave Zadie and Gray a crash course in pruning.'

'*And* persuaded the Colonel to sign 'em on for a day a week at an agricultural college down the road. They're picking it up pretty quick, as a matter of fact. We had our own veggies in the summer.' She squeezed Nancy's hand. 'Did she tell you Wolfie was here? The social lets him come on a visit once a month. He's doing great . . . got a grand home . . . coming on a treat at school . . . grown about six inches. He's always asking about you, wants to be in the army when he grows up.'

Nancy took a sip of the champagne. 'Is he here today?'

'Sure is . . . along with his foster mum 'n' dad.'

'Does he talk about what happened?'

'Sometimes. He wasn't fazed about Fox dying.

Told me it was a good thing if it meant none of us would have to go to court. I guess it's what we all feel one way or another.'

'Yes,' agreed Nancy.

Bella went back to arranging her canapés. 'Did Mark tell you Julian Bartlett got sent down a couple of weeks ago?'

Another nod. 'Said he changed his plea out of the blue and claimed personal problems in mitigation.'

'Yeah, like trying to run a wife and a mistress at the same time.' Bella chuckled. 'He's been doing it for years, apparently . . . got cold feet when the cops unearthed a couple of ex-bimbos in London and some swindle he'd been operating against his old company.'

Nancy was amused. 'Did Eleanor know?'

'Probably not. She lied about how much he earned, but Martin reckons she was just trying to keep her end up. Your granddad has no sympathy for her. He says the more she lied about how much Julian was worth, the more attractive she made him to encroaching females.'

Nancy laughed. 'I expect she's regretting it now.'

'Must be. Stuck in that great big house on her own. She don't come out much, that's for sure . . . far too embarrassed. The biter bit, that's what I say. Serves her right.'

'What about the Weldons? Are they still together?'

'Just about. Dick's a nice bloke. He came and

apologized after you'd gone, said he didn't expect the Colonel to forgive Prue but hoped he could accept she was completely ignorant about what was going on. There's no doubt she was shocked rigid when it all came out. Hardly opens her mouth these days for fear of saying the wrong thing.'

Nancy shook her head. 'I still don't understand how Julian thought he'd get away with it.'

'Martin says he tried to put a stop to it by phoning Vera when he found out Mark was here. There was a record of the call on his mobile, but either Vera didn't pass the message on or Fox wasn't playing.'

'Why didn't he phone Fox?'

'Never did, apparently. Knew enough about mobiles to keep Fox's number well out of it.' She opened the oven and took out some warmed sausage rolls. 'He's a stupid bugger. He did OK out of Ailsa's jewellery and the bits and pieces Vera nicked from the rooms the Colonel never went into . . . then he got greedy. You know what Martin reckons? He says it's because Julian wasn't punished for the swindle . . . instead his firm paid him off to keep it quiet. *Bad* lesson. He gets the idea nicking's easy . . . skedaddles down here, meets up with the likes of Bob Dawson and Dick Weldon and reckons Dorset folk have sawdust between their ears. He keeps his nose clean till his money starts running out . . . then he bumps into Fox in the woods one day and thinks: "Bingo! I recognize this bad penny." '

'Surely he must have guessed Fox had something to do with Ailsa's death?'

Bella sighed. 'Martin says he wouldn't have cared once the coroner accepted natural causes. In any case, it gave him a lever. Vera rabbits on endlessly about how Mr Bartlett said he'd go to the cops if her boy didn't steal for him. Poor old Colonel. He was a sitting duck . . . all on his own . . . didn't talk to his kids . . . no neighbours . . . senile cleaner . . . bolshie gardener . . . solicitor in London. Easy-bloody-peasy to clean him out behind his back. That's what they reckon the encampment was about. Fox was gonna strip the place, then do a runner and leave us in the firing line.'

Nancy nodded. Mark had told her most of this. 'I wonder which of them thought of it.'

'Who knows? One thing's for sure: you and Mark weren't supposed to be here. They wanted the Colonel alone and thinking Leo was behind it. Martin reckons Fox was gonna kill the old boy, anyway, so there wouldn't have been a witness.'

'What did Julian say?'

Bella grinned. 'Nothing. Just shat himself when Monroe told him how many people they think Fox murdered. The reporters don't know the half of it, Nance. The tally's up to thirty so far . . . and rising. Fox was one sadistic bastard. The cops reckon every sodding brush in his bus represented a person as well as a fox. It makes you think, don't it?'

Nancy took another sip of Dutch courage. 'Do you see Vera?'

'No, but everyone who visits the nursing home hears what she has to say.' She reached over to take Nancy's hand again. 'There's something else she's saying, darlin', and I'd rather you heard it from me than on the grapevine. I know Mark's told you about the photos the police found in the Lodge, the ones of Fox and Elizabeth when they were in their teens. Seems like he hooked up with the travellers that came to mend Mr Squires's fences. It don't mean nothing as far as you're concerned . . . but Vera talks about you being Fox's daughter quite a lot.'

Nancy swilled the champagne in her glass and watched the bubbles pop. Mark had told her in January. He, too, had said the photographs meant nothing but she'd spent hours on the Internet researching brown–blue alleles, blue–green alleles, dominant gene colours and colour variations. She had expected confirmation that it was impossible for blue-eyed parents to have a brown-eyed child. Instead she had learnt the opposite.

She guessed Mark had done the same research, because he had asked her once or twice if there was anything she wanted from Elizabeth. They both knew what he was talking about, but each time Nancy had said no. He never pushed it, and she was grateful for that. He understood that in this one instance uncertainty was more bearable than certainty.

Now it was too late. Elizabeth had died in April, having made her peace with her father but not with the child she gave away. Her only gift to Nancy, other than life, was a handwritten note saying: 'I have so much to regret, but I don't regret giving you to John and Mary Smith. It was the best thing I ever did in my life. With love, Elizabeth.'

'Well, let's hope Vera's wrong,' she said lightly, 'otherwise I've inherited a brain tumour on one side and cirrhosis on the other.'

'Don't be an idiot,' said Bella roundly. 'Cirrhosis ain't inherited . . . it's self-inflicted . . . and you know Fox ain't your Dad. Yours was a tall, handsome sod with brown eyes, a good brain and a kind heart. Anything else'd be going against nature.'

Nancy smiled. 'So how are things with Martin?'

'Brilliant,' said Bella, accepting the change of subject easily. 'He's in there, as well.' She nodded towards the drawing room. 'Leo, too. They're all dying to see you, darlin'. Are you gonna let me take you in now?'

Nancy felt a terrible shyness creep over her. They were all expecting far too much. Apart from Mark, she hadn't seen any of them for nearly a year and she'd never met Leo. 'Maybe I should go out again and come through the front door?'

She felt a coat being draped across her shoulders. 'I have a better idea,' said Mark, taking her hand and leading her into the corridor. 'We'll go for a walk and blow the cobwebs away. In half an hour we'll take a discreet look through the drawing-room window and see how everyone's getting on. How does that sound?'

Nancy relaxed immediately. 'As good as it did last time,' she said simply.

www.panmacmillan.com